Songbird's Remembrance
L.S. TAAL

L.S. Taal Publishing

ISBN: 978-1-7381227-2-1

Dedication

To the goddess trapped inside me, who perpetually haunts my dreams with visions of the person that together, we could be . . . I hope one day to fully set you free.

Note From The Author

Songbird's Remembrance is an adult fantasy romance novel, book two in the Celestial Songbird Series. It is intended for audiences 18 and over and does contain physical violence, crude language and explicit sexual content.

Contents

ANCIENT CELESTIAL STAR ETCHING

When the Celusian Moon is no more and the light of Selayne disappears from the heavens, the Cradle of the In-Between will birth the child of celestial love, who will grow and dwell in obscurity until Selayne rises in the Sangelis again, lifting the veil to dissolve the season of celestial mourning.

By a shard of the Old, Arcane Magic, she will be summoned—her rebirth ushering in a new age to the Sangelis. Born of light and darkness, born of love and music, born to rule . . . she will rise. All-consuming love and power she will command with the High King of the Light Age, and war they will wage against the daughter of the Laureal Moon and dark Gods of the ages.

The truth of her nature is two-fold: The High Queen of the Light Age and the Celestial Songbird, guided by the Anchor—Catraia. Without Catraia, darkness will prevail and will swathe the Sangelis in doom. Catraia is the guardian; Catraia is the bridge.

If she, whose name is lost, can claim the Ankhira and harness the power of the Ethereal Harmonies, she will have dominion over Shadow and Light and will take her rightful place in the Sangelis.

Ancient Celestial Star Etching
Written in the stars by the Mavigos
at the end of the First Age of the Sangelis

A RIADNA: ONE DAY AGO . . .

The world was my fucking oyster. Ripe for the taking.

Outside the arched windows of my ornate chamber, the expanse of dusky nothingness sprawled on for miles and miles in every direction.

Clawkier Dreve.

The perfect spot to erect my fortress in Ariadna. Unreachable. Impenetrable. Here, nestled within the deserted barrens of Deadlands in southern Proscette, I was untouchable. My dark magic had seen to that.

I shifted my gaze, my glittering reflection in the gilded mirror smirking back at me. I deserved to shine. No one was ever locking me away again. Bloody Pashket—that barbarous hellhole—Ariadna's dominion of banished *evildoers*. Two agonizing stints there, with barely seven months in between, and Gods, I was still beautiful. Even more so with the black, menacing lightning bolt burned into my right cheek.

It was fierce. I was fierce.

A penance for what I'd stolen during my first incarceration after trying to overthrow my imposter Sovereign father one hundred and sixty years ago? Ha. Fuck that. The jagged scar was a long-standing badge of honor, a declaration to everyone who looked upon my face that I had accomplished what no one had before—I had infiltrated the Phantom Pocket Between Realms and kicked it in its metaphoric cunt, absconding with its most treasured possessions. Possessions that were instrumental in my triumphant escape from the Dark Dominion after being locked away for sixty years.

1

The caress of cool, smooth sleekness brushed against my legs, weaving through my planted feet. "Zaval," I tutted, reaching down to lift the banguar off the marble floor. The four-legged terror whimpered softly as he scrambled onto my shoulders, his diamond-shaped scales glittering like jewels as the light from outside glinted off them.

He was barely four, I reckoned. Still a lot of growing to do. Banguars didn't reach maturity until they were half a century old. But even fully grown, they were no larger than a house cat. Such fascinating creatures. So much of their power came from their small size and eye-catching aesthetic. Being underestimated was a mighty weapon—I would know. Their true killing power, though, lay in their tears, of all things. Those haunting, plaintive eyes—so deceptive, it was devious—drew their prey in, closer and closer, before they pounced, shooting jets of corrosively lethal venom that they secreted from their eyes at will.

Saddling myself with a *pet* had never been my intention, but the moment I'd set eyes on Zaval in the forests of Nesda almost three years ago, I knew I had to have him. The poor thing was orphaned and barely alive. The fucking symmetry was not lost on me. It was a banguar, after all, that had killed the mother of Ash's beloved beyngyle baby.

I frowned as Zaval's claws gripped my shoulders. His honey-colored eyes bore into mine, attentive and discerning, his double-forked tongue darting out to swipe my face. "We'll play later, darling." I stroked his head gently. "I promise I'll bring you a tasty treat from Kindrik when I return."

I lowered him onto my bed, and he unwound his body from around my shoulders before burrowing between my sheets. Turning toward my vanity, I picked up a hefty pair of dangling, gem-studded earrings from a gilded box and fastened them to my lobes.

For as long as I could remember, I'd had a taste for luxury and an eye for beauty. My parents had seen to that in my early years. Ruskil and Lydia Tandor—Sovereign and Queen Consort of Tandor—well, they'd indulged me and catered to my every whim. Surrounded by opulence, showered with extravagance, and lavished in excess, I was a princess in every sense of the word.

So what if I had spent more than three-quarters of my life locked away? At two hundred and four years old, I was still pretty much a cub. Still lots of living ahead of me. And this princess had her sights set on being crowned a queen.

My heartbeat quickened as a charged frisson of electricity, interlaced with a salty-sweet musk, stormed my honed senses. I wasn't alone. I inhaled and sighed, reveling in the quantum supernova of power seeping into the luxurious chamber. It never ceased to render me weak in the knees.

An ancient weapon. Lethal and cold. Gargmoin. *Mine.*

Massive, over eight feet tall, draped in billowing swaths of black, he was terrifying and spectral. Gods, his eyes were dead as fuck—onyx, soulless—and his skin a sickly shade of green—leathery and wrinkled. The vertical slashes gouged into his forehead flashed silver, pulsing slowly with slivers of his power.

"Shadow sorceress." His deep voice reverberated through the chamber, sending a tremor of excitement careening to my core.

All that ancient magic. Intoxicating. Arousing. By the Gods, I wanted to tangle limbs with him, but the emotionless prick was frigid and empty, his desire for retribution and power the only forces that evoked any response in him. His power might be mine to use, but his cock was off limits. A godsdamned bloody tragedy.

In my entire life, I had been denied nothing—well, almost nothing. There was one thing—one pure, precious thing I desired above all else in the world, one beautiful possession that had thus far eluded me. But not for long. The day was soon coming when Asher Valkyse would be mine, and together we would conquer and rule over all of Ariadna. Why settle for a quarter or even half when I could have the whole bloody realm?

I'd known the truth since I was eight years old. A random embrace between Ash and his mother had set it all in motion. Just one glimpse at the look of unadulterated love and adoration in his eyes was all it had taken to rouse the whispers that lived inside me, for the burning conviction to burrow into my soul and take root. Ash would look at me like that; I would be his world and reason for being. He just didn't realize or accept it yet.

Gargmoin adjusted his stance, folding his massive tree-trunk arms across his expansive chest. "The generals of Tynor's army await your command." His voice was flat, detached, the words clipped. A bored smirk skirted his lips, a momentary flash of menace sparking his eyes.

Holy fuck, his tenebrous affect was unnerving. And that coming from me—the queen of fearless and twisted.

I waved my hand in dismissal. "I'll get there when I get there." Tynor might be the King of Kindrik, ruler of the Dark Shen, and my true sire, but none of that meant shit to me. Fuck—without me, that precious crown on his head would have still been a dream begging to be realized.

Gargmoin's eyes narrowed, a low growl rumbling in his chest, causing my skin to prickle at the nocuous admonition. I tamped down my unease, flinging it into the bottomless crevasse inside me where I condemned all my fears and insecurities to die.

An intrepid, unforgiving bitch. That's who I was. I owned that shit.

I didn't have to turn around to know he was gone. Only a wisp of his tainted power lingered in his wake.

I glanced in the mirror once more. Face flushed and full of color, ivory hair voluminous and silky, body golden and supple. A far cry from the pale and sickly-looking sack of shit I had been when I was released three years ago. One hundred years I had spent locked away in Glanag—that dismal abyss in Pashket—powerless and broken, with nothing but time and spiraling shadows to keep me company.

But killing Ash's parents had been worth it. It had paved the way for him to become Sovereign, after all. Set events in motion for us to take our rightful places as rulers over Valkyse—and eventually, Ariadna. A bloody shame that my pure-hearted love was too short-sighted to recognize the precious gift I'd given him.

Locked away in Glanag, the only things that had kept me from losing my mind, from smashing my head in on the dank, cold walls of my prison, were the whispers in my head and the knowledge that I would one day be released. The Mavigos and Cloryals—sanctimonious vipers and shrews that they were—had deemed that I had not yet fulfilled my destiny. Well, they were right about that. I hadn't. My great destiny, as I saw it, was to rid not just Ariadna, but the Sangelis, of the Divine and those conniving demi-goddesses once and for all. And I'd have some fun in the process.

Baby steps.

Patience.

Six regions made up the Sangelis—the *Elterien Realms*, as they were known, with Ariadna the prized jewel at its nexus. One at a time, I would conquer them. Once Ariadna fell, the others would come tumbling down. All starting with the Convergence.

Thirty-six days to go.

The moment the constellations of Sorin and Eolith aligned, my war drums would thunder across the Sangelis. The vortex of power unleashed during the Convergence was critical to my plans.

I closed my eyes, exulting in the surge of power rippling through my veins. It required no effort at all now to summon it to the surface. Like muscle memory, it had returned to me quickly upon my release three years ago.

Staring at my reflection, I admired my naked body. My breasts were full and high, my waist slender, my curves accentuated by the ample breadth of my hips. I reached inside and summoned my power, watching in delight as my body shifted and Ash stared back at me in the mirror.

Shape-shifter, skin thief, *diabomattise*—it made no difference to me what they called me. It was simply who I *was*. Sometimes, when my lust for Ash was so overwhelming, I would change into his skin and pleasure myself by looking at his form in the mirror, imagining that it was my hands on his beautiful body, that it was me bringing him to climax. It was almost as thrilling as the rush I'd experienced when I'd shifted into his skin and murdered his parents.

In Kindrik, I often used the shape-shifting abilities of the lesser princes in my father's court to feed my sexual appetites, to achieve my most powerful releases. Whenever I had them wear Ash's skin and pleasure me, my orgasms were always explosive. It would be even more intense when I had Ash for real—which, if everything went according to plan, would be in short order.

The human wretch was the only obstacle standing in my way. I thought I'd taken care of the wispy bitch. Fucking Great Creator. If it weren't for Arazul's power barring me from venturing to Earth, I'd have killed the cunt myself. At the time, it didn't matter that I had no idea who she was, or what, if anything, she had done to garner Ash's attention. The mere fact that she had captured his notice was all the cause I needed.

The God of Gods was no match for Gargmoin, though. That magnificent fuck had power that the Gods of the Sangelis couldn't even fathom. He'd opened the way for my Manatocht warriors to destroy the simpering creya, but when they failed, Gargmoin himself went, returning to me with assurances that he had splintered the usurper's mind and ground her body into dust just because he could before leaving that primitive realm.

So how was she here? In the Sangelis. With Ash. *My* Ash. I had no doubt Arazul and the Mavigos had something to do with it. Only they were powerful enough to deceive Gargmoin.

I clenched my jaw, the tension nearly severe enough to crack a tooth. Poisonous fumes of jealousy and rage melded together to leave a bitter taste in my mouth.

Ash's *Gloweyen Queen.*

Even the thought of it made me want to retch. Caz had been utterly gleeful when he came to see me earlier today after the Ethereal Harmonies read the bitch for a giln. It had taken every ounce of my willpower not to rip his dick off and shove it down his throat before he ambled away to see for himself who she was.

But I had knowledge the God of Chaos didn't. I knew about the ancient celestial star etching. As much as I was loath to believe it—and even more so to accept it—the Mavigos had bound the three of us together—the cunt, Ash, and me—and now I needed to reevaluate my next steps.

My objectives remained the same, despite her existence—claim Ash, claim Ariadna. She was just in my way. And I showed no mercy to anyone or anything standing in the way of what I wanted. I'd make an example of the bitch. She dared to lay a claim on what was mine? She would beg me to end her, plead for death, but her fate was sealed. Unending torture. I'd take her to the brink and bring her back. Every. Fucking. Time.

Death was a mercy. One that she would never be allowed.

My nails dug into the palms of my hand as Ash's enraged glare stared back at me in the mirror. Shape-shifting back into my own body, I walked to my closet to get dressed. I settled on a black, gauzy blouse, studded with emeralds down the front, and flared, red leather pants. I slipped on a pair of diamond-encrusted slippers with a five-inch heel, then cinched a gem-studded belt around my waist. All the jewels were real. I would settle for nothing less.

Moving on. I was to meet my father in Kindrik. He had assembled his war council and had requested my presence. I looked at myself appreciatively and smiled. Who said that one couldn't look spectacular when planning a war? I giggled in pleasure as I imagined the look on Tynor's face when the realization dawned on him that I, not he, would be calling the shots, and that his armies had already sworn allegiance to me. One demonstration of Gargmoin's power had been all it took to convince them whose side they needed to be on. Perhaps if my father toed the line and did as I commanded, I would let *him* have a place at *my* side.

The thought filled me with delight, and I burst into laughter. He was such an intransigent prick, the hard-assed pile of dung. I was done seeking his approval. I answered and bowed to no one. I would be queen of Ariadna, and everyone would bow to me by the time I was done.

I checked myself again in the mirror and smiled at my radiant reflection. Lifting my hand to touch my swirling dark giln, I shifted into mist and slipped into the air.

Chapter 2

ELEYSE

MAY 2: ONE YEAR, ELEVEN MONTHS AGO . . .

Shit. There was a frigging hole the size of Australia in my pantyhose.

Okay, that was probably an exaggeration, but barely. After carefully lifting my legs out of my SUV, the heel of my right stiletto had snagged my left calf, ripping a god-awful crater in the delicate nylon. Crap. I'd only just changed into a new pair at lunch after catching the old one on a jagged edge of the filing cabinet in my office. Useless pieces of garbage, that's what they were. Why the hell did we even need them?

Completely self-conscious now, I hurried inside and made a beeline for the ladies' room. Crusoe's wasn't too packed for a Friday night. It was a long weekend, plus it was unseasonably warm for the beginning of May. People were probably heading out to cottage country to take advantage of the mild spring weather.

With the same sour shock as a shot of concentrated lemon juice, my sullen face greeted me in the mirror as I opened the washroom door. Great. I'd only just gotten here and already my mood was shit. The sharp smell of pine-scented cleaner hit my nostrils as I turned toward the stalls. Slipping into an empty one, I hurriedly peed, peeling my ruined hose off at the same time, all the while hovering and keeping an eye on my aim. Who said women weren't good at multitasking?

I exited the stall, tossed the useless hose in the trash, washed my hands, and forced a somewhat pleasant look on my face. Pushing the door open, I sighed and headed out into the belly of the beast.

Hip-hop music blared from the speakers above as I slid onto a polished stool at the bar and ordered a vodka martini. The bartender smiled and made loud small talk for a minute before moving away to serve a group of ladies who were clearly out on a girls' night. Their raucous laughter and shrill voices reverberated over the blasting music, and their happiness made me sad—sad for myself that I was alone and didn't have friends to help ease the anguish I felt.

That wasn't exactly true, though, and I knew it. Alice and Maya had tried to get me to go out with them after work and I had turned them down. Instead, I stayed at work until 6:30, long after everyone else left, and then drove to Crusoe's, intent on drowning my sorrows in a few drinks before heading home.

I was twenty-eight years old, and what did I have to show for it? Yes, I was successful at work—the youngest director of marketing in the company's history—but that was the extent of my successes, as I saw it. I had no family, no significant other, no children, no one to love or love me back. The friends—well, more like acquaintances—I did have, I chose to keep at arm's length, and although they made attempts to include me and bring me out of my isolation, more often than not, those efforts were futile.

I was *trying*, though. Trying to be less closed off, less sad, less alone. First off, it really wasn't my fault that resting bitch face was my default look. It was something both my late fiancé, Liam, and my former best friend, Charlotte, had constantly teased me about, but no matter how hard I tried, that mask always slipped back into place when I wasn't paying attention. When it came right down to it, it was the face that a life of tragedy and loss had molded for me, stripping away any traces of laugh lines, lightheartedness, and unschooled contentment.

Ever since that sobering night almost a year ago, I had vowed to turn over a new leaf, to make a real attempt at truly living. *Your entire life with a paramount future awaits*, the violet-haired woman from my dream had said, and I believed her. She'd planted a strange conviction in me, sowed the tiny seeds of hope that life held more than just heartache and misery. And so, I gave up on trying to die. It wasn't easy—I was still bloody miserable—but I was *trying* to be better.

Yet, as I sat at the bar sipping my martini and listening to the women at the table laughing and regaling themselves with personal stories that meant nothing to me, I felt myself sinking deeper into despair. I ordered another drink and decided that I was going to get good and drunk—drunk enough to forget my sorry life for a few moments—and then I would call a cab and go home.

As I reached out my hand to take the drink from the bartender, someone bumped into my stool, sending my glass flying across the bar.

"Crap, I'm so sorry," an apologetic voice said from behind me. I turned around to see a man with sandy brown hair staring at me intently. He looked to be in his twenties, dressed in a teal shirt and chinos, his shirt sleeves rolled up to his elbows.

"It's okay." I reached over the counter and grabbed some napkins to wipe up the spill.

"No, it's not." His face furrowed in a frown. "Please, let me get you another one."

"Josh, you're such a klutz," another man piped in, coming over to stand on the other side of me. He was wearing a ball cap and was dressed in jeans and a collared T-shirt.

I shook my head. "Seriously, it's not a problem."

"Please, I insist." Josh lifted his hand to hail the bartender.

He wasn't bad looking—decent built, medium height, and easy on the eyes. Same with Ball Cap, but I wasn't in the mood to socialize; I just wanted to be left alone and not have to talk to anyone.

"What were you having?" Josh asked when the bartender came over.

"A vodka martini." I adjusted my position on the stool. My butt was starting to fall asleep.

"Vodka martini for the beautiful lady," Josh said to the bartender, a smile lighting up his face.

The minutes passed by in awkward silence until finally, the bartender brought the drink over, winked at me, and moved on to someone else trying to get his attention.

"You out by yourself on a Friday night?" Ball Cap asked.

Wonderful. They thought I wanted to hang.

"No. I'm waiting on someone, but thanks for replacing my drink." Turning away from them, I pivoted to go find a booth.

"Whoa!" Josh said. "The night's still young. Where are you going? The least you could do while you wait for your friend is have a drink with us for getting you a drink." He grabbed my arm, and I immediately froze.

"Let go of me," I growled, my eyes glaring daggers into him as I set my drink down.

"You bitches are all the same." Ball Cap sauntered forward, getting close my face. "Tight dresses, all dolled up—nothing but a bunch of cock teases."

I gritted my teeth. "Listen, jackass. I didn't ask you to come over, and I didn't ask you to get me a drink. So get out of my way and leave me alone."

"I don't think so, sexy." Josh sidled closer, a smirk on his face. "Not before I sample what you have on display." He reached out his hand and grabbed my ass.

Was this dickhead for real? Who spoke like that anyway? I didn't think; I just acted. I punched him squarely in the face, a surge of satisfaction flaring inside me at the crack of bone crunching, even as pain flared through my knuckles. Blood spurted from his nose.

"You broke my nose, you crazy bitch!" Josh screamed, while Ball Cap yanked my hair from behind.

I whirled around and kneed him in the groin. He fell to the floor, doubling over in agony. As he rolled onto his back, his knees to his chest, I smacked him in the face with my purse and then kicked him, the sole of my four-inch pumps digging into his side. I'd taken enough self-defense classes to know how to protect myself.

"I told you to leave me the hell alone, assholes!" I picked up the drink they got me and hurled the contents into Josh's face. "You can keep the vodka martini, you sick douche!"

I spun on my heel, my eyes searching for the exit.

Shit. A crowd had gathered around us. The cheers and whoops of the girls' night group drifted in from behind me. "Serves them right, girl," one of them yelled, reaching out a hand to yank me closer.

"Some guys are entitled idiots," a pretty redhead said with an emphatic nod. "You're more than welcome to sit with us if you'd like. No one will dare mess with you here. Safety in numbers, girl."

I smiled in acknowledgment at their group of six. The energy trailing off them was tantalizing, heady. A wave of longing crashed over me. How easy would it be to say yes, to sit and soak in the happiness and excitement they exuded? Gosh. To let go, laugh, and just have *fun*? How awesome would that be?

I gritted my teeth and swallowed, the bitter scorch of disappointment and resolve coating my throat. "Thanks, but I think I'm done for the night." It was for the best. Plus, the last thing I needed was new friends. I was pretty shitty to the ones I did have.

"If you change your mind, you know where to find us," a voluptuous brunette with pouty red lips piped in. "We'll be here till closing."

I smiled and walked away, making a beeline for the door, my eyes alert as I searched for Josh and Ball Cap. No sign of the assholes. As I exited the bar, I looked behind me once more to make sure they weren't following, and with my head still swiveled in the other direction, I barreled into someone, my purse flying onto the sidewalk.

"Shit! I'm so sorry." I dropped to my knees to grab my bag. "I wasn't watching where I was going."

"No harm done."

I froze. The husky, rich timbre of the speaker's voice commanded my attention, the hint of amusement grazing his words brushing against my senses. Out of the corner of my eye, I saw him move closer.

"Besides," he continued, "I wouldn't want to get on your bad side. I saw what you did to those two guys inside."

An outstretched hand appeared before me. I looked past the hand up to his face and my mouth dropped open. I was staring into the face of a god. There was no other way to describe it. The man was hands down the most magnificent creature I had ever seen.

Dark hair, chiseled face, unnaturally beautiful emerald-green eyes, full lips—and so broad-shouldered and tall. I felt my insides going to mush. He had barely said five words to me, but I could already tell what kind of man he was. Confident, with a commanding presence—it oozed out of him with every movement he made.

Oh God, Eleyse, in the name of all that is sweet and holy, close your mouth, my mind screamed at me, but my body refused to obey. I shook my head vigorously to snap out of it, but a rush of emotion bowled me over—excitement, joy, longing, relief. *Mine*, a voice deep inside me roared.

Shit. What was happening to me?

"I'm sorry, what?" I took his hand and he pulled me to my feet. I almost jumped out of my skin as a blast of electricity jolted me when I touched him. What the hell was wrong with me? So he was gorgeous. Big deal. It wasn't as if I hadn't seen gorgeous men before. Hell, half the men I worked with were gorgeous.

Much to my chagrin, my eyes started doing a slow perusal of their own accord. He was wearing a dark leather jacket, a V-neck fitted T-shirt, and jeans. Damn, he was fine. Everything he wore hugged him in *all* the right places. Oh God, I was done for. Lust, pure and unadulterated, coursed through me.

Over the past few years, I'd had lovers, but if anything, it had been more out of a basic need for fulfillment than anything else. I had been in charge. I had taken what I wanted and moved on. I had perfected the act of being in control. This—what I was experiencing right now—defied all explanation. My heartbeat was erratic, my thoughts going in places they hadn't before. I wanted to do dirty—no, nasty—things to this man, with him. Oh crap. I had to get out of here.

"Are you all right?" the man-god asked, his eyes flashing with genuine concern.

And why shouldn't he be concerned? I was acting like a frigging lunatic in the middle of the street, for heaven's sake. *Pull yourself together, Eleyse,* my mind screamed at me. *Put on your bitch face and stare this gorgeous fucker down.*

I closed my eyes and took a deep breath, willing steel into my nerves. Flicking my gaze up, I raked my eyes over his face, my mind poring through clever and sophisticated things to say. The moment I opened my mouth, my thoughts glitched and short-circuited.

"Holy shit, are you an angel?" I blurted out. My brain raged at me.

He laughed, his eyes crinkling at the corners. It was the laugh of a man who was used to this kind of reaction from women. Of course he was. He was sex appeal personified. Everyone had a type, and I was pretty sure he was everyone's type.

His teeth were white and straight, his lips even more sensuous when parted. An image of those lips on my body flashed into my mind, and I blushed violently, looking away, trying to push the picture out of my head. But it was there, burned in my brain, and so I refused to meet his gaze.

"I'm sorry," I mumbled, staring at his chest. The next second, I was picturing him with his shirt off. *No!* I screamed to myself.

I flicked my eyes upward for a fraction of a second, my heart thudding when our gazes met. "I have to go." Without another word, I turned around and darted out into the street, almost getting run over by a bicycle in the process.

Don't you dare look back, Eleyse, I warned myself sternly. *Just get out of here.*

I fumbled in my bag for my keys, almost running to my car now. Clicking my remote to unlock the door, I jumped into the driver's seat, starting the engine in record time. I leaned my head against the headrest, the blood pounding in my ears. What the hell was that? I had never reacted to a man like that before. My body still tingled from thinking about him, wanting to feel his sculpted sexiness all over me.

God, I had made a complete ass of myself in front of him, practically drooling as I ogled him, as if he was a double—no—triple serving of the double fudge chocolate chunk ice cream I loved to devour so much. Only he'd taste much, much better. Of that, I was entirely certain.

I shivered as the image of me licking said ice cream off that sinful body teased my overstimulated senses. Fuck. I put my car in gear and hightailed it out of the parking lot, tearing home like a crazed bat out of hell.

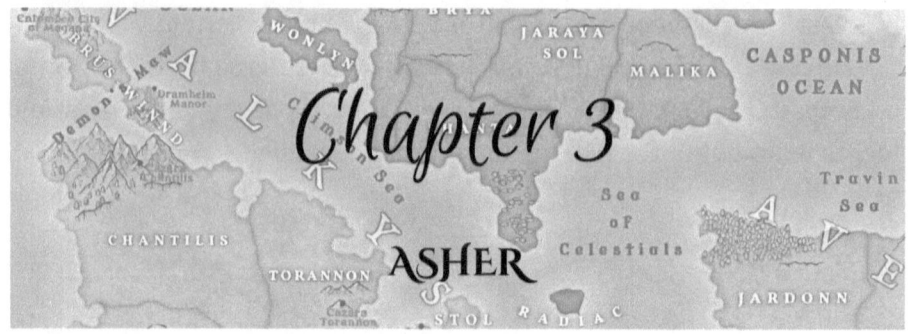

Chapter 3

ASHER

P RESENT DAY SOLNIESS, THE VOID . . .

A pang of longing clawed at my insides, slowly squeezing the breath out of me. Could anything be more painful? Wavy, violet hair spilled onto the silken pillow in front of me, cascading delicately in a mass of gossamer softness.

She was here, but not here.

Our physical bodies were still safe and secure at Cazara Torannon with my sister and my uncle, but our shadow selves existed here in the Void with our consciousness. Elle was even further removed from me. Sending her consciousness back to the past through the back door of her mind was the only chance we had for her to regain the memories the rebounding curse had ripped from her when that ancient fuck, Gargmoin, hit her with his magic five days ago.

I cringed. The presence of the dark sway of the Old, Arcane Magic around her soul was the last thing I'd expected—a possibility that hadn't even occurred to me. Fuck, I was so grateful that Tora had discerned what was happening. It made sense that she had. She was the prime elemental spirit of Ariadna, after all, an ancient being who wielded the light strain of the Old, Arcane Magic. She had recognized the ancient magic's signature when I couldn't. But how could I, when the magic I wielded was different? The Ethereal Harmonies were a different power source altogether, the source of life and balance in the Sangelis.

I released a shuddered breath. Gargmoin's darkness had spread its inky wings around Elle's soul, preventing her from accessing the light inside her when she used her magic. It had to go. The rebounding curse had to be destroyed or she would not be able to complete her transformation into the Celestial Songbird. She was strong, my goddess—strong and resilient, like I always knew she was.

A frown pulled my brows together as I stared at her beautiful face. Gods, it was hard to believe that it had only been five days since she arrived in Ariadna. So much had happened in that time. I could only imagine how overwhelming it all must have felt for her, especially not being able to remember the last two years of her life.

Her entire world had been turned on its head since she'd arrived here. It irked me that her introduction to Ariadna was horrific—assaulted and almost raped in Torannon. It made me furious that in Torannon—my city—such an unspeakable fate had almost befallen her. Thank the Gods Gwynn had been able to save her in time, banishing the vermin to the Dark Dominion, the shadowlands of Ariadna. If my sister hadn't been there . . . I shuddered at the thought.

In Pashket, I'd found the culprits and meted out my retribution, obliterating them off the face of Ariadna. No one would ever again hurt someone I loved and go unpunished.

Her violent welcome to Ariadna was only the tip of the iceberg, the first swirl in the dizzying vortex of events that had yanked her into the path of its unforgiving funnel. Not only had Elle discovered that she was in an entirely different world from the one she had lived all her life, but had found out that she *belonged* here.

In the span of a mere two days, she'd been visited by my deceased mother, was bestowed with the mantle of Songbird of Valkyse, and had learned that she was part of a future written in the stars millions of years ago. She had been taken—not once, but twice—by Cazril, God of Chaos, in his attempt to learn more about the mysterious human who had been chosen by the Ethereal Harmonies to be my Gloweyen Queen—not just of the Dominion of Valkyse, but all of Ariadna. The two labrals identical to mine that had been returned specifically for her when she was read for a giln at the Giln Keeper's Sanctuary had proclaimed the truth of it all.

Fuck. Just thinking about everything she had gone through was enough to make my head spin.

The truth of her identity had been the final revelation, one I wasn't quite sure she had come to terms with yet. Her parents were Gods of the Sangelis—she was the daughter of Eolith, Goddess of the Ethereal Harmonies, and Sorin, Summoner of Light and Darkness. She was a goddess in her own right. And she was mine—my eternal soul's shadow—just as I was hers.

My gaze flicked up at the Lonefera on the wall above the bed. Golden light streamed from the magical artifact, skimming Elle's serene features, scanning her mind for any traces of instability.

Nothing.

I hoped to fuck it stayed that way. We'd barely even begun.

Closing my eyes, I rippled my power and reached for our Gloweyen bond. Even in her slumber, that all-powerful connection between us was still active, a reminder that the Mavigos—the divine will of the cosmos—had tethered us together for a greater purpose.

Catraia, I whispered in my mind.

I am here, Asher, the entity that resided within Elle answered at once.

Thank the Gods our Gloweyen connection allowed me to communicate with Catraia, even in Elle's current state.

All is well, she assured. *Eleyse's consciousness is back where she needed to go. Her journey to retrieve her lost memories has begun.*

I breathed a sigh of relief, my eyes flitting to the Lonefera's visual countdown on the wall.

Six hundred and ninety-eight.

Seeing it in writing made it all the more bleak. Six hundred and ninety-eight days before I would see those slate-gray eyes again. A bloody lifetime. Time might be inconsequential here in Solniess—the Goddess Eolith's sanctum in the celestial plane of consciousness in the Void—but the Lonefera's painstaking display of the passage of time unfolding in Elle's mind—day by day, hour by hour—Gods, it was like swimming against the tide through viscid treacle.

Beneath the day marker, two lines etched in gold pulsed softly on the wall. Two hours. She'd only been gone for two hours. Sweet, merciful Medra. This was torture.

If memory served me right, though, by now, she would have already collided with me outside of Crusoe's. I couldn't help the smile that lifted my lips at the recollection. The moment those beautiful gray eyes of hers had met mine on the sidewalk, it had taken every ounce of my self-control not to pull her into my arms and kiss her.

That wasn't the first time I had seen her in her world, though. No, the first time I set eyes on her—four months before Crusoe's—time itself had slowed to a halt, and Magnus—as the little minx so facetiously named the beast of our Gloweyen bond inside me—completely lost his godsdamned mind.

I smiled and let the memory carry me away.

TWO YEARS, THREE MONTHS AGO . . .

"*Are you ready, Asher?*" *Eolith, Goddess of the Ethereal Harmonies asked, her silver eyes flashing calmly.*

I clenched my hands at my side. Was I ready? Fuck, yes. After ninety-seven years of waiting, I was finally going to see Elle in the flesh again. That night before my coronation—when she had slipped into my room through the Senshifter the Goddess Eolith had summoned—had stayed with me all these years. I knew why the Gods had sent her back in time a century to me; I'd known since the day of my coronation. Whether she knew it or not, she'd saved me. Now it was my turn to return the favor.

"*You have less than a minute to cross over before the portal closes.*" *The Goddess Mother's voice was calm, but I detected a hint of worry in her tone. "Remember, your power will only last for a maximum of two days; less than that the more you use it. It will be the same every time you go. You'll never be able to stay longer than two days.*"

I nodded. The Ethereal Harmonies were the source of my magic. I couldn't afford to be away from Ariadna when my power drained or I would not be able to summon the portal to return home. I couldn't be that reckless.

It had been nine months since the Mavigos lifted the veil. Nine months since Kaliope had been released from Glanag. Nine months since I became capable of seeing Elle in her world from mine—to use my labral to conjure her at will.

With the lifting of the veil, restlessness became my constant companion. Sleepless nights, scattered thoughts, short fuse—I was a ticking time bomb. The beast of our Gloweyen bond was agitated. My eternal soul's shadow was within reach. It sensed her; even worlds away, it recognized her presence, her existence. It wasn't enough to conjure her through my labral, to see her from afar. She consumed my thoughts, and I struggled against the primal need to go to her.

"There is nothing more we can do to prepare you," the Goddess Eolith said, her eyes wide as she took my hands. "As much knowledge as you have recently absorbed of Earth, the actual experience will be different, will take some getting used to. Get a feel for the world, the life there. Assimilate. The beast of your Gloweyen bond will react strongly, and you'll have to learn to control it. Take as much time as you need before you're sure you can approach Eleyse. And don't be disappointed if you're unable to do so the first time. Or even the next."

Her silver eyes seared into mine. "Bring her back to life, Asher. I know it will take time, but we cannot fail."

I nodded, the aching in the Goddess Mother's voice piercing my heart. We both knew. We both had seen. Elle was a husk of a person.

Her world was not like the Sangelis, where I was well versed in all the realms and civilizations in existence. It was unfamiliar. And so, the Great Creator, Arazul, and the Goddess Mother had gifted me with knowledge—knowledge of Earth. Its chronicled histories, geography, cultures, politics, societal norms, financial conventions, technology. Thousands of years of an entire civilization delivered to my mind in a matter of seconds. Astonishing.

I'd greedily absorbed it all.

Stepping toward the swirling spiral of golden light, I squeezed the Goddess Eolith's hand. "I know what's at stake, and I will not fail."

I crossed the threshold into the portal, and a cocoon of warmth and light enveloped my form, spiriting me away. To Earth. To Elle.

The blaring of horns pierced my ears, spiking my heart rate.

Where was I? I squinted in the glare of the early morning sun, trying to get my bearings. Patterned brick tiles lined the sidewalk under my feet, and behind me, cars zoomed by on the bustling street.

Up ahead, a slow-moving vehicle edged against the curb, lazily sauntering in my direction. I searched my mind for the knowledge. A street sweeper. I watched in fascination as the powerful rotating brushes cleared the debris from the road as it ambled by.

On both sides of the street, a mix of sprawling skyscrapers and older brick buildings vied for attention, the former screaming out for notice, the latter a lesson in understated charm.

The middle of a city. That's where I was. The Goddess Eolith had said the portal would take me where I needed to go, but what that meant, I wasn't entirely sure. I had to trust that finding Elle would not be a problem.

Hargrove, Ontario. That's where she lived. Not a large city by Earth's standards, but a humming one nonetheless, located in central Canada. On the sidewalk to my left, a handful of food vendors were setting up their stalls.

"Please, sir, can you spare a dollar?" a ragged voice wheezed from behind me. A wizened, outstretched hand greeted me as I turned around, and my gaze coasted over the human it belonged to. Faded blue jeans hung low on his too-thin hips, and a stained, gray T-shirt clung loosely to his chest. His shoulder-length, light-brown hair was limp and flat against his head, a smattering of wayward strands plastered to his stubbled face.

Intense blue eyes regarded me, but it wasn't his eyes I couldn't stop staring at. No. It was the jagged scar carved into his cheek, so reminiscent of another scar on another face, but at the same time completely different.

Kaliope's leering visage flashed in my mind, and I gritted my teeth. Even worlds away, I was not free of the bloody creya. My blood boiled and writhed in my veins. The bitch's mangled cheek was a proclamation of what she had done, her face permanently marred by the Hagdern—the three fearsome beasts who guarded Glanag—because of the Scimion magma she had stolen from the Phantom Pocket Between Realms. Magical, malleable, magma that she had used to both escape the Dark Dominion the first time and to forge the scimitars she'd used to murder my parents.

I blinked, pushing the bitter glimpses away. My gaze shifted back to the man in front of me, and reaching into my pocket, I pulled out a brown, leather wallet. I was prepared. Money, credit cards, identification. Cell phone, transportation, lodging. It was all thought out and taken care of.

Pulling out the first bill my fingers closed around, I placed it into the man's waiting hand. "Here you go."

He looked down in disbelief before flashing surprised eyes at me. "A hundred dollars? Are you sure you didn't make a mistake, sir?"

Integrity. I hadn't expected that. I reached into my wallet once more and pulled out the remaining bills. "You know what, good man, you can have it all." I folded the bills and added it to the one already in his open hand.

His face lit up with shock, then excitement, as he shook my hand vigorously. "Thank you so much, sir. God bless you."

"You're most welcome," I said, smiling at him.

Behind me, the loud roar of a motorcycle drew my attention, and my head pivoted toward the blur of chrome and shiny red paint. I walked along the sidewalk to the intersection, where the bike was stopped at a traffic light. It really was a thing of beauty. Exhilarating. Freeing. That's what I imagined it would feel like to ride one. I'd have to see for myself.

I stopped abruptly as a wave of excitement coursed through me. The beast of my bond was stirring.

"Roger, I didn't forget," a faint voice called from behind me.

I froze. I'd know that voice anywhere. The creature inside me reared, whipping my power into a frenzy.

Elle.

I turned around just in time to see her strolling toward the man I had given the money to, her dark hair braided and swishing as she walked, her body clad in a fitted tank top and leggings. Bright-blue sneakers adorned her feet, and a cross-body bag hung from her shoulder.

I glanced up at the building behind her. Full Life Fitness. A gym. I couldn't tear my eyes away from her, devouring as much of her stunning face as I could. A wistful smile lifted her lips as she gazed at the man walking toward her.

"I got you the Berry Blast smoothie, without the kale this time, as promised." She handed a tall plastic cup to the man, who bowed his head gratefully and took the drink from her.

"Thank you, sweet Eleyse," the man said. "You are too kind to me."

"It's nothing at all. But seriously, frigging kale? What the hell are they thinking? Who needs that shit in a smoothie?" She threw her head back and laughed, and my heart stopped.

Even if I lived four thousand more years with her at my side, I'd never get tired of that laugh, the look of pure joy on her face.

My power surged inside me as the beast of my bond roared, fighting to be free. A tidal wave of heat and desire bowled me over, and I gripped the lamppost beside me, scrambling for support. Fuck. What the bloody hell was this? I was losing control. This had never happened before. My skin was clammy and hot, and to my horror, my body began responding to her. Sweet, merciful Gods! I was getting a certified erection in the middle of the city street.

I'd given in to my desires the first time we met. Not again. As much as I wanted her, the need to know her was stronger. I would take things slow; although my soul claimed her as mine, we were strangers. I wanted a deeper connection with her, to learn everything there was to know about her.

Once more, the beast inside me keened and thrashed, and I wrangled for control, forcing my power into submission. My beast was having none of it.

23

It twisted and writhed inside me.

I had to get out of here. Now.

Although shielded and invisible, the labral on my wrist was still clasped there, and with one last look at Elle, I swirled my giln with trembling fingers, my knees almost buckling as I slipped into the air, getting as far away from my eternal soul's shadow as I could.

The Goddess Eolith was right. I'd have to get the beast of my bond under control before approaching her.

Chapter 4

ELEYSE

M AY 2: ONE YEAR, ELEVEN MONTHS AGO . . .

As soon as I got home, I put the kettle on, coiled my hair into a bun, stripped off my clothes, and jumped into the shower. My nerves were shot. The encounter with the beautiful man-god on the sidewalk had left me . . . frazzled, for lack of a better word.

Are you an angel? Shit. Had I actually said that? God, he must have thought I was a frigging dolt.

I blasted the water on cold, intent on washing away the burning thoughts from my mind. A hysterical titter escaped my lips as I pictured the steam rising off my body in thick, frustrated waves.

I had just stepped out of the bathroom into my bedroom when the chime of the doorbell pierced the silence.

What the— Who the hell was here at this hour? My eyes flicked to the clock on my bedside table. Ten minutes past nine. I hurriedly yanked on a tank top and yoga pants and tiptoed down the stairs.

I looked through the peephole and almost fainted. It was *him*. My man-god. My heart thudded like a confusion of stampeding wildebeests, that wild excitement from earlier tumbling me once more. Sublime contentment. A staggering sense of familiarity and possessiveness. Where were these feelings even coming from?

I shook my head and refocused my thoughts. Shit. Was he following me? Should I be worried? What if he attacked me?

You'd probably like that, the smug voice in my head blurted out.

Oh shut up, I retorted. My eyes darted around the room for something

I could use as a weapon. I grabbed my yellow umbrella from the stand in the foyer and slowly opened the door a crack.

"Umm . . . yes?" I peered up at him, my mind swirling with questions.

"Hi again," he replied, reaching something out to me. "Full disclosure—I'm not stalking you; this was on the sidewalk after you made your frantic getaway." He smiled that irresistible smile again, his eyes twinkling with humor.

He was holding my wallet. I reached out my hand and took it from him.

"Your driver's license was in it and I figured it would be easier to drop it off to you rather than taking it to the police station. I hope that's okay."

"Th—thanks." I stared at him blankly, my mind at a loss for words. Shit. He knew where I lived.

"I'm Asher, by the way."

Oh, God. This was ridiculous. Even his name was sexy. I closed my eyes and sighed to myself. I had to snap out of it. He would think something was wrong with me. And for some reason, it mattered to me what he thought.

"I'm Eleyse. I, uh . . . I feel like I owe you an apology for my strange behavior earlier."

"None needed. I just caught you at a bad time, you having just pulverized those guys in the bar and all—which let me say, was highly entertaining."

"They were jerks," I stated simply. "They deserved worse."

"I was fully prepared to smash their faces in for you, but you did a fucking spectacular job of that all on your own."

I shrugged. "I know how to deal with assholes. I learned the hard way that the only one I can rely on to protect me is me."

A flicker of emotion flashed across his face, but it was gone as quickly as it appeared, and he smiled and reached out his hand again. "Well, I won't keep you any longer. It was nice meeting you, Eleyse."

I looked down at his outstretched hand. I didn't want him to leave. I was lonely, and every fiber of my being screamed out to be close to him, to feel some connection in my cold and withered heart.

"Would you like to come in for a drink?" I blurted out, hoping against hope that he would not sense the desperation in my voice. Even as the words left my mouth, my brain screamed at me. *What on God's green Earth are you doing, woman? We don't let strange men into our house.*

He looked at me long and hard, and I burned under the intensity of his scrutiny.

"Only if you want me to."

"I do." I opened the door wider for him to come in, tossing the yellow umbrella back into the stand behind me. A sliver of doubt enveloped me. Shit. My brain was right. What the hell was I doing? He could be a serial killer for all I knew.

But even as I thought it, that inexplicable certainty inside me scoffed at the notion, whipping its hair so militantly in my face to show its displeasure. *Not him,* it declared. *He belongs to us.* I whimpered as a blossom of sanguine calm unfurled inside me, dissolving my unease.

Serial killers can be hot, too, you know, my brain quipped sarcastically. I swatted the thought away.

The sheer breadth of his frame hugged the doorway, and I swallowed, marveling again at how stunning he was. He slid his jacket off, and I took it from him and hung it on the coat rack in the foyer. I bit my lip to keep from swooning at the heat emanating off his body.

I led him to the kitchen and gestured to a bar stool near the kitchen island, my heart pounding like a sugared-up toddler banging a bucket. He slid onto the stool and leaned his elbows on the breakfast bar, leisurely studying me. Shy and self-conscious with his eyes on me, I absently turned off the burner for the kettle. I opened the fridge and peered inside nervously.

"Beer or wine?" I asked over my shoulder. Jeez, why was I so nervous? I'd never reacted like this to someone before. I turned around quickly. "Wait. Do angels drink beer or wine?"

His lips tipped up, his green eyes crinkling at the corners. "Beer's fine."

I grabbed a can of beer and a bottle of wine and closed the fridge. When I turned around, he was still looking at me, a curious smile on his face.

"Do I make you uncomfortable, Eleyse? I can leave if I do."

God, I loved the way my name sounded on his lips. It gave me goosebumps just hearing him say it.

I sighed and placed the drinks on the counter. "No, I don't want you to leave." I peered up at him, feeling suddenly brave. "But seriously, you can't tell me that other women don't get all starry-eyed and tongue-tied around you. I mean, look at you." I gestured toward him with both hands.

A smile tugged at his lips and he shrugged. "Perhaps, but I've never found any of them as alluring as I find you."

I threw my head back and laughed. "That's a really good line." I handed him his beer. "Really good. I bet it works all the time too."

He laughed, and I delighted in the sound of it.

I leaned against the counter in front of him. "In all honesty, I'm not an easy woman to get to know. I don't let people in, and that's the way I like it. I think it's safe to say I'm a loner."

What was wrong with me? Why was I telling him this? This was stuff serial killers would definitely want to know when scouting their victims. But I couldn't help myself. Something about him called to me in a way I'd never experienced before. I *wanted* to be vulnerable with him, which confused the hell out of me, because I was vulnerable with no one.

He arched an eyebrow. "So this is a bold move for you, then? Asking a complete stranger into your house to have a drink with you seems out of character for a loner."

"Oh, it's completely uncharted territory." I poured myself a glass of wine and took a quick sip to steady my nerves. My eyes unfocused, distorting his face into a hazy blur as I retreated into my scrambled thoughts to chase the truth. "You make me uneasy, but a *good* uneasy. How can I explain? It's an uneasiness that makes me feel like I'm still alive."

His gaze burned, those emerald eyes stripping me bare, as if peering into the desiccated emptiness inside my soul. It hurt, that scrutiny. I didn't want him to see too much, to discover the toxic ugliness that lived in me. He would run for the hills, and I didn't want that. I wanted to keep him a little longer.

"So what did you have in mind when you asked me to come in?" He leaned back in his chair and folded his arms across his broad, muscular chest that I simply could not tear my eyes away from.

"Umm . . . honestly, I don't know." I shook my head and forced myself to look up at his face. "I just didn't want you to leave. It's been a very long time since I've felt something that warmed me inside."

"And I looked like I could warm you inside?" He was clearly teasing me now.

I blushed furiously, trying to rid myself of the mental picture that his words had created.

I shrugged and stared at him boldly. "I have no doubts that you could. My body jumped ship and swam over to your boat the moment I laid eyes on you."

He chuckled softly, and a riot of goosebumps skittered across my skin as he touched my wrist with his hand. "All teasing aside, Eleyse, I do know a thing or two about feeling dead inside, so I can relate to what you're saying. Here's to feeling alive." He lifted his beer.

I raised my glass and clinked it against his can. "To feeling alive," I replied, taking a sip of my wine.

Holding onto my glass, I beckoned for him to follow me into my sunken sunroom, just off the kitchen. I placed the glass on the coffee table, folding my legs under me as I sat on the couch.

He stopped to admire my piano in the corner of the room. "Do you play?"

"I used to."

He raised an eyebrow. "Not anymore?"

I paused for what seemed like an eternity before answering him. "There's too much sadness in the music this piano has given life to. Too many echoes of a time when there was happiness, laughter, and music in my life."

I could tell that I had thrown him with my words. Heck, I had thrown myself too. It was like I couldn't help myself. I was never this loose-lipped about my past or my feelings with anyone.

"Sometimes I wish I could smash it to pieces," I heard myself say, my voice cracking from the emotion slowly creeping up on me. "But it's all I have left of someone who loved me very much a long time ago."

"I'm sorry, Eleyse," he said, sitting next to me and squeezing my arm softly.

I stiffened, my arm burning from where he had touched me. Everything was heightened with him, relegating my brain to mush in its struggle to process my body's response to him. I picked up my wine glass and took a sip, desperate for any kind of distraction.

"I feel it, too, you know," he said, as if reading my mind. "The attraction runs both ways."

My stomach flipped into somersaults again.

"I'm sure I can be many things to you, and you to me." He brushed a thumb against my knuckles, sending a shiver through my entire body. "But tonight, I think that what you need more than anything is friendship."

I furrowed my brows, my eyes flying to his.

"I saw you earlier at the bar, before the altercation," he said. "You sat there, lost in your own pain, and your grief and agony emanated off you in waves." When I didn't answer, he tilted my face to look at him. "I've been there before. I know what that kind of pain feels like, what it looks like."

I held his gaze, startling at the flicker of recognition there, at the kindred emotion in his eyes that he let me see.

He had known. When I had asked him to stay, he had looked right through me and seen my decaying heart. I hadn't been able to hide my desperation after all.

Feeling a sudden sense of temerity, I put my wine glass on the coffee table and turned to face him, studying his handsome face, committing his features to memory before locking my eyes with his. It was a long time before I spoke. "I've lived my entire life jumping from one tragedy to the next." I made no attempt to hide the bitterness in my voice. "One by one, I lost every single person I loved in my life. There's a hole inside me, and it's there by design, to remind me that love is pain, and to warn others that to love me is to welcome death. No one can fix me anymore—I'm beyond redemption.

"Years ago, I shut off that part of me that lets me feel. But tonight, you've made me realize that I *need* to feel something or I will go mad. Not love, no, but lust—well, lust is the closest thing to feeling some connection with another person that I'm willing to let myself feel. As for friendship, that can lead to caring, and caring to love. It's a fine line to balance."

"So if not love, and if not friendship, what about music? Is that welcome in your life anymore?" He reached for my hand and covered it with his own.

It was a simple question, but it jolted me to a place buried deep inside my heart, where a dam had been plugged a long time ago.

I choked on a sob, not sure how to continue without losing control. I closed my eyes and let myself remember. I remembered my parents, whose lives were filled with music, love, and laughter. What few memories I had of them were of those three things. It was the same with my aunt Mags and Liam.

I opened my eyes and looked at Asher through my blurred vision, glimpsing the emotion on his face as he bore witness to my pain. The bloody dam had broken and I wasn't sure how I was going to plug it back again.

"Music is even more dead to me than love." It pained me to say that. Music had once been my entire life, my reason for existing, but now, it only brought back painful memories. "There is no beauty or purpose in my life anymore." I was crying in earnest now. "What did I do? Why did I have to suffer the deaths of *all* my loved ones? Why couldn't I have died too?" I balled my hands into fists in my lap. "There is nothing left for me in this world anymore."

With that last statement, all the emotion came rushing out of me and I covered my face with my hands, sobbing uncontrollably. Asher's arms encircled me, pulling me against him. I let him, craving, needing his closeness, comfort. I placed my head on his chest and let the flood carry me away, my heart for the first time in a long time feeling less weary and tight. He held me as I cried, stroking my hair gently with his fingers. I must have cried myself to sleep in his arms, because the next thing I knew, it was morning, and I was in my bed, and he was gone.

On the nightstand, was a small note written in elegant cursive.

Eleyse, it's not too late to bring the music back to life—Ash.

Chapter 5

ELEYSE

MAY 3: ONE YEAR, ELEVEN MONTHS AGO . . .

Crap. What had I done? My feet pounded the trail as I ran, my mind completely preoccupied with the events of last night. All day, I'd kept replaying what happened.

Who was I, even? That person—the one I'd turned into the moment I laid eyes on Asher—wasn't me. On so many levels, what had transpired between us was strange, and it both terrified and fascinated me.

Swatting a branch out of my path, I plodded forward, the sticky-sweet air whipping against my skin, hot and stifling. High overhead, the trill of birdsong reverberated through the trees, the tranquility I always felt in these woods enveloping me like a dear friend.

I was at the halfway mark. Touching the large oak and turning around, I started on my way back, my troubled thoughts sweeping me away once more.

It had been almost a year since I had given up my quest for death. I thought about that dream every day—the woman with violet hair, the things she had said. That dream had kept me clinging to the promise of something I wasn't even sure existed because it was infinitely better than the alternative of seeking out death.

Deep inside, I wanted to hope. I wanted to live.

He comes, and on his heels, your future.

I'd never forgotten those words, had spent many a night wondering what they meant. And all day, they'd kept replaying over and over in my head like a stuck record. I couldn't put my finger on it, but something about my encounter with Asher gave me strange vibes, vibes very reminiscent of that dream and the woman in it.

The way he had looked at me last night, the things he said, the way my body and heart responded to him—I didn't know what to make of it. It was as if all the rigid rules I had implemented to deal with the world didn't apply to him. He'd walked in and simply slipped past my defenses, wrangling out of me feelings and thoughts I had locked away a long time ago. I didn't like it one bit.

The rules were in place not just to protect me, but to protect others. To get close to me was to entice death, and I couldn't allow that to happen to anyone else. No matter how handsome and irresistible they were.

That beautiful man—quite likely an angel—is danger, my brain chided me. Of course, my brain was right. The path that led to Asher was the same one that led to pain and loss. I needed to avoid it all costs. Shouldn't be too hard to do. He was gone, and apart from the small note on my bedside table, he had left no number, did not mention wanting to see me again.

It was a good thing. I'd probably scared him off anyway. I'd practically projectile vomited all my depressing emotions into his lap. Everything about me screamed, *Keep out. TMB!*—too much baggage. He was probably thanking his lucky stars he'd dodged that bullet.

Precisely twenty-seven minutes later, I exited the trailhead. My ears perked up, and I froze in my tracks. Was that a hiss? It sure sounded like a hiss. My head swiveled around, searching for a pair of terrifying, blue, crossed eyes.

Nothing.

Maybe I'd just imagined it. Yeah, that was it. After all, it had been about four months since I'd seen that mangy terror. I'd just assumed the sad excuse for a cat had slunk off somewhere and croaked. For almost a year, it had terrorized me, always darting out somewhere along this stretch of the path and scaring the shit out of me before chasing me home.

It was a foul little beast, although I had to admit—begrudgingly—that the hellcat had saved me from getting nailed by a drunk driver once. After my run one evening, the fleabag had darted out of the bushes and bit my calf, and in the melee that ensued with me flipping out and screaming, trying to pry its teeth out of my skin, I narrowly missed the pickup truck that barreled onto the sidewalk a stone's throw away from me.

I had marched myself straight to the emergency room and gotten a rabies shot. I hadn't just narrowly escaped death by truck only to die from the bite of a rabid cat. How ironic would that have been? That just when I gave up trying to die, death came looking for me?

Now, as I ran through my tree-lined neighborhood, my head on a swivel, I made it all the way to my house without incident. No surprise critters hiding in the bushes.

"Ovi," a voice called from up ahead.

I smiled and changed direction, jogging toward the house across the street from mine. In rural Hargrove, the houses on my cul-de-sac were set a bit apart from each other, just the way I liked it.

Standing at the edge of her long driveway, hands on her hips, looking at me critically, was my neighbor, Aggie. "I see you're not wearing a bra again," she said dryly, narrowing her gaze as she studied my chest.

I clucked at her. "I've told you. These tops have built-in support. They're made like this so you don't *have* to wear a bra."

"Tell that to your nipples," she quipped, pointing at my chest. "I don't care what you say. You're out every day, traipsing through the woods, those ample breasts of yours bouncing around with not a care in the world. It's not goddamn Mardi Gras, Eleyse. One day, you're going to get to my age, and you'll look down, and *phloop*, there they'll be, keeping your arthritic feet company."

I burst out laughing. "Geez, Aggie, you make it sound like I have enormous boobs. I'm only a C-cup, for god's sake. I don't think I'll ever have to worry about them tripping me up when I walk."

She snorted, pointing to my chest. "Keep up this nonsense, and they definitely will. That's how time and gravity work."

I chuckled. Good old Aggie. Blunt as fuck. She was in her seventies and still a force of nature. She glared at me, her back ramrod straight, her short, mahogany hair perfectly curled. Her skin was flawless—she made no secret of the boatload of plastic surgery she'd had.

As always, she was dressed to the nines. Today, she was wearing a blue silk blouse and charcoal slacks, with expensive-looking, low-heeled slingbacks on her feet. How she walked in them at her age, I had no clue. Her signature string of pearls hung around her neck, and a massive diamond glittered on her ring finger. It didn't matter that the only place she was going was her gorgeous wraparound porch.

"Always dress to impress," she constantly told me. "You never know when Prince Charming might make an appearance."

Ha. What would she have said last night if she saw me opening my door to a real-live Prince Charming? My hair in a messy bun, wearing nothing but flip flops, yoga pants, and a tank top. And—gasp—no bra.

She loved to impart her *pearls of wisdom* to me, running the gamut of topics such as the importance of Kegels, the merits of anal bleaching, and the delights of tantric sex. She was a powerhouse of knowledge and took every opportunity to share it with me.

I honestly had no idea what I did for entertainment before she moved in eight months ago. After her husband, Jack, passed away, she'd sold off their entire estate, donated the vast majority of her money to charity, and downsized to rural Hargrove. She still kept a penthouse in the city, but she never visited. Said it reminded her too much of the wild sexual adventures she and Jack had lived out.

She called me Ovi—on account of my resting bitch face—having learned that word on a trip to the Amazon with her late husband. According to her, it meant, "the one who sucks on lemons." Even if it did—which I highly doubted—that she called *me* by that name was in itself the biggest irony, given that I was sure if I looked up the definition of resting bitch face on the internet, Aggie's scowling face would be emblazoned right next to it.

"Have you been to see Nina?" she asked, cocking her head and regarding me appraisingly.

I rolled my eyes. "I'm not sure about her, Aggie. I swear, she slathered the wax *inside* my vagina last week before ripping it out. And then she laughed at me because I almost passed out on the table. She's a sadist."

Aggie tsked at me. "Nina's the best at what she does. Suck it up. Don't you dare stop going to her. Any day now, you might get laid, and you'll have me to thank for your smooth and aesthetically pleasing nether regions."

"Oh absolutely, you'll be the first on my gratitude list," I sassed.

"I can only hope getting laid will also do something about that attitude of yours. No word of a lie, sometimes I think all that ravishing beauty is wasted on the likes of you."

I stuck my tongue out at her.

"Anyway," she said, reaching for my hands. "Your reckless bralessness and pathetic pain tolerance aside, I called you over because I wanted to warn you about a man lurking about in front of your house." Her voice was hushed as she pulled me closer.

I froze. Was she talking about Asher? Had she seen him last night after all?

"What man?"

"He was there about an hour ago, standing on your curb after you went for your run. He looked right at me and walked away before I made it up the driveway to ask him what he was doing there."

I frowned. "What did he look like?"

"Tall, shoulder-length, light-brown hair, handsome face." She squeezed my hands tightly. "But the thing that startled me were his eyes. Silver. Bright. Paranormal."

My heart thudded in my chest. No, it couldn't be. I looked at Aggie, terror ripping the breath from my body. Please, God, no. I knew exactly who she was talking about.

Death.

My stomach churned, and my skin grew hot and clammy. I was going to be sick. My horror must have been reflected on my face because Aggie tilted my chin, forcing me to meet her gaze, her eyes wide with concern.

"Eleyse, what is it?"

Tears blurred my eyes. Please, not Aggie. I'd kept her at arm's length ever since she introduced herself to me the day she moved in, but I'd grown fond of her all the same. She was funny and feisty, and although she'd never admit it, she was lonely, just like I was. She made me laugh, and I felt a little less alone knowing she was across the street.

You can't lose someone if you have no one. That was my mantra. I should have known better.

But what if it wasn't Aggie? What about Asher? Could it be a coincidence that the day after I met him, Death showed up at my door? Asher was still a stranger to me, but the way I'd responded to him? The feelings he had roused in me? What if that was enough to seal his fate?

"Eleyse, you're scaring me," Aggie said. "You're as white as a sheet."

"I'm so sorry, Aggie. I have to go." I didn't want to leave her, but I couldn't stay. There was nowhere she could go to escape if it was indeed her that Death had within his crosshairs. I knew that firsthand, had learned that lesson well.

"No, you don't, Ovi," she demanded. "Tell me what's going on."

Helplessness washed over me in writhing waves, and once more, like it did last night with Asher, my emotions overpowered me. I was so tired of living like this. Closed off, locked away, scared to live, to feel.

I took one look at the worry and affection in Aggie's light-brown eyes, and it all came tumbling out. I told her everything.

Chapter 6

ELEYSE

"Oh, my dear girl." Aggie shifted her position on the love seat to wrap her arms around me. We were sitting on her front porch, where for the past hour and a half, I had revealed to her all the details of my sad life. My eyes were sore and swollen, my nose bruised from the countless tissues I'd abused.

The entire time, Aggie had sat silently, listening, not interrupting, just letting me release all the sorrow, guilt, and pain I had locked away inside. I couldn't deny the lightness in my body, as if a huge weight had been lifted off my chest and shoulders.

"You don't really believe that, do you?" she asked, squeezing my hand. "That the deaths of all those you loved were your fault?"

"It's all too much to be a coincidence. First my parents, then Mags, then Liam. Almost Charlotte. And every time one of them died—*him*. Death. And he was there every time I tried to take my life. Except the last time."

"There has to be some other explanation." She crossed her ankles and stared off toward the road, her expression wistful. "I am sorry that you felt so hopeless that you thought ending your life was your only choice. I wish I could have been there for you then."

"It wouldn't have mattered if you had been here then, Aggie. I was in a terrible place."

"And that all changed when you had that dream?"

I furrowed my brows. "I know it sounds stupid, but I can't explain it. It was a life-changing moment. And maybe I was just so desperate at that point that I was clinging to any shred of hope, but that dream saved my life and has kept me going since." I crossed my arms over my chest. "I mean, it's not like my life has changed in any significant way. It's more of a mindset change than anything."

Aggie squeezed my fingers. "Well, I, for one, am glad that you did change."

I nodded, rubbing my temples with my fingers.

"Do you believe in fate, Ovi?" Aggie asked, arching a brow. "The supernatural?"

I grimaced. "I think it's all bullshit, really."

Her brows lifted. "Do you, now? You just told me that you believed yourself to be cursed. That Death has followed you for most of your life. That a mysterious woman came to you in a dream and gave you hope. That sounds to me like someone who believes in the existence of forces bigger than themselves at work."

"I don't know what I believe," I said softly.

Aggie toyed with the pearls around her neck. "You said the man you saw never talked to you, but did you try talking to him?"

I frowned. "Why on Earth would I do that? What would I have said? 'Hey Death, fuck off and leave me alone?'"

She shrugged. "Maybe that's why he never talked to you. Maybe he was waiting for you to initiate the conversation."

I gaped at her. "That is literally the most insane thing I've heard."

"Why?"

"Because he's bloody Death, Aggie."

"But what if he isn't? That's who you *think* he is on account of when you've seen him. But he always appeared to you *after* your loved ones died, not before, and he appeared every time you tried to take your life, but yet you're still alive."

"That's because he's a sick asshole and is playing games with me."

Aggie shook her head. "Listen to yourself. You're so blinded by your preconceived notions that you won't entertain any other possibilities."

"Like what?"

She twisted the diamond on her finger. "Well, for starters, that he's not Death. That maybe he's here for another reason. To protect you. Maybe he's responsible for you *not* being able to take your life all those times."

"You just told me that he was creepy as hell, standing there, watching my house."

"I never said that. I said he was hanging around in front of your house."

"Same thing. Either way, I think there might be a chance he's coming for you."

Aggie chuckled. "Ovi, dear, even if he is Death—which I don't think he is—I am not afraid to die. I have lived a full, rich life, and it will be a blessing to be reunited with my Jack. Trust me, outliving the love of your life is its own living death. So, please, my sweet girl, keep your conscience clear. My death, whenever it occurs, will not be your fault."

"Aggie—"

"And what about this handsome stranger you met last night? I have to admit, I didn't think you had it in you."

I shifted in my seat to glare at her. "How can you be so calm after everything I told you? I'm not crazy, Aggie."

"I never said you were," she said, taking my hand again. "Listen, Eleyse, all I'm saying is that sometimes we can make ourselves believe truths that are grounded in the unreliable confines of our own thoughts. I asked you if you believed in the supernatural. Well, I do. And I think that yes, there is something *other* happening with you, but based on everything you've told me, I don't see things the same way you do."

"What would you have me do?"

"Well, I certainly don't want you to stay away from me because you feel like you're not allowed to care about people. And I definitely don't want you to stay away from your handsome stranger. He could be the key to getting you laid. I told you Nina's wax jobs would pay off."

I blushed at the image of Asher being anywhere near my wax job. "Cut it out. I don't think I'll ever see him again, anyway."

"Hmph. I'm holding out hope, Ovi." Her face softened as she tapped my chest with her fingers. "Listen, Eleyse. You might be tough and hard on the outside, and try your hardest not to let anyone in, but you can't help caring about people. As a person, that's who you are. You're compassionate and kind-hearted, no matter how hard you try to hide that. And that's something to be celebrated, not shunned."

"What about the man, Aggie? What if he comes back? You said it too. His eyes were flashing silver and strange. He might be dangerous."

She looked at me with a grim look on her face. "If you see him again, Ovi, don't run away. Confront him. At this point, what do you have to lose? You already believe he doesn't want *you* dead. Do the one thing you haven't done yet—talk to him."

Chapter 7

ASHER

P *Six hundred and eighty-four days.*

The Lonefera kept pace, steadfastly counting the time down, its presence a reassurance that progress—although slow as fuck—was being made. Fourteen days Elle had already relived, our first two encounters behind her. It would be weeks before she saw me again.

I stared at her as she lay there. Her face was peaceful, thick lashes framing her soft cheeks, her lips parted gently in slumber. I enfolded her warm hand in mine, my thumb stroking her wrist gently.

Turning my attention inward, I reached for our Gloweyen bond. *Catraia,* I called in my mind.

I am here, Asher, she answered without hesitation.

I sat on the edge of Elle's bed. *There's something I've been curious about for a long time.* There definitely was, but how to frame the question? I ran my fingers through my hair. *At what point did you come into existence within Elle? Was it at her conception?*

Ever since I'd learned of the ancient celestial star etching and the entity that lived inside Elle, I was flooded with questions about how Catraia's existence and presence would work. Who better to go to than the source?

I have existed within her from the moment she came to be inside her Goddess Mother, but just as she lay slumbering in the Cradle of the In-Between for thousands of years, so did I. There was a latent sense of awareness, but nothing strong enough to understand what was happening around me.

The Cradle of the In-Between. A hallowed sanctum in the celestial plane of the Void accessible only to the Great Creator, Arazul. It still blew my mind that although Elle was only just approaching thirty years old, she had existed before her human birth for many millennia. The God of Gods himself had removed her from the Goddess Eolith's womb and nestled her in the Cradle of the In-Between to protect and ensure the future written in the stars by the Mavigos.

I turned my attention back to Catraia. *You remained in this stasis, so to speak, even in the human world?*

Yes. My awareness snapped awake when Eleyse arrived in Ariadna, her return to the Sangelis being the catalyst, but I only fully awakened upon her transformation into the Songbird of Valkyse in Falayen with your mother.

A pang of longing washed over me. My mother. The former Queen Consort of Valkyse. She had been dead for over a hundred years, but had somehow been sent back to pass her Songbird of Valkyse mantle to Eleyse in Falayen, the sanctum of Sovereigns. I had no doubts the Mavigos were involved. Who else had the power to summon the dead and imbue them with purpose?

I swallowed the lump in my throat. *And as long as Elle lives, you will be with her?*

Until the end. She and I are Nalios.

Nalios. Hasheyn for conjoined. I knew the term. So deeply connected and interdependent. One unable to exist without the other. Only contained within beings of extreme power.

And if anything were to happen to you? I asked.

That is the wrong question, Asher. I exist to protect Eleyse. I am the anchor and steward of her power. I will cease to be only when she does.

Knowing that Catraia could never leave Elle and would always protect her filled me with relief. But there was something else that still puzzled me.

In the entire Sangelis, I know of only one being with an entity such as you inside them.

Is there a question there? she asked.

Arazul, the Great Creator is the only one who has a Nalios connection.

It's only natural that he would, she said. *He is the God of Gods in the Sangelis. In other parts of the universe, the order of things, as ordained by the Mavigos, would also follow suit.*

But why Elle? I prodded.

Because she was chosen by the Mavigos to usher in the Third Age of the Sangelis—the Light Age. To restore the balance. To do that, she would have to contain more power than even the most powerful of the Gods.

More powerful than Arazul. I glanced down at Elle's beautiful face, so fragile and innocent as she slept. That a colossal vortex of power lay inside her was mind-blowing.

Don't forget your place in all of this, High King of the Light Age. The Mavigos bestowed on you the ability to slay Gods. That is no trivial thing. Eleyse might be the one to usher in the new age, but that is only possible with you at her side. Some might say that your Gloweyen bond is even more powerful than Nalios. She is your eternal soul's shadow. In the depthless expanse of the universe, Gloweyen defies all odds, crosses all barriers, to bring such souls together. Forever. From one life to the next.

My head snapped up. *You're saying that our souls will find each other even after we pass on from this life?*

That is the nature of your bond. Two halves of a whole that will always make their way back to each other.

The nature of our Gloweyen bond. It made sense when I thought about the history of our relationship. The overwhelming rightness I had experienced the very first time I saw her when she came through the Senshifter, the way she had reacted to me when she first saw me in her world, and every time afterward. The way I had reacted to her. Always drawn to each other on a subconscious, primitive level, unable to stay away.

Happiness and fulfillment hummed within me but tangled with my fear and worry. The bitter soil of war and bloodshed was hardly nurturing for love to blossom. I hated that this was our reality.

You believe this war will extend to the Gods? I asked Catraia.

It already has. The wheels are in motion.

Fuck.

"Asher," a voice said from behind me. I turned to see the Goddess Eolith standing in the doorway, her eyes flashing silver as she regarded me. "We must talk." Her face was somber as she walked toward the balcony overlooking the ocean.

I followed her out onto the stone overhang, brilliant sunlight streaming onto the expansive space around us. Here in Solniess, the sea that yawned before me was the most intense shade of blue I had ever seen. Along the shore, the sand itself glittered like it was made of crushed diamonds. Not a cloud drifted by in the sky. God magic.

The Goddess Mother turned to face me. "We must discuss WorDalg."

I groaned inwardly. The last thing I wanted was to think of the threats awaiting us in the real world. Time didn't exist here in the celestial plane of the Void, but the moment Elle was finished reliving those lost two years through her consciousness and returned to me, our shadow selves and consciousnesses would leave Solniess and be reunited with our physical bodies, where reality beckoned.

It really was incredible how the timeless planes in the Void worked. At the entrance to the Void, once the gates to a timeless plane were opened and entered, time in the real world ground to a halt for that person, resuming at the exact spot they left off when they exited the timeless plane. Two years, ten, a hundred—it made no difference. Time was an illusion here, completely disconnected from the constructs of reality.

"Has something happened?" I furrowed my brows, my thoughts returning to the Goddess Eolith's earlier statement.

WorDalg was a powerful shadow wraith—a Sykrilix—an ancient being, perhaps as ancient as Gargmoin, although I couldn't say for sure. He was doomed to guard Valkyse's Phantera, but how he met with that demise was a mystery to me.

Buried within each dominion in Ariadna was a magical weapon of powerful proportions—a Phantera. The Cerulean Embers in Valkyse, the

Viridian Tide in Averon, the Sandstone Shadows in Solanis, and the Sable Tempest in Tandor. Each Phantera's respective burial place was known only to the dominion's ruling Sovereign. Valkyse's Phantera was buried deep within the Entombed City of Magana, located in the far-flung reaches of Brus.

The only thing holding WorDalg's power in check was his subjugation to the entombed city and his conscripted allegiance to me as the Sovereign of Valkyse.

The Goddess Eolith frowned. "Kaliope might have turned him to her side, but WorDalg is incapable of harming you; he is bound to do whatever you command of him. He might hate every second of it, but he has no choice. That being said, it doesn't mean that he couldn't betray you. The most likely scenario is that he will aid you in retrieving the Phantera, but will lead Kaliope to you and let her do the rest."

I folded my arms across my chest. "The Phantera is not safe there if Kaliope knows about it. We can't risk it falling into her hands. As soon as Elle retrieves her memories and we destroy the rebounding curse, I will leave for the Entombed City of Magana."

Eolith studied me, not saying anything, and immediately, I sensed there was more she wasn't saying. "What is it?" I asked.

"WorDalg is not the only complication you will encounter in the territories of Brus-Winnd." Her eyes flitted toward the ocean. "Kurglokh, prince of the Soulshredders has pledged his allegiance to Kaliope as well. Undoubtedly, both he and WorDalg were lured by Gargmoin's power. He is, after all, as ancient as they are."

Streaks of black clouded my vision. This just kept getting better and better. The heaviness in my chest pressed in on me like a vise. Passing through Demon's Maw—the narrow sea crossing separating Brus from Winnd—to get to the Entombed City of Magana was inevitable. But the cursed place was the abode of the Jiacotie Soulshredders, aptly named for the deepwater wraiths who fed off the souls of those unfortunate enough to venture unsanctioned into Demon's Maw.

Fuck. Feeding was putting it nicely. Those voracious fiends were pack feeders, ripping their victims' bodies and souls to shreds before consuming them. When they were done with a living being, there was nothing left for the afterlife.

The Goddess Eolith sighed. "We both know that just because every living thing in the Dominion of Valkyse is bound to obey you, it doesn't mean they will make it easy for you. Especially the dark, ancient ones. They are predators, always looking for an opportunity to pounce, to gain an advantage. Kurglokh is ruthless and clever and cannot be trusted. He will try to find a way to ensnare or make you beholden to him."

She wasn't telling me anything I didn't already know.

"This war won't just be fought amongst mortals, Asher." Her gaze fastened on Eleyse's form in the chamber in front of us. "The Gods and ancient ones will join the fray, and sides will be taken."

I grimaced. "Which Gods do you think will be on our side?"

She blinked, as if thrown by the question, her delicately arched brows furrowing together. "Arazul, of course; the Goddess of the Elements, I hope; and Sorin . . . well, that depends."

I stared at her, noting the trepidation and doubt etched on her face.

"You know he will find out about Elle soon enough," I said softly. "Undoubtedly, Kaliope knows about the celestial star etching. Everything she is doing—going after the Phanteras, seeking out ancient ones and Sovereigns as allies, amassing her father's armies—it's clear that she knows. I got the distinct sense that the God of Chaos had no clue who Elle was, so he is still in the dark, but it won't stay that way for long. The Gods *will* learn of the ancient celestial star etching, and when Sorin does, there will be no hiding that you and the Great Creator kept the knowledge of Elle's existence from him." I sighed and placed my hands on the balcony railing. "I wouldn't deign to tell a powerful goddess such as yourself what to do, but for Elle's sake—for all our sakes—it would be better if he learned the truth from you. He is her father. He has a right to know."

She lowered her head, her hands clenched at her sides. "I know." After a moment of silence, she lifted her gaze to meet mine. "The Veil of Aegis is in jeopardy of being destroyed, Asher."

"What?" I said, my eyes wide. I had to have misheard. I gave my head a shake and looked at her. Fuck. This conversation was just brimming with horrible news.

The Veil of Aegis, a knitted fusion of light magic—a union of the light strain of the Old, Arcane Magic and the Ethereal Harmonies—kept the dark sway of the Old, Arcane Magic contained. It was ancient, as old as Ariadna itself. There was no way it was in jeopardy of being destroyed.

"But that would mean—"

"That the dark sway of the Old, Arcane Magic will run wild in the Sangelis, spreading unchecked, usurping the Ethereal Harmonies, and there is nothing the Gods of the Sangelis will be able to do to stop it." Her lips were pursed in a thin line, her expression grim. "Arazul believes that it was an event such as this that brought about the destruction of the First Age. He believes that this is the basis for the ancient celestial star etching. This is ultimately what Elle was meant to prevent from happening."

Her words settled in my gut like a barrel of rocks. The way ahead was dark and dismal. Gods, ancient beings, and mortals. Thrown together, unsettling the natural order of things. Millions of years of co-existence about to come undone.

War. At the very heart of it, the celestial star etching proclaimed it an inevitability. And Elle and I were instrumental in how it would unfold. But what of the Ankhira the star etching told of? If it was indeed a weapon, crafted from the joining of all four Phanteras, then yes, it would be possible to harness the power of the Ethereal Harmonies. And in doing so, then the Goddess Mother was right—it would be possible to destroy the Veil of Aegis.

The Goddess Eolith placed her hand on my elbow. "Although this is the safest place for Elle to be while her consciousness travels back through time, we must be careful. The other Gods could come calling."

"Who, specifically, are you referring to?" I asked. "The Great Creator? Sorin?"

"Arazul will certainly come. He has watched over Elle since the very beginning. As for Sorin, I will go to him. Like you said, it is best he hears it from me, but he might also want to see his daughter for himself. And I don't think I can deny him that."

I clenched my jaw. "I can't let that happen if he means her harm."

The Goddess Mother's eyes flared, the silver churning in her irises like liquid smoke. "Elle is the child of our love. I know his heart. He could never hurt her."

"Are you sure? I am not willing to risk her safety if there is even the slightest chance that he might harm her."

Eolith nodded. "I am sure, Asher. It is Cazril and Jaraya that we need to keep an eye on. Their penchant for darkness and cruel games makes them the biggest threats we face in this timeless plane."

I nodded in agreement. Both the God of Chaos and the Goddess of the Night had a reputation for callousness and cruelty. I didn't want them anywhere near Elle. I couldn't be trusted to keep my composure a second time.

"What of the Goddess of the Elements?" I asked, rubbing my knuckles.

The Goddess Eolith frowned. "Twylos tries to stay neutral in matters of conflict concerning the Gods."

"There is no neutral ground here," I growled. "This is no trivial matter. Life in the Sangelis as we know it is on the line."

"Arazul will make her choose," Eolith said with certainty. "In the meantime, Asher, I think it would be wise if you enlist the aid of one or two of the most trusted in your inner circle. Just as a precaution. I will grant them access to Solniess and imbue them with some of my magic."

I nodded grimly. The fact that she was asking this of me told me that she was worried about the Gods interfering. And if she was leaving to go to make her confession to Sorin, then I would be alone with Elle. I had absolutely no fear of the Gods; they were not a threat to me. The Mavigos had seen to that. It was Elle I was worried about. The more eyes on her in this vulnerable state, the better.

Gwynn, Uncle Andreo, and Lorien were at Cazara Torannon with our physical bodies. I needed them to stay there. Faron and Treye were my two most skilled warriors and closest friends. I trusted them with my life, and with Elle's. Faron and Treye, it would be.

Chapter 8

ELEYSE

MAY 17: ONE YEAR, TEN AND A HALF MONTHS AGO

My stomach rumbled loudly, echoing through the silence of my office. I looked away from my computer and glanced at my phone. Almost noon. I hadn't had breakfast this morning. After the gym, I'd been in a rush and didn't have time to stop for anything. Where the hell was Joe? He'd gone to the deli next door over half an hour ago.

As if sensing he was being summoned, Joe Randall appeared in the doorway of my office, two bags dangling in his hands. His dark hair was mussed from the wind, his comb-over a sad, sorry disaster.

"Sorry, boss." He slid one of the bags onto my desk. "The lineup was insane today, and then Sheila talked my ear off while she put the order together."

"Well, thank God you're here," I said. "I was just about to dig out that package of old, mangled crackers from the bottom of my purse. Doesn't Sheila know by now that she gets a bigger tip when she puts a rush on the order?"

"I think she has a thing for me." His lips quirked in a smile. "She kept touching my arm while she was ringing me in." He waggled his eyebrows and rocked back on his heels as he hooked his fingers through the front loops of his pants. "Plus, she always gives me extra pickles on my sandwich. The guy before me ordered the same thing, and she only put two pickles on his. I got five."

I laughed. "I think you're on to something, Joe. Thanks again for grabbing my food."

"No problem. Later, boss." He waved his index finger over his head as he barreled out of my office and down the hallway.

I grabbed my phone and purse, along with the bag Joe had deposited on my desk, and headed to the lunchroom. My mouth began to water from the smell. The Rueben sandwich at the deli was the best—so good, in fact, that it was all I ever ordered there.

Maya and Alice waved me over from their spot near the window. The two communications specialists were the closest things I had to friends at work. Ever since we'd been randomly assigned to the same group at a company team-building event a year ago, they'd been relentless afterward, refusing to back down when I brushed them off or made excuses if they tried to include me in their plans. More often than not, I said no, but once in a while, when I couldn't stand the loneliness, I'd say yes. They were bubbly and full of personality—everything I was not, although a part of me itched to give in and be as carefree as they were. And although we never made plans to eat lunch together every day, if they were in the lunchroom when I got there, I'd sit with them.

I headed toward their window seat and smiled in greeting. "I'll be back. Just gotta run to the washroom." They nodded as I placed my purse and lunch on the table and continued chatting as I walked away.

A flash of tousled, dark hair at the table in the back caught my eye as I approached the lunchroom door, and my heart did an erratic flip-flop.

Goddamn it. It was the new girl from accounting, not *him*.

The sharp sting of disappointment settled over me as I walked down the hallway. It had been two weeks since the night I met Asher, and I was unable to get the man out of my head. I thought and fantasized about him constantly, found myself looking for him everywhere, longing to catch a glimpse of him, but he had left as mysteriously as he had appeared.

In the back of my mind, always lurking in the shadows, was Aggie's sighting of the man with silver eyes. *Death*. Although Aggie had scoffed at the notion that he truly was Death, I couldn't shake the fear that at any given moment, loss would strike again. Thus far, Aggie was still as colorful and cantankerous as ever, but what about Asher? He had completely disappeared. What if it *had* been him? Could he have been the target of Death's withering embrace?

And if he wasn't, why hadn't he made an attempt to see me again? He knew where I lived.

I spied my face in the mirror as I stood in front of the bathroom sink, unable to deny the dejection reflected in my gray eyes. I sighed, washing my hands quickly before heading back out the door.

When I returned to the lunchroom, Maya and Alice were engrossed in conversation, Maya's hands animated as she explained something to Alice. "I swear, it works," she was saying. "I was so good at it that it scared the shit out of me and I stopped doing it."

Alice burst out laughing. "You're so full of shit, Maya. There's just no way."

"No way what?" I asked, sitting next to Alice. I opened the brown bag and pulled my sandwich out. God, it looked even better than it smelled.

"Maya says that when she was in college, she used to read palms, and that she had a gift for seeing the future, but she was so great at it that it scared her."

"It's no joke." Maya's curly black hair bounced around her face in her excitement. "When I was home from college my second year, my great-aunt Penelope was visiting, and she taught me how to do it. By the end of the summer, I'd gotten really good, so I put it to the test when I went back to school that fall. I was dating Jesse Armstrong at the time. Good Lord, he was hot. He used to do this crazy thing with his tongue—"

"Focus, Maya." Alice rolled her eyes and looked at me with amusement.

"Right," Maya continued. "Anyway, so one night, we're lying in bed, and I'm telling him about my summer, and I mentioned my great-aunt Penelope and the palm reading. So he asks me to read his, and I did. As my fingers traced the lines on his hand, I saw a great loss of fortune and I told him that. He laughed and shrugged it off. His family was loaded, so losing their fortune seemed inconceivable. I read his other palm, and, well, same thing. Two months later, the real estate market crashed and his family lost everything. His father had to declare bankruptcy."

"No way," I said, my voice muffled between sandwich bites.

"That has to be a coincidence." The skepticism in Maya's voice was evident.

Maya arched a brow. "That's what I thought, but then it happened two more times and it freaked me out so much that I stopped doing it." She paused for dramatic effect, taking in the silence her words had created. "The second time was a few days later with my roommate, Sara. We were hanging out, eating pizza and watching a movie. Remember, at this point, I didn't know that my prediction about Jesse would be true. So I read her palm, and told her that she would find something precious that had been misplaced or lost. A week after Jesse's father went bankrupt, Sara's little brother, who had been missing for over ten years, was found in the takedown of a kidnapping ring."

"You have to be making this shit up, Maya." Alice's voice went up an octave.

"Seriously, Maya, did that really happen?" I asked, echoing Alice's skepticism.

Maya nodded. "As God as my witness. And I haven't even told you the craziest one. A few weeks after Sara's brother was found, I was a mess. I was struggling to believe that I had really predicted these two things that had come to pass. So I decided to do it one more time and see what happened. I was working at a café downtown at the time, and I was on a smoke break out back with one of the chefs. He had been having a really hard time. His wife had suffered three back-to-back miscarriages, and they weren't sure they were going to try again.

"I asked him if I could read his palm, and when he placed it in front of me, I saw the three losses immediately, but they were followed by three new lifelines, and another two further down. This is where you guys are really going to lose your shit. His wife did get pregnant again a couple months later . . . with triplets!"

"No frigging way." My eyes widened as Alice and I exchanged jaw-dropping looks.

"Yes way." Maya looked between Alice and me. "Once he told me the news, that was it for me. I stopped with the palm reading. My heart couldn't take it. And you know what's even crazier? I ran into him about two years ago, and we got to chatting. He told me that he and his wife had just welcomed twin girls a year before! I had read that in his palm as well."

"You're in the wrong profession." Alice shook her head as she popped a handful of trail mix into her mouth. "You should have joined the circus."

I laughed. "She'd be perfect with those dark, mysterious eyes and curly black hair. Fortune-telling gypsy woman."

Maya joined in the laughter. "All joking aside, though, I do believe that it's in my ancestry. Aunt Penelope used to tell my sister and I all sorts of stories about the nomadic travels of our ancestors."

Alice stuck her hand out. "Read mine. It'll be fun."

"Didn't you hear what I've been saying for the past half hour?" Maya shook her head at Alice. "I don't do that anymore. Aunt Penelope warned me about having a healthy dose of respect for the gift, but at the time, all I heard was, 'blah blah blah.' I do think she was on to something, though. I just don't understand enough about it to use it properly."

"Do you believe in that stuff, though?" Alice squinted her eyes and pursed her lips. "I mean, at the end of the day, it's a cool party trick, but one that doesn't show rewards right away."

"I kinda agree with Alice." I scrunched my sandwich wrapper into a ball. "I don't know if I believe that the future is set, that it's all decided ahead of time. It would be pretty shitty if that were true. It would mean that when I was born, it had already been predetermined that I would lose all the people in the world closest to me before I turned twenty-five. I like to imagine that we do have some control over our lives and the decisions we make, and that we do have some influence over our future."

As soon as the words were out of my mouth, I grimaced. Where the hell had that come from? I'd never talked about those I'd lost with Maya and Alice before. I was friendly with them, but aloof. Arm's length. I never got too close.

"I didn't mean for this to upset you, Eleyse," Maya said softly. "I'm sorry if I did."

I shook my head. "You didn't upset me, Maya. I enjoyed your story. I just choose to believe that there must be some rational explanation for it."

"I agree," Alice interjected. "Because the alternative would be to believe in the supernatural—otherworldly deities or entities that play the role of puppet masters, dangling us about as we go about our daily lives, when they already know how the story ends."

The supernatural. Immediately, my mind flashed back to my conversation with Aggie when she'd asked if I believed in fate. I had scoffed at the idea, but she was right, as much as I hated to admit it. There were things about myself and my life that defied rational explanation. That being said, I wasn't willing to concede that our lives weren't our own—that we were all just living out a predetermined destiny. I refused to believe it.

"This turned deep real fast," Maya said.

I cocked my head. "Alice and I are simply skeptics. Natural-born rebels."

"Hey. There's no bigger rebel than me!" Maya laughed, gathering up the remnants of her lunch from the table.

"Says the fortune teller," Alice piped in, bursting into laughter.

I grabbed my purse and the empty paper bag and got to my feet. The heel of my stiletto caught on the leg of my chair and I lurched forward. Maya grabbed my hand to stop me from falling, and she immediately froze. Her face blanched, her expression blank, as if she was in a trance.

"Maya?" I shook her gently. "You okay?" For a moment, she didn't reply, but then the color flooded her face once more and she looked at me, her eyes wide and wild. She grabbed my hand and turned it over to look at my palm. She gasped and dropped it as if she had been burned.

"Maya, what's wrong?" Alice asked, coming to stand beside her.

Maya was staring at me as if she had seen a ghost. "I have to get out of here." She pivoted on her heel and dashed out of the lunchroom.

"Maya, wait!" I hurried to catch up with her, Alice right behind me.

"What happened?" Alice reached for Maya's hand as she slowed down.

"I . . . I don't know." Maya's eyes flitted back and forth between me and

Alice. "I just saw something strange when I touched you. And then your palm confirmed it."

"Confirmed what?" I asked, perplexed. "What did you see?"

Maya's eyes were filled with terror, a thin sheen of sweat beading her forehead. "I saw death, and not just death following you, but you . . . you are tied to death somehow. And your palm . . . you have the longest life line I've ever seen, but there are a shit-ton of death lines on the edges of your hand. It's the freakiest thing I've ever seen."

None of this made any sense to me, but Maya was clearly rattled. She paused, wringing her hands and staring apprehensively at me. "There's something else, something weird that I don't know how to explain. When I touched you, I saw a vision of you dressed in a stunning gown and cloak, holding some kind of scepter in your hand, climbing a long, crystal staircase. You looked like a . . . queen. Then I heard a voice . . . barely a whisper." She swallowed hard, her throat bobbing with the movement.

The hair on my skin prickled. "What was it?"

Wide eyed, she stared at me. "I don't know. But it filled me with chills all over. I heard just one phrase, but it makes no sense at all . . . *Renala cotur precvi.*"

Sitting in my office an hour later, I stared out the window. *Renala cotur precvi.* What did it mean? My mind latched onto one word. *Renala.* The woman in my dream had called me *Renala Cielta.* It couldn't be a coincidence. It had to be related.

Maya was right. It was frigging weird. I didn't know how to explain any of what she had said. Whatever she had seen and heard had scared the shit out of her.

Her comments about me and death unsettled me. It hit too close to home, and if anything, only served to strengthen my own beliefs about being responsible for the deaths of everyone I loved.

As for her vision of me wearing a gown and holding a scepter, I didn't know what to do with that.

Maya had gone home after lunch, citing a fever and headache. Perhaps, she was coming down with something, and that was responsible for what she had seen. Sometimes high fevers could cause hallucinations. Yes, that had to be it, right? Because if not, what the hell else could it mean?

Chapter 9

ELEYSE

J UNE 4: ONE YEAR, TEN MONTHS AGO

Were people really so desperate for love?

I stared at the television screen, watching Ben propose to Lisa on bended knee. We were on a first name basis—Ben, Lisa, and I—but I neither knew nor cared who these sex- and love-starved crazies really were. They had met the day before at a sexy singles island retreat. I rolled my eyes and flipped to another channel. Reality TV shows were the worst—so theatrical and orchestrated, and far, far, far removed from reality.

I took a sip of my wine and checked the time on my phone. Almost seven. Another rocking Saturday night for me. Cracking open the tub of Chocolate Death ice cream—a brand-new flavor I'd picked up while I was out—I sank my spoon in and scooped out a heaping chunk. It was the perfect blend of cold, velvety softness. I hated when the ice cream was too frozen or there were icy shards throughout, ruining the texture. Gross.

I brought the spoon to my mouth, savoring the creamy goodness as it melted on my tongue. Oh my god—were those brownie bits? And chocolate fudge? My eyes rolled back in my head and I sank into the cushions. Yes, please. I'd choose a chocolate death any day.

I'd just reached into the tub for another decadent spoonful when the shrill chime of the doorbell pierced the air, almost giving me a heart attack. I jerked upright, a dollop of ice cream splattering onto my shoulder, the startling cold prickling my skin. Licking it off, I stuck the half-filled spoon back into my mouth and headed to the foyer, just off the TV room.

I opened the door and almost choked.

Holy. Frigging. God. There he was—the object of my obsession and dirtiest fantasies this past month—standing in front of me like some kind of powerful dark angel conjured from the well-loved, over-read pages of a steamy fantasy novel.

Asher.

A myriad of emotions washed over me—relief, happiness, confusion, excitement.

He was alive!

That thought pounded wildly in my head. Death hadn't stolen him away from me before I got the chance to know him. He was alive. And he was here, standing in front of me.

I was painfully aware of my appearance and what I was wearing—sweatpants, tank top, loose ponytail, no makeup. If Aggie could see me now, she would shake her head and groan in embarrassment. Always dress to impress, indeed. As it stood, I was rocking the *don't-give-a-shit* look hard tonight.

Asher, on the other hand—casual, but pure perfection. A light, leather bomber jacket, jeans, fitted T-shirt. I fanned myself as I drank him in greedily.

Pulling the spoon out of my mouth, I swallowed the remaining glob of ice cream. "Angel," I said in greeting, my voice a breathy whisper. Shit.

A sexy smile hovered on his lips. "Eleyse."

Goddamn, that voice.

"So, where've you been hiding?" I leaned against the door casing, twirling the spoon in my hand.

His emerald eyes twinkled with mischief. "Why? Did you miss me?"

Holy crap, that intense green was out-of-this-world gorgeous.

"Maybe." I shrugged, placing my hand on my hip.

"I know it's last minute and entirely out of the blue, but would you like to have dinner with me?" His eyes swept over me slowly. "By the look of things, it doesn't appear that you have plans."

"Hey!" I folded my arms and scrunched my face into a scowl. "I'll have you know I was having a very enjoyable Saturday night before you showed up. Bottle of wine, fireplace on. Melted chocolate on skin that required licking off. There was moaning and everything; it was *that* good. I thought I'd died and gone to heaven." I arched a brow at him. "Can *you* guarantee a better time than that?"

A flash of surprise flitted across his face, and then he smiled, the tip of his tongue, then teeth, catching on the side of his lower lip. I gawked, mesmerized, wrangling all my self-control not to pounce on him.

"The chocolate would just be a nuisance for me." His lips curled as his eyes flitted to my shoulder, where I had missed a spot. "You'd taste far more delectable without it."

My stomach did a delirious little somersault and I gulped, unable to tear my eyes away from his mouth, my body ablaze with wanting him. I lifted my gaze to meet his, his eyes gleaming with playfulness and the hint of something gloriously wicked.

"I deserved that," I said.

He shrugged arrogantly. "Two can play that game."

"Promise?"

He laughed, and the sound was so intoxicating that I couldn't help but laugh with him.

"So dinner is a yes?" he asked.

"Why don't we just skip ahead to dessert?" I suggested, shamelessly flirting. Goddamn it. How did he have this effect on me? I hadn't seen or heard from him in a month, and then he unexpectedly shows up, and I melt like butter, practically offering myself to him as tribute?

"Stop trying to lure me into your bed." He folded his arms and leaned against the door casing, the twitch of a grin dancing at the corners of his mouth.

He made my blood thrum, I had to admit. Something about him spoke directly to the carefree person I used to be a long time ago. And it wasn't just the way he looked—which, yes, was sinful and breathtaking—it was *him*, what I sensed simmering beneath the surface. It called to me like a bloody siren's song, made me feel alive, and I was here for it all.

"Oh, it doesn't have to be my bed," I said. "Right here will work just fine too. I'm sure the neighbors would enjoy the show."

"Stop tempting me and go get dressed," he growled, his eyes crinkling as he smiled.

I moved aside and beckoned for him to come in. "I'll be as quick as I can."

He stepped inside and I led him into the TV room, the remnants of my Saturday night activities on shameful display on the coffee table.

He sat on the sofa, arching an eyebrow as he picked up the tub of ice cream. "Chocolate Death? Sinful Saturday night indeed."

I threw my spoon at him. "Oh, shut up."

His laughter followed me up the stairs as I raced to my room to get dressed.

I tripped over myself in my haste to get ready, but I also wanted to completely blow his mind. I settled on a low-cut chiffon blouse and a short, ruffled skirt that showcased my legs. Slipping on a pair of open-toed sandals, I thanked the stars that I'd had a pedicure a few days before.

It took me forty minutes to pull everything together, but as I stared at my reflection in the mirror, I sighed in contentment. Makeup, hair, outfit and jewelry—check, check, check.

I headed down the stairs, my heart trilling in anticipation. I stepped into the TV room, and he looked up at me from a spoonful of ice cream.

His jaw dropped open as his gaze swept over me. "You look . . . fucking incredible."

"Thanks." A warm flush spread over my skin as his eyes snaked over me again.

He got to his feet and gestured to the tub of ice cream. "Want me to put this in the freezer?"

I reached for the container. "I've got it. We can save it for later." I winked suggestively, and he smiled and shook his head, sauntering toward the door.

"You might want to grab a light jacket," he said. "I wouldn't want you to catch a chill."

I stuffed the ice cream back in the freezer and slid the drawer shut. "What? Why?"

"You'll see." He opened the door and stepped outside, and I hurried from the kitchen after him. Parked on the curb was a sleek, black motorcycle. Why wasn't I surprised? It was beautiful, shiny, and dangerous—just like him. "Yours?" I asked.

He shook his head. "Rental."

"Very sexy."

"I have to agree."

"The bike's not half bad either."

He threw his head back and laughed, his broad shoulders shaking as he turned to face me. "You are relentless." His smile was affectionate and light.

I winked. "A girl's gotta try." I stepped back into the house and opened the hall closet. "Maybe I should change. Not sure if this is bike attire."

"Don't you dare. You look perfect."

"Ha. You just don't want to have to wait for me to change again." I reached into the closet and grabbed a leather jacket.

"We can always take your car if you don't want to take the bike."

"And give up the chance to get my arms around you and feel you up? Hell no."

He cocked his head to the side and looked at me. "Are you always this open and direct?"

I paused in mid-action and lifted my eyes to his. "Truthfully? Never. Would it surprise you to hear that I don't even recognize myself with you?"

His green eyes glittered in the recessed porch lighting. "Yes, it would. The banter and flirtation seem effortless, second nature."

"Trust me when I say that's *all* you. You're the most excitement I've had in my life in a long time."

I felt his stare on me but I refused to meet his gaze. I didn't want to see the pity I was certain I'd find there.

I zipped up my jacket and pushed the closet door closed with my foot. "Ready?"

He nodded and reached for my hand. When I slipped mine into his, he lowered his head and brushed his lips against my knuckles. My entire body erupted in chills at his touch.

"I'm really happy you said yes," he whispered.

"Me too."

Chapter 10

ELEYSE

H e had come prepared with an extra helmet, and I slipped it onto my head and fastened the strap under my chin. True to my word, I made sure to move as close to him as I could when I straddled the bike and sat behind him. As I slipped my arms around his waist, every part of me was acutely aware of how hard and powerful his body was against mine.

He turned the engine on, and I clenched my muscles at the vibration beneath me, tightening my grip on his chest. The fact that there was only a thin layer of clothing between me and the seat did not make it easier.

He turned his head toward me. "Are you okay?" His voice was low, soothing, intoxicating.

Hell no, I wasn't okay. I was sitting behind the sexiest man alive, my legs open wide and my body pressed against his, the roaring vibration of a powerful machine under me. I had never been so turned on in my life! Every nerve in my body was on fire.

I rested my head against his back and breathed deeply. *Pull yourself together, Eleyse,* my brain screamed at me. *You're coming across as a sex-starved junkie, for god's sake.*

"I'm okay." My body shuddered as he covered my hands with his.

"It's not too late to change your mind."

"Definitely not. I'm fine. Let's go."

He lifted his feet off the ground, shifted the bike into gear, and off we went.

I loved every exquisite moment of it—the wind in my hair, the rush of the world whizzing by, the heat of his body next to mine, the way his muscles tightened when he moved, the exhilarating, crisp smell of him. Every one of my senses was hyper-alert. I didn't want it to end.

When we arrived on the promenade about twenty minutes later, I swallowed my disappointment that it was over already. At least I'd get to do it again on the way back home. He eased the bike into a parking spot and shut the engine off. I unclasped my helmet and slipped it off my head. Holding on to his arm, I slid my leg over the side of the bike and stepped onto the sidewalk. Asher took my helmet and attached it to one of the handlebars.

He reached for my hand, and we walked amid the twinkling lights that hung all the way along the promenade in the heart of downtown Hargrove. The evening was warm, and all around us, people were milling around, enjoying the balmy Saturday night. The restaurants on either side of the promenade were packed and full of life—talking, laughter, music. It was invigorating.

"Where are we going?" I asked.

"Starlight Bay. Been there before?"

"Yes. Amazing food, and they make killer margaritas."

When we got to the trendy, crowded restaurant, the hostess led us to a private spot outside, away from the bustle and noise of the other patrons. Flowering vines climbed a slatted trellis on the far side of the patio, the aroma of jasmine and honeysuckle mingling with the intoxicating scent of Ash's cologne. My breath caught in my chest as I glimpsed the hanging lanterns above us, the fiery wicks flickering with buttery, warm light. Everything about the moment—the beautiful man sitting across from me, the setting, music, ambience—was an assault on my senses, dousing me in a dopamine-drenched cornucopia of contentment.

I lifted a brow and nodded. "Wow, I'm impressed. Prime table on a Saturday night, on short notice? How did you manage to score that?"

He shrugged. "I have my ways."

"Clearly."

Our waitress sashayed to the table, shamelessly ogling and flirting with Asher as she took his drink order. Finally, she ripped her eyes away from him and turned to me. The disdain was apparent and immediate. Her lip curled and she gave me a disapproving once-over, her thoughts written all over her face. *How did you land someone like* him?

Asher reached for my hand across the table, intertwining his fingers with mine. My gaze flew to his. He brushed his lips against my fingertips. "Margarita, perhaps?"

"Hmm?" I watched as his lips moved from one finger to the next, his eyes glued to mine. It was clear that he was putting on a show for the waitress, but I was giddy, unable to concentrate on anything but the sight and feel of his mouth against my skin and the blazing heat surging through my body.

I shook my head and cleared my throat. "Yes. That's right. A double, please."

The waitress nodded, a muscle clenching in her jaw as she wrote it down, and then she turned to Asher, a seductive smile on her face. "I'll get those right out," she purred, batting her false eyelashes at him. He didn't tear his eyes away from me.

"Are you trying to get me killed?" I hissed when she walked away.

"What do you mean?" His mouth quirked in amusement, lips still pressed against my fingers.

"I would like very much *not* to get shanked in the parking lot. And yes, you're that hot."

He laughed dryly. "I'd like to see her try." He cocked his head. "You could take her." His eyes grew serious and forbidding. "No one minimizes you."

The force of his words hit me, and my fingers shook as I struggled to keep from melting into a puddle under the intensity of his gaze. "Well, to be fair, I don't blame her. I'd want to shank her in the parking lot, too, if roles were reversed. She's gorgeous. Definitely the kind of woman I could see you with."

He tilted his head to the side. "You really don't see yourself, do you?"

"What do you mean?"

"You are a fucking goddess. Don't let anything or anyone make you feel less than that."

I snorted, my eyebrows shooting upwards. "Okay. I know I'm attractive, but a goddess? By what standards and in whose eyes?"

"Mine."

I swallowed as I stared at him, shadows dancing off his handsome face in the muted lighting.

"I'm not saying it to flatter you, or to earn points with you, Eleyse. I'm saying it because it's true."

I smiled shyly. "Well, thank you for the compliment. And please, call me Elle."

"Only if you call me Ash."

"I have a lot of other names I'd like to call you," I replied, not missing a beat.

He smiled, his lips curving upward provocatively. "I'm sure you do."

I dragged my eyes away from his mouth and slowly untangled my fingers from his, placing my hand on my lap. I couldn't think straight when he was touching me; the feel of his skin drove me to distraction.

I cleared my throat. "I thought a lot this past month about what I would say to you if I saw you again." My fingers twirled in my lap, fussing with the ruffles on my skirt.

His brows raised. "You did?"

"Yes." I swallowed and lifted my eyes to his. "I didn't know if you would be back, and although that made me a little sad and disappointed, it did help me figure out what I would do if I saw you again."

"Lure me to your bed with a tub of ice cream?" he quipped, a teasing smile on his lips.

I blushed. "God, no. That was entirely my body talking. If you haven't noticed, it's been your biggest fan since the moment I laid eyes on you."

"I noticed."

I flushed even deeper, the fervor in his gaze causing my heart to stutter. Goddamn it! What the hell was wrong with me? I lifted my eyes to his. "No one could ever accuse you of lacking in confidence, that's for sure."

His lips tipped up, and he leaned back in his chair, folding his arms across his chest. "Would you have given me a second glance if I wasn't confident?"

I shrugged. "Maybe." I tasted the lie the moment it left my lips. He was right. I was drawn to his charismatic presence, the silky self-assurance he exuded. It elevated his physical beauty, made him more than just a pretty—a *very* pretty—face.

"Why did you give me a second glance?" I asked, running my finger across the edge of the menu.

His eyes crinkled as he smiled. "After you beat the shit out of those two guys at the bar? How could I not? That was both spectacular and titillating at the same time."

My face heated, my heart racing at his blunt flattery. "You like your women feisty?"

"Among other things." His gaze lazily dipped to my mouth as he studied me. "I'm willing to bet you deliver on everything I like."

Oh god. A rush of desire rolled over me, sending fluttery tingles across my skin. I clenched my fists, struggling to keep it together.

He leaned forward and took my hand, his fingers brushing gently over my knuckles. "Why did you say yes to me tonight?" His voice was serious, tinged with curiosity.

I closed my eyes, savoring the electricity coursing through me at his touch. "I wanted to see you again," I admitted as he interlaced his fingers with mine.

His lips twitched. "So you did miss me."

I cocked my head. "I don't know, to be honest. Can you miss something that you're not even sure exists?"

His smile froze on his mouth, his fingers squeezing mine tighter. "I've been asking myself the same question since I first laid eyes on you, but here, in this moment, nothing has ever felt more real."

I nodded. "I'm scared that if I blink, you'll disappear."

"I promise I won't."

My body tensed, my heart pounding in my chest. I exhaled slowly, unable to ignore the question swirling in my mind. "I'm sorry to turn this all serious, but I have to ask. Do you plan on seeing me again?"

His voice was low and quiet. "Only if that's what you want."

My heart leapt at his response. I looked up as the waitress returned with our drinks.

"Are you ready to order?" she said cheerily, setting our glasses on the table.

"Can you give us a few minutes?" I asked, and she nodded stiffly in my direction before stealing a glance at Ash as she walked away.

He brought his glass of whiskey to his lips. "You were saying?"

I smiled nervously and took a sip of my margarita. "I haven't seen you in over a month. You came into my life that night and then disappeared. I'd resigned myself to the fanciful notion that you were either a figment of my imagination or an angel who intervened to save me from myself. Either way, although I hoped I would, I didn't think I'd ever see you again.

"The night we met, I told you that I wasn't looking for anything that resembled a commitment or relationship, and I meant that. I can't get attached to you or anyone. I need to be able to cut the cord at a moment's notice and walk away."

There. I'd said it. It didn't matter that Aggie thought I was mistaken in my beliefs and that there was some other explanation for the tragedy in my life. I knew what I knew, and I couldn't take the chance.

I looked at him and shrugged. "I mean, this conversation might be moot; you might not be looking for anything serious either." Even as the words left my mouth, they hurt my heart. I *wanted* something more with him, despite my convictions. And I wanted him to want me back. I was a frigging mess.

He grazed his fingers against my wrist. "Listen, Elle. This can be whatever you want it to be. The reins are in your hands. You lead, I'll follow."

Slowly, I slid my hand into his, and he wrapped his fingers around mine. I leaned forward in my chair, wanting to be closer to him. "Ash, you probably think I'm crazy for believing the things that I do, but it doesn't change the facts. I love, people die. I can't let that happen again. I don't need to know specifics. As much as I might be curious, I don't need explanations of who you are or where you go when you're not here, or anything else you don't want to tell me. I need to stay detached. I just want to live in the moments that I share with you. Nothing more. That being said, I need you to promise me that there isn't someone else you're betraying by spending time with me. I couldn't live with that."

"There isn't anyone else," he said without hesitation, and I exhaled in a rush, surprised that I had been holding my breath.

He leaned back in his chair, steepling his fingers on his chest. "Elle, I hear everything you're saying, and my question to you is, what exactly is it that you want from me?"

"I . . . I don't really know," I replied, looking away. "I just know that I like the way I feel when I'm with you, and I need that."

"What way is that?"

"Alive, hopeful."

His eyes flashed, heated emotion stealing over his handsome face. "The feeling is mutual."

I looked away as the sting of tears burned my eyes.

"What is it?" His warm fingers squeezed mine gently.

"I am frigging terrified," I whispered. "I don't want to hurt you or get hurt, but I can't live one more day feeling like I'm dying inside. I don't want to play games or give you mixed messages, and I don't know how else to explain it except to say that I need you in my life. For however brief that might be. In whatever limited capacity. And I know that's a selfish thing—I don't want to put any burdens or expectations on you."

"Elle." He brushed his knuckles across my forearm. "There is nothing you can throw at me that I can't handle. You're right, though. There are things about me that I can't explain. I can't stay here with you, I can't tell you where I go or when I will return. My life is complicated, and I know I'm being selfish by wanting you in it. If that is too much for you, just say the word and I will walk away."

I shook my head, panic swarming at the prospect of not seeing him again. I knew what I didn't want to go back to. I'd have to be careful that I didn't start feeling more, wanting more. That wouldn't end well for either of us. I was playing with fire, but the overwhelming need to *live*, to *feel*, trumped everything.

"Now I have something to say to you." He leaned forward in his seat, coaxing my gaze to his. "You're probably not going to like it, but I want you to really listen before you respond."

I nodded and waited for him to continue.

"As much as I would thoroughly enjoy being physically intimate with you, I get the impression that sex is a tool for you—a way for you to maintain control and fill the void inside you."

"What's wrong with that?" I felt suddenly exposed and under attack.

"Everything," he answered. "You deserve more than that."

My eyes narrowed. "So what are you saying? Sex is off the table?"

"I'm not saying that." His thumb gently circled the back of my hand. "I want us to get to know each other before blindly jumping into bed."

"But why?" I asked, my frustration rising. "People have meaningless sex all the time with people they don't *really* know. We're two consenting adults with a mutual attraction for each other. Or are you saying that you're not attracted to me?"

His eyes flashed. "That is not what I'm saying. On the contrary, I've never wanted another woman the way I want you." He paused, his heated gaze making my face flush. "And that's not just a line that I'm feeding you. This thing between us—it runs both ways. Don't for one second think that I'm not affected just as much as you are."

"Then what's the problem? This way, we both get what we want and neither of us gets hurt."

"It's not about one of us not getting hurt." He looked away, staring off into the bustle of the promenade for a long moment. "Elle, I've been in a dark place before. And in the midst of that, sex was a way for me to numb the pain I felt inside, but it only exacerbated my emptiness and self-deprecation. It took the pleasure and joy out of the experience."

An ember of jealousy flared in my gut at the thought of him with someone else, but I tamped it down.

His gaze swept over me, a multitude of emotions blazing there—sadness, remorse, resolve, pity. "I came to detest it. Not for what it was, but for all the things it *wasn't*."

Fuck. *All the things it wasn't.* This was hitting a little too close to home for me. I wasn't ready for this kind of introspection. I didn't want to face all the things that were *wrong* with me; didn't want to dwell on all the ways I was messed up.

I quietly cleared my throat. "What happened to change things for you?"

He reached for his glass of whiskey. "You could say I had an epiphany. A gift from the Gods. I found a purpose and a reason to live."

I sighed softly, a pang of longing twisting my insides. "I'd be lying if I said I wasn't disappointed—you have no idea." My eyes flicked to the sensuous curve of his full lips. "That night I met you at Crusoe's, it was the first time in years that I felt alive. And although we only spent a few hours together, it was enough for me to know I was *dying* for more. Since then, I've fantasized about you shamelessly. Every time I touch myself and imagine it's your hands and your mouth on my skin, when I picture that it's you and not my goddamned vibrator moving inside me, I come completely undone, and the orgasms that rock my body are like nothing I've ever experienced. So yes, *fucking yes*, I want the real experience with you." My breath hitched as I lifted my eyes to meet his. "I want all the things it *could* be."

He stared at me for a long moment, his eyes dark and murky as they swept over my face. The energy emanating off him was palpable, and I swore a crackle of electricity sizzled where our hands touched.

"You know, sometimes reality doesn't live up to the fantasy," he said softly.

I met his gaze full-on. "That's absolutely true. But we both know that when it comes to you and me, that's bullshit."

He smiled. "I'll make a deal with you. I know you laid your cards on the table—you need to stay detached—but we can still be *real* with each other. I'm not looking for something shallow and surface-level, and everything you've said tells me you're not either. So let's be *real* with each other. Authenticity is a rare thing to come by. I promise that the day *will* come when you tell me that you're ready to take a chance on life again, that you're ready to let the pain and emptiness go. When it does, I'll oblige you in making all your sinful fantasies come true."

Right away, my brain launched its silent protest, spouting all the reasons why I *could* never be ready for any of that, but that strange, calm certainty stirred inside me once more, tuning out the noise, lapping up Ash's words as if they were gospel, urging me to believe.

"You never know," I answered. "I might wear you down before that."

His lips tipped up. "I have strong willpower."

"We'll see."

As much as I didn't want to admit it, my heart was soaring. Ash and I stayed at the restaurant until closing, talking and enjoying each other's company.

We were both cognizant of the boundaries I had set around divulging the details of our lives and kept the conversation in neutral territory—our likes, pet peeves, interests, our favorite seasons, the type of music and books we liked. And bloody hell, although I was the one who had drawn the line in the sand, I found myself hungry to know more about him, biting my tongue to keep from prying, from asking him to tell me everything about who he was.

When he mentioned that his favorite season was fall, for instance, my mind swirled with personal and inappropriate questions—*Do the seasons change where you're from? If so, where are you from? Do you take long walks in the woods to watch the leaves change? Does your soul feel peace simply from sitting at a lake and watching the pure blue of the sky as it showcases that breathtaking kaleidoscope of radiant color? Can I do both of those last two things with you every fall for the rest of my life?*

Instead I went with, "Don't you just love pumpkin spice?" Grrr. I hated my stupid rules.

I felt at ease and content with him, like I didn't have to wear a mask the way I did with everyone else. He called to something dormant inside me, stirred my resident restlessness to frenzied heights. Although I couldn't deny his jarring physical beauty, it was his intensity—so terrifying and magnetic—that commanded my focus and kept me coming back for more. When he looked at me with those piercing emerald eyes of his, it was if he possessed the unnerving ability to see straight through me. Heck, within an hour of meeting him, I'd given him a front-row seat to the grief and self-loathing that I'd kept to myself for years.

Danger! Danger! Danger! my brain screamed. But god help me if I didn't just want to throw caution and fear to the wind and just crash and burn and go out in a blaze of glory. And if it was just me that I was worried for, I would, but I couldn't risk something tragic happening to *him*, and so I vowed to keep my head screwed on tight.

By the time he brought me home a little after midnight, I didn't want the night to end. He walked me to the door, and I froze, suddenly uncomfortable and shy, angry with myself for being so forward and blunt earlier about my attraction for him. He must have sensed the shift in my energy because he grabbed my hand and pulled me closer, his hand resting on my waist.

"I had a lovely time," I said, painfully aware of the warmth of his body.

"So did I." His face was inches away from mine.

I wanted to kiss him so badly, but I stiffened and pulled away, tearing my eyes from his lips. I grabbed my purse and began rifling around for my keys.

"Elle, I don't want you to feel awkward around me." He tugged a lock of my hair with his fingers.

"I can't help it," I whispered. Tears sprang to my eyes, and I swiped them away. "You must think I'm pathetic."

"Never." He moved one step closer. His fingers brushed my tears away and drifted down my jaw to tilt my chin up to meet his gaze. "I see the warring sides of you: the bold, funny, outspoken, and spontaneous you—your true self—and I also see the broken, lonely, scarred, and anguished you that grew as a result of your life experiences. And I can't look away from either one. Each side calls to me in a different way, touches a different part of me."

I stared at him for a long moment, then lifted my hand to touch the side of his face. I ran my palm along his cheek and across his jaw, savoring the feel of his smooth skin. My heart flip-flopped when he caught my fingers in his and kissed the back of my hand. His mouth was warm and soft, sending a jolt of electricity shooting through to the very core of me.

"I know I said no specifics. I don't need you to tell me when I'll see you again, only that I *will* see you again." My voice was barely a whisper.

"You'll see me again." His eyes never left mine.

"Promise me that if that time ever comes—when you know you won't be back—that you'll tell me."

"I promise." He kissed my hand once more.

I looked at his mouth and shivered, a wave of desire swelling inside me. When I lifted my eyes to meet his, I found myself trapped there. Conflict swirled in those emerald orbs—control warring with need—and for a moment, time stood still and it seemed we were at a stalemate, but then he lowered his head and brushed his lips against mine, his lips moving gently, a slow caress, stoking the embers simmering inside me.

The tip of his tongue slid between my lips to trace the edges of my teeth, and instantly, the fire roared to life. My mouth parted, welcoming him in. His tongue swept in and swirled against mine, sending shivers through my body that made me pull him closer to me. His fingers tangled in my hair, and I kissed him back with all the pent-up need coursing through me.

I slipped my tongue into his mouth, and a sharp ache of desire tore through me when he sucked on it gently and then twirled his over mine. Fuck! I wanted more! My hands trailed down his neck and came to rest on his chest. I moved my palms lower, over his abs, feeling his muscles tighten under my touch. Everything about this man kindled my senses, sent me careening through space, luring me higher, begging me to come closer, to ignite and combust in the flame he so deftly wielded.

A ragged moan escaped my lips, and I grimaced as his sharp exhale. I knew the exact moment he regained control. His body stiffened and he slowed the kiss, the movement of his lips becoming tapered and gentle. He sighed and pulled away, resting his forehead against mine. His heart thudded against my fingers, his breathing short and ragged as he wrapped his hands around mine against his chest.

"That was a hell of a first kiss." I fisted my fingers in his jacket.

"It's even better than I re— imagined it would be." His lips flitted across my jaw.

I didn't want the moment to end, but of course, it had to. I hated the dull aching that throbbed inside at the thought of him leaving, at the prospect of an unknown stretch of time without seeing him again. This was exactly what I didn't want to feel, but at least I would see him again.

We stayed like that for a long moment—heads and hands together—neither of us making an attempt to move. Finally, I inhaled deeply and pulled away, stepping up on tiptoes to brush my lips against his one last time.

"Don't be a stranger, Ash," I whispered.

"I won't." His mouth grazed my forehead. "Good night, *Tialla mata.*" His voice was soft, filled with tenderness.

I cocked my head. "What does that mean?"

He stroked my cheek gently, his mouth lifting in a wistful smile. "I'll tell you the next time I see you."

I traced his lips with my fingers, and he kissed my fingertips, sending a ripple of heat tingling through me. I lowered my hand and turned away. Finding my keys, I unlocked the door and stepped inside, closing it behind me without looking back. If I dared to look at him again, I'd beg him to stay, and I couldn't bear the thought of him telling me no.

Chapter 11

ASHER

P RESENT DAY SOLNIESS, THE VOID . . .

"You've made your choice?" the Goddess Eolith asked.

She stood outside in her garden, a flock of jorandas and mycelias tittering around her excitedly. Sprays of light trailed from their tail feathers, their melodic trilling soothing the anxiety twisting in my chest.

Both species of birds were magical—jorandas contained healing magic, and mycelias mind-soothing magic—and were symbols of the Goddess of the Ethereal Harmonies. They were two of the creatures known to travel between the real world and the Void—zaragals—gifted with that ability by the Gods they served. Less than fifteen different species of zaragals existed, each one of them bonded to a God or Goddess of the Sangelis. To capture or harm one of them carried an automatic sentence to the Dark Dominion for a mortal. The life force of the jorandas and mycelias was connected to the Goddess Mother herself, and every last one of them was personally accounted for by her.

Curtains of moss and floral blossoms climbed the columns of the sprawling gazebo we stood in, and around us, squat rasienda and tall buswyn trees flanked the perimeter of the colorful and lush grounds.

"I've decided on Faron and Treye." I leaned my shoulder against one of the sun-drenched columns, taking care not to disturb any of the delicate blossoms.

She nodded. "Good. Once I retrieve them, I will leave for Madwen, Sorin's sanctum in the celestial plane. It is as you said. He should learn the truth from me." She stretched her hand out, and a blue and orange joranda flew to her, perching on her index finger. "This little one carries a message from Tora. Came here straight from Dramhelm Manor in Winnd."

My eyes flicked to the tiny creature's shimmering tail feathers, where a sheer ribbon of magical parchment fluttered loose. I caught it in my hands.

I furrowed my brows. Tora was in Dramhelm, safeguarding the source of the light strain of the Old, Arcane Magic while Lorien Reo, keeper of that ancient magic, waited in Torannon, ready to destroy the darkness surrounding Elle's soul once she regained all her memories. Tora and Lorien both wielded the light strain of the Old, Arcane Magic, but because Lorien was the only one who could destroy Gargmoin's magic inside Elle, and the source of the ancient magic could not be left unprotected, Tora had switched places with him so that he could be in Torannon.

Tora might be in the territories of Brus-Winnd in real time, but the prime elemental spirit had the ability to slow and pause time around her to suit her purposes, even if they were as trivial as writing a letter. I had seen her do it on many occasions, the most recent being the encounter with the God of Chaos at the Torannon market. Hard to believe that in real time, that was just earlier today.

"I'll give you some privacy," the Goddess Eolith said, and in the blink of an eye, she was gone.

I unfurled the ribbon slowly, the familiar scrawl of Tora's handwriting illuminating the surface.

My Dear Smolders,

I meant it when I said that everything would be all right. Baby queen—Agaia—your unrelenting storm, will return to you, to us, restored, and the dark effects of the rebounding curse will be destroyed. There is no room in your mind to entertain any other possibility. Please don't let your fears about that dirty, mangled-faced cunt, Kaliope, not even for one second, sway your resolve and take your eye off the goal.

I know time will be as slow as a wounded snail carrying a slug uphill until Elle returns, but I promise to seal and soundproof the entire south wing of

Cazara Torannon when she's by your side again so you can release all that pent-up sexual frustration to your heart's content. (Although can you truly have a full release if you're not allowed to fuck until Elle's coronation?) But I digress.

The reason I am writing . . . I have a confession. The day you found out that Kaliope had learned about your visits to Earth, a series of events unfolded, and I used my magic to take something from you. A memory. You didn't see it coming, and afterward, you didn't even realize you had lost anything.

To commit such an act upon a Sovereign is treason—I know that—but I could not, in good conscience, leave you with the weight of that memory and the consequences that might have ensued had you kept it. Especially in that volatile time.

I give it back now, but only because of the important truths it contains that you need to know. Pay close attention and keep your eyes wide open. My lips are sealed, as you will see, and I cannot speak of it again, at my own peril.

The memory can only be unlocked with your voice, when you read the words at the end of this letter. I am truly sorry for violating you that way, but it could not be helped. I trust when it is restored, you will understand why, and you will find it in your heart to forgive me.

I have been loyal to the House of Valkyse since its inception, for I have always known that greatness would arise from within. You and your Gloweyen Queen are that greatness, Ash. I will forever remain loyal to you both.

Yours,

Tora

Cedwa MigoLix Vorbelim

Confusion and surprise bubbled inside me. Tora had taken a memory from me? Had I been completely blitzed not to have realized what she'd done?

In my entire life, Tora had never given me a reason to distrust her. She had been the first one I told about Elle after she came to me through the Senshifter. *Agaia*, she had whispered then, eerily echoing what my senses had told me about Elle. A storm. When I'd asked why she said that, she'd smiled mysteriously and said that the stars had whispered it to her.

I had always confided in Tora, and she had never betrayed my confidence. So why would she do this? Granted, she was confessing, but why now? It had been five months since Kaliope learned about Elle. She'd had all that time to tell me and didn't.

Tora did nothing without a reason. As upsetting as this was, I owed it to her to give her the benefit of the doubt. I'd never once questioned her loyalty. That being said, would I feel the same way after I saw what she took?

I lifted the ribbon and read the words out loud.

Cedwa MigoLix Vorbelim.

My voice unlocks the truth.

Tora's words faded before my eyes, and the ribbon slowly disintegrated into a cloud of green smoke, swarming my face, seeping into my skin, my pores, mercurial slivers of cold and heat flooding my mind.

I closed my eyes and let it settle, my body rigid as the pieces of the memory knitted back together. Once complete, I summoned it to the surface.

FIVE MONTHS AGO . . .

I stared at the ceiling, my eyes unfocused as my mind reeled.

She knew.

The sickening churning in my gut refused to abate, my heart thudding in my chest. Fear—so all-consuming—leached the strength from my body. Treye had been very clear when he was here earlier. There was no doubt about it.

She fucking knew.

I'd been so careful. Planned my goings and comings, accounting for every possibility. But she'd still found out. She knew I'd been off-world, and specifically, Earth. How? It was infuriating. Exhausting.

Reaching for the drink on the bedside table, I drained the glass, relishing the warmth blossoming through my chest. Every other part of me was frigid and numb.

It was not safe anymore.

The time had come. I couldn't go back. I couldn't reach for her in my mind. To protect Elle, to make sure the creya didn't learn about her, I had to break off all contact. Yes, Earth was a massive world with over eight billion souls, but where Kaliope was concerned, I could and would not take any chances.

A low hiss in the corner of the room drew my attention, and I squinted at the shards of light sparking near the window. The hair on the back of my neck rose, my magic flaring to life inside me, coiled to attack. Reaching into myself, I connected to my power source, siphoning and storing it within grasp, waiting.

In front of my eyes, a tall, monstrous figure took shape by the window, but before I could move, a hand calmly touched my shoulder from behind me—firm, but gentle.

"No, Smolders," Tora's voice rang out, deathly still.

What the fuck?

The full form of the figure in the corner materialized, and I blinked as a behemoth, otherworldly life-form stared at me with flat, stygian eyes. The beast of my bond stirred restlessly, its curiosity and cautious scrutiny of the abomination in front of me unnerving.

"Lyria," the creature said, shifting his focus to Tora. His voice was a deep baritone, gravelly and emotionless, reminiscent of the gloom-steeped foghorn in the Torannon harbor.

I stared at Tora, my mind whirring with speculation. Lyria? What in the Sangelis was happening?

"Gargmoin." Tora's body was unnaturally motionless.

Gargmoin? The monster of myth? He was real? My eyes flew toward the creature and I pushed forward, but Tora stepped in front of me, impeding my path.

The anger and utter contempt emanating from the gargantuan menace blasted me full-on, and the beast of my bond roared inside me in response.

Tora glared at Gargmoin pointedly. "You cannot touch him." Her magic glowed and radiated around her form, her voice cold.

My anger flared. What was Tora's game? I did not need her protection, or for her to speak for me. The arrogant fuck was in my dominion, my home; I was well within my rights to end him. I sensed the unrelenting darkness in his soul, cold and acerbic, putrefying every part of him.

Those dead, sable eyes found mine again, a smirk hovering at the edge of his peaked lips. Slitted gashes on his forehead pulsed with unnatural light, expanding and contracting like the gills of a floundering fish.

"Not yet," the monstrous creature rasped, his gaze flicking over me with disinterest before returning to Tora. "But neither you, nor he, can stop what's coming." His eyes met mine once more, and he sauntered forward, the fabric of his black robe billowing as if stirred by a wayward breeze. "You cannot escape your destiny, *Sovereign*. Past, present, and future will come full circle."

"We are all but slaves to destiny, is that it?" I folded my arms across my chest. "Devoid of choice, bound to obey its uncompromising call? Is that what you would have me believe?"

"I care not what you believe," he sneered. "What you think means nothing to me."

"Why the fuck are you here?" I flexed my fingers, my power begging to be unleashed.

He grinned, baring sharp, fanged teeth at me. "I am here to deliver a message. A place and a name from your *recent* adventures. *She* wants it."

The blood slowly drained from my face. Fuck no. Rage flooded my veins and I blindly unleashed my power, blasting a hole straight through his chest.

"Ash," Tora cried. "Stop. Don't do this."

"Get out of the way, Tora," I growled, watching in shock as the hole in

Gargmoin's chest fused together effortlessly.

"I am sorry, Ash." Tora lashed wrists together and a heated blast grazed my skin as I flew backward onto my bed.

Invisible restraints pinned me down, and I roared with rage, summoning my power to me once more.

Gargmoin took a step forward.

"Don't come any closer, you venomous plague." Tora shot a blast of her magic toward him.

With lightning speed, he dodged her attack and then lurched forward, lifting her by her neck.

"No," I roared, staring at Tora in horror, her face contorted as Gargmoin squeezed harder. With a simmering rush of my power, Tora's restraints disintegrated around me, and I leapt onto the bed and jumped, hurtling through the air toward Gargmoin.

He dropped her and smiled, his eyes flashing with twisted delight.

"No, Ash," Tora's scream rang out. "Don't touch him."

Too late. I aimed a fist at his chest and released my arm, sending the twisted fuck reeling backward.

I stopped in my tracks, a paralyzing heat consuming me. He had barely moved. I had blasted him with everything I had, and it did *nothing*. How was that even possible? What kind of cursed creature was he?

He turned his gaze on me, but where his eyes were black and dead before, they were now a pale shade of blue, the intense gaze piercing straight through to my soul, exposing me bare.

No. This was impossible. Something was amiss. But my senses were never wrong. The wellspring of my power responded to those eyes, a warming hum stirring the surface.

His gaze flitted to Tora, standing aghast next to me. "An ember still lives, Lyria, even though the darkness consumes me."

A different voice. Softer. Gentler. The fuck?

Tora gasped out loud, shock and sorrow on her face. "Alvar," she whispered.

"Find the hearts of the Siccharis," he wheezed. Shuddering, he squeezed his eyes shut, a pained expression contorting his face. "He returns."

His eyes opened, replaced with that black, hateful glare.

He growled, low and deep, and stepped backward, the ragged sound shifting to a taunting, coarse laugh. "Oh Sovereign, what have you done? It will be a pleasure to find out what secrets await us in Hargrove."

His laughter boomed throughout the room even after he disappeared in a haze of searing light.

I stared in horror at the spot where he had stood, my heart in my mouth, my mind blasting a multitude of warning bells. Gods, what had I done?

I turned toward Tora, panic rising in my chest. "What the fuck was that? Gargmoin is real? And how is he working with Kaliope? Where did she even find him?" I gripped the edges of my desk, my knuckles straining under the pressure. "How did he get through our wards? What exactly just happened? Who was that . . . *other* presence?" My mind dissolved into a haze of panic. "Gods, Tora. Now Kaliope knows. How did he get the name from me?"

"I lowered the wards," she said softly.

"You what?" I stared at her in disbelief. "Why in the name of the Gods would you do something so reckless?"

"Because of this. It arrived shortly before he did. I had no choice once I viewed the message it contained." She waved her hand, materializing a flat, shimmering parchment.

I narrowed my eyes. "A *paplyrel*? Who sent it?"

"Watch." The magical parchment folded in on itself before exploding into a tiny vortex of fluttering sparks.

"Tora, darling." Kaliope's voice rang out through the room, sending my skin crawling. The sparks moved in time to the creya's words as they poured out. "Be a good little guard dog and do as I say, will you? It seems my powerful love has been a naughty boy behind my back, world hopping. Earth—a rather archaic realm . . . I wonder what could be so interesting there?"

My heartbeat boomed in my ears, a dizzying surge of heat rushing to my head.

"Now, I'll only ask once. I'll even say pretty please. Lower the wards on Cazara Torannon. My pet comes with a message. If you refuse, how do you think Ash will feel about you after I kill his sweet, feisty, baby sister? He will hate you forever."

Dread, so incomprehensible, coursed through me.

"And just in case you think I'm bluffing . . ."

The sparks shimmered, only to be replaced by a moving image of Gwynn laughing as she strolled through the cobblestone town square in Chantilis with two friends.

Kaliope's voice rang out again. "So clueless, don't you think? Such threadbare wards. It would take no effort at all to rip through them and get to her. You should know me enough by now to understand I never bluff. I trust you'll do the right thing, despite you being a brainless, waspish bitch."

The image of Gwynn disappeared and the parchment materialized once more.

Rage streamed into my chest until it swallowed me whole. "Why can't I just be rid of her?" I roared my frustration, my fingers clenched so tightly they burned indentations into my palms. If she touched even one hair on Gwynn's head . . .

Blindly, I reached for my labral, using my senses to pinpoint Gwynn's location as I shifted into the air, appearing right in front of her. She was alone, standing on the old stone bridge overlooking the Sangwene valley.

A high-pitched squeak escaped her lips, her body jerking when she saw me. "Shit, Ash, you scared me. What are you doing here?"

"No time to explain." I reached for her hand. "We need to leave for Cazara Torannon now."

"Why?" Her eyes were wide with confusion. "Did something happen? Is it Uncle Andreo? Is he okay?"

I said nothing as she pulled her coat tighter around her, her face lined with worry.

"Damn it. Say something, Ash. You're scaring me."

I grabbed her elbow and touched my labral again, and in a flash, we appeared in the main living room at Cazara Torannon.

"Ash!" She yanked her arm away from my grip. "What in the Sangelis is going on?"

I pulled her into an embrace. "I'm sorry, Wynn. I . . . I just got word that Kaliope threatened your life. I needed to get you here, where it's safe."

"What?" she cried in outrage, her eyes as wide as saucers.

I took a step toward her, anger and irritation seeping through me. "Why are your wards not at full strength?"

Her eyes flared. "I was out for dinner in Chantilis. What in blazes have I ever had to be cautious about there? Why would Kaliope threaten *my* life?" Immediately, her facial expression slackened, and she furrowed her brows. "To get to you."

I clenched my jaw. "I need to talk to Tora to make sure our wards are at full strength here. I'll come find you as soon as I'm done."

"Ash." Her voice was low, her eyes flashing with a mix of frustration and anger.

"I know," I said, kissing her forehead. "I'm tired of living like this too."

"I had no choice but to lower the wards," Tora said a few minutes later as I paced the floor of my study. "We both know that bitch is deranged enough to make good on her threat."

"I know." I rubbed my hand across my face. "She can't get to Elle, Tora. I can't be the reason something happens to her. I am so tired of the constant fear and paranoia that define my life because of Kaliope. Always on the alert, waiting for her to make a move, to hurt someone I care about."

Tora put her arm on my shoulder. "I know this sounds clichéd, love, especially coming from me, but you have to trust that the Mavigos know what the fuck they're doing."

I folded my arms across my chest. "You didn't tell me you *know* Gargmoin. All those stories you used to tell me when I was a boy—they weren't made up, were they?"

"They were made up," she said quietly. "The truth about Gargmoin is much worse, but something I can't talk about."

My eyes narrowed. "He called you Lyria. Is that your real name? I don't understand. What happened when I collided with him? Was that someone else? And what's a siccharis?"

Her eyes flooded with anguish. "Ash, I literally cannot answer any of that. The craleic oath binds my tongue."

I frowned. *Craleic.* "What are you talking about, Tora?"

She leaned against my desk, clutching the dark wood tightly. "Every surviving living being at the dawn of the Second Age of the Sangelis was bound by an oath prohibiting them from speaking of the First Age. And it's not a choice. We are *incapable* of speaking of it with anyone else. The craleic oath *binds* our tongues."

I lifted my brows. There were two known ages of the Sangelis. The First Age and the Second Age, the latter also known as the New Age, which we lived in now. The ancient celestial star etching had foretold the Third Age—the Light Age—of which Elle and I played a significant role. "I always suspected you were as old as the First Age, given that you wield the light strain of the Old, Arcane Magic."

She was silent.

"You said you are incapable of speaking of the First Age with anyone else. Does that mean you can speak of it with others like you?"

She nodded.

"But what about the ancient celestial star etching? Any living being from the First Age would know about it. It was there before the Great Creator appeared in the heavens at the dawn of the Second Age millions of years ago. Is that part of the oath? That it cannot be spoken of?"

She was quiet for a moment, as if thinking how to answer me. "We can speak of the ancient celestial star etching freely with anyone who is a part of it."

Anyone who was a part of it—Eolith, Sorin, Elle, Kaliope, Catraia, me. Someone had clearly told Kaliope. But who? Gargmoin? Some other unknown ancient one?

"Who is Alvar?" I asked, and her eyes flew to mine, the same pain I had seen before flashing there. "The moment Gargmoin's eyes changed to blue, my sense of perception responded to him with welcome. Is he a different being from Gargmoin?"

She wrung her hands. "I cannot speak of this, Smolders."

"Fuck, Tora." I raked my hands through my hair. "Give me something to work with. What's a siccharis? Why did he ask you to find the hearts?"

"Ash," she said, pleading.

"Tell me this, then. Does the craleic oath have an end date?"

She nodded. "When the Celestial Songbird absorbs the light strain of the Old, Arcane Magic as part of her transformation, the binding will be broken."

I was silent, processing her words. It was only a matter of time before Elle found her way to Ariadna. How? I still had no clue. A lot about the celestial star etching was cryptic. Now all of this. Gods, I didn't know anything about anything.

Tora moved toward me and grabbed my hands. "Smolders. Listen to me. The oath prohibits me from speaking of the First Age. So I won't speak of the First Age." She looked at me, her eyes wide, conveying something secret in their depths. "Beings of extreme power like Arazul, like Elle will be one day, carry sentient life inside them to anchor the power they wield."

She looked at me as if waiting for me to say something. I narrowed my eyes. "Right. Nalios . . ."

She was trying to tell me something, although she *couldn't* tell me.

I looked at her abruptly, understanding dawning. "This Alvar and Gargmoin are Nalios?"

She neither affirmed nor denied. "What did I tell you not to do when Gargmoin was here?"

I furrowed my brows, confused. "You told me not to touch him." What did that have to do with anything?

"Remember what happened when you did."

What the fuck? Was I simple? What was she trying to tell me? I replayed it all in my mind. The first time I blasted a hole through his chest with my power, he had healed right away. When I physically rammed my fist into his chest, nothing had happened. Wait. Not nothing. *That's* when he'd changed.

"I summoned this Alvar?" I asked. "But I felt his goodness. Are you trying to tell me that Gargmoin is not all evil?"

Tora sagged, frustration lining her face. Clearly, I wasn't seeing the whole picture. "I need you to remember what happened here when the time comes, Smolders. Remember everything. For I will not speak of it again. Even now, I feel the castigating sting of the oath threatening retribution." She took a step forward. "You can't know any of this now. Not until Elle is here in the Sangelis will it truly be safe for you to possess this knowledge. I have known you all your life, my love, and I know that you will be relentless in trying to get answers. You will stir too much trouble, draw too much attention. You will also want to take action against Kaliope for threatening Gwynn. That cannot be your focus right now."

I shook my head. "Tora, you can't expect me to sit back and do nothing."

She reached up and touched my cheek. "Precisely. Forgive me, Ash. I have never once used my magic against you, and I did that tonight in an attempt to protect you. I do it again now, for the same reason. I promise to give back what I take."

"Wha—"

She quickly rested her fingers against my temple, a searing heat instantly bleeding into my mind, and then everything faded to black.

Chapter 12

ASHER

P RESENT DAY SOLNIESS, THE VOID . . .

I walked into Elle's chamber, instantly gazing at the wall.

Six hundred and seventy-one.

Close to a month she had relived through her consciousness. The Goddess Eolith's sanctum in Solniess was expansive, but I found myself never wandering far from Elle. In this celestial plane, the need for sleep and food was unnecessary, given that my physical body wasn't here, but that only made the time pass slower. Elle's stasis, on the other hand, was unavoidable given that her consciousness was not present in the Void, but was in the past.

Ever since Tora's letter, I had been replaying the memory she had returned over and over in my mind. Despite what she had done, I couldn't bring myself to be livid with her. Yes, it was a betrayal of trust and an abuse of her power, but I myself had taken liberties with those I loved to protect them in the past, so how could I be angry when I understood her motivations? Perhaps that's why she had done it in the first place—she knew I would see everything more objectively through the lens of hindsight.

Tora was one of the precious few who knew how far I fell after Kaliope killed my parents. I had been a ghost, numbing the horror of their loss with physical pain, sex, restless wandering, and mind-numbing magic that took away the sorrow, took away my ability to feel anything. I'd alienated those who loved me and was selfish and hurtful in my grief.

Was I in dereliction of my duty? Absolutely. I delayed my coronation for two years, and when the Cloryals issued their edict that it could be put off no longer, I agreed to a date and put into motion what I had been planning in the shadows for over a year, only to have Tora get wind of it.

I still remembered our heated row the evening before my coronation. The callous things I'd said, the tongue-lashing she gave me, the retribution I promised if she intervened—it was terrible. It made me sick to my stomach to think of what would have likely happened had Elle not stepped through the Senshifter into my room that night. I'd have gone through with it—my blood-soaked vengeance—and at this very moment, I'd be where Kaliope was up until three years ago—locked away in Glanag.

I had Tora to thank for lowering the wards at Cazara Torannon and granting the Senshifter access. Her magic could have easily blocked the Goddess Eolith's attempt that night. She could have turned a blind eye, left me to self-destruct and blow up my entire life, but she didn't. For leading Elle to me, I could and would forgive her anything.

It was clear now that Gargmoin was always meant to be the catalyst for Elle's arrival into Ariadna. Perhaps I might have altered things if Tora hadn't taken the memory from me. I couldn't truly say. Where Kaliope was concerned, my anger and frustration were volatile. If I weighed the events of that night—Kaliope threatening Gwynn's life and sending Gargmoin to retrieve information about my earthly visits, him finding out the name of the city Eleyse lived in, all the things I learned about Tora regarding the craleic oath, Alvar, Nalios—I couldn't say what I would have done. I just knew it wouldn't have been nothing.

Had she done the same to Gwynn? My sister had never mentioned that night to me, so perhaps Tora had taken that knowledge from her as well. Gwynn was even more of a loose cannon when it came to Kaliope, so it wouldn't surprise me if Tora had wiped it from her mind.

Remember everything, Tora had said to me that night. And I had. It played out in a loop in my thoughts, but I was nowhere closer to uncovering the truth of it all.

From what I gathered, Tora was from the First Age—no surprise there; I had always suspected as much. That would mean so was Lorien. They both wielded the light strain of the Old, Arcane Magic, and Lorien was the guardian of that power in Ariadna. By that reasoning, WorDalg, as well as Kurglokh, prince of the Soulshredders, and his kin, also belonged to the First Age. They all wielded the dark sway of the Old, Arcane Magic.

Next to nothing was known about that time, and it made sense now why that was the case. The craleic oath Tora mentioned had erased all knowledge of an entire age. The question was why? What had happened to wipe out an entire age in the Sangelis? Why was it kept secret?

As for Gargmoin and his Nalios connection—Tora's reaction had me rethinking whether I'd gotten that right. *Remember everything.* When I touched Gargmoin, that had brought about the change in him, summoning this Alvar whom Tora clearly knew. My magic responded warmly to his presence, which told me that he was not the same entity as Gargmoin, and he was good.

The entire time Gargmoin was in the room, Tora's main objective had been to keep the two of us away from each other. *You cannot touch him,* she had said to him; *Don't touch him,* she had said to me. Gargmoin learning Elle's location had to be because I touched him. Did that knowledge transfer to him then? Had he retrieved it from me somehow?

So if my reasoning was right, by touching each other, he had somehow gained knowledge from me, and I had summoned an entity inside him. But how? Why? It still didn't make sense. I was missing something.

I reached for my Gloweyen bond in my mind. *Catraia,* I called.

Yes, Asher.

If we fail in destroying Gargmoin's magic around Elle's soul, and the darkness consumes her, what happens to you?

I told you before, she answered, *the only way to end my existence is to end hers. As long as she breathes, I exist, but if she is consumed by the darkness, I will do, what as the anchor to her power, I must.*

A chill went down my spine. *What do you mean, you will do what you must?*

If I determine that Elle is too far gone to be saved, and is instead swallowed by the darkness, as the guardian of her power, I will destroy her from within. I am duty bound to ensure that her power is staked in the light. Anything else will prove detrimental to all life in the Sangelis.

I staggered, gripping the edge of the bed for support. The possibility that Catraia could end Elle's existence had not once crossed my mind. I'd always figured that as long as Catraia was with her, she would be safe, protected. And yes, in a sense, that was true, because when it came right down to it, Catraia would always keep her safe and protected, even from *herself.*

We will not fail, Asher. She will walk in the light freely again.

"I know." It was as simple as that. There was no room for any other beliefs. The alternative was terrifying, unacceptable. We would not lose her.

My mind snapped back to Gargmoin and Alvar. In trying to understand the dynamics of the Nalios connection, I'd gone straight to the source of one, but Catraia's answer only left me with more questions. If the entity within a being of great power could not be destroyed, but instead had the power to destroy the being it resided in, then who the fuck was Alvar? He was powerless, weak—there was no way he had the ability to destroy Gargmoin. What was I missing?

At the sound of melodic trilling behind me, I turned to see an *olianette* standing in the doorway, her electric-blue wings shimmering behind her. The ethereal creature's delicate face lit up in a smile as she regarded me, her large ochre eyes fluttering shyly.

"The Goddess Mother awaits your presence in the solarium," she said, before bowing her head and flitting away.

I sat on the edge of the bed and brushed my knuckles against Elle's cheek. I'd do whatever I had to do to ensure she came back to me with the darkness around her soul from the rebounding curse destroyed.

It was time. The Goddess Eolith had intended to go to Sorin after I read Tora's letter, but she'd received word that the Summoner of Light and Darkness was not in Madwen, his sanctum in the celestial plane. And so, we had waited, holding off, as well, on retrieving Faron and Treye. Before

I'd entered Elle's chamber just now, one of her messengers had arrived bearing news of Sorin's return.

I lowered my head and pressed a kiss against Elle's brow before leaving in search of her mother.

"Sorin was with the Goddess of the Night, I was told," the Goddess Mother said to me as we faced each other in the solarium. It was hard to miss the sadness in her voice. "But he's in Madwen now, so I will go. Faron Cardinin and Treye Wolvett, correct?"

I nodded, folding my arms across my chest. "Treye had just arrived in Cazara Torannon before I left, so both he and Faron should be there."

The Goddess Eolith walked to the center of the room where a golden bowl was perched on a marble pedestal. Inside was a recognizable substance—the essence of the Ethereal Harmonies. It was the same aqueous matter that was found in Alonai, the lake of rejuvenation in Falayen.

"Not even a second has passed in real time since you left, so pulling them into the Void will be jarring for them."

I nodded. "They'll recover quickly. But before you retrieve them, I have a question." I regarded her carefully. "Is there any way for Kaliope and Gargmoin to enter the celestial plane?"

"Not if Arazul has anything to say about it," she said without hesitation. "The entire fabric of the Void was constructed with the Great Creator's power. Nothing moves in here without his knowledge. I can assure you that his power and mine surround Solniess, making it impenetrable to any living being who is not granted access. As well, the pure essence of the Ethereal Harmonies themselves lines the perimeter of the sanctum. In the Void, there is no safer place to be than here. I am the Goddess of the Ethereal Harmonies, after all.

"As for Gargmoin, the Old, Arcane Magic has no effect in the Void, and that includes the light strain as well. Only Gods and Sovereigns were ever meant to enter the Void."

The memory of Gargmoin at Cazara Torannon had left me unsettled and filled with worry. My power had had no effect on him. He hadn't used his power against me, so it was hard to say what kind of damage he would do, but I didn't want to find out here, in the Void. For the moment, I was relieved to hear that he could not enter this place.

"One last thing, Asher," she said.

I turned to look at her. "Yes, Goddess Mother."

"I'd like it very much if you called me Eolith," she said with a soft smile. "You and my daughter have a powerful future ahead of you, and I could not imagine anyone else at her side. Your love and commitment to her is more than any mother could ask for her child." She took both my hands in hers. "Elle will one day be your queen, and I am happy and proud to know that in such a short time, not only have I gotten my daughter back, but I've also gained a son."

I lowered my head and squeezed her hands. "I would be honored, Eolith."

She smiled and touched my cheek gently. "Now, let's get Faron and Treye here." She dipped her index finger into the golden bowl and stirred the rippling essence gently. A slow humming melody issued from her mouth, and her lips moved quietly as the essence inside the bowl changed to a glittering blue.

In a thick cloud of swirling mist, Faron and Treye appeared in front of us.

"What in the name of the Goddess Moth—Fuuucck," Treye's voice rang out. His slitted eyes opened wide as he stared at the Goddess Eolith, and he stumbled backward, his short, cropped hair looking more red than chestnut in the sunlight.

"Ash?" Faron exclaimed, his brows furrowed in confusion. "What's happening?"

"Sorry for not giving you any notice," I said, stepping forward. "But I need you both here. Welcome to Solniess."

Chapter 13

ELEYSE

JUNE 9: ONE YEAR, TEN MONTHS AGO

God, I was winded. My six-mile route had felt like ten today. Up ahead, the entrance to the trailhead beckoned, slowly creeping closer. Almost there. Another thirty seconds and I would be done. Ugh. Maybe I shouldn't have eaten the rest of that burrito as a mid-afternoon snack. My body was heavy and sluggish as I forced myself forward.

I yelped as something darted out of the trees onto my path before skittering into the bushes on the other side. Shit. Bear cub? Coyote? Chicken? All I'd seen was a dark blur. I stopped, tiptoeing past the spot, staying as close to the edges of the trees on the opposite side as I could.

Leaves rustled in the cluster of bushes, and slowly, a familiar figure sauntered out.

The mangy, cross-eyed cat.

I'd thought for sure the bastard was dead. I hadn't seen it in months. I watched as it strolled across the path in front of me and came to sit on its haunches, its light-gray fur matted and patchy-looking. With not a bloody care in the world, the menace lazily lifted its front paw and began licking it as if it had nowhere else to be.

I stood with my mouth agape, my mind racing to figure out a way around. I had to be clever. The little bugger was a scratcher. Abruptly, the cat finished its grooming and turned its crossed blue eyes on me, tilting its head slowly as it regarded me.

A staring contest—at least I was pretty sure it was. I couldn't really tell because the critter was cross-eyed, its gaze bugging out in opposite directions. I would have laughed if I wasn't scared shitless that it would pounce on me and claw my eyes out.

But as we continued our stare down, the strangest thing happened. Its eyes *uncrossed*, and Mangy Cat . . . smiled—it bloody smiled. I blinked, my brows furrowed as I struggled to make sense of what I was seeing.

"Hello, Eleyse," the cat said, literally almost scaring the shit out of me. It spoke with a strange voice—no—voices, neither feminine nor masculine. Like nothing I'd ever heard.

I'm out, my lily-livered heart roared. I turned around and took off running in the other direction, but inexplicably, there the cat was, blocking my path again.

It sashayed toward me. "We can do this all day."

"B—but you . . . you're a cat," I stuttered, my heart thumping in my chest. Holy shit. I had to be hallucinating.

"Today we are," it replied matter-of-factly. "Same as every other day we've watched you since you moved to Hargrove." It sauntered toward me, weaving its way between my legs, its surprisingly soft fur brushing against my skin. "But this is just a vessel, one of many we've assumed over the years to observe your human journey."

What the hell was Mangy Cat talking about? It was a cat, for God's sake. And who was this *we* it kept referencing? A talking cat with multiple personality disorder? Fuck my life.

"The veil has lifted, Eleyse. It's almost time to return home."

"What on Earth are you talking about?"

Stop it, Eleyse. Stop it, my brain screamed. *Stop encouraging these delusions.*

"What we speak of does not exist on Earth." The cat sprawled in front of me, its front legs stretched long as it lay on its belly with its back legs splayed behind it. Its gray tail swished back and forth lazily.

I took a step back. "What are you?"

Mangy Cat cocked its head. "Do you see that tree? Or that patch of wildflowers? They are all manifestations of the universe—infinite energy, pure consciousness—as are all living things."

My mind reeled. This was nutty as hell.

"All living things are one with the universe, which is what *we* are."

Was I really standing in the middle of the woods getting a bloody philosophy lesson from a *cat*? And not even a nice cat—as if that really mattered.

I stared at the cat, my lips quivering as I struggled to find the words. "So . . . you are the universe . . ."

"As are you." Its blue eyes stared at me, unblinking and serious.

"All right, then," I said, desperate to extricate myself from the utterly bizarre situation. Gooseflesh tore across my skin, and I suddenly felt very, very small and cornered, despite towering over the feline at my feet.

The cat sat back on its haunches, its gaze holding mine captive. "In all things, there must be balance. We are the life force of the universe, arbiters and overseers of that balance."

I shifted uneasily under the creature's burning scrutiny. What in blazes was it going on about? What did any of this shit have to do with me?

Mangy Cat sauntered over, lifting onto its hind legs and pressing its front paws against my thigh. "Listen carefully, child of celestial love. Three earthly tragedies defined your human life. The past will come calling, and you will be powerless to resist. Three tragedies, three visits, three voices of reason."

"What are you talking about?" My voice was shrill, panicked. How did whatever this thing was know about the tragedies in my life? "And what do you mean, the past will come calling? What kind of visits? Like with *Scrooge*?"

The cat cocked its head. "We always did like that story. Oftentimes, it takes something drastic to break entrenched, toxic beliefs, and you, Sviyen, are as mired as they come. From great sorrow comes redemption. See past the heartbreak and pain of each loss and focus on the happiness, the love. Open your heart to love and music once more. Use the magic within you to weave the words, create the melodies, sing the songs. *Sing the songs, Eleyse.* Your voice gives them power."

My mind reeled. I had to be hallucinating. What melodies was I even supposed to create? What songs to sing? How did the feral little runt know so much about me?

The cat continued, the myriad of voices spilling forth from its unmoving lips. "You were made from pure light, created to wield the light. But even that which is pure can be corrupted. Here, cut off from the source of your light, you have slipped into darkness, a dangerous path for one such as you."

For one such as *me*?

"As the adage goes, to thine own self be true. The truth of who you are lies deep inside, buried under smothering layers of loss. You must strip each layer away to uncover your truth."

I stepped backward and the cat dropped its front legs to the ground, sitting back on its haunches.

"Darkness was never meant to be your path. The way forward is treacherous, and alas, you *will* suffer loss again. Do not succumb to the darkness, Sviyen Cielta. Trust in love to save you. Only when you see and accept love for what it is—a beautiful risk worth living *and* dying for—will you be free from the chains that bind you, and steer the course of your future. Never forget that. The moment you give up on love, all is lost."

And with those words, the cat turned around and sauntered toward the tree line.

"Wait," I called, my mind reeling. "I have so many questions."

"Don't we all," the cat called back over its shoulder. "*We'll* be seeing you soon, Eleyse."

It trotted off, disappearing into the trees, leaving me standing on the path with my mouth hanging open.

A wave of nausea hit me. Where did I even begin unpacking all of . . . that? I mean, did any of it really even happen? Who would ever believe me anyway? The truth was, my entire life was filled with bizarre, unexplained occurrences. Weird things happened to me. There. I said it. My life was a rainbow of weird. And I had no clue what to do with that.

Was there anyone who would?

Aggie sat on her porch—as classy as usual—staring at me with a blank expression. "So you're saying that the same fleabag-infested stray that chased you home every day for months *said* all these things to you?"

"You think I'm nuts, don't you?" I hung my head and moaned. "Maybe I am going crazy. Maybe I'm hallucinating it all. See, this is why I keep to myself."

"Now, now, I never said that." Her eyes grew bright. "You didn't hallucinate the handsome stranger you told me about. I caught a glimpse of him as he rode in on his shiny motorcycle last week. If I were even twenty years younger, I'd teach him a thing or two."

"Back off," I growled. "I will fight you to the death for him. He's my man-god; you can find your own."

She chuckled. "Well, did you take him for a ride?"

"Aggie," I gasped, my eyes wide. "A lady never tells."

"Get off your high horse, Ovi. We both know you're no lady."

I sighed. "I did not take him for a ride, if you must know." She opened her mouth, but I lifted my finger to silence her. "But it wasn't because I didn't want to."

She leaned forward in her glider armchair. "Wait. *He* turned you down?"

I nodded sheepishly.

"Oh, Ovi, please tell me you weren't wearing sweatpants and a tank top like a goddamned hobo when you were with him?" She shook her head, clucking her tongue quietly.

"That was only when he rang the doorbell," I said in protest. "You would have been proud, Aggie. I got dolled the hell up. His jaw almost hit the floor when he saw me. He took me out to dinner, and it was lovely. We talked, we laughed, and enjoyed each other's company. But then he said we should take things slow, get to know each other." Yes, I was leaving out some details, like how he pretty much thought I was sad and pathetic, but Aggie didn't need to know that.

"Child, are you telling me that in this day and age of fast sex and fast love, there's someone out there who still believes in taking things slow?"

"Right?" I exclaimed. "My thoughts exactly. I'd have jumped his bones right there on the front porch if he had let me."

"Don't be crass, Ovi," Aggie chided. "This one might be a keeper. He didn't run for the hills at your signature vagabond look, *and* he respects you enough to want to get to know you before *knowing* you, if you get my meaning."

"Are you saying that I don't respect him because I wanted to get down and dirty with him?"

She cocked her head. "I'm not saying that. For someone as emotionally closed off as you, sex doesn't have any meaning. And there's a time and place for that kind of blunt release. But your handsome stranger, in just the few things you've said about him, and the way your eyes light up when you talk about him, he's different. You *like* him. Really like him. And maybe that has a lot to do with him looking past your tough, cynical exterior, searching for the real you, the one you locked away after your Liam died."

"So, back to the cat," I said, not wanting to venture into deep emotional territory.

Aggie shook her head, her exasperated look telling me she knew exactly what I was doing. "At least tell me his name."

"Ash," I said quietly, unable to stop the fluttering of my heart.

"There," Aggie said with a smile. "That look on your face. It speaks volumes. There's hope for you after all, my girl."

I frowned. Hope. Wasn't that what I'd been searching for since my dream that night? *He comes, and on his heels, your future.* Could Ash be that *he*?

So much of what the cat had said—God, it sounded nuts to even say that—had hit home for me. The tragedies that defined my life. Opening my heart to love and music again. Ash had practically told me the same thing about music the first night I met him. The cat had spewed a lot of gobbledygook, too, but what it said about love being worth it and setting me free—I couldn't get it out of my mind.

"Back to the cat." Aggie's expression grew thoughtful. "Certain indigenous cultures believe in spirit guides—oftentimes in animal form—who guide a person through different phases and trials of their lives. Perhaps, there is some truth to that. You already know that I believe in the supernatural. Sometimes, you simply have to accept that there are things that defy reason and logic. Maybe that's what the cat represents. It's clear that strange things have happened to you. And are still happening."

She squeezed my fingers and tucked a strand of hair behind my ear. "I have lived my entire life following this philosophy, Ovi, and it has gotten me this far. Maybe you should try it. Don't fight the tide. Go with the flow."

Chapter 14

ELEYSE

D *on't fight the tide. Go with the flow.*

Aggie's words stayed with me long after I left her. Hours later, I sat in bed with my laptop, trying and failing miserably to read through a strategy document for work. I'd read over the same sentence at least ten times and it still hadn't registered. Shutting the lid on the computer, I shifted onto my side and placed the laptop on the floor next to the bed.

I stared blankly at the wall. When was the last time I'd gone with the flow? When I was a child? After my parents died, I'd spent the rest of my life always waiting for the next shoe to drop. Never allowing myself to be completely happy, to let go and live in the moment. Being carefree was a luxury I'd never permitted myself. What did that kind of freedom even feel like?

My thoughts drifted to Ash, a dull ache throbbing inside me. More than anything, I wanted to let go with him, to go with the flow, to experience what it would be like to allow myself to be happy.

Conflict whirled around in my mind. Mangy Cat had told me to open my heart to love and music again. Had said that love was worth the risk. But it had also said I *would* suffer loss again. If—and this was an astronomical if—there was any truth to anything to do with the cat, I wasn't strong enough to endure another loss. Mentally, I was not equipped to deal with that. I'd be nuts to open myself up to love again with the certainty that it would be ripped from me. I just couldn't do it.

The bitter sting of tears burned my eyes and a surge of rage flooded my senses. Why was I not worthy of love? Of happiness? It wasn't fair.

The image of Ash flashed in my mind, and I closed my eyes and let myself *feel* the whirlwind of things he roused in me—excitement, curiosity, desire, contentment, acceptance, hope. I thought of our kiss, and how the moment his lips had touched mine, something inside me had roared to life and rejoiced. *Mine*, it had declared, just as it had the first night we met. What right did I have to stake any kind of claim on him?

Tialla mata, he had called me, his voice filled with so much devotion and reverence that it floored me, confused me. He didn't even know me, but—and maybe this was just my own wishful thinking—he made me feel like I was precious to him. And I loved every moment of it.

Despair consumed me and I gave in, allowing the rush of grief to sweep me away. I didn't even know what it would feel like to be loved by him, and already, I was mourning the loss of never having it.

In my heart, I knew that if I let myself fall in love with Ash, I would never come back from losing him. He evoked emotions in me on a scale of magnitude I'd never experienced before. My salvation and destruction both at the same time—that's what he was, and I was a fool for wanting any part of him. I didn't know when—and I knew it should be sooner rather than later—but I would have to push him away. Not yet, though. I wasn't ready.

"Come with me, Eleyse," a voice whispered.

I opened my eyes groggily. Strange. I knew that voice somehow. But from where?

"Take my hand," the voice urged, and amid the blanketing darkness of my room, phantom fingers emerged, tendrils of light trailing from them.

"Back we go, my love, but this time, I will be with you every step of the way."

The melodic lilt of the words brought the realization crashing down on me—the woman from my dream a year ago. That's whose voice was in my head. She had come back.

"Where are we going?" I asked, my voice a ragged whisper.

"To the beginning. To the day loss plunged your life into grief. We bear witness through your eyes."

Shit. *The past will come calling*, Mangy Cat had said. *Three tragedies, three visits, three voices of reason.* Oh god. It was real. I hadn't hallucinated it all.

"Don't be afraid, Eleyse." The voice was soothing, calming the fear twisting my insides. "I am right here with you."

I reached out and slipped my fingers into the hand in front of me and screamed as I hurtled forward, as if into space and time itself. The sickening, gut-churning drop of a roller coaster—that's what it felt like—and in front of me, images spun and zoomed by until they became a swirling spiral of light. The spinning gradually slowed, and before my eyes, a scene began to emerge. A dark room. A solitary window. And beyond that, a glistening winter wonderland.

The clock on the wall in my pink, frilly bedroom chimed eight times. I bolted out of bed, my five-year-old heart racing excitedly at the sea of white outside my window. Thick, fluffy snowflakes drifted down magically, sparkling and ethereal as the morning light glinted off them. Last night, I had knelt at the side of my bed and prayed and pleaded for a white Christmas, given that not even an inch of the white stuff had fallen yet all season. It was a miracle. God had been listening and granted my wish.

Filled with glee, I raced into my parents' room, diving onto their bed.

"Wake up, wake up, it's snowing." I jumped into my father's arms as he cracked open a sleepy blue eye to look at me.

"Ellie, do you know what time it is?" he groaned, covering his face with a pillow.

"Come on, sleepyhead Daddy! It's morning, and it's Christmas Eve."

"Ellie, love," my mother said, pulling me off my father and into her arms. "Why don't you snuggle in with us for a few more minutes and then we'll get dressed and go out."

"No, no, no, silly Mama. It's Christmas Eve. There's so much to do today. Come on, come on. Up, up, up!"

I proceeded to jump on the bed, until finally, my father darted up and grabbed me around my middle, swooping me into his arms and over his shoulder as he got out of bed.

"Come on, Ky, you heard our little commander." He lifted me high over his head, and I spread my arms, zooming through the air like an airplane.

"Oh, all right." My mother yawned and stretched slowly. "I'm coming."

"Why don't you go wake Mags?" my father said, setting me onto the floor. "She loves playing in the snow."

"Yes!" I ran full speed ahead toward my aunt's room.

My father's younger sister, Mags, had arrived the day before and I was excited that she would be staying until New Year's Day. Next to my mother and father, Mags was my favorite person in the entire world.

Once everyone was up and dressed, we headed outside and spent most of the morning playing in the snow, having a snowball fight, making snow angels, and building a snowman. Afterward, we drank hot chocolate with jumbo marshmallows on top and had blueberry pancakes with whipped cream and maple syrup.

My parents sang me snippets of the pieces they would be performing at the Christmas Eve concert at the opera hall that afternoon. By the time they were ready to leave for the city—my mother smothering me with kisses and my father sweeping me into a tight hug laced with tickles—my little heart was full. All was right with the world, and it wasn't even Christmas yet.

"Be good, my sweet girl," my mother said as she slipped her coat on.

"Give your aunt hell, Ellie." My father winked at me conspiratorially.

"Oh, you," Mags said, pushing my father's shoulder. "I'll give you hell."

My father laughed as he closed the door behind them, and I ran to the window to wave as they drove off.

Mags and I whiled the afternoon away baking—sugar cookies, chocolate macaroons, apple pie, and her famous Christmas fruitcake. I helped her set the table for dinner as she put the finishing touches on the meal she had whipped up after we were done baking. Christmas carols blared in the living room, and I belted them out at the top of my lungs, looking out the window every few minutes for my parents' car in the driveway.

"When are they going to be back?" I asked, sneaking a cookie from the plate on the coffee table.

"Any minute now, Elle." Mags walked over to sit beside me. "Don't you worry. They wouldn't miss our Christmas Eve dinner for the world." She kissed the top of my head and ruffled my hair.

They had assured me that they would be home in time for dinner, and I had no reason to question that. But as the shadows outside grew longer, and the snow deeper, restlessness set in. Where were they? Maybe they had made a detour to pick up a Christmas gift for me. Perhaps the violin I had been asking for every day since the summer.

Mags assured me that they were just running late, but she kept casting anxious glances out the window, chewing on her lip the way she did when she was worried about something. My stomach rumbled in protest, but I ignored my hunger, more concerned with why my parents weren't home yet.

The grandfather clock in the living room chimed seven times, and a few minutes after that, my world exploded. I stood at the living room window, staring in confusion at the flashing lights outside. The snowflakes looked eerie and peculiar lit up in blue and red as they drifted to the ground. But perhaps it was the image of the police car in the driveway that my brain processed as chilling, and not the blue and red snowflakes themselves.

The doorbell rang, and Mags rushed to answer it. I heard snippets of words as the officers spoke to her in hushed whispers. ". . . terrible accident . . . didn't make it . . . so sorry . . . ."

Still, I didn't know what was going on, but I was sure that something was very wrong. Mags's wrenching sobs as she turned her grief-stricken face to look at me filled me with fear, the likes of which I had never known before.

I peered out the window and caught glimpse of movement near the tall *spruce tree in the far corner of the front yard. A figure stood there, looking back at me. Silhouetted in shadow, I could not make out specifics. Tall. Broad. Shoulder-length hair. A man. But the thing that held my gaze hostage were his eyes. In the darkness, they glowed silver, piercing through me, sending a shiver down my spine.*

"Everything will be all right, precious Eleyse," a voice spoke into my mind. "Hold on to your light, Sviyen."

My heart thudded in my chest, and I turned around to call out to Mags, but when I fixed my gaze on the tree again, the figure was gone. My eyes scanned the front yard, but only shadows and falling snow moved outside in the darkness.

Unease settled over me like a frigid blanket, and I knew with every fiber of my being that from this moment on, my life was never going to be the same again.

My heart raced, and a dull ache pulsed in my head. Everything had been so vivid, so real. Just like that—with the chime of a doorbell—my childlike trust and faith in a lifetime of happy tomorrows had crumbled and faded to dust.

How does a five-year-old comprehend the magnitude and finality of death? How does a brain that young process a loss of that scale? At the time, I remembered thinking I was in a bad dream, that it was all a mistake or a joke, that any minute now, my parents would breeze through the door, my mother's lilting voice and my father's deep laughter lighting up my world the way they always did when we were together.

I was so lost without them; they were the center of my universe. Without them, the sunlight drained out of my life, leaving only darkness and an emptiness that ate away at my heart, gnawing its way into the hallowed, warm place inside me where my memories of them lived.

Months later, after I had gone to live with Mags, she had given me the

Christmas present my parents had bought for me—the violin I had asked for. I gingerly put it back in the box and hid it in the attic when she wasn't looking. I didn't deserve it. I was the one who had prayed for snow. It was the snow that had caused the avalanche that had caused the accident that killed them. It was my fault. I never prayed for anything again after that.

I gritted my teeth. What was the purpose of this *visit* to the past? Did I really *need* a reminder of the loss that had changed the trajectory of my life? What was this supposed to teach me? I had spent all my life trying to move on from the events of my tragic past, had focused on burying the pain and sadness that had defined so much of my life since that moment.

And what of the man in the shadows? All these years, I had thought of him as Death, never for a second questioning that he could be anything else until Aggie planted the seed in my head a few weeks ago.

What if she was right? What if he was there for another purpose? *Everything will be all right*, the voice—his voice—had said in my head. *Don't lose your light, Sviyen.* I hadn't remembered his words from that night. Only that I had seen him.

Sviyen. Mangy Cat had called me that too. *Sviyen Cielta.* And the feline had rambled a lot of stuff about light as well. *You were made from pure light, created to wield the light.*

"Wake now, Eleyse," the woman's voice from my dream called to me, sending my thoughts scattering.

My eyes flew open and my heart lurched. She was here—curly violet hair and silver eyes flashing—sitting at the edge of my bed. Her face softened in a warm smile and she reached out her hand and stroked my hair.

"Who are you?" I asked, my voice a hoarse whisper.

"All in good time, *leida mata.*" Her face grew serious as she took my hand. "Right now, who *you* are is more important."

I frowned. "Me? What do you mean?"

She cupped my cheek gently. "You are more than the sum of your losses, my love." Her eyes shone even brighter as her gaze pierced through me. "You are a blessing, not a curse; hope, not despair; light, not darkness. When the new day dawns, step into it with fresh eyes. Celebrate the ones you lost that night instead of mourning them. Wrap their love and warmth around you; that long-forgotten happiness deserves to walk in the light, not to be banished and locked away in the dark reaches of your unrelenting grief."

Her words sounded eerily similar to those Mangy Cat had spoken to me earlier. *See past the sorrow and pain of each loss and focus on the happiness, the love. From great sorrow comes redemption.*

"And lastly, my heart, do not be afraid of love. Of the thought, the possibility, the reality. The weight of so much rests on it. Believe me when I say that happiness is but a thought away. The mind is a powerful thing. Reality is merely the fruits of your thoughts. Remember that."

She leaned forward and brushed her lips against my forehead. "Until we see each other again, *leida mata.*"

I closed my eyes and savored the warmth of her breath against my temple, the melody humming inside her enfolding me in a cocoon of enchanted serenity. When I opened them again, she was gone.

Chapter 15

ASHER

PRESENT DAY SOLNIESS, THE VOID . . .

"So this is the violet-haired beauty who owns our Sovereign's heart . . . and will soon be our queen." Treye's voice echoed through Elle's chamber, undertones of awe hanging off his words.

"Yes, this is Elle." A rush of emotion swept through me as I looked at her serene face on the pillow.

Treye turned his slitted gray eyes on me, a trace of playful insolence flashing there. "I have to say, Bash, she is even more gorgeous than I pictured. Perhaps even too gorgeous for you. And that's saying something, given that you are quite the looker yourself."

Bash—short for Basher. The name Treye had given me after witnessing me use my powers on someone hurting two Tandorin women in a tavern in Tasma the first time we met. At the time, he didn't know who I was, but even after he learned my identity, he refused to call me anything else. But then again, Treye refused to call anyone by their given name.

Faron chuckled beside me. "His head is fat enough, Treye. No need to swell it any more than it already is."

I smiled, shaking my head at the two of them—two of the most trusted in my inner circle, my two closest friends. Treye, commander of my Dulogrien, was one of countless others in Ariadna who were half Shen. Born to Ariadnan mothers during the time of the Dark Shen infiltration, he, and those like him, although Ariadnan citizens, had seen themselves as outcasts, with no place to call home.

Anti-Shen sentiment was high after the war, regardless of allegiances.

There was no hiding or disguising those slitted eyes, predominant in all those born with any Shen genes, and so, many of those born to Dark Shen fathers went into hiding. Some of them turned to a life of crime and violence, but there were those who clung to their Ariadnan heritage and rejected the legacy of their fathers.

I'd met Treye, Gilham, and Ovix on a visit to Tandor about ten years after the war. Upon hearing their plight and that of others like them, I proposed an alliance and offered them my protection. Soon after that, the Dulogrien was born. My cabal of spies had grown in number since then to what it was now—sixty-five—and every one of them were half Shen. Only the most elite and loyal were within their ranks.

"I can't shake the feeling that I've seen her before, though." Treye furrowed his brows. "It's the strangest thing—I can even picture the sound of her voice in my head. Isn't that weird?"

Faron grinned. "Better be careful, Treye. Don't give Ash the wrong idea."

Treye propped a shoulder against the bedpost, his eyes sparkling with humor. "I'm telling you, Bash, once news of your union is made public, the wailing in the streets all across Valkyse will be terrible. Hopeful mothers, dreamy-eyed daughters—crushed that the most eligible bachelor in Ariadna is spoken for." He inclined his head toward Faron. "Luckily, Ice and I will be there to pick up the pieces and provide comfort to the heartbroken fairer sex."

Faron snorted. "As if anyone in their right mind would come anywhere near Ash with Kaliope claiming him as her own."

Treye frowned. "Speaking of Queen Cunt, O reported that she has won the allegiance of Papa Tynor's armies. All of them. Five Dark Shen army commanders under her thumb. Tynor will shit himself with rage when he finds out."

I clenched my jaw. "Are you sure?"

"That he will shit himself with rage? I think it's pretty safe to assume so." He snickered at his own jape before turning serious eyes to me. "I am sure. She's racking up allegiances like a greedy siginil collecting shiny baubles. With Gargmoin at her side, no one will refuse her. And that asswipe, Madio, has visions of grandeur in his eyes. I'd love to know what glory the bitch promised him for relinquishing Averon's Phantera."

Faron grunted with distaste. "Ovix is sure she won't raise the war cry before the Convergence?"

Treye nodded. "Certain. He heard it from Kaliope's own lips. She needs that surge of power during those three days to strengthen and channel her power."

"Fucking Ovix." Faron shook his head. "I swear, he has balls of trinzum. The chances he takes to keep us in the know. I shudder to think of what Kaliope would do to him if he ever got caught."

I scrubbed my hand across my jaw. "Trust me. I think about that every day."

"O chose his post willingly." Treye folded his arms across his chest. "He knows and accepts the risks, as does every single member of the Dulogrien."

I placed my hand on Treye's shoulder and squeezed lightly. It wasn't just Ovix. No one could do what *any* of my Dulogrien did. Being half-Shen made them the perfect spies in Kindrik. The kingdom of the Dark Shen was a cutthroat, savage place, and I was fully aware of everything Treye and the others risked and sacrificed for Valkyse and Ariadna in their missions there, and at Kaliope's fortress in Clawkier Dreve.

I exhaled softly, my fingers digging into my palms. "I'm afraid I have even more bad news. Kaliope has turned both WorDalg and Kurglokh."

A weighted silence filled the chamber as Treye and Faron absorbed my words.

"The Sykrilix *and* the fucking Soulshredders?" Treye shook his head, disbelief clouding his features. "This just keeps getting better and better."

"Are you certain?" Faron fixed his pale blue eyes on me. "Could it just be a rumor?"

I shook my head. "No. This came straight from the Goddess Eolith's lips." I looked at Elle's shadow self on the bed. "At least neither Kaliope nor Gargmoin can gain entrance to the Void. The Goddess Eolith confirmed as much to me."

Faron shifted his stance beside me. "But the fact that we're here must mean that danger still lurks."

I nodded. "The Gods come and go freely in the celestial plane of the Void. Solniess is protected by both the Great Creator's and the Goddess of the Ethereal Harmonies' power, but not all the Gods are on our side. I almost killed the God of Chaos earlier today, and he will be smarting from that humiliation. The Goddess of the Night is also a threat. Once she learns that Elle is Sorin's daughter, her wrath will surely follow. There is a very strong likelihood that Kaliope will sway them to unite with her."

"How did it come to this?" Faron muttered. "I've heard many arguments that evil is made, not born, but in Kaliope's case, I don't believe that. Ever since we were children, she carried that festering darkness inside her."

A chill went down my spine. From the moment I was old enough to sense the nature of living beings, I had known the truth about Kaliope. I might not have understood how terrible it truly was when I was a child, but that darkness, as Faron said, had always been a part of her.

Treye furrowed his brows. "So, from what the Goddess Mother briefly explained before leaving for Madwen, she bequeathed us some of her power in the event the Gods make their way here?"

"That's right," I said. "Protect Elle at all costs. That is our main objective. I am the only one who can stand against the Gods, and if I get swept up with that, I need eyes on Elle."

"Were you ever going to tell us you have that power?" Treye exchanged glances with Faron.

"I don't know." That was the truth. "The Mavigos bestowed them on me shortly after I started visiting Elle in the human world. I never told anyone, but it's something the Gods of the Sangelis . . . I don't know—*sensed* about me afterward. Same with Tora and Lorien. They just knew."

"Why would the Mavigos give you the power to destroy a God?" Faron asked. "Did they explain?"

I frowned. "Is anything ever straightforward with the Divine? It's all tied in with the celestial star etching. All part of maintaining the balance, ensuring that darkness does not prevail."

Treye cracked his knuckles. "That is a tremendous amount of power, Bash. To be able to slay a God. You would think that you would have an entity like Elle does inside her to anchor you as well."

"I don't. Elle and the Great Creator are the only two beings I know of with a Nalios connection." Not to mention what I'd just learned about Gargmoin, which I still did not understand. "It should give you some indication of the kind of power *they* wield."

"But wait," Faron said, his brows furrowed. "If you have the power to destroy even the Great Creator, would that not make you more powerful than he is?"

I opened my mouth to say something but quickly shut it. I'd never thought of it that way, but in theory, that sounded right. "I've never had a problem controlling my power. Even in my dark days, it was always under my command."

Treye and Faron glanced at each other again, something unspoken passing between them.

"What is it?" I asked softly.

"Those were uncertain times, that's for sure," Faron said. "Your obsession with vengeance and self-destruction was terrifying."

Treye nodded. "We were fully committed in our support of you, but Gods, there was so much relief in the ranks when you didn't go through with your plan. None of us wanted that path for you."

It wasn't meant to be; that's what it came down to. Tora lowering the wards to let the Senshifter gain access to Cazara Torannon, the Goddess Eolith sending Elle back to that specific night, meeting my eternal soul's shadow for the first time. It had changed everything. Only Elle could have saved me from myself, from the vengeful plans I had carefully plotted, and that one night with her had transformed everything.

"So the power the Goddess Eolith imbued us with," Faron said, changing the subject, "they amplify our own abilities?"

I nodded. "That's right. That's how she explained it to me. Your ability to melt and control matter with your thoughts will extend to the constructs of the Void. You'll be able to hold your own against a God."

Faron touched the crystal vase on the console near the door and it, along with the flowers inside, melted in on themselves. I watched as he began to mold it with his mind, and in a matter of seconds, a multicolored cresting wave formed, spilling over onto the top of the console before receding, only to be frozen solid in its curved wave shape.

Treye rose his eyebrows. "Impressive, Ice."

My lips twitched at his nickname for Faron. Ice—on account of his silver-blue eyes.

"Let's see what I can do." Treye took a step backward, and in the blink of an eye, he disappeared, his stealth abilities activated. I watched as the balcony door opened and blue shadows rose around the railing, squeezing the marble balustrades together until they cracked.

Faron stepped onto the balcony, and with his mind melted the broken sections before reforming them the way they were.

"This is insane." Treye materialized in front of me. "It feels like my power, but like something completely new. Like when you first bestowed my abilities on me, Bash."

As Sovereign, I had the power to gift the magic of the Ethereal Harmonies to those I held close to me. What form that power would take, however, was wholly up to the Ethereal Harmonies when it bonded with that person. It was similar to a giln reading that way.

Treye had been bestowed invisibility and shadows of strength, while Ovix and Gilham, the other two in my Dulogrien, had received completely different abilities.

Faron, whose father was a great-uncle of my own father, had been born with his abilities, as was his twin, Astrid.

"So, do you think it's a matter of when, not if?" Treye crossed his arms over his chest.

I grimaced. "I do. Elle is too much of a risk for those who oppose us to leave her alone. And right now, she is at her most vulnerable, unable to defend herself or use her power."

Treye grinned. "So we're the brawn. Don't you worry. We'll protect your Gloweyen Queen with our lives."

"Absolutely," Faron said. "Valkyse deserves a Sovereign union as solid as your parents' before you. Not only that, but we are on the verge of witnessing history in the making. The first ever High King and Queen of Ariadna. Mind boggling."

Faron was right. It was mind boggling. As a child, I'd always known I would replace my father as Sovereign when he passed on, but I had always been unsure of myself, always worried that I wouldn't live up to my father's legacy. And after my parents' death, that fear became a reality, and I'd found myself on a collision course with failure.

Tora had once told me that she believed that regardless of that night with Elle and the Senshifter, I would have never gone through with my plans, and as much as I would have loved to believe she was right, perhaps Tora had more faith in me than I did myself.

Regardless, I had accepted my duty and sworn to protect and rule over Valkyse with the dedication and devotion of my father before me. To make my parents proud—that's what I'd always wanted, and through Elle, I had received that validation from my mother, and it meant the world to me.

My dreams of vengeance, though, still lingered, and with every fiber of my being, I would have it. Kaliope would not walk away from this battlefield unscathed. This was a fight to the death. In her eyes, I was a prize to be won, but her delusions were always grandiose and far-fetched. Only one of us would walk away alive, and I would do everything within my power to ensure it wasn't her.

Chapter 16

ELEYSE

JUNE 19: ONE YEAR, NINE AND A HALF MONTHS AGO . . .

The rain hammered the windowpanes in my sunroom. I closed my eyes and listened to the frenetic thumping, sinking into the tranquility and hypnotic inertia that rainy days delivered in droves.

Curled up on the couch with a book in my lap, a cup of tea, and a plate of cookies on the side table, it was the perfect way to while the afternoon away. I turned on some soft music and shifted onto my side, opening the fantasy novel to my page crease on chapter two.

Anya, the main character, had just been warned by her best friend, Tali, to stay away from troublemaker Kai, Prince of Shadows. Yes! Anya was definitely going to get it on with him. Only question was when. Hopefully, there'd be some steamy sex in the pages to come. I wasn't getting any, but that didn't mean sweet and feisty Anya couldn't enjoy some toe-curling orgasms. In fact, I was banking on it.

Anya was just admiring Kai's powerful physique, her traitorous gaze lingering on his firm buttocks, when my doorbell rang. I jumped, my heart leaping into my throat.

Ash. Please be Ash.

I chided myself for hoping. A week ago, the doorbell had chimed, and oh, the bitter, bitter disappointment that had engulfed me when I opened the door to find two old church ladies handing out pamphlets for a food drive they were organizing. I had smiled sweetly and donated generously to their cause, but the disappointing encounter had put me in a shit mood for two days.

Ever since the woman with violet hair had visited me again, I'd been a mess, my mind constantly obsessing over the events of the past month and a half since I'd met Ash. What the hell was happening to me? And did any of the strange occurrences have anything to do with him? Or was it just a coincidence that all the bizarre situations had escalated since I met him?

Today was the first day since my "visit" back to the night I lost my parents that I'd managed to turn my brain off and just concentrate on doing something as mundane as enjoying the sound of rain and reading a book.

As I walked to the door, I slowed my pace and willed my heart to settle, all the while thinking, *Old church ladies, old church ladies,* so I wouldn't get my hopes up. Shit. What to do? Look through the peephole or just rip the Band-Aid off and open the door?

Rip it off, girl.

I pulled the door open and almost melted in a puddle on the floor.

Ash. Fucking Ash.

Standing in front of me, soaking wet, beads of water dripping off his handsome face. Be still my wild heart. I looked past him to his gleaming bike in my driveway before sweeping my eyes back to him, thanking the heavens for this glorious piece of eye candy they had gifted me.

"Holy shit, Angel. You look good wet." I bit down hard on my lip as I stared at him.

"I imagine you do, as well," he drawled softly, his lips curving in a wicked smile as his gaze flitted over my body.

My face flamed, and suddenly shy and self-conscious, I shifted on my feet and avoided his eyes, fighting the urge squeeze my thighs together.

Invite him in, you lunatic, my brain chided, and I snapped out of my haze, whipping into action.

"Crap, let me get you some towels." I darted up the stairs to my linen closet, grabbed a handful of bath sheets and headed back to the door, opening it wide. "Please, come in."

He stepped inside the entryway, water pooling at his feet. "I don't want to get water all over your floor."

"Honestly, don't worry about it. I have lots of towels." I dropped one of the flannel sheets onto the floor, sliding it on the wet tiles with my feet. I grabbed his shoes as he slipped them off, flipping them over and placing them on the air vent in the foyer.

"The powder room is right through there." I handed him the remaining two bath sheets and pointed to the door near the kitchen. "Take your clothes off and I'll throw them in the dryer. You'll have to make do with a towel. I have absolutely nothing that will fit you."

"This was your plan all along, wasn't it?" he said, his voice teasing. "To get me out of my clothes?"

I smiled. "Busted. I commanded the rains, knowing you were going to be here, just so that it would lead us to this very moment."

His lips twitched with humor. "I have no doubt you are powerful enough to do that and more, *Tialla.*"

Tialla. That word again. Before I could ask him what it meant, he turned around and headed to the powder room. I stared at his broad back, his wet T-shirt plastered against his skin, his pants molded to his muscled legs. All of a sudden, I was Anya from my book, admiring *my* dark prince's sculpted physique and firm buttocks.

I slowly closed my gaping mouth and padded to the kitchen, sliding the towel along the floor in front of me to soak up the water that had dripped off him. My heart thudded in my chest. *Get a hold of yourself, Eleyse,* I growled. *When he opens that door, do not lose your goddamn mind.*

Too late. The door opened, and he stepped into the hallway, with nothing but a towel wrapped around his waist. The breath whooshed out of me in a rush, like I'd been kicked in the gut with a steel-toed boot. The man was so breathtaking, it should have been a crime. His hair was wavy and damp, curling softly around his face, his tall frame dwarfing me as he towered more than a foot over me. I couldn't tear my eyes away. His muscled chest, arms, shoulders, abs. God, he was well put-together. Even the bloody veins on his hands and forearms were sexy.

I didn't dare dip my gaze any lower. I glanced up at his face to find him staring at me with a strange look I couldn't read. Swallowing slowly, I took the wet clothes and towel from him, woodenly walking toward my laundry room.

"I'll be right back," I croaked, my movements heavy and mechanical. "You can wait for me in the sunroom."

When I returned, he was sitting on the couch with my book in his hands.

"*The Light Beyond the Shadows*," he read out loud, arching a brow at me. "Any good?"

I shrugged. "Can't say yet. I just started."

He flipped through the pages with his thumb, stopping somewhere in the middle of the book. A roguish smile coasted across his face as he read silently, his eyes widening slowly. "This sounds promising." He lifted the paperback and cleared his throat. "'Do you want me to show you how glib this tongue of mine really is?' the Prince of Shadows asked, his gaze skating over me like a wicked, wanton caress. 'I will have you screaming my name in four seconds flat. I might be your sworn enemy and darkest nightmare, baby, but I sure as fuck can take you all the way to paradise. Don't for one second think you will be able to walk away without wanting more. The pleasure I can bring you will haunt your dreams. And yes, I am that good.'"

I laughed, grabbing the book from him. "Hey. Don't ruin it for me. Kai has to take two women to paradise tonight."

Ash chuckled. "Damn that Prince of Shadows and his glib tongue."

"It's his confidence in his own abilities that's sexy."

"Well, he can take a woman to paradise in four seconds flat. Definitely something to gloat about. And the way he tells it, he's *that* good."

I laughed. "I believed him. I'm not usually a fan of the word *baby*, but when Kai said it, I got chills." That wasn't a lie. But it was Ash's voice saying it that made me shiver. Forget about Kai.

"He definitely seems to be gifted with the ladies."

"A gift you have in common, I'm sure."

And just like that, the lightheartedness of the moment was sucked out of the room, replaced with weighted silence, the soft, sultry music still playing in the background only strengthening the tension in the air between us.

"Are you going to sit?" Ash asked, and it was only then that I realized that not only was I standing, but I was slowly backing away from him, keeping my eyes averted.

"I'm sorry," I whispered. "It's really hard for me to focus with you sitting there with nothing but a towel on."

Ash frowned. "Should I go? The last thing I want is to make you uncomfortable."

"No," I blurted out, a moment of panic gripping me. "I don't want you to go."

He reached his hand out to me, and tentatively, I stepped forward and took it, my fingers curling around his as a blast of sizzling energy shot through my body. Pulling me forward, he guided me to the couch next to him, and I sat there, every nerve in my body aware of his glorious display of bare flesh so close to me.

"As soon as my clothes are dry, I promise to change right into them. Until then, just take a breath and try to relax." He brushed his fingers against my temple, his thumb circling gently. His touch was hypnotic, and I found myself unwinding, arching into the warmth radiating where his skin touched mine.

"Better?" His emerald eyes glittered as he studied me.

I nodded. "Everything about your presence makes me feel better."

For a moment, I swore a flash of fire sparked in his eyes, but by the time I blinked, it was gone.

He tucked a tendril of hair behind my ear. "How have you been since I last saw you?"

"All right, I guess." I fought the urge to close my eyes as I reveled in the feel of his fingers. "The past week and a half especially have been . . . strange."

His brows lifted. "How so?"

"You wouldn't believe me if I told you. I'm not entirely sure I believe it myself."

"Try me." He shifted his body toward me.

My gaze flew to the ripple of muscle on his chest as he moved. I shook my head and glanced back up at him again. A glimmer of amusement twinkled in his eyes.

"Sorry, what?" I mumbled.

"You were going to tell me what was so strange."

"Right," I said, snapping out of it. "You'll probably think I'm nuts."

"I'm sure I won't."

I stared at him, his warm gaze focused wholly on me, as if nothing else in the world mattered to him. An uncontrollable shiver rocked me as I struggled to decipher my feelings. Consumed with an inexplicable ease, my senses were secure and confident that I was *safe*, something I had not felt in a long time. It was as if an invisible thread—powerful and unyielding—tethered us together.

And so, in the doleful gloom of the late afternoon, as the rain rattled the windowpanes and the wind howled and beat against the house, I found myself word-vomiting my crazy into his lap again, just as I had that first night I'd met him. I told him about Mangy Cat and my encounter with the violet-haired woman. I told him about my "visit" back to the day my parents died. About the man in the shadows and what he had said to me. Then I backtracked and told him about all the strange and unusual things that had happened to me since the death of my parents. My beliefs about being cursed. The man who had appeared to me over and over again. My dream a year ago that changed my life. Aggie's sighting of the man with silver eyes recently, and her views on his presence. What Maya had seen and said when she touched me.

In between my ceaseless babbling, Ash changed back into his clothes once they finished drying, helped me in the kitchen as I made dinner, set the table as I transferred my chicken and shrimp stir-fry into a serving dish, uncorked the wine in the fridge and poured us two glasses. Not once did he appear bored, distracted, or skeptical. He listened to me with rapt attention, just letting me get it all out, asking questions every now and then, but for the most part, he was quiet and supportive as I talked.

By the time I was done telling him everything, we were back on the couch, wine glasses in hand, dishes already washed and kitchen tidied up.

"I'll understand if you want to quietly slip out the door and never return," I said with a deprecating smile.

"Did I give you the impression that I felt that way?" he asked quietly.

"No, but you have to admit it's all far-fetched."

"What do you think?" he asked. "Do you believe you're crazy?"

I frowned. "I don't know, Ash. I don't know what to believe."

He cocked his head. "Do you really believe you're cursed?"

"I don't just believe it, I know it. Deep inside me, I know I'm the reason I lost my parents, Mags, Liam. And almost Charlotte. Everyone I loved lost their lives. Love is the reason they're all gone."

"So how did it make you feel to hear the cat tell you otherwise? To open your heart to love and music, the two things you shut out of your life? How did you feel when the woman from your dream said all the things she did?"

"Do you think I imagined it all?"

He stared at me intently. "I don't think you imagined any of it."

"Aggie thinks that the cat might be some kind of spirit guide, here to guide me through an important phase of my life."

"And Aggie is your next door neighbor?"

"Yes. She's the only other person I've confided in." I took a sip of my wine and tucked a leg under me as I faced him. "Sometimes, I feel like I'm living a life that isn't mine. I can't explain it. Sometimes it feels like this is an existence, a passage of time before my real life starts. Does that sound crazy? I know that there are lots of people who would tell me that we only get one life to live and I am squandering mine, but if this is my one life, is it really worth it? I'd rather it be over as opposed to having to live out the vicious cycle of love and loss again."

Ash's fingers brushed my jaw, tilting my face toward his. "Don't give up on love, Elle. And don't give up on music."

"I don't know how not to," I said, furrowing my brows. "There is so much about all of this I don't understand. Mangy Cat, the woman from my dream, the man with silver eyes, even Maya that day—they spoke to me like I'm someone else. Someone I don't know, belonging to a life that isn't mine. They spoke words I don't understand, said things about me I don't recognize."

I put my wine glass on the side table and reached for his hand. "Even you, Ash. What I feel when I'm with you is like nothing I've ever felt before. I've never had to fight *not* to feel. Shutting myself away has always been easy. But you light me up like a bloody Christmas tree, and I love it, crave it, need it. You make me want to let go, but I'm so frigging terrified I'll fall."

"You might surprise yourself, *Tialla*." He trailed slow circles with his thumb on the back of my hand. "You might fly."

"But what if I don't?"

"Then I'll catch you." He lowered his head and kissed me, his lips featherlight against mine. "You were meant for more than a life of sorrow, Elle." His fingers fluttered against my cheek as he trailed kisses along my jaw. I moved toward him, climbing into his lap, taking the wineglass from his hand and setting it on the table beside me.

For the longest moment, we just stared at each other, neither of us moving. Slowly, I rested my hand against his chest, feeling the steady thud of his heartbeat beneath my palm.

"What does *Tialla* mean?" I asked, my voice a low whisper.

He clasped my neck gently. "In an ancient language, it means goddess."

My eyes widened as a rush of heated emotion washed over me. He had called me a goddess when he took me for dinner. I hadn't forgotten.

His hands moved around my waist and settled in the small of my back.

I ran my hands through his dark hair, luxuriating in its softness. Trailing my fingers down the sides of his face, I lowered my head and kissed his cheekbone, slipping lower to graze my lips across his jaw. Finally, I brought my lips to the lushness of his, tracing the outline of them with my tongue.

My body flamed as his mouth parted and he grabbed the back of my head, crashing my lips onto his. Slow and teasing turned to hard and desperate, our tongues and teeth colliding as our mouths moved feverishly together. His tongue plundered the recesses of my mouth, and I sucked him in greedily, tangling my hands in his hair.

His hands drifted up my thighs to cup my ass and I ground my hips against his, reveling in the feel of his erection between my legs. That he wasn't unaffected by me made me feel confident, powerful.

"Ash," I whispered, the brittle threads of my control snapping loose.

"Yes, *baby*?" He emphasized the endearment, his voice low and teasing.

I sucked in a breath and placed my hands on his shoulders. "Please don't stop calling me that. It's even better when *you're* the one saying it, and it's directed at *me*."

"Noted, *Tialla*."

"That one too." I trailed my hands across his chest.

I sat back on my knees and drank him in, exploring his face with my fingers—his smooth brow, the tiny laugh lines at the corners of his eyes, the sharp planes of his cheekbones and jaw, his straight, perfect nose, the deep groove leading to the top of those lips, so pillowy and soft.

My breathing was short and ragged, the pulsing between my legs driving me to distraction.

"Please don't go tonight," I said, unable to bear being alone. "I promise to behave."

"Fuck, Elle." He frowned, his hands circling my waist. "I don't want you to feel that you can't be yourself with me."

I looked at him long and hard, furrowing my brows. "Ash, the woman I am with you feels like someone else, someone trapped inside me who you awakened, and I wish she would stay. I don't want to be myself when I'm with you. I want to be her." I ran my fingers down his chest. "I'd be lying if I said I didn't want you to take me all the way to paradise, as Kai so perfectly put it, but I respect what you said before. I want sex to mean something, to be more than just a release, but I'm not ready for the rest of it, to open myself up to life again, to let go of the pain. The pain is all I have left of *them.*"

He pulled me to him, burying his face in my neck. "It's not, Elle. I know it might feel like that, but the happiness, the love—those are the things you need to carry in your heart with you."

"Will you help me?" I pulled away to look at him, the sting of tears burning my eyes.

"In whatever way I can, *Tialla.*" The back of his hand grazed my cheek. "And just because I'm not taking you all the way to paradise doesn't mean I can't give you a glimpse of it."

The blood heated in my veins at his words, and I rose onto my knees, my head higher than his in that position. He gripped my torso and pulled me closer, his thumbs lazily tracing the underside of my breasts. His mouth sauntered down my neck, the press of his tongue warm and tantalizing as it slid against my skin.

All the while, my heartbeat pounded in my ears, the rush of my arousal burning its way through my body like a bloody fever. I threw my head back to give him better access, biting my lip to keep from moaning when he sucked gently on the hollow near my collarbone.

His fingers slid under the straps of my tank top, gripping them lightly but not easing them off my shoulders. Letting out a frustrated moan, I arched into him, the tips of my breasts rubbing against his chest. I closed my eyes at the glorious friction and whimpered at the searing contact.

"The Prince of Shadows can work his magic in four seconds flat," I rasped, my voice heavy with want.

He chuckled. "I haven't even touched you yet."

"My point exactly." I levelled him with a glare.

"Trust me, baby, the anticipation only heightens your arousal."

I looked at him through half-lidded eyes. "When you call me baby, it sends a jolt of pleasure straight to my clit."

His eyes flashed and he inhaled sharply, his fingers digging into my skin, shaking slightly, as if he was fighting for control.

"And when I call you *Tialla?*" His voice was a guttural caress.

I clasped the sides of his face, stroking his cheekbones with my thumbs as I shook my head slowly. "That one evokes a different response. That one goes straight to my heart."

We stared at each other for what seemed like an eternity, unspoken thoughts and emotions swirling on our faces, until slowly, our lips met. My hands dropped to splay wide on his chest as his fingers pulled the elastic free from my hair before threading through the wavy length of it.

"You're so Goddamn beautiful, Elle." His mouth claimed mine again, his teeth gently nipping on my lower lip. His hands cupped my breasts through my tank top, and I rose to my knees, my chest almost eye-level with his face.

"Please, Ash," I murmured, pressing myself into his palms.

"Tell me." His fingers traced the top swell of my breasts.

"Touch me. With your fingers. Your mouth."

His lips curved in a small smile, the irises of his eyes dark as he gripped the fabric of the tank top at my chest, slowly yanking it down before slipping his hands in to scoop my breasts out. All the while, his gaze remained glued to mine. It was all I could do not to shove my tits in his face.

Beads of sweat dotted my forehead, the throbbing between my legs growing more intense with each second. Slowly, he lifted his hands to slide the straps off my shoulders and down my arms, only then dipping his gaze.

A ragged inhale reverberated through him as he traced a path across the top of my chest with his index finger before swirling wide circles around my breasts with both hands.

"Perfect," he whispered.

Gooseflesh erupted across my skin, every inch of my body tingling with his touch, my nipples growing tight and achy with anticipation. My fingers gripped his T-shirt, my body rigid and still as it waited for more.

His hands moved down to grip my torso, and slowly, ever-so-fucking-slowly, he pulled me closer, his mouth a hair's breadth away from my right breast. He lifted his eyes to meet mine, and involuntarily, my body shook, the tension inside me about ready to combust.

He smiled as he swirled his tongue and closed his mouth around my nipple.

I closed my eyes and lost my goddamned mind. "Ash," I cried out as an orgasm tore through me, erupting from the depths of nowhere, and I dug my fingers into his chest as wave after wave rocked my body. His lips were warm and soft against my skin, the suction of his mouth and tongue intoxicating, driving me wild. I pulled away from him and sank back into his lap, seeking out the hardness of his cock against my clit, and I ground myself against his length through his pants, using the friction and pressure to intensify and prolong my climax.

My heartbeat was wild and erratic as I came down off my high, every nerve ending in my body reactively sensitive to touch. I shuddered and opened my eyes to find him watching me intently, desire and hunger swirling in those emerald pools.

"Gods, Elle," he growled, sliding his hands onto my hips. "That was . . . the sexiest thing I've ever seen. I barely even touched you."

"You're the one who said anticipation would heighten my arousal." I wrapped my arms around his neck.

"Yes, but I didn't expect you to explode like a powder keg at the slightest touch."

"Take the win, baby," I said through a sated smile. "The Prince of Shadows needs four whole seconds to have women screaming his name. You did it in one."

He laughed, placing a kiss on my lips. "That's right. Prince of Shadows. Fucking amateur."

Chapter 17

ELEYSE

AUGUST 13: ONE YEAR, SEVEN AND A HALF MONTHS AGO . . .

I sat on my back deck, exhausted after a long hike through the Bluetail Trail earlier. It had taken me six hours to complete the full loop. Summer was in full swing, and every chance I got, I was outside. God knew it would be over all too soon, the icy wrath of winter always lurking in the wings, biding its time.

As I lay back on my lounge chair, a glass of wine in hand, a splendid sunset swept across the sky, taking my breath away. Thoughts of the violet-haired woman arose in my mind, as they often did since the night she had come to me again.

You are a blessing, not a curse; hope, not despair; light, not darkness.

What did she mean? Who was she really? Both times I had encountered her, she had looked at me with such tenderness in her eyes? Why?

. . . do not be afraid of love. Of the thought, the possibility, the reality.

Shit.

Trust in love to save you, Mangy Cat had said. *The moment you give up on love, all is lost.*

Those were the words I kept obsessing over, my heart soaring with longing and hope every time they played out in my mind. I was falling, in over my head, and didn't know what to do.

Ash. He was always there, hovering on the fringes of my thoughts, oftentimes the sole focus of my shameless fantasies. My longing for something more tormented me like nothing else, shaking the foundations of my long-standing resolve.

Since that rainy afternoon in my sunroom, I had seen him three times. The first time, he'd shown up at my office and taken me out to lunch, and I had taken the rest of the afternoon off and gone bowling—of all things—with him. I couldn't remember the last time I'd felt so carefree or laughed so hard.

The second time, we'd gone on a hike together, and the morning had unfolded perfectly until I tripped on a tree root and stumbled into a patch of poison ivy. The hike had been cut short with a trip to the pharmacy for some anti-itching medication, but afterwards, we'd ended up at a pub across the street, where we'd whiled the afternoon away drinking cocktails and talking.

The third time, we'd gone to a hockey game, and I'd immersed myself into the experience, screaming and cheering on the Hargrove Mooseheads with as much enthusiasm and vigor as I used to when Liam was alive and we would go to games. The excursion was bittersweet, flooding me with mixed feelings. Being with Ash made me feel giddy and carefree, and that scared the shit out of me.

Each of those three times I was with him, I purposefully avoided initiating any physical intimacy. I'd been a mess since he'd made me come in my sunroom with a flick of his tongue. I'd spent that night in his arms, fighting my feelings as my heart threatened to bottom out from the utter happiness and contentment he made me feel. Although I ached for more, my brain struggled to process and reconcile my volatile emotions.

Screw loneliness and heartache. He made me want to live. To feel. I was so tired of being dead inside. He was brilliant sunlight, and wilted flower that I was, I chased after his flame, craved his life-giving light.

Although I'd kept him at arm's length physically the past few times he was with me, he never pushed me, seemingly content to let me take the lead. I had to admit, though, not once did I ever feel like I wasn't the object of his undivided attention. The man had the ability to make me feel like I was the only person who existed, the only one he had eyes for.

My intimacy avoidance didn't extend to goodbyes though. No frigging way. In those moments, I clung to him like he was life itself, my desperate kisses grounded in the fear that I might never see him again, and he returned my fervor and need with reassurance—every look, every touch, every caress of his lips against mine a promise that he would be back.

No doubt about it, I was in trouble, swimming toward the raging rapids, and god help me, part of me desperately wanted to tumble over.

As I stared off into the shadowy woods at the edge of my backyard, my eyelids grew heavy. I hadn't slept well last night, my dreams troubled and morose. Slowly, my eyelids drooped, and I relaxed, sinking into the pull of my fatigue.

A few seconds later, my eyes flew open, and I sat up straight in my lounge chair, the hair on the back of my neck rising.

I wasn't alone.

My gaze found the source of my unease immediately, settling on the silhouette of a figure slowly striding from the woods toward my house.

Fuck. It was him. *Death.*

I didn't even need to see him up close to be sure. His shoulder-length hair lifted gently in the breeze as he moved, a white tunic clinging to his broad, tall frame as he walked. From where I sat, there was no mistaking the silver flare of his eyes as he looked at me purposefully.

My heart clenched in my chest, but I sat there frozen, unable to peel myself off the chair.

Do the one thing you haven't done yet. Talk to him. Aggie's words echoed in my mind. Oh god. Could I? What the hell would I even say? My tongue was stuck to the roof of my mouth, so who even knew if I was capable of speaking.

As he drew closer, the air around me grew heavy with an unmistakable substance.

Power.

Dreadful, heart-stopping, mind-melting power.

It exuded from Death, dripping from every pore, even as it settled around him like a warm familiar. It was the same every time I had encountered him, and like nothing I had ever experienced with anyone else before. He was something to be feared, worshipped, no mere mortal.

From day one, I'd instinctively understood that. There was no doubt in my mind that he held the power to end me.

And yet, in all of the times I had encountered him—fifteen, to be exact—he hadn't. Was Aggie right? Was there a chance that he wasn't Death? But if so, then who was he? And what the hell did he want with me?

He came to a stop at the edge of my gazebo, the intense silver of his eyes unnerving as he gazed at me. He was so breathtaking, it *hurt* to look at his face. High cheekbones, angular features, a magnificent mane of light-brown hair any woman would kill for. His was an ethereal, spectral beauty—hauntingly majestic and terrifying at the same time. I gasped, shaking in a full-body tremor as the urgency to drop to my knees and beg for mercy overwhelmed me. My skin erupted in gooseflesh as the power pulsing off him rippled around me.

He had never approached me before, had always watched from a distance. Why was today different? I dared to look in his eyes, and again, that compulsion to fall prostrate rocked me, but this time, I couldn't stop it. I dropped my head, sliding off the chair onto my knees in front of him. As I lowered my face to the ground, a blast of electricity shot through me as his hand touched my hair.

"No, Eleyse." His smooth, deep voice sent shivers through my body. "A queen does not bow to a subject, and a queen you are, Sviyen Cielta."

What the— I lifted my head and shot a fleeting glance upwards. Those stunning eyes ensnared me, holding me hostage. Swirls of liquid silver churned and shimmered in their depths. I couldn't have looked away if I tried.

"The time for your awakening is at hand, little bird." He reached down to grasp my hand and pulled me to my feet. The power surging into me at his touch almost drove me to my knees again. He steadied me with his hands. "This world can no longer provide sanctuary."

Confusion rushed in. Sanctuary? What on Earth was he talking about? Who exactly did he think I was? My neck strained as I looked up at him. Holy crap, he was tall. Even taller than Ash, and that was saying something because my angel/man-god was tall.

"Wh—who are you?" I asked, my voice a breathless whisper.

"The one who, at the dawn of the New Age, was entrusted to ensure your ascension."

"My what?" My eyes widened. God, this had to be a dream. That was it. I was dreaming. Because this made absolutely no sense.

"The past has come calling again, Eleyse." His eyes softened as he looked at me. "To the second great tragedy of your life, you must return."

"No, please no." My breath constricted as the memory of my parents' deaths I had revisited bubbled up. "I don't want to remember."

He touched my cheek, setting my skin ablaze with the contact. "Hold on to the love, the warm memories, the strength of the bond that bound you. Let the pain go." It was the same thing Mangy Cat had said. Death's fingers drifted up to the center of my forehead, grazing gently against my skin. My eyes grew heavy, the world slowly spinning around me as my body went slack and the darkness consumed me.

"Liam, hon, can you get your tongue out of Ellie's throat? You're going to hockey practice, not off to war."

I blushed, pulling away from Liam to peer at Mags's face on my computer screen.

Liam pressed a kiss to my forehead, his light-brown eyes sparkling with mischief. "But Mags, every time I'm away from her, I miss her like crazy. Plus, she'll be gone a whole week visiting you, so I've got to steal as many kisses now as I can."

Mags rolled her eyes, even as her smile betrayed her affection. "Oh, you. Get going before I stick my foot through this screen and boot you in the ass."

Liam chuckled, slipping into the chair in front of my laptop. "Stop playing, you know you love me."

"Like a bad case of hemorrhoids."

"You can be a hemorrhoid on my ass any day." He winked, brushing a lock of ash-blond hair off his forehead.

I laughed at the incredulous look on Mags's face.

"Boy, you're lucky you're pretty," she said, shaking her head. "And that you make Ellie laugh."

Liam got to his feet and wrapped his arms around me. "Making our girl laugh is my life's calling, Mags." He planted a kiss at the top of my head. "I'll let you two catch up." Tugging his ball cap onto his head, he hugged me once more before heading out the door.

Mags sighed, her perfectly arched brows pulling tight. "I'm so happy you have him and Charlotte there." She flipped her dark-brown hair behind her. "It eases some of my anxiety to know you're not alone."

"Yeah, yeah. Enough about me," I said, unable to contain my excitement. "How was the audition?"

Over the past few months, Mags had talked my ear off about auditioning for the coveted piano concerto in the upcoming symphony orchestra performances at the Orpheus Symphony Hall in Toronto. In my mind, there was no way she wouldn't get it. She was that talented.

Her excitement bled through the screen as her face lit up and her eyes grew bright and animated. "I got it, Elle."

I screamed, jumping up from my chair and doing a happy dance at the desk. "Oh, Mags, I'm so happy for you." I looked at the screen. "I'm so proud of you, and I know Mom and Dad would be too."

Tears sprang to her eyes, the deep blue of her irises shining like polished glass. "Thanks, baby girl. I can't wait to see you tomorrow. We have so much to catch up on."

"You're picking me up from the airport, right?"

She nodded. "8:15. Already in my calendar. I'll be there with bells on." The sound of the doorbell chiming carried through the screen and Mags looked off to her left. "Gotta run, Elle. I'll see you tomorrow morning, okay? Love you."

"Love you too, Mags," I echoed. "See you tomorrow."

I pulled my carry-on behind me as I headed up the front walk. The morning sky was overcast and grim, throwing a ghoulish haze over the entire neighborhood. Eerie silence hung in the air, rattling my nerves and sending my senses on alert.

Mags hadn't shown up to get me at the airport. It wasn't like her. She hadn't texted me back this morning before I boarded the plane either. The last time I had seen her in person was two months ago, when she had shown up on campus to surprise me for my nineteenth birthday.

Her car was in the driveway, the top of her convertible down. I tiptoed closer and stopped in my tracks, my body stiffening. Small puddles of water and tree debris pooled all over her leather interior. I turned my head and looked around. The ground was wet, strewn with fallen leaves and branches. It wasn't like Mags to leave her baby unattended in the rain.

Alarm bells sounded in my head as I hurried to the front door. Fishing my keys out, I unlocked the deadbolt, quickly stepping inside.

Silence.

"Mags?" I called out. "You here?"

Nothing.

My heart thudded, a feeling of pallid foreboding snaking down my spine. "Mags?" My movements were frenzied and uncoordinated as I ran into the living room. The room was neat and undisturbed, with not even a throw pillow out of place. Her beloved piano stood quietly in the corner, shrouded in shadow. I rushed into the kitchen. What was that smell? I pinched my nose, looking around for the source. The entire space reeked of it. It smelled like rotten eggs. Oh no. No!

"Mags." My voice rose an octave higher as I raced toward her bedroom. Her door was open, and I sped inside. The room was dark—curtains drawn shut—making it impossible to discern anything. I flipped the light on and instantly, horror and disbelief ripped through my chest.

She was lying on her side, her body stiff, her face and lips blue—so fucking blue. I rushed to her side and touched her cheek. Icy cold.

"Mags," I cried. "No. Please don't go."

No! No! No! This couldn't be happening.

I grabbed the phone near the bed, my fingers shaking as I dialed 9-1-1. Tears blurred my vision and I swiped them away. I turned to look at her and almost jumped out of my skin. She was sitting up in bed, her bloodshot eyes wide and wild as she looked at me. "You did this, Elle," she rasped, her blue-black lips curled in a snarl. "You're not welcome here. As long as you walk in this world, death will always be one step behind you. All who love you will die. The veil has lifted. The Sangelis awaits your return."

The room spun and shifted, and my body catapulted forward, hurtling through a turbulent sea of undulating light. My body slowed, floating in suspended animation, encapsulated within a halo of pulsing radiance.

How many times had I relived this memory in the past nine years? Too many to count. The last bit was new—the grisly specter of my beloved Mags. It was both macabre and sickening.

The veil has lifted. The Sangelis awaits your return. Mags's chilling words were almost word for word what Mangy Cat had said to me. But what was this veil? And what the hell was the Sangelis?

Mags . . . My heart ached with the weight of my grief, the heaviness of it threatening to suffocate me. She was gone, her loss the third stake in my chest. The trauma of finding her the way I did had never left me. At any given moment, I had but to close my eyes and think of the scene and it unfurled, vivid and untouched as the day it had happened.

She had installed a natural gas stove a few months before the incident. The investigation had shown that a break in the hose hooked up to the back of the stove had caused the leak. Mags had simply gone to bed and hadn't woken up. She'd been dead almost sixteen hours when I found her.

Something critical to my existence had been annihilated the day she died. I had loved her fiercely my entire life. She had been my doting aunt for five of those years, and parent, sister, friend, therapist, teacher, the rest. She had only been twenty-four when I'd gone to live with her, and although she'd never once said anything, I knew the sacrifice she had made to raise me. She had put her budding career as a concert pianist on hold because of me. It was only after I started high school that she began focusing on her passion again.

Losing her had completely devastated me. When my parents died, she was the one who saved me from the darkness and roaring emptiness that had threatened to devour me. She'd gathered the pieces of my broken heart and spirit, and akin to the Japanese art of mending broken pottery with precious metals, she had painstakingly fused each piece of me back together, an amalgam of love, music, and laughter her lacquer and gold. Her pseudo-Kintsugi restoration was always on display when I looked at myself in the mirror—every mended crack and fissure a painful but beautiful reminder of the power of love.

With her death—and for the second time in my young life—my world crumbled around me, and I shattered with it. Liam and Charlotte had salvaged what pieces they could, but there were some parts of me that had been obliterated—scattered to the four winds, forever lost to me.

As I floated there in my cocoon of light, haunting strains of cherished melodies echoed softly in my mind, and I closed my eyes and allowed myself to remember. I was overcome by the force of her love for me, felt it absorbing into my skin, my heart, soothing my weary soul.

Live, Eleyse, a voice whispered, and I swore it was hers. The air swirled around my face tenderly, and I allowed myself to sink into the moment. Tears, unbidden, spilled freely, my heart bursting with aching sorrow, poignant remembrance, and the overwhelming need to create. I hadn't felt that spark, that pull to write, to make music, for a long time after she died.

My heart lurched as the light surrounding me snuffed out and a warm breath of air drifted across my face. I opened my eyes to find Death sitting at the edge of the lounge chair where I was lying, his silver eyes piercing through me. His handsome face was serious as he studied me.

"You betray the ones you love with your self-loathing and contempt for life," he said quietly.

A flash of anger sparked inside me, causing the words to spill from my mouth in a rush. "Ironic that you would say that to me, seeing that you're the one who ripped them from me."

His expression softened and he tilted his head, contemplating my words. "Who do you think I am, little bird?"

"Death," I said between gritted teeth.

His brows lifted, and a sad smile touched his lips. "I can assure you, Eleyse, I did not take them from you."

I stared at him. "But you don't deny that you are Death?"

He looked away, his gaze drifting off in the distance. "The power of life and death is mine to command, but I have no dominion over this world."

His words filled me with unease and confusion. I sat up straight, unable to tear my eyes away from his face. No dominion over this world? What did that mean? Who the hell was he? And what was his interest in me?

As if reading my mind, he turned his silver eyes back to me once more. "I am the protector of your future, Sviyen Cielta."

An overwhelming rush of despair and helplessness barreled into me. What was happening to me? I was losing my goddamn mind. And it had all started with *him*. When I lost my parents, Mags, Liam, he was there. When I was drowning in sorrow and tried to die, he was there. Every time. Then the woman with violet hair had come to me, imploring me to stop seeking out death, assuring me that a great future lay ahead for me. And I'd believed her. For a whole year, I'd held on to the hope she gave me that night, and then I'd met Ash, only to have Death show up again. The strange encounters with Alice and Maya, with Mangy Cat, only exacerbated the situation. Something was happening to me. Something I couldn't make any sense of. It went beyond any rational explanation my mind could grasp.

The specter of Mags and her cruel words rang out in my mind. *You're not welcome here. As long as you walk in this world, death will always be one step behind you. All who love you will die.*

She had said I caused her death. Wasn't that what I believed? That I was cursed?

As if sensing the conflict churning inside me, Death reached for my hand. "If you search yourself, Eleyse, you will *know* the truth of my words, feel it deep within your soul. You were born for greatness, but that greatness does not extend to this world. Here, you cannot blossom and thrive."

"What do you mean?" My heart thudded in my chest.

This was no ordinary man; anyone with half a brain could see that. But was he *real*? Were all these things truly happening to me, or was I going crazy? Talking cats, ethereal creatures with silver eyes, impossible revelations about me. I was going out of my goddamn mind.

And what about Ash? His presence in my life was shrouded in mystery, but everything about him *felt* right. I couldn't explain it—the pull, the belonging, the primal desire. I knew next to nothing about him, and yet it was as if I had known him my entire life. For once, I wanted to simply let go and let this thing between us sweep me away.

Death leaned closer to me. "Here, only death and hopelessness beckon, and darkness will destroy you." He gripped my chin with his hand, his blazing eyes searing into me, as if peering into my soul. "Listen to me, Eleyse. From this moment forward, let go of logic and reason, and let your senses guide you. There is a wellspring of great power within you waiting to be awakened. Expand your understanding and heed the voice that stirs in the deep reaches of your soul."

"So it's true then?" My voice was a raspy whisper. "I am cursed."

His eyes grew thoughtful as he considered my question. "You are anything but a curse, little bird. One day, when circumstances shift, the tragedies that defined your human existence will make sense. I promise you that."

I stared at him in disbelief. For as long as I lived, nothing about losing the people closest to me would make sense. Their deaths were senseless and cruel.

Slowly, he stood to his feet, and the soft fabric of his dark trousers brushed against my fingers. "Fear has held you captive for too long, Eleyse." He reached for my hand, and as my fingers slipped into his, he pulled me to my feet. "Close your eyes for me, little bird."

I stared at him hesitantly, but at the silent urging in his eyes, I did as he asked.

"Conjure the images of the ones you lost." His voice was soft and soothing.

Why? It was on the tip of my tongue to ask, but I didn't, instead focusing on the faces of my parents, of Mags and Liam.

"I want you to imagine that it was you who died, and not them. Ask yourself this question—would you want them to live their lives swallowed by grief, pain, and guilt the way you do?"

"Of course not," I blurted out, my eyes flying open. "I would want them to move on and be happy. I'd want them to be free."

He stared at me with a sad smile on his face. "Wouldn't they want the same for you? How do you think they would feel if they could see you now?"

"I . . ." I closed my mouth, unable to find the words. If things were reversed and I was the one who had died? It made me sick to think of my parents, Mags, Liam enduring the kind of pain I had. I'd meant what I said. I would want them to move on, to find happiness and purpose in their lives without me.

"Honor them, Eleyse. Cast aside your grief and pain and live in the moment. When you think of your loved ones, focus on the happy memories, not the sorrow. That is how you set the darkness free."

"Will you tell me who you really are?" I fought against the tears burning my eyes.

Gently, he tilted my chin upwards. "I have known you your entire existence. When you were but a growing seed within your mother, I watched over you. I am the guardian of the Sangelis. My name is Arazul. We will meet again, little bird, but for now, this is goodbye. Heed what I said, Eleyse."

Before I could even protest him leaving, I blinked, and when I opened my eyes again, he was gone, the only proof that he had even been there the lingering scent of mint and evergreen in the evening air.

P RESENT DAY SOLNIESS, THE VOID . . .

I tracked the steady path of a locarel as it soared across the cloudless sky. Another one of Eolith's zaragals, it was majestic to behold. With a wingspan over twenty feet wide, it was one of the largest and rarest creatures in Ariadna. From this distance, it was simply a blur against the backdrop of the brilliant sky. A shame really, because locarels were glorious specimens, with their glittery green and blue feathers and the bright teal color of their heads. Their eyes were the richest hue of amber I had ever seen. Their song was magical—known to lull a listener into a state of euphoria, a gift they used sparingly. In all of Ariadna, they were one of the two most formidable zaragals in existence. Well, in living existence, anyway.

In front of me, the sand along the beach was blinding in the sunlight, shimmering like cut diamonds along the water's edge. From the colorful trees on the grounds behind me, the chittering of birds and other critters erupted in a tranquil melody.

At the sound of approaching footsteps behind me, I turned to see Faron headed in my direction. My eyes flitted to Elle's balcony where Treye sat on a chair, his head in a book, his feet crossed and perched on the railing.

Faron followed my gaze as he came to stand beside me. "He found the Goddess Eolith's library. He jumped around like an excited schoolboy when he found two texts on the Shacquiri Rebellion and the Pirthenon Wars. We'll never hear the end of his findings."

I chuckled quietly. "I know it's tedious—the waiting—but I'm glad you both are here with me. I can't shake the feeling that things are about to get complicated."

Faron frowned. "If it wasn't for the Lonefera counting down the days as they pass by in Elle's consciousness, I'd have no fucking concept of time at all. There is no night, just day, no need for sleep, food, anything. It's jarring, really."

I nodded, crossing my arms over my chest. "That's the way it works in the timeless plane of the Void—an endless expanse of nothingness."

Faron frowned. "It would be easy for a normal person to go mad here."

"At least we have something to focus on and count down to."

"Speaking of counting down," Faron said, cocking his head, "based on the Lonefera's time keeping, it's been close to eighty days since the Goddess Eolith has been gone. Should we be concerned?"

I shook my head. "The celestial plane is tricky. Hard to keep track of time when it doesn't exist here. Plus, time means nothing to the Gods. If there was something wrong, she would have sent word. Elle is her main concern."

Faron shook his head. "I still can't believe it. Elle is the daughter of the Goddess Eolith and Sorin, Summoner of Light and Darkness himself. She is a goddess in her own right."

"I know." My lips lifted in a smile. "I've known for close to a century and I still find myself blown away by it."

Faron's expression darkened. "And now Kaliope knows about her. Do you think she knows she's in Ariadna?"

I clenched my jaw, staring off at the water again. "The moment the Ethereal Harmonies read Elle for a giln, the Gods would have been made aware of her presence and what we are to each other. I'm sure that worm, Cazril, was all too eager to tell Kaliope. Up until then, she probably believed that Gargmoin had killed Elle. Now she knows the full breadth of who Elle really is. I have no doubt the vengeful bitch is aware of the celestial star etching."

Faron stroked the scar on his upper lip absently. "To think there was a time when I thought she hung the moon. What a bloody fool I was."

I touched his shoulder. "Far, you were young. Don't be too hard on yourself. Kaliope can be very alluring and persuasive when she wants to be."

He turned remorseful eyes to me. "You never fell for that. Neither did Ari. You both barely tolerated her. Even after I saw her cruelty with my own two eyes, I dismissed it and made excuses for her."

I frowned as I looked at my closest friend. Some wounds never healed, and it was clear his history with Kaliope tormented him. We were so young then, though. Barely out of our teens when things turned sour between them. Some days, our friendship with Kaliope seemed like a lifetime ago; other days, it felt like just yesterday.

"You never told me what happened between the two of you to change things," I said, facing him. "And I would never pry, but just know that I'm always here if you want to talk."

"I think it's time. I've been carrying this around for too long." His eyes looked at me beseechingly. "There are two things I never told anyone about Kaliope, and sometimes, I wonder. What if I'd said something about one of those things? Is there a chance that it might have prevented any of the havoc she ended up wreaking?"

"Far." I touched his arm reassuringly. "Trust me, my friend. Nothing anyone could have done would have prevented Kaliope from turning into the monster she is. It took me a long time to accept that. From day one, my sense of perception told me the truth of her nature. Even Shanya Tandor—powerful Madgion witch that she is—saw the toxic darkness in her from the very beginning. She knew the truth, too, and it mattered not one whit that Kaliope was her grandchild—she was powerless to do anything about it. Kaliope is touched by the Mavigos, and everything she has done—as heinous as they might be—was meant to happen."

A gentle breeze drifted off the ocean, fanning breaths of salt and sand warmed by balmy sunlight in our direction. I welcomed the calming assault on my senses, inhaling deeply. Crossing my arms over my chest, I shifted my stance to look at Faron. "Pirovala, Far. On Earth, they call it Karma. It's coming for her. She will get her comeuppance, will face the consequences of her actions. I will see to it if it's the last thing I do."

"You can count on me to help make that happen." Faron looked down at his feet, shifting uneasily. "I think it's better that I *show* you, rather than tell you what happened with Kaliope. Take it, Ash."

I lifted a brow. "You want me to *siphon* the memory?"

"Yes, it would be easier for you to witness it as opposed to me telling you."

"Are you sure? You don't have to do this. A memory is something you have to freely share for it not to cause pain when I use my power."

"I'm sure." He met my gaze, a desperate look in his eyes. "Even if it is just to appease my own guilty conscience for never having said anything all these years. I freely release it."

I nodded. "All right then. You'll have to close your eyes and think about the memory you want to share. Go back in your mind to that moment and then let me in when you feel my power probing. Let me know when you're ready."

Faron closed his eyes and sighed. "I'm ready."

I lifted a hand to touch his temple. The moment my fingers connected with his skin, I released a tendril of my magic and let his mind open to me willingly. This was a part of my Sovereign powers I rarely exercised. The first person I'd used it on . . . fuck, that was over a century ago. And they hadn't given the memory freely, so it wasn't a pleasant experience for them. Not that I'd cared at the time, but I was a different person back then, driven by rage and vengeful motivations.

As my power seeped into Faron's mind, a rush of magic coursed through my fingers, and a flash of light pulsed behind my closed eyes. My awareness was yanked in and I was sucked into the memory he had opened up to me.

A ripple of excitement coursed through me as I headed to the beach with

Ari. Kaliope Tandor had come with her parents to Cazara Somel for a visit, and Goddess, I was in love. She was eleven, only three years older than Ash, Astrid, and me, and oh, how I was captivated by her. She had a larger-than-life personality and the most beautiful smile I had ever seen. I couldn't take my eyes off her when Ash had introduced us three days ago. With her ivory hair and pale, slitted eyes that called to me like nothing else, I was in heaven.

Since she had arrived, the four of us—Ash, Kaliope, Ari, and I—had been inseparable, and with each moment I spent in her company, I found myself falling deeper under her spell. She was adventurous, carefree, and funny, and so unbelievably regal. No doubt, she would be Sovereign of Tandor one day. She carried herself like a queen; anyone could see that.

As Ari and I trekked to Sazbe Beach on the Zidiurrh Strait, not too far from Cazara Somel, my heart raced with anticipation. Up ahead, I could see Kaliope and Ash wading in the surf.

"Hey, Far," Kaliope said cheerily when we grew closer. A part of me soared that she had called me out, and not Ari. Not that it bothered Ari. She made a beeline for Ash, ignoring Kaliope altogether. I'd gotten mad with my twin last night when she'd told me she found Kaliope stuck up and rude. If anything, Ari was the stuck up and rude one.

The tide was low as we played in between the rocks on the shore, looking for twinklefish and other sea life in the shallow tidal pools scattered sporadically across the length of the shoreline.

Ari, Ash, and I were watching a herd of seahorses flitting in and out of one of the deeper pools when I looked around to find Kaliope gone. Leaving my sister and Ash, I headed further down the beach in search of her. I heard her talking before I saw her. She was kneeling in the sand behind a hedge of tall rocks, looking at something in a shallow pool that funneled directly into the ocean. She was so engrossed in her conversation that she didn't hear me coming, and I didn't announce my presence. The words out of her mouth were Tandorin, which I spoke fluently.

"You look so beautiful fighting for your life." She stared intently at something wiggling on the sand in front of her. "I'd like to take you apart

149

and see if each piece of you will continue to thrash around like that."

I moved closer, curiosity flooding me. My heart thudded as I stared in confusion. She had trapped a lagriet, a protected species found only on the western region of Somel along the Zidiurrh Strait. The tiny creatures made their homes in the shionut trees scattered across Somel, burrowing deep, meandering passageways into the massive, wide trunks of the deciduous behemoths to insulate themselves from predators. They were purported to have magical abilities and were in the past hunted—almost to extinction—for their crowns of tapiur, a pale indigo dentin-bone composition, which contained the source of their power.

It was rare to see one, and even rarer that it was so close to the beach. The creature flailed frantically on the sand, its furry tail whipping back and forth in a frenzy as it struggled to lift its head out of the water. Every time it managed to pull itself out, Kaliope pushed it back in.

She jabbed at its head with a stick, keeping it submerged under the water. Finally, the lagriet's strength flagged, and Kaliope reached out and laid it on the sand, talking gently to it as she watched it twitching slowly. "Ah, I see it," she said, almost reverently. "There it is—the light leaving your eyes." She sighed quietly.

The lagriet let out a plaintive, chirping cry as its eyes rolled back in its head. Its breathing was shallow and faint, and my heart shuddered at the creature's distress.

I must have made a sound, because without missing a beat, Kaliope's voice changed and she said gently in Valkyn, "You poor dear." She quickly scooped the lagriet up in her hands. She turned to me then, and with tears in her gray eyes, she looked at me sadly. "You should have seen it, Faron. I found a lagriet flailing around in this shallow pool. Thank the Gods I was here to rescue it. No creature should ever have to die like that, fighting to breathe."

"Far!" a voice called from behind me, and I turned to see Ash and Ari headed in our direction.

"Oh, Ash." Kaliope rushed toward him with the lagriet in her hands. "The poor thing is dying."

Ash looked at her, his emerald eyes flashing with a mix of disbelief and . . . disgust. He quickly took the lagriet from her hands. A surge of rage washed through me at Ash's iciness toward her.

"I'll take it to my mother." He stroked the failing creature's fur gently. "She'll know what to do." Without another word, he turned on his heel and broke into a run toward Cazara Somel.

"What did you do to it?" Ari turned accusing eyes on Kaliope. "Everyone knows lagriets don't like water. There's no way it would have made its way down here."

"I didn't do anything, Shadow," Kaliope said, venom lacing her words. She'd taken to calling Ari that on account of her always being one step behind Ash wherever they went.

Ari narrowed her eyes before turning and walking away in the direction of Cazara Somel. "You should stay away from her, Far," she muttered over her shoulder.

Kaliope stared daggers into Ari's back as she walked away.

"I'm sorry about her," I said, "and for Ash. But really, if there's anyone who can save the lagriet, it's Ash's mother. Her healing powers are incredible."

Kaliope whispered something under her breath and for the life of me, it sounded like, "Shame," but I convinced myself that I'd misheard. It just all had to be a terrible misunderstanding. Kaliope had been so sincere and broken up over the plight of the lagriet when she scooped it out of the water. I must have imagined the whole thing. There was no way she could have done anything to willingly hurt a helpless creature. That's not who she was.

As I retracted my power, the rush of it sluiced through me as it ebbed back to the wellspring inside me.

Faron opened his eyes and looked at me, guilt shining in his icy-blue gaze. "I'm sorry, Ash. Even back then, she was a psychotic shit, and what did I do? I turned a blind eye, made excuses for her. Pathetic."

"Enough, Faron." My voice was stern as I stared at my friend. "You have nothing to apologize for. You were eight, for Medra's sake. You were innocent, and not used to seeing cruelty in people, so of course your natural inclination would have been to dismiss what you saw. She immediately showed empathy, going out of her way to convince you that she did indeed try to save the lagriet from dying."

Faron clenched his jaw. "You and Ari saw right through her, though."

"My own senses exposed her to me," I said. "As for Ari, she's always been the type to never accept anyone until they proved themselves. It was no different with Kaliope. Not to mention, from day one, Kaliope was a bitch to Ari. Condescending and rude. Dismissive." I sighed, running my hand through my hair. "Far, Kaliope took your fascination with her and used it against you. That's what she does. It's a game she plays, making sure her mask stays in place at all times. She's masterful at that—being different things to different people, letting them see what she wants them to see, changing the narrative to suit her purposes. None of this is on you."

"I can't believe that once upon a time, I fancied myself in love with her." A look of disgust stole over his face. "There's one more memory I want to share. This one will show what happened for me to finally see her for who she was."

"Far, you don't need to explain."

"Please, Ash." His eyes were pleading. "Just take it."

I nodded gently and placed my fingers on his temple once more.

I entered the town square, my heart thudding in my chest. I was supposed to meet Kaliope near the dais. With every breath of my being, I was in love with her. I would marry the ivory-haired beauty one day; no doubt about it. It wasn't like I was a nobody; my father was Lars Cardinin, Governor of Somel and great-uncle to Ash's father.

So what if right now she favored Ash? Why shouldn't she? They were equals—it was common knowledge that both sets of Sovereigns hoped they would marry one day. But there was no way Ash would let that happen—he didn't want anything to do with her—and that was perfect for me. I would sweep her off her feet and show her the kind of worship and loyalty worthy of a queen. Soon, she would realize that no one could shower her with fervent devotion like I could. I was seventeen; she was twenty. Still lots of time to woo her and win her heart.

It was the last day of Cadavweira, the Celebration of Light and Harmony, and everywhere in Ariadna, festivities were in full swing. On Somel, activities were planned in Bethama, the capital city. All across Valkyse, tributes to the patroness Cloryal, Medra, and the Goddess Mother were made. Lanterns of azulight floated through the skies and were set adrift on the ocean around the island in a profusion of light and magic, while laughter, merriment, and music drifted in everywhere.

As I approached the dais, I nodded to Ash, helping his mother with the festivities. Kaliope glared at him from her seat near the stage, probably upset that he was not paying attention to her. She was bored—I could see that—but not for long. I'd take care of that.

"You look beautiful, Kal." I snuck around her and kissed her cheek. I truly meant it. She looked like a goddess in her form-fitting blue gown, with silver blossoms woven into her ivory hair.

"Aw, thanks, Far." She interlaced her fingers with mine. She loved to be flattered and fawned over. That much had never changed over the years.

"Want to take a walk on the beach?" I asked.

She nodded, springing to her feet. I noted the extra lengths she took to walk by Ash so he would see the two of us leaving together, her arm linked tightly through mine. It was clear that she was trying to make Ash jealous, but I didn't care, and by the looks of it, neither did he.

The beach was packed with festival-goers. Children ran across the shoreline, trying to catch nearby lanterns bobbing on the water. Couples walked hand in hand on the sand, enjoying the beauty of the night.

We walked further down the beach, away from the crowd and festivities, toward the dark cliffs at the end of the inlet, and with each step we took, my heart galloped faster. She led me through a maze of rocks at the base of the cliffs and then stopped, leaning back against one and looking at me invitingly.

"Is this what you wanted, Far?" she said, her body beckoning seductively. "To get me alone? To have me to yourself?" She arched her back and looked at me through heavy lashes. "Have you even been with a woman before?" she asked, moving closer to me.

I trembled as she brushed her lips against mine, her hands moving slowly across my chest.

"You certainly have grown these past few years," she continued, her hands trailing across my stomach. "So muscular and tall . . . and very handsome. I'm sure all the girls on the island lie awake at night moaning for you."

My blood heated at her words. My breathing was shallow, and I tried not to focus on her hands moving down my body.

"Of course, they probably all lust after Ash, but surely they have better sense than to think they could actually have him. You, however, are a prize more attainable. And don't get me wrong, you are a prized stud indeed."

She slipped her hand into my pants then, rubbing the hard length of me with her fingers. I sucked in my breath at the roar of pleasure coursing through me. Cupping her head with my hands, I brought my mouth down on hers, but she pushed against my chest and clicked her teeth at me.

"Whoa." She took a step back and wagged her finger at me. "I want to make sure you don't misunderstand me. You can have any girl on this island; they would be lucky to have a fine catch such as you. And while we might tease and play with each other, that's as far as it goes. Don't lose sight of that and start thinking that you are worthy of me."

Her hand gripped my face, and with excruciating slowness, she dragged her index finger—the nail long and pointed—across my upper lip, gouging my skin forcefully as she scored her finger upward. A slice of pain tore through me and I yanked my face away, the copper tang of blood dripping in rivulets past my lips into my mouth.

With one quick motion, she twisted her head toward mine, her tongue *darting out to lick the blood off my lip. "I will be a queen one day, and a queen needs an equal. All you can be to me is a happy distraction. I wouldn't want you doing something so stupid as falling in love with me."*

Her tone was cold, mocking even, and any shred of the passion that coursed through me just moments before fled instantly at her words. I pulled away from her, dabbing at my lip with my fingers.

"Don't be like that." She tutted and smiled at me. "We can still have fun; I have no doubt you'd be a good ride. I just want to make sure you know where the boundaries are. Once Ash and I are officially together, though, you're out. I won't have time for trifling distractions then."

"I think I'll pass." My voice was cold as I pushed her off me and walked away.

"Come on, Far," she called after me. "Don't be such a baby. You wanted it a moment ago." Her laughter floated on the breeze behind me. "Now I feel bad. I got you all worked up and hard. Let me finish you off. It's the least I can do." Her laughter kicked up a notch, the derision in her voice deafening.

I was sick and disgusted with myself for being such a fool. I kept on walking up the beach and didn't look back once, abandoning everything I ever felt for her back there at those rocks, along with my trampled heart and shattered pride.

What did I expect? It wasn't as if she'd said anything to me I didn't already know deep inside. So why did it hurt so much? It wasn't so much what she said but how she said it—the care she took to humiliate me and put me in my place. Trifling distraction, she'd said. That's all I was to her, all I would ever be. Well, I'd be damned if I ever let myself become so vulnerable again for someone to make me feel like a worthless piece of shit. Never again.

As I slipped out of the memory, a wave of sorrow crested over me. Siphoning a memory didn't just let me see a past event; it immersed me in the memory itself—thoughts, emotions, sensory focus. I'd felt it—how deeply Faron cared for Kaliope, how completely gutted he was after she'd said what she did. Back then, he'd been smitten with her, but at the time, I was relieved whenever she was with him, particularly because it meant she wasn't with me.

For Ariadnans, the ability to giln-shift only happened after the age of fourteen, and Kaliope used that to her advantage once she came of age, often traveling wherever I was. In those years, I spent most of my time in Somel with my mother, and so Kaliope followed suit. As selfish as it was, I was happy when Faron was around. He'd pandered to her need for attention and flattery and alleviated the pressure on me when I was around her.

I placed my hand on his shoulder. "I'm so sorry, Far. I didn't know." My apology sounded hollow to my own ears. It couldn't change his humiliation and hurt. I remembered that night all those years ago, how relieved I was when Kaliope went off with him. I'd finally been able to relax and enjoy the celebrations. I hadn't seen Faron again until the next week, and when I did, I was surprised to see the gash on his lip. It hadn't been healed. The skin was red and puffy, and when I asked about it, he'd brushed me off.

He'd pulled away from me for a while after that, and even Ari had no idea what was going on with him. A few months later, he was back to being his usual cheery self, and happy to have my friend back, I didn't push the issue.

"Why did you never get it healed?" I asked quietly. "My mother would have happily rid you of the wound."

"No." His eyes glittered with anger as he absently ran his finger along the jagged mark. "Yes, healing magic could have completely removed all traces of the gash in a heartbeat, but I didn't want that. I wanted it to heal and scar on its own, so that every time I looked in the mirror, every time I touched the marred skin with my fingers, I would be reminded of who Kaliope really is."

His eyes flicked to mine. "I loved her, Ash; I truly did. We were friends for nine years. In all that time, how could I have been so completely blind to who she truly was? I could never understand why you and Ari disliked her so much. I thought for sure that once she and I were together, everything would be perfect with the four of us. I imagined that it would be Kaliope and me, and you and Ari—the inseparable foursome to the end." He laughed bitterly. "How disillusioned I was. Of the four of us, you're the only one who found love, and what a love it is."

I nodded, my thoughts drifting to Elle. Never in my life could I have imagined to feel the depth of emotion for another person that I felt for her. There was nothing I wouldn't do to keep her safe.

Faron tilted his head to the side, his pale-blue eyes serious as he looked at me. "Despite everything the celestial star etching proclaims, one thing we can count on is for Kaliope to play dirty. She will do whatever she has to do to get her way. We need to be as ruthless as her if we want to defeat her."

I gritted my teeth. "Trust me. I know. Elle is still so new to this world. Not to mention, her powers are untrained and unstable. We need to be her strength and protection while she learns and hones her abilities."

"You're worried that we won't have enough time."

"I'm worried about everything." I folded my arms across my chest, a tremor of fear racing through me. "Things aren't just going to be difficult. They're going to be downright nasty."

Chapter 19

ELEYSE

AUGUST 26: ONE YEAR, ALMOST SEVEN MONTHS AGO . . .

"Oh, thank god you're back," I said as the door opened and Aggie's face came into view.

"Well, fuck me, it's nice to be missed." She stepped aside and beckoned me in.

She was wearing a pair of classy, tailored palazzo pants and a gray silk blouse. I stared at her appraisingly. Hair? Check. Jewelry? Check. Makeup? Check.

"Geez, Aggie, do you roll out of bed looking like this?" I slipped my sneakers off at the door. "Like where are you even going? Don't you have a casual, don't-give-a-shit, hanging-around-the-house look?"

Her light-brown eyes flicked over me with barely-concealed distaste. "You mean like the one you're currently rocking? And what's the excuse today for not wearing a bra? That flimsy tank top has absolutely zero support."

I rose to my full height and placed my hands on my hips. "Would you cut it out with trying to shame me into wearing a bra? I hate them. They make me feel like I'm suffocating."

She shook her head. "You're going to regret it one day when your nickname is saggy tits."

"Nuh-uh. That's why I make sure to focus lots of attention on my chest when I work out. Pushups, chest press, flys, you name it. Exercise will keep my girls nice and firm."

She snorted and beckoned for me to follow her to her kitchen. "So where's the fire, Ovi? You seemed anxious when I opened the door."

"You were gone for two months," I exclaimed. "I've had no one to talk to since you left. And so much has happened."

"What about your man-god, as you so affectionately called him?"

"He doesn't count. Plus, he's half of what I want to talk about anyway. But I'll get to that afterward. How was your trip?"

"It was incredible." A bright smile lit up her face. "Europe in summer is simply delightful. London, Paris, Nice, Rome, Tuscany, Brussels, it really was a whirlwind. The girls and I had a blast."

"Aw. That's awesome. Did you take lots of pictures?"

"I sure did." She rooted around in her bag for her phone. "Got some great shots at a nude beach in Nice. Carolyn, Daphne, and I had a wonderful time."

She shoved her phone in my face and the image of two sculpted, nude men burned my eyes. "Gah!" I said, staring at the photo. "What the hell, Aggie? Did you make that your screensaver?"

"Absolutely." She smiled wickedly. "Look at Horatio. Hung like a horse, that one."

"Oh god." I shoved the phone away. "I change my mind. Show me pictures later."

She shook her head and put her phone on the kitchen island. "Can I get you a cup of tea?" She headed toward the stove.

I slid onto one of her dark mahogany barstools. "That sounds lovely."

"So tell me, what have I missed?" She leaned forward, resting her forearms on the edge of the island.

"Geez where do I start?"

"Well, before I left, the cat had cornered you on your run and talked your ear off."

"Right. It doesn't sound crazy at all when you put it like that." I proceeded to fill her in on what had happened with the woman with violet hair and Death—or as he had introduced himself, Arazul. I told her how Mangy Cat's warning about reliving my life's tragedies had unfolded with the reliving of my parents' and Mags's deaths.

159

We moved to her sunroom after the tea was poured, and the entire time I talked, she was quiet, simply listening to everything I said.

"Am I going crazy, Aggie?" I asked after I finished telling her about Arazul. "Do you think this is all in my head? It's so far-fetched."

"Do *you* think you're crazy?"

My eyes flew to hers. "That's the same thing Ash asked me when I told him about Mangy Cat and the woman with violet hair."

"Ash." A smile tugged at her lips. "Your handsome man-god. Things are evolving on that front, I take it."

"I don't really want to talk about it," I mumbled, staring into my half-empty cup of tea.

She cocked her head. "Why is that?"

I lifted my eyes to meet hers, my mouth suddenly dry, my throat tight. How did I even explain? I cleared my throat, swallowing the lump lodged there. "I'm scared of what he makes me feel."

Aggie sighed. "Fear is the killer of hope, Ovi. Fear is a vicious master when you let yourself be ruled by it. Haven't you learned anything from your three encounters thus far? Let go of the fear. Of the hurt and pain. Open your heart to love. It will set you free."

"Or destroy me," I whispered.

"The biggest tragedy is living a life without love." She leaned back on the plush sofa next to me. "Everything you've told me so far is proof that you've buried your happy memories and love for those you lost under the horrendous weight of your grief and guilt. It has crippled you to the point where you're barely even recognizable as a person." She reached for my hand and squeezed my fingers gently. "Your Ash," she said, looking at me intently. "He is a game changer."

I furrowed my brows. "What do you mean?"

"I have eyes. It's glaringly obvious. Ever since you met him, you've changed. Your aura and energy is so much lighter, airy. You smile more. And when you talk about him . . . magic."

I stared at her blankly, before bursting into tears a few seconds later. "What if the curse is real? What if something horrible happens and he dies because of me? I don't think I can survive losing another person."

"Sweet girl, there are no guarantees in this life." She squeezed my shoulder. "Every choice comes with risk."

Risk. What was it that Mangy Cat had said? *Only when you see and accept love for what it is—a beautiful risk worth living and dying for, will you be free from the chains that bind you, and steer the course of your future.*

Could I love Ash? I was trying—as much as I could—to avoid learning more about him, trying to keep him at arm's length, trying not to let him in, but it was a battle I was losing. I wanted him, and not just physically. I wanted him in every way a woman could want a man, and that terrified me. He called to a place inside me I didn't even know existed, and whenever I was with him, I swore something answered back.

"Enough about Ash for now." I shook my head and changed the subject. "What do you think the Sangelis is? Mangy Cat, Maya's vision, the woman with violet hair, Arazul, what the ghost of Mags said to me—I feel like I'm losing my mind. Who am I? What am I? Where do I belong? Maya said when she touched me, she saw a vision of me with a gown and scepter. Mangy Cat called me the child of celestial love, alluded to me being something *other*. And then this Arazul—fuck—he called me a queen, told me that this world could no longer provide me sanctuary. Like what the hell does that even mean? Nothing he said makes any sense."

"What did Ash have to say about it?" Aggie took a sip of her tea.

I frowned. "I haven't seen him since Arazul visited me, but everything else I told him about—he said that he didn't believe I imagined any of it. He also told me to listen to Mangy Cat and not give up on love or music."

"Smart boy," she said.

"What do I do, Aggie? Should I go see someone?"

"Someone?" Her forehead creased in a frown.

"Like a professional. These are some serious delusions, don't you think?"

"Only if you don't believe that they can be a possibility."

"Do you seriously think any of it can be a possibility?" I asked, my eyes wide. "Any rational person with any reasoning or logic would call me crazy."

"Fuck them." Aggie placed her teacup on the coffee table. "I've been around a long time, Ovi, and I have seen some incredible things that have defied explanation. Tell me something. What does your gut tell you?"

Without hesitation, the answer rushed to my mind. "It tells me to . . . it tells me to believe."

"Ask any deeply religious or spiritual person and they will tell you that faith is at the core of their beliefs. Heaven, hell, angels, demons, a plethora of deities, reincarnation, nirvana—can any of it truly be proven? Who's to say what the *truth* really is?" She patted my hand lightly. "I'm not telling you to blindly believe everything that was said to you. Trust your gut. I think intrinsically, our intuitions are powerful tools designed to help us make our way through the world. Listen to what it tells you and keep an open mind, no matter how batshit crazy it might sound."

"Some things are easier said than done," I whispered.

Aggie sighed, shifting her position on the sofa to face me more. "Let me tell you a story. It's something I haven't spoken about for a very long time. I think it will explain why I'm so open-minded about a lot of things that seem implausible."

She pursed her lips, swallowing slowly before she continued. "Many years ago, Jack and I lived on his family's estate in the English countryside. Our housekeeper, Mariane, and her daughter, Sela, lived with us at the house. Mariane's husband had run off with another woman and left her with Sela, barely even one at the time. She had nowhere else to go, and Jack and I gave them both a home. Mariane became my closest friend and confidante, and Sela, well, I loved her like my own daughter. One day when Sela was five, Mariane and I were in the front garden pruning the roses. I was never one for getting my hands dirty, but when it came to my garden, I loved and cared for it myself."

That took me by surprise. Aggie absolutely came off as someone who had lived a cultured and pampered life. It was evident that she had a deep love of flowers, though; the blooms in her front beds outside were beautiful. There were fresh-cut flowers in every room on her main floor. She had to have a caretaker—I was sure of it—although I'd never asked or really paid attention. As hard as I tried, I couldn't picture Aggie out there on her hands and knees in her pearls and pumps and perfectly manicured nails, pulling up weeds and deadheading her plants. I stifled a giggle at the thought.

"Mariane loved the garden as much as I did," Aggie was saying, "and that morning, we were both absorbed in what we were doing when a sickening feeling of foreboding crept over me." Her face turned somber as she wrung her fingers in her lap. "Somehow, I just *knew* that something had happened to Sela. We searched the house for her, and then the grounds. We found her at the bottom of the pool at the other end of the house. She'd been helping Cook in the kitchen and somehow managed to slip away from her. She must have been in the water for at least twenty minutes when we found her."

I gasped. "Oh my god, Aggie." I didn't even think she heard me. Her eyes were haunted, her face pale, as if she was reliving the moment in her mind.

Her expression twisted in anguish. "Sela was gone. We tried unsuccessfully to revive her. Mariane—well, she was devastated, and in that moment, I did the only thing I could think of. I dropped to my knees and prayed—begged, pleaded—to whichever god or entity was listening, for a miracle."

My heart clenched in sorrow as I stared at Aggie. The loss of a child. I couldn't even fathom that kind of pain.

"As I kneeled there on the ground, surrounded by my household staff, I felt the warmth of fingers on my head." Aggie's eyes flitted to mine. "A woman, Ovi, the most beautiful and majestic creature I had ever seen, was standing over me, a halo of light around her, and kindness in her eyes. Even now, I can see her in my mind, as plain as day." She sighed quietly. "The woman stepped toward Sela, who was still lying lifeless on the ground, and she placed her hand over her chest, barely even touching her. Light drifted from her fingers into Sela, and in the next moment,

Mariane's little girl gasped and *breathed*."

"What?" I exclaimed in disbelief, my eyes wide as I looked at Aggie. "How?"

She nodded. "Crazy, right? As for the how of it, I truly believe that there are things that defy reason and logic. Was she an angel, a saint, a goddess? In that moment, it really didn't matter. All that mattered was that she brought Sela back to life. Sela, who grew up to live a long and prosperous life." She lowered her head and interlaced her fingers together. "I will never forget the woman's words to me. 'Light must always prevail over darkness. Do your part, as I just did, as we all must, to make that a reality.' And then she was gone."

"I don't know what to say," I whispered, in shock over what she'd revealed. "How could something like that happen?"

"Does it matter? If by some wondrous miracle, you were able to get Liam, Mags, or your parents back, would you care?"

"No." What an unbelievable notion—the possibility of having my loved ones back. "But I think I would always be afraid of what the consequences would be for cheating death."

Aggie shrugged. "There's that, yes, but life's too short to live in constant fear of *something*." She stood to her feet and took my empty teacup from me, along with hers, and headed to the kitchen. I followed her soundlessly.

"I told you about Sela for a reason." She opened the dishwasher and deposited the teacups. "So you could understand why I believe that just because something seems improbable or impossible, it doesn't mean it is. There are forces beyond our understanding alive and at work all over the world—heck, the universe—and to simply dismiss everything that is happening to you by thinking that the only explanation is that you're crazy? Well, that's a tragedy. Be a little more open-minded than that. You live your life shut away, afraid of even your own shadow, for god's sake."

I winced, the harshness of her words cutting deep. She wasn't wrong, though.

Aggie stared at me with steely eyes. "Time to go grow a pair and kick your fear to the curb, to get up and fight, and actually give a damn about *living* your shitty life. You might surprise yourself at the beauty you find there." She tilted her head up and met my gaze with challenge in her eyes. "Seriously, what do you have to lose? Enough wallowing in the past. Death, Arazul—whoever the hell he is—is right. You dishonor the memory of the ones you love by living like a bloody ghost."

My frustration mounted. "What would you have me do, Aggie?" Shame and anger washed through me at her blunt appraisal of my life choices. Yes, I was squandering my life, but it was mine to squander, wasn't it?

"What would I have you do? Dear god, Ovi. Be happy. Dream. Travel the world. Fall in love." She squeezed my hand firmly. "*Live*, Eleyse."

Chapter 20

ASHER

PRESENT DAY SOLNIESS, THE VOID . . .

I stepped out of Elle's chamber and headed down the atrium to the library. Five hundred and ninety-six days left. The restlessness and anxiety were beginning to take their toll. When I wasn't with Elle, I found myself spending most of my time with Treye and Faron poring over the ancient texts in the Goddess Mother's collection. Two rooms over from Elle's chamber, it was within quick reach if I needed to get to her in a rush.

Treye looked up as I walked in. "Bash, did you know that Brus-Winnd is not the only place in Ariadna with a connection to the First Age?"

"In what way?" I asked.

Treye leaned back in his chair, interlacing his fingers behind his head. "Well, according to this manuscript, Deadlands in Tandor also contains a small concentration of the Old, Arcane Magic. Right around where the Sigril Portal is located."

I frowned. This was news to me. The Sigril Portal was the most powerful of the three known portals in Ariadna used for dual travel between worlds. After the Dark Shen Invasion, all three portals were locked down, with special dispensation from one of the four Sovereigns being the only way to gain access.

"It makes sense if you think about it." Faron slid open one of the crystal cases to return the text he had been studying. He stepped back as the case lifted off the floor and rose to its assigned spot adjacent to the window.

"What makes you say that?" My gaze flitted to the hovering crystal cases located all around the library in layered tiers.

"Well, it would explain why there is so much magic powering the Sigris Portal," he mused. "The other two portals have but a fraction of the range and accuracy."

Treye cocked his head thoughtfully. "It would be interesting to know how much of that power comes from the dark sway of the Old, Arcane Magic as opposed to the light strain."

Before I could answer, a ripple of power surged through the room, scattering streams of light everywhere. My power answered in response, poised to attack if warranted. In a sizzle of crisscrossing sparks and lilting music, the Goddess Eolith appeared in front of us.

Eyes wide, she found my gaze. "Quickly, Asher." Her voice was tinged with urgency. "We don't have much time. Sorin is on his way."

At my nod, Treye and Faron sprang to their feet, darting down the hall to Elle's chamber.

I searched her troubled face. "What happened, Eolith? I take it he knows she's his daughter?"

She nodded. "I told him. As you know, after the Ethereal Harmonies read Elle for a giln, all the Gods and Goddesses were made aware of the Gloweyen proclamation. Apart from Arazul and me, none of them have any clue who Elle is, so you can imagine how curious they were, Sorin included."

"Yes." I thought of the God of Chaos and his brazen pursuit of Elle to get answers. "Does Sorin mean her any harm?" I clenched and unclenched my fists.

"No, but he is livid, and he can be volatile when he's angry." Her body grew rigid as she looked at me. "He's here."

"What's the plan?"

"Have Treye and Faron stay with Elle while you and I meet with Sorin. I need to make sure he's calmed down." As if seeing the hesitation in my eyes, she added, "He will not hurt her, Asher."

I nodded silently, gathering my power to me. I hoped she was right. I didn't want to destroy a God today.

Her eyes met mine just as a loud crack of thunder pierced the air and all of Solniess was thrust into darkness. Thunderbolts of crimson lightning streaked through the sky, illuminating the sanctum in ominous red light. The Summoner of Light and Darkness was making a hell of an entrance.

Another crack of thunder boomed, and in the blink of an eye, bright sunlight streamed through the library windows once more. An indigo mist materialized in front of us, and as I stared into the billowing waves, it was as if I was staring into the cosmos, a plethora of stars swirling around in the expanse of a night sky.

Next to me, Eolith stood tall, her back ramrod straight, lips fixed in a grim line, silver eyes flashing. She exuded power, and I had no doubt that she was capable of holding her own against any of the Gods of the Sangelis.

In a blinding flash of light, the mist dispersed, and Sorin, Summoner of Light and Darkness, stood before us. His brilliant white essence clung to him, wafting around him lazily. His eyes blazed with fire, a thin ring of amber visible in their depths. He was shirtless, his signature white trinzum breastplate the only thing across his chest. His legs were clad in mid-calf boots and form-fitting breeches that were a thin fusion of trinzum and corilian silk.

I bowed my head in a show of respect before lifting my gaze to meet his. "Are you expecting to go to battle, Great One?" I met his scrutiny full-on.

"You bet those pretty green eyes I am, Godslayer." His voice was soft, even as a muscle twitched in his jaw. "The God of Chaos was quick to tell me about the hole you blasted through his body with your fist."

I narrowed my eyes. "Good. Now you know the lengths I will go to protect the woman I love."

His eyes flashed, and a small smile lifted his lips. "I've been watching you with interest your whole life, son of Valkyse. Noble blood, noble heart. And yet a little bird once told me about a dastardly plan forged in the shadows—one that was orchestrated by you, but never seen to fruition."

My lips twitched. "Even the Gods aren't infallible, and I am but a mere mortal. Is it really a surprise that I have ugliness in my past?"

The massive God crossed his arms over his chest, rising to his full height. "I guess like any father, I just want the best for my child, and no, it isn't lost on me that I've known about her for all of five seconds." He turned to look at the Goddess Eolith. "I'd like to see this daughter of ours who will shake the foundations of the Sangelis, leida mata."

My treasure. It was obvious by the way he looked at the Goddess Mother that he was in love with her. He reached for her hand, pulling her to his chest.

She cupped his face gently. "You promised, trihlo mata."

My heart. In the time she had been gone, had they rekindled the passion between them? Or had it never been extinguished in the first place?

"The only one who can incite my rage is Arazul, Eo. I would never do anything to endanger our child. Am I thrilled that the Mavigos chose the Godslayer to be her Gloweyen King? No, but if he will protect her with his life, then I can look past who he is."

I gritted my teeth. How noble of him to accept me. But this wasn't about me. This was about Elle. And Sorin was her father. He deserved the chance to see her.

The Goddess Eolith turned silver eyes to me, and I nodded, stepping aside so they could walk past me.

He leveled me with a glare as he brushed by, but I met his gaze unflinchingly, not in the least bit intimidated by his towering presence. As the Gods crossed the threshold into Elle's chamber, Treye and Faron looked at me for confirmation, and I nodded quickly. They both dropped to their knees in a show of fealty to the Summoner of Light and Darkness. Next to the Great Creator, he was the most powerful of the Gods of the New Age.

"You may rise." His body was rigid as he stared at the bed where Elle lay. He tread forward slowly, coming to a stop at the side of the bed. I made my way to the other side of the room, my gaze fixed on Elle.

"She is even more beautiful than I could have imagined, Eo." His voice was reverent as he reached out to touch Elle's face, his knuckles grazing her cheek. "Soladeo," he whispered, a look of awe and sadness on his face.

Daughter. The moment was touching and intimate, and for a second, I felt like I was intruding, but in no reality was I letting Elle out of my sight.

"Born of light and darkness, born of love and music—is that what the celestial star etching said, Eo?" His gaze did not leave Elle's face, so transfixed he was as he stared at his daughter for the first time.

"She is the child of our love, Sorin." Eolith linked her arm through his and rested her head on his shoulder. "Have you ever seen anything more perfect?"

"Only you, leida mata." He brushed his lips against her head.

At the far end of the room, Treye and Faron exchanged glances, Treye's eyebrows lifting in surprise at the Summoner of Light and Darkness's declaration.

Sorin stared at Elle for a moment longer, and then his body stiffened and his facial expression grew stony. He turned on his heel and walked out of the room. Eolith hurried after him, her forehead creased in a frown. A prickle of unease caused the hair at the back of my neck to stand on end.

I gestured for Faron and Treye to stay with Elle as I left the room. Out in the atrium, Sorin was pacing, his agitation glaringly apparent.

"Arazul, I summon you," Sorin cried out. "You will not deny my call, God of Gods."

Fuck. This was not happening.

Sorin's voice echoed through the cavernous atrium. "If you do not want me to plunge all of Ariadna into darkness, you will heed my call, *Great Creator.*"

His use of Arazul's title was mocking, awash with ridicule. Even though I knew what to expect, I still couldn't brace myself for the onslaught of power that blasted through the space in a fury. A sandstorm whipped around in front of me, making it difficult to see. Thick, reedy vines snaked around my legs, threatening to pull me down. My power went on the offensive, buttressing me against the raw magic battering everything in its path. Streams of water poured down the walls from the ceiling, just as flames erupted in a circle around us. The heat licked at my flesh, causing perspiration to bead my skin.

A loud, howling wind tore through the atrium, and with it, the chaos erupting around us was sucked away. Arazul, the Great Creator, stood in front of us, a dark-blue robe covering his imposing form. His light-brown hair was tied loosely at his nape.

"Sorin." His silver eyes blazed as they clashed with the fiery stare of the Summoner of Light and Darkness.

Without uttering a word, Sorin speared a crimson lightning bolt through Arazul's chest. The Great Creator flew backward, but quickly recovered, using his essence to encase himself in a shield of light. Shit. I needed to keep them as far away from Elle's chamber as possible.

"You coward!" Sorin hurled multiple blasts of lightning, as well as waves of oily darkness, at Arazul.

I stepped between them. "Enough of this." I moved toward Sorin. "One ricochet of your power could have devastating consequences for your daughter's shadow self in the next room. I will put you down myself if I have to. Don't give me a reason. I would hate to destroy her father before she has a chance to know him."

He flashed angry eyes at me, but lowered his hands. His gaze flew to Arazul's once more. "You kept my child from me. I let Eolith go, believing it was what was best for the inhabitants of the Sangelis."

"It was what was best," Arazul said firmly. "If you had known about the existence of the child, you would have not been able to let Eolith go. You would have broken your bond with Jaraya, and in so doing, condemned two worlds to extinction."

Sorin's eyes flared. "You don't know that."

"Oh, but I do," Arazul said softly. "As does Eolith, which is why she agreed to keep the child a secret from you." The Great Creator took a step forward. "You are angry, and you have every right to be. I took your choice from you, and for that, I am truly sorry, but there was no other way. What do you think Jaraya would have done when she found out about the child? Your love for Eolith has always been your weakness. You know the bitterness the Goddess of the Night harbors for her. Then to learn that you did the impossible? Fathering a child with someone who was not her? We Gods are made, not born, Sorin. To know that a miracle was created from your union with Eolith? That would have been too much for Jaraya's pride to bear."

"All hypotheticals," Sorin gritted out, his fists tight at his sides.

My heart clenched in my chest. Did I feel for Sorin? Absolutely. He had every right to be angry and upset. But anger was driving him, making it hard for him to see reason.

Arazul inclined his head toward the Goddess of the Ethereal Harmonies. "Ask Eolith if she believes that."

Sorin's gaze flicked to Eolith, and she met his eyes with sadness. "I told you, Sorin. I know your heart, just like you know mine, and if you had learned I was with child, all the repercussions in the entirety of the Sangelis would have meant nothing to you. You would have burned it all to ashes if it meant you could have me and our child. Look at you now. You would have your revenge on Arazul, consequences be damned."

Arazul sighed. "This wasn't an easy decision to make, Sorin. This was bigger than just you and Eolith. You were fulfilling the will of the Mavigos as was foretold in the ancient celestial star etching. I saw the signs, and did what as Great Creator I had to do. The time with your daughter that truly matters is now. She will need your help and support more than ever. The fate of the entire Sangelis is resting on her shoulders, and yes, she has a powerful king at her side, but she will also need the might of the Gods behind her. I don't need to tell you that sides will be taken. The dark Gods and ancients of the Ages—that is what she will be up against. I don't need to tell you that the dark sway of the Old, Arcane Magic is surging. The ancient ones are stirring; some have already allied with Kaliope Tandor. We must ensure that your daughter and her Gloweyen King have the best chance for success."

Warring emotions flickered on Sorin's face, his wavering body language suggesting that he saw the wisdom of Arazul's words. In this coming war, Elle and I would need all the help we could get.

Arazul released his hold on his magic and the shield around his form dissipated. "In the entirety of the New Age of the Sangelis, there has never been a Celestial Songbird, a Godslayer, and a Sovereign King and Queen over Ariadna. The Ethereal Harmonies have spoken. Eleyse and Asher will usher in the Light Age to the Sangelis. The Mavigos foresaw this at the end of the First Age, long before you and I came into being."

Arazul reached out his hand and touched Sorin's shoulder. "All her human life, I did what you weren't given the chance to do—I watched over her and kept her from mortal harm. Now that she is here in the Sangelis, which is always where she was meant to be, I hand those reins to you. For the sake of your daughter and the perilous future she faces, will you put aside your anger and join with us to fight for her?"

Sorin was silent, his eyes flitting between Arazul, Eolith, and me. Finally, he turned to look into Elle's chamber and exhaled deeply. "You're right, Eo. For her, the beautiful child of our love, I would burn the entire Sangelis to ash if I had to." He turned to face me. "You have my pledge, Godslayer. I stand with you."

Chapter 21

ELEYSE

OCTOBER 10: ONE YEAR, SIX MONTHS AGO . . .

My eyes flew open, and I turned my head to look at the clock on my bedside table. Almost nine. I rolled onto my side and swung my legs out of bed. I'd been snoozing my alarm since eight. Outside the window, the sky was blue, shafts of sunlight peeking through the clouds.

My spirits soared. Finally. It had been raining non-stop for the past eight days, a dreary, soul-shattering sort of rain. Sunshine was long overdue. I grabbed my phone and checked the temperature. Fifty-three degrees, with an expected high of sixty-four for the afternoon. Beautiful for the beginning of October.

I got to my feet and shuffled over to the window. Outside, my back lawn was littered with soggy leaves, the ground still brutally sodden from all the rain. A run on the trail was out. Would be too muddy and slippery. If anything, I'd have to stick to the sidewalk.

On the bedside table, my phone vibrated, and I yawned, reaching for it. My heart raced at the name on the screen.

Ash.

We had graduated to phone messages a month ago. I was trying to take Aggie's advice about opening myself up to living and love. I'd given him my number and he'd given me his. Baby steps. I could count on one hand the people who had my phone number; it was not something I gave out lightly.

Now, instead of just showing up on my doorstep, he would message me when he was in town. Of course, the curious part of me wondered why he never messaged me when he was gone, which, of course, sent me down a rabbit hole of speculation. Where did he go when he left? Did he miss me? What was his real life like? Was there someone else? Did he have a family? Was he truly a good guy? But instead of spiraling, I chose to push those thoughts aside and trust my instincts and what they told me about Ash.

He would never hurt me.

I unlocked my phone and touched the screen to expand his message.

Elle, I just got into town. Are you free today? I can pick you up in an hour if that works.

My heart soared as I read his words.

My fingers flew across the keyboard. *One hour works fine, Ash. See you soon.*

I headed to the bathroom to get ready, pausing to look at my smiling face in the mirror. I'd caught myself doing that more often since I'd met Ash.

I showered quickly, straightened my hair, did my makeup, and then debated on what I should wear. I settled on a blue V-neck sweater, fitted jeans, and calf-length, camel-colored leather boots. I grabbed a light jacket and made my way downstairs. I'd managed to get ready with ten minutes to spare. I wolfed down a muffin and a smoothie before making a quick phone call. I'd just put my dishes in the dishwasher when I heard the doorbell.

My heart leapt into my throat, and I grabbed my purse before opening the door. I gulped as I drank him in. He was wearing dark, boot-cut jeans, a form-fitting gray sweater, and a black bomber jacket. Right on cue, I found myself swept away by my physical response to him. I forced my eyes away from his broad chest and looked up at his face. The air whooshed out of me. Damn, he was gorgeous. Those insane emerald eyes did it to me every time. And holy frig, he smelled glorious. I didn't think I was ever going to get used to how beautiful he was.

His teeth grazed his lower lip. "You look ravishing." It was my turn to watch him appraise me. My body tingled everywhere, basking in his eyes roving slowly over me.

I reached for his outstretched hand. "Thanks."

He pulled me to him and I wrapped my arms around his neck, brushing my lips against his.

"I missed you, Tialla." Arms wound tightly around my waist, he rested his forehead against mine.

I ran my fingers through his dark hair. "Ditto, angel."

We stayed like that a bit longer, lost in each other, savoring the intimacy of the moment.

"So, where to today?" he asked, shaking me out of the reverie. He took my hand and guided me down the driveway to where a black SUV idled.

"Another rental?"

He nodded. "Not exactly bike weather anymore."

"I have a surprise for you," I said, as he opened the passenger door for me. I climbed into the seat, lifting my legs in. He closed the door and walked around the vehicle to the driver's side. As he slipped into his seat, I caught a glimpse of myself in the side mirror, once more struck by the pure contentment on my face.

I turned to look at him. "Just drive. I'll tell you where we're going."

He put the car in reverse and backed out of the driveway. We made our way across town, parking at the top of Heart Avenue near the city center. The sidewalks were lined with people strolling around, enjoying the beautiful fall day. All the shops and cafés were open, people weaving in and out. The bistro patios were all bustling on account of the mild weather, filled with people having a leisurely breakfast under warm patio heaters.

I loved this part of town. Sometimes, I would walk down here on a Saturday morning or sit at a café just to feel alive—to feed off the energy of other people.

"It's just up ahead." I took his hand and led the way.

We stopped in front of an old theater, and I peered up at the shabby exterior, covered with faded paint and old posters, the marquee sign rusted and dingy. "This is the place," I said brightly, noting the questioning look in his eyes. "I should explain. Shortly after I moved here, I met the owner of this theater at my office. He became a client of mine, and he told me about this place. He had bought it for his wife more than fifteen years earlier, but she passed away suddenly shortly afterward, and he shut it down. He didn't have the heart to sell it, though."

I walked up to the front gate, pausing in front of the panel affixed to the side wall. I keyed in the access code and the gate unlocked with a click. Pulling it open, I beckoned for Ash to follow me, and when he did, I locked the gate behind us.

We headed down a dark corridor until we came to the main lobby. The air was stuffy and musty, a thick layer of dust coating everything. We crossed the lobby to a pair of grand oak doors, and when I opened them, the auditorium came into view. I flicked on a light switch on the wall and the room was flooded with soft light. The upholstery on the seats were worn and dusty, the smell of it cloying as we walked, but I breathed it in deeply.

I made my way toward the stage, where a solitary grand piano stood at an angle facing the auditorium. I led Ash down to the edge of the orchestra seating.

"Sit here." I pointed to a chair in the front row.

Curiosity sparked in his eyes as he sat down. "Like I was saying, I know the owner of this place, and I guess you could say that we bonded over our respective tragedies. This piano belonged to William's wife, and just like he couldn't sell this place, he couldn't sell her piano, so he kept it tuned regularly and let me come here and use it when I wanted. I've told you that I don't play my piano anymore, but sometimes, especially when I felt lost and alone, I would come here and play this one."

I moved in front of Asher's chair and kneeled in front of him. "Up until a month ago, it had been while since I was here—since I played or sang anything. But I've been thinking a lot about what you said about not giving up on music, and what Mangy Cat told me about creating the melodies, singing the songs. Ever since I was visited by Arazul and went back to the memory of Mags's death, I've been plagued with the need to write, to sing. I've been here a couple of times since, and today, I want to play for you. It's the first song I've written in more than a year, and I want to share it with you."

"I'm honored, Elle." Ash reached for my hand and brought it to his lips.

I smiled and squeezed his fingers. "I'll be right back." I made my way off to the side to the stage entrance. My nerves were rattled, but the moment I stepped onto the stage, sat at the piano, and my fingers brushed against the keys, I was home. I closed my eyes and touched the keys lightly, and started playing the opening chords. The melody sprang to life, and the piano became an extension of me, and I gave myself over to the music and started singing.

Even in the gloom of the early morning light
When the shadows fill each room and the dawn unmoors the night
There is beauty in the dreary, although the day might feel cold and weary
If you only look closer, you'll find that happiness lies behind an open mind

In the cry of a crow as it welcomes the morn
In a shimmer of snow, in a storm cloud that's born
In a blast of cold air as it rattles the trees
In the reverent fear of magnanimous seas
Just open your eyes, you'll see what's always there
Majesty and splendor, beauty everywhere
And it shatters the darkness inside, throws the doors open wide

When the winter melts into spring and the world erupts with life
And the finch and nightingale sing and the days grow long and rife
With radiant blossoms and glorious greenery
And the breathtaking pomp of spectacular scenery
Breathe deeper, dream weaver
There's nothing you can't do, the world belongs to you

In the cry of a crow as it welcomes the morn

In a shimmer of snow, in a storm cloud that's born
In a blast of cold air as it rattles the trees
In the reverent fear of the magnanimous seas,
Just open your eyes you'll see what's always there
Majesty and splendor, beauty everywhere
And it shatters the darkness inside, throws the doors open wide.

Though hurt and pain may flay your soul
Make you lose your way, leave you lost and cold
Look up, break free from the sinking sands
Sometimes salvation comes with an outstretched hand

To pull you out of the dismal night
To hold you close, lead you back to the light
To fill you with hope, be a balm to your heart
To show you it's possible—you deserve a new start
It's always darkest before the dawn.
The shadows draw closer, pull tighter until they're gone
Then the sun in its splendor, shines bright, wrapping you in its light

I played the last few chords, then let the music die slowly. I looked at Ash leaning forward in his seat, his hands steepled together over his mouth. I walked off the stage and made my way back to him. When I reached the end of his row, he got out of his seat and came over to me. He placed his hands on both sides of my face, his emerald eyes wide.

"Elle, that was unbelievable." He brushed his lips against my forehead. "The words, the melody, your voice . . . I'm fucking floored." His voice was tinged with such reverence that it brought tears to my eyes. "Thank you for sharing that with me."

He lowered his head and kissed me, his hands tangling in my hair. I reached up on tiptoes, wrapping my arms around his neck, kissing him back with burning intensity.

"Thank you, Ash," I whispered against his lips.

"For what, Tialla?" He brushed a thumb across my cheek.

I swallowed the lump in my throat. "For finding me, for being you, for showing me that I don't have to live my life like a ghost, for showing me that there is wonder in life if I look for it. I wrote this song for you. Music has always been my go-to mode of communication—the language of my heart—and for a while, I thought it was lost to me forever, until I met you."

His eyes burned with emotion and he grabbed the back of my neck and crushed me to him, holding me tightly against his body. Tears blurred my vision as I buried my face in his chest. My heart was light and airy, as if a huge weight had been lifted from me. All the anger, grief, pain, guilt, misery—gone. Love was worth the pain, I saw that now. Although my life had been filled with heartbreak after heartbreak, the memories and experiences I had shared with those I lost were so precious and sacred to me, and I wouldn't trade them for anything. I didn't know how things would end for Ash and me, but Mangy Cat was right. *Love was a beautiful risk worth living and dying for.* I just needed to step past my fear and take the plunge.

Chapter 22

ELEYSE

OCTOBER 28: ONE YEAR, ALMOST FIVE MONTHS AGO . . .

It was late when I left the gym, and as I drove through the thoroughfare, my mind was preoccupied with thoughts of Ash. I hadn't been able to get him out of my head since that day at the theater.

Almost six months had passed since we met at Crusoe's. Although he never stayed longer than a day or two, we were inseparable when he was here. I had more questions than I cared to admit, but as much as I wanted to know, I also didn't want to know, as ridiculous as that sounded.

I didn't want the bubble to burst, for reality to sweep in and take away my small sliver of happiness, and so I contented myself with ambiguity. There were times when I still wasn't sure that he wasn't entirely a creation of my imagination.

I was seriously contemplating introducing him to Aggie. She had only seen him that one time from afar, but I was anxious to hear what her opinion of him would be. Aggie was a straight shooter and would give me her honest impressions. Although, from what I had told her about him thus far, she was definitely Team Ash all the way.

Even though she joked that she was in support of anything that would get me laid, make me give a shit about my appearance, and make me less cranky—in that order—she genuinely had my best interests at heart and wanted me to be happy. And Ash truly made me happy.

In the time I had spent with him, I made several quiet observations: he was generous and kind, a man used to the finer things in life. Money was no object to him, and yet he was also content with the simple pleasures life had to offer. He paid attention to everything around him, immersing himself into his surroundings in a way I had never seen before. He lived in the moment, experiencing everything with wonder, and I was envious of his refreshing, vivacious approach to life.

He was an enigma to me. He never asked for anything, never pressured me, never made promises he couldn't keep. I didn't understand what his motivations were. It wasn't clear to me why he would even choose to spend time with me—I had nothing to offer him.

Out of the corner of my eye, I spotted the rural exit turnoff coming up on my left. Goddamn it. I'd been so caught up in my thoughts, I'd forgotten to stop at the drugstore down the street from the gym. That meant I'd have to stop at the grocery store.

Shit.

I gripped the steering wheel and forced myself to relax. *Calm down, Eleyse. Piece of cake. You've done this lots of times.*

Of course, I knew what the problem was, and I was trying my hardest not to think about it. Mangy Cat had said I would revisit the three tragedies of my past, and the first two were behind me. That left one more.

Liam.

It made me sick. I didn't want to go back there. That loss had completely destroyed me. If there was anything that was going to trigger memories of losing him, the grocery store would be it.

Crap. The other things on my list weren't so important, but I needed tampons, so I had no choice but to stop. Taking the next right, I pulled into the Wholesome Foods parking lot. I grabbed my purse from the passenger seat and slid out of the car. Slinging my bag across my shoulder, I locked the door and headed toward the store.

At the entrance, I squared my shoulders and inhaled deeply. Just a quick in and out. Bread, eggs, ice cream, tampons. One-stop shop. I could do it in five minutes tops. I grabbed a basket, feeling my heart rate ramp up as I walked past the produce aisle. *You've got this, girl. Just keep moving. Shut your brain off and keep going.*

I speed-walked to the bakery section, grabbed a loaf of multigrain bread, and tossed it into the basket. Three more to go. I was almost running now as I approached the dairy aisle. Quickly sliding open the refrigerator door, I reached for a carton of eggs. *You're doing great. Just beautiful. Now go get the ice cream.* My heart was hammering, my breaths shallow and ragged as I moved down the aisle.

A few feet in front of me, a woman was yelling at someone on her phone while balancing her toddler on her hip and trying to wrangle her small son running circles around her. The commotion set my heart racing again and the blood rushed to my head. I swayed as my vision blurred. *No. No. No. Don't freak out. Just abort. Get the hell out of here.*

I shook my head to clear the fog and stepped around them. I grimaced at what the boy was holding in his hand. A carton of milk. Fear gripped my heart like a vise. It all happened in slow motion. The woman darted out to take the milk from her son, and in the ensuing scuffle, the carton hit the ground with a soul-shattering thud. It exploded on contact, milk spraying everywhere, and I dropped to my knees and screamed as blackness engulfed me.

"Can you grab the milk, babe? I might be a while. At least ten of these bags of potato chips are calling my name."

Next to me, Liam chuckled. "Ellie, we play this game every week, and every week, you pick the same ones—jalapeño cheddar and spicy barbecue."

"Yeah," I said as I examined a bag of butter chicken-flavored kettle chips, "but doesn't it seem like every week they come out with at least five new flavors? I mean, there is such a thing as too much variety."

Liam's light-brown eyes sparkled with humor as he crossed his arms over his chest. "Here's a thought—why don't you take a walk on the wild side and pick two new ones we've never tried before?"

I gasped and looked at him in mock outrage. "Why the hell would I ever do that? What if I hate them?"

He flashed me a grin, baring those dimples I loved to trace with my tongue. "What if you love them?"

I rolled my eyes and sighed. "I'll consider your request."

"How generous of you." He brushed his lips against my forehead. "If I get back and I see jalapeño cheddar and spicy barbecue in the cart, they're going right back on the shelf. I'll pick two myself."

I narrowed my eyes. "Yes, master," I muttered with mock vitriol.

"Good girl." He chuckled, heading down the aisle toward the dairy section.

I smiled and returned to the task at hand, staring at the international flavors section of chips. Good Lord, this truly was overwhelming. Scanning the shelf, I slowly read the various names. I reached for a salmon-colored bag. Pad Thai flavor? What the hell? Although . . . that might not be half bad.

A woman's horrendous scream split the air, causing me to jump and drop the bag in my hand. My heart pounded in my chest. Another shrill cry rang out, followed by yelling and panicked voices.

"Security!" someone screamed.

Oh god. What was happening? A robbery? I grabbed my purse from the shopping cart and raced down the aisle to find Liam.

"Someone call 9-1-1!" a man's voice yelled hysterically.

My heart thudded and my pulse pounded in my ears. As I rounded the corner to the dairy aisle, my blood ran cold and everything slowed down, as if I was watching in slow motion. Liam was splayed on the ground, two people leaning over him, pressing their hands against his chest and stomach.

I flew down the aisle, skidding to a halt and dropping to my knees at his side, vaguely registering that the floor was wet and sticky. "Liam!" I cried as two arms grabbed me from behind. I shrugged them off and scrabbled on my hands and knees to get to him.

Fuck! Blood. There was so much blood. Blood everywhere—gushing out of his stomach and chest, and spurting out of his mouth. No, no, no.

I crouched against his side, reaching for him. His eyes were open, staring blankly at the ceiling above him.

"Liam, please don't go," I pleaded, tears streaming down my face as I shook him gently. "I'm here. Stay with me."

I couldn't breathe. The walls were closing in on me. It was so fucking hot.

I reached for his hand, slick and wet, but still warm. "Please don't leave me."

I screamed as two arms pulled me away and two paramedics dropped to their knees to tend to him.

Not even twenty seconds later, they shook their heads. "He's gone," one of them announced.

The world around me swayed. "No!" A keening wail ripped from my throat. I closed my eyes, but nothing could make me un-see Liam's blank and lifeless gaze. It was burned into my mind. How could this be happening? Not even five minutes ago, we were laughing and joking. Why had I asked him to get the milk? Why couldn't I have just waited until I was done and then we could have gone together? I slammed the back of my head against the freezer door and kept on banging it. This was a mistake. A horrible mistake. I opened my eyes, my gaze snapping to Liam's empty stare. Pain, more severe and crippling than I'd ever known, cleaved me in half.

"Liam," I cried, my voice hoarse and shaky, my body wracked with heaving shudders. "I'm sorry. I'm so sorry." I covered my face with my hands and surrendered to my grief.

"Elle . . ." a ragged voice whispered.

My eyes flew open and my heart lurched. Liam lay convulsing on the floor, the blood sputtering out of his mouth as he tried to speak. Abruptly, his body relaxed and he sat up calmly and looked at me, blood seeping out of his eyes. I shuddered and screamed, unable to make sense of what I was seeing.

He moved slowly toward me. "The Shadow King and Queens breathe again, Agaia. Winther comes. Catraia stirs. The Third Age looms. The Bells of Galeseira call you home."

The world around me shook and spun, and then darkness claimed me.

Just as Mangy Cat had deemed, the past had come calling. The three tragedies that had shattered my life had been revisited, leaving me numb and empty inside.

I sat in the back of an ambulance with a blanket around my shoulders. The store manager had called the paramedics and police after I blacked out, and after examining me and determining that I'd suffered a terrible panic attack and was still suffering from mild shock, the EMTs had advised that I was okay to go home, but not to drive.

I'd made a terrible scene at the store, apparently—had scared the shit out of the mother and her two kids in the dairy aisle. I felt bad about that. I shouldn't have even gone.

Tears rolled down my face as my mind swarmed with memories of Liam. Him standing up for me the first day we met in grade seven. Him refusing to let me eat at the lunch table alone. Liam, Charlotte, and I on the roof of Charlotte's house gazing at the stars. Our first kiss at the town fair when we were sixteen. Him telling me he loved me at prom. The devotion in his eyes the first time we made love. Him holding me every night after Mags died when I was broken and inconsolable. Him sweeping me off my feet in elation after he proposed and I said yes.

Liam—my beautiful, kind, loving, loyal Liam—had died in the dairy aisle of a grocery store—had bled out while I knelt there hysterical and helpless, unable to do a single thing to save him. His death had been senseless and tragic. And all because he had chosen to stand up for someone.

In those two minutes he was away from me, the unthinkable had happened. After getting the milk, Liam witnessed a man slipping a woman's wallet from her purse while she was grabbing something out of the freezer. In fearless Liam fashion, he'd boldly confronted the thief, who'd pulled out a knife. A scuffle ensued, and Liam was stabbed four times.

The fourth stake to my chest. I could still remember staring at the floor as I leaned against the freezer after they pronounced him dead, thinking to myself what a strange color blood and milk blended to make. What a ludicrous thought to have. I hadn't bought a carton of milk since.

As the voice of the paramedic pulled me back to reality, I shivered at the familiar sense of gloom seeping in. I nodded numbly when the police officer to my right asked if I needed a ride home, and when he dropped me off in front of my house, I didn't even remember unlocking the door and going inside.

The moment that little boy had sent the carton of milk crashing onto the floor, it was inevitable. The spiraling darkness had come for me again.

The emptiness inside me was a monster with a life and will of its own. Sometimes it was lax and dormant, floating just beneath the surface, watching me through heavy-lidded, slothful eyes, and then other times, it was a roaring beast, slashing and raging, devouring me entirely.

God-knows-how-much later, I lay on my bed—my body slack and unresponsive—staring at the ceiling. My head was leaden and my thoughts scattered, and all I wanted was to sleep, to close my eyes and feel nothing. The last time I'd felt like this, I hadn't gotten out of bed for three days.

I didn't want to think. Thoughts whirled around in my mind, but I detached myself, not focusing on any one in particular. That was crucial. The moment I started tuning in to the voices in my head, the paranoia would begin. That, too, was inevitable, but I wasn't ready for it yet.

My eyes drifted shut—for how long, I wasn't sure—but through the dark haze that had settled over me, I heard footsteps and someone calling my name. The mattress shifted next to me, and fingers brushed against my hair.

I groaned, moving my face closer to the source of warmth. Forcing my eyelids open, I sucked in a breath at Ash's face above me, his green eyes wide with worry and fear.

"Elle," he whispered. "Are you all right? Your front door was wide open." The slight tremor in his voice and his mouth against my forehead was my undoing. Ever since Liam, I'd been alone, with no one to comfort me or be strong for me or to lift me out of the darkness. Since I had lost Liam, I'd suffered in silence. But not tonight. He was here. I wrapped my arms around his neck and completely fell apart.

The roaring in my ears grew louder as the tears rushed to the surface, and I let it all out—the anguish and rage, the loneliness and fear, the guilt and regret. Not once did he let go. He held me tightly, pulling me into his arms as I cried, and I cried harder because of it. His fingers stroked my hair and my back, his movements grounding and calm.

I wasn't sure how much time passed, but when finally the tears subsided, I lay in his arms, listening to his heartbeat against my ear. He eased me onto my back and shifted onto his side next to me, wrapping one arm around my waist.

"Tell me, baby. What happened?" He gently tucked my hair behind my ear.

"Stupid talking cat," I rasped, my voice gravelly and raw. "Liam." I closed my eyes as the tears spilled out once more, the hot splash of them like acid against my cheeks. "It just hurts so much, Ash."

"Elle." His voice was clogged with emotion. "If I could take all your pain away, I would. I know what it's like to hurt like you're hurting. To walk around with so much emptiness inside you, your soul shuttered and cold."

I squeezed my eyes shut, my throat tight as I fought against another wave of tears. "I don't think anything can take this away," I choked out.

"I want you to do something for me, Tialla." He ran his fingers through my hair.

"I don't know if I can."

"Yes, you can." His voice was steady and calm. "Focus on the memories, the happy moments. Remember *why* you loved Liam. Tell me why."

I opened my eyes to find him looking at me with tenderness and compassion. "He. . ." I said, not sure where to start, not sure if I should even talk about Liam with Ash.

"I won't get upset. This is about you and your healing."

Why did I love Liam? I think it was more like, how could I have *not* loved him? I swallowed and closed my eyes. "The first time I met Liam, he punched another kid in the face for calling me an ugly orphan. Then he looked at me, winked, and said, 'I got your back, new girl,' even as he was being yanked to the principal's office. I loved him from that moment. I remember thinking that he was sunshine. He just had that way about him—so full of life and energy and happiness. He always had a smile on his face, always knew how to make me laugh. It was infectious, you know?"

Ash nodded, his fingers still threading through my hair gently.

"I craved being around him because of that. And I know Mags did her best to give me a happy childhood, but there was a gaping hole inside me after my parents died. Liam flooded that emptiness with his spirit and his light. It's like I *forgot* to be sad when I was with him." My voice cracked, tears flowing freely again. "Liam and Charlotte were my best friends, but Liam and I always had a deeper connection. He was fiercely protective of me, and loyal, and so unbelievably patient. I loved him for making me feel like I was both normal and treasured."

Ash reached out his fingers to brush away the tears running down my face. I grabbed his hand and held it tightly near my head. "It was only after he died that I realized how much of a crutch he was for me emotionally, how much I leaned on him, how much I *took* from him." I bit my lip to keep it from quivering. "That's what kills me, Ash. To think that I took from him more than I gave. That maybe I didn't love him as much as he loved me. That I should have shown him more how much he meant to me."

I wrapped my arms around myself, looking at Ash through the blur of tears. "I don't know how to explain this. The feelings I had for Liam are different from the ones I have for you. Liam was a tornado of energy who blew into my life and swept me along for the ride—long haul. I *grew* in love with him. Laughter, tenderness, loyalty, friendship—that's what I had with him, and those were the reasons I loved him. But you—you are the first . . . *anything* I've ever laid eyes on that I *wanted* for myself."

I shifted on my side to face him. "Liam fed me his strength and love, and I was content to let him lead, so long as he was by my side. It's like my entire existence was wrapped up in him." I traced a finger along his jaw. "You, on the other hand, make me want to be strong on my own, to harness that power within myself and be the person I've always dreamed of being. I chained that girl up after my parents died, and she's been suffocating all these years, locked away so deep inside me, I forgot she even existed. She took her first breath in twenty-three years that night I locked eyes with you on the sidewalk outside Crusoe's, and her restlessness has been growing ever since." I reached down and threaded my fingers through his. "Part of me feels that I am betraying Liam's memory because what I feel for you is on an entirely different level than it was with him."

Ash clenched his jaw and exhaled softly. "Elle. Don't think like that. What do you think Liam would want for you?"

"He would want what he always wanted," I said without hesitation, a wave of emotion washing over me. "To see me happy, to see me smile." I burst into tears, covering my face with my hands. "I wish I could have told him how much he meant to me, how much I loved him. I wish I could have thanked him for protecting my heart and always safeguarding my mental health." I gulped, taking in a huge breath of air. "And more than anything, I wish I could have said goodbye. I never got to say goodbye to my parents, to Mags, or Liam. That feeling—being robbed of a last moment with someone you love—is the worst feeling in the world."

"I know," Ash whispered, and as I looked up at him, his eyes glittered with unshed tears. He pulled me into his arms, and I clung to him as if he was life itself.

My tears were like a river that could not be plugged. They kept on coming, even as I tried to stem them.

Ash exhaled slowly and reached for my hand, stroking my fingers gently. "When I was a boy," he said softly, "my mother always knew how to make me feel better. Always." He lifted his hand and cupped the back of my head. "She loved music—just like you—and whenever I was sad or hurt, she would sing to me. Now, this might sound crazy, but I swear her voice had the power to heal, because every time she sang to me when I was feeling bad, it would make me feel better."

I reached for his hand, weaving my fingers through his. His voice was lulling, and I moved closer, focusing on his words. This was the first time he had spoken of his family, first I'd heard that he had a mother who loved music as much as I did.

His voice wavered slightly. "She's been gone a long time, but I still hear her song in my head when I'm in a dark place. Her words, though distant and faint, still contain the power to soothe me. Let me try and do that for you."

I lifted confused eyes to his as he smiled wistfully and pulled me closer. Inhaling deeply as his fingers tangled in my hair, he began singing softly, the lilting strains of a mesmerizing melody sending tremors through my entire body, even as the gentle rumbling of his voice reverberated against my palm on his chest.

I promise, it won't last, the piercing pain you feel inside.
Like sea-washed glass, tumbled smooth by steady tides,
Let the sand and currents shape you,
As time, with its power, transforms you,
And you emerge changed,
Your jagged edges polished and planed,
The burning truth imprinted on your soul,
A broken spirit can always be made whole.

So close your eyes and let the pain and sorrow go.
Let the evening star's light surround you in its healing glow.
And when the darkness fades with the coming dawn,
You'll awake at peace as you find yourself reborn.

I stared up at him, my mouth agape, my eyes wide with wonder. His singing voice was rich and hypnotic. I had never heard anything so haunting and exquisite in my entire life, never felt with such clarity that I'd found the other half of my soul. Chills peppered my entire body and tears stung my eyes as I reached up to touch his face with my fingers.

"It wasn't meant to bring more tears," he whispered.

"I can't help it. That was beautiful. You're so fucking beautiful," I choked out, my sobs muffling my words.

He tilted my chin gently. "You're the beautiful one, Tialla."

I stared at him for a moment, then lifted my head and brushed my lips against his. His hands cradled my face as he lowered me back onto the pillow.

My head pounded, the throbbing radiating down through my neck and shoulders. My eyes were swollen and sore, and I squinted to keep them from burning. "I'm so tired Ash," I cried as shivers swept through my body. "Everything hurts—my body, my heart. I just want it to stop. Please make it stop, if only for a little while." The tears were hot and angry as they slid down my face.

His lips brushed against my forehead, and his fingers grazed my temple. "I will, Elle," he whispered. "Just close your eyes."

My body relaxed against his, and a soothing warmth seeped from his fingers as he stroked the side of my head. A sense of calm enveloped me, and my eyes grew heavy and relaxed as I drifted off to sleep.

Chapter 23

ELEYSE

My eyes fluttered open, and I squinted against the sunlight filtering into the room. Something heavy was resting against my stomach. I looked down to see a large, tanned forearm around my middle. *Ash*.

His eyes were closed, his long lashes fanned out across his lids, softly framing his cheekbones. Even in sleep, he was magnificent. Powerful. I squeezed my fingers, fighting the urge to touch him. Memories of last night came flooding back, and mixed emotions washed through me—sadness and devastation when I thought of Liam, but also hope and longing when I thought of Ash. He'd comforted me, urged me to remember the beautiful bond I'd had with Liam. He'd sang for me. And the song, his voice—both mesmerizing and unforgettable.

As if sensing my attention, his eyes slowly opened and focused in on me.

"You stayed," I whispered.

His hand cupped my face gently. "Of course I stayed. I couldn't leave you like that."

I inched closer to him and slid my arms around his neck, resting my head on his chest. "Thank you."

His fingers threaded through my hair. "Did you sleep okay?"

I nodded. "I did. I don't think I've slept that peacefully in a long time."

He smiled and touched my earlobe. "What would you like to do today?"

My heart wobbled in my chest. "What do you mean? You don't have to leave?"

"Not until later."

I stared at him. "You don't have to stay with me just to make sure I'm okay." I tugged on the edge of his sweater. "I'm better now. I promise."

"I know. I can see that. I just want to spend the day with you."

My stomach did a happy little flip-flop as my gaze flitted to his. "What about a hike? The weather's supposed to be nice today. We can do the Avalon Trail. The views from the top are breathtaking, especially with the leaves changing."

"Whatever you want." He kissed the top of my head. "Why don't you take a shower and get dressed and I'll meet you back here in an hour. I'll pick up some breakfast on my way back."

"Where are you going?" I twisted to look at him as he got out of bed.

"Into town to grab a couple of things. I didn't come prepared to go hiking. I'll be back in a flash."

"Okay," I said, as he grabbed his shoes and headed out the bedroom door.

I made my way to the bathroom and turned the shower on. I stared at my face in the mirror as I waited for the water to heat up. Last night had been a close call. Guaranteed, if Ash hadn't shown up, I would still be curled up in a pathetic little ball on my bed. I hated how volatile I still was. It only took one small thing to trigger me and send me unraveling. Sad thing was, the list of small things was long.

Most of the time, I felt in control—aloof and detached, but still in control. Moments like last night—they scared the shit out of me. I didn't know who I was in those situations. My trauma had given birth to sightless demons and ghouls who'd built their roost in the haunted watchtower of my mind. As long as nothing stirred or unsettled their rayless nest, they left me alone. But at the slightest provocation—a memory, an event, an object, a place—in a whirlwind of hysteria and chaos, they were quick to descend and rip me to shreds.

After a long, soothing shower, I made my way to my closet to get dressed. I'd just pulled on my leggings when my mind flashed back to the memory of Liam. I'd come so completely undone I'd forgotten about the strange vision of him talking to me. Just like the vision of Mags, it was dark and sinister.

The Shadow King and Queens breathe again, Agaia. Winther comes. Catraia stirs. The Third Age looms. The Bells of Galeseira call you home.

What the hell did any of that mean? Who could I even ask?

I ran to my bedroom and grabbed my phone from the bedside table. Quickly, I opened my note-taking app, jotting down the words. I'd started doing that after the encounter with Mangy Cat, writing down everything about all the strange occurrences thus far.

A few minutes later, I heard the chime of the front door as it opened. "I'm back," Ash called from the foyer.

"I'll be down in a second." Grabbing a hair elastic off my dresser, I pulled my hair into a ponytail, stuffed my phone into my little backpack, and hustled down the stairs. I could hear Ash moving around in the kitchen, and when I walked in, he lifted his head from where he stood at my kitchen island.

His eyes trailed over me slowly. "Seriously, Elle, no matter what you wear, you always look incredible."

I laughed, feeling suddenly self-conscious in my activewear leggings and long-sleeved fitted top. "Aggie would totally disagree with you. She thinks I look like a wild hobo when I dress like this."

"I need to meet some more hobos," he said with a mischievous smile.

I laughed and opened my fridge. "We should ask Aggie where you can look."

He chuckled. "Well, I've never seen you look anything but perfect."

I cocked my head. "Even that night when you came over and my mouth was full of ice cream?"

"Especially that night." He pulled me toward him. "That was my favorite. The ice cream you were wearing just completed the look."

I shoved him playfully, and his eyes crinkled with amusement as he took two takeout containers out of a bag on the island.

"You're the one who always looks perfect in whatever you're wearing." I gestured to his long-sleeved T-shirt and hiking pants. "Everything you wear just molds to you in all the right places." Before I could stare at his crotch, my eyes flitted to the open container in his hand. "Oh my god, did you get the egg and peameal bacon special from Terry's?"

He grinned. "I've only heard you talk about it at least ten times."

"You're my hero, Ash." I sighed as he handed me a plate. My mouth watered just looking at it—a massive kaiser bun stuffed with a double layer of peameal bacon, two kinds of cheese, a fried egg, avocado slices, and spicy aioli. "I apologize in advance. Look at the size of this thing. Me eating it won't be pretty, baby, so look away."

"Not a chance," he said with a wink.

I was quiet as we made our way through the trail about an hour later. Screwing the cap back on my water bottle, I looked up at the forest around me. The weather was mild for late October, and the changing foliage was still spectacular, the brilliant yellows, oranges, and reds suffusing the world around us in a warm, mellow glow. Here, amid the tranquil stillness and untamed beauty of nature, with Ash next to me, my heart was content. Painfully so.

My mind reeled. How could a moment be so perfect and hurt so much at the same time? I was scared to breathe, my heart clenching with dueling feelings of longing and fear.

I stepped over a gnarled tree root in front of me. "We're almost at the top."

"I feel your emotions leaking out of you as if you're a sieve." Ash reached out to touch my shoulder. "Want to tell me what's playing out in that head of yours?"

"Do I have to?" I swatted a stray branch out of the way as I plodded ahead.

"Of course you don't have to," he said quietly, "but I'd like it if you did. I know how you can get caught up in your own thoughts and go to a dark place."

"I don't really want to have this conversation." I pushed forward, picking up my pace.

"Whoa. Wait. What conversation is that?" Ash grabbed me by the waist, spinning me around to face him.

I looked away, staring at a dead tree to my left. He gripped my chin lightly, his gaze piercing as he studied me.

"Tell me, Elle."

I bit my lip, a million thoughts rushing through my mind. "The conversation where we talk about how little I really know about you, where we confront the fact that this thing between us is getting too huge to contain within the boundaries we set when we met, where I tell you that I die inside a little every time you leave, only to be reborn when I see you again. That conversation."

Ash stepped forward, his expression stormy. My heart thudded. I backed up until the hard bark of a birch tree ground into my back. He placed his hands on either side of the trunk, caging me in.

"Let's get a few things straight, Tialla." He trailed his fingers up my neck. "First of all, you were the one who insisted that you didn't want to know anything about my life. Second, you wanted boundaries—needed them—and third, I die inside a *lot* every time I leave you." His thumb traced my lips, his eyes flashing with a mix of longing and sadness.

"Ash," I whispered, clutching his shirt with my fingers. "Just tell me this is real, that I can give myself permission to fall and you'll catch me. Tell me I won't lose you, that letting myself be happy won't destroy me. Tell me that I'm not cursed, tell me that we have a future."

He brushed his lips against mine, gripping each side of my face in his hands. "You *are* my future, Elle. In more ways than you know."

His emerald eyes flashed, and I gasped at the soft flame I swore flared to life.

"This is real, Tialla. You can let go. I'll catch you, I promise. You won't lose me. We are stronger together or not at all. As for happiness, it's your salvation, baby, not your destruction." He gripped the back of my head. "You are many things, but a curse isn't one of them."

My hands shook as I clenched my fists tighter against his chest. My heart soared, rejoicing in his assurances. The heat of his body next to mine, mingled with something else I couldn't quite grasp, inflamed my senses, and I reached up and kissed him, dragging my teeth against his lower lip, biting down.

He pulled away and looked at me, his eyes sparking with untamed hunger. "Don't incite the beast, Elle," he rasped. "Once he comes out to play, it's hard to put him back in his cage."

I snaked my arms around his neck, trailing kisses across his cheek, stopping to brush my lips against his ear. "Here, beasty, beasty."

He growled, reaching behind me to grip my thighs. Throwing my backpack on the ground, I wrapped my legs around his waist as he lifted me, the hardness of the tree trunk against my back long forgotten.

I ran my fingers through his dark hair, tightening my grip. "If I'd known that being out in nature like a wild animal was the key to making you lose control, I'd have used that to my advantage months ago."

His lips curled in a smile. "It'll take more than your teeth sinking into my skin and your pretty legs wrapped around me to make me lose control, Tialla."

"Yeah?" I whispered. "What about this?" I tightened my hold around his waist, grinding my core against his erection.

"Silly girl." His eyes twinkled with amusement, even as he pulled me tighter. "You have no idea what makes me lose control."

Ha. He wasn't as unaffected as he was pretending.

"I'm sure I can find out." I slipped my hands beneath his T-shirt and ran my palms up his hard stomach.

A rush of desire coursed through me at the feel of his bare skin against my fingers, and I moaned, flattening my hands against his bare chest. His heart thudded a wild staccato against my palm. "I don't know, baby," I whispered. "For someone who's in control, your heartbeat feels pretty erratic to me."

He chuckled, his lips snaking down my neck. "Excitement and control are mutually exclusive, Tialla."

"I bet you want to fuck me against this tree, though." I reached my hand between us to stroke the outline of his cock through his pants. "I bet you want to rip my clothes off and throw me to the ground and fuck me on my hands and knees like a wild animal."

He groaned, his eyes glued to my hand still moving against his crotch. "Is your plan to dirty talk me into losing it?"

"Is it working?" My voice was husky, even to my own ears.

His hand moved up to cup my ass. "Try harder." His lips curled in a smile.

I swirled my finger around the head of his dick. God, I wanted my hand on his bare skin so bad. "I told you before what it does to me when you call me baby."

"Remind me." He dipped his head to graze the pulse at my neck with his tongue.

"It makes me wet," I said, my voice a low rasp.

"Are you wet, baby?" he teased, his eyes crinkling at the corners.

"Drenched." I tightened my legs around him. "Wanna check?"

He inhaled sharply, lowering his head to my neck, his tongue tracing a path to my ear. "I would, but you're wearing these ridiculously tight leggings."

"It's a good thing they come with a zippered gusset for easy access." My breathing was ragged as his cock grew even harder around my fingers.

His jaw clenched. "I don't even know what the fuck that is. The only thing that registered were the words 'easy access.'"

I touched the hidden zipper just above the crotch of my leggings. "It comes in handy when you're out in the middle of nowhere like this and need to tinkle." I lifted my gaze to meet his. "Or fuck. Convenient, right?"

He swore softly under his breath.

"Shall I demonstrate?" I asked innocently. "You'll have to put me down."

His hands tightened around my thighs as he pushed me harder against the tree. "Not a chance. Figure out how to make it work right where you are."

I lowered my gaze, my fingers probing for the top of the zipper in the hidden seam, sliding it down, shifting my body to get as much of the track open as I could. Ash's fingers dug into my skin, his body completely rigid as I lazily reached past the opening and pushed the flap of protective fabric to the side, leaving my skin exposed. With my legs open wide, it left nothing to the imagination.

"Fuck," he ground out. "Wrap your legs around me tighter. I need to free one of my hands."

I hooked my feet around him, pushing back against the tree for more leverage.

His breathing was shallow as he looked down at me, lightly trailing his fingers down my waist ever so slowly. My skin heated, a rush of desire pooling in my core. I arched my back, impatient for him to touch me. Finally, his fingers connected with my bare skin, gently caressing the top of my clit as he moved down to the warm rush of wetness on display for him.

He groaned as his fingers slid through my slickness, and my entire body shuddered, the feel of his fingers on my skin a million times better than I had ever imagined.

"Ash." I whimpered as he slipped a finger inside me. "Don't fucking tease me." A burning supplication. That's what it was.

"Do you want to come, Tialla?" He slipped another finger inside me as his thumb stroked circles around my clit.

"Yes," I cried, my hips moving of their own accord as he continued his slow ministrations.

"Fuck it," he growled. "You told me before that you wanted to climb me like a tree and see what the view was like from the top. You're going to get your wish, baby." With one quick movement, he gripped both my thighs and hoisted me up, swinging my legs over his shoulders.

My heart lurched at the abrupt movement, my arms flailing, gripping his head for balance. Then the strangest thing happened. I couldn't feel the tree at my back although I was still pressed against it. My body was weightless and free, as if no gravity was pulling me down. It was as if I was just hovering there across his shoulders.

I peered down at Ash, and his lips curved wickedly as he looked up at me, his hands parting my legs wider. "Just relax, Tialla. Be a good little goddess and let me worship at your temple."

I laughed, slipping my fingers between my legs. "Is that what this is?"

"Fuck, yes." His voice was low and guttural. He moved my hand away and parted me with his fingers before clamping his lips over my pussy, the suction making me cry out. His mouth and tongue worked in tandem, licking, sucking, until finally, he shifted his attention to my clit, flattening his tongue as he licked me slowly, then closed his mouth over the bud and sucked sharply.

"Oh god," I cried out, my fingers digging into his hair.

He groaned and released my clit, swirling his tongue over it slowly before settling on a steady pace, with just the right amount of pressure, working me into a frenzy.

I had to admit, the view from the top was fucking amazing. I couldn't tear my eyes away, completely captivated as I watched him devouring me like I was his own personal buffet. He lifted his eyes and met my gaze, and I gasped, unable to look away as the pleasure built, as my hips thrust forward, riding his face.

"Let go, Elle," he urged. "Come hard for me."

His words sent a jolt of desire straight to my clit, and I closed my eyes and reached for my breasts, squeezing them to relieve the aching in my nipples. I whimpered as a flutter pulsed low in my core—my orgasm announcing its impending arrival. It was going to make one hell of an entrance, I was bloody sure of it. I moved my hips faster, focusing on the feel of Ash's warm mouth and tongue on me, and right on cue, my release galloped in, like a mob of stampeding racehorses crossing the finish line, bowling me over.

"Ash!" I ground my hips on his face as my body jerked and spasmed, wave after wave of pleasure rocking me. I slowed my movements, my fingers gripping his face lightly. The tremors pulsed through my body even after he lifted me off his shoulders and lowered me to the ground.

"Please," I groaned, gripping his arms. "You've got to hold me up. I don't think I can move yet."

"Good." He smiled, wrapping his arms around me before lowering his head to kiss me. I tasted myself on his lips, and that in itself excited me. Slipping my tongue into his mouth, I pushed my body closer to his, moaning as he sucked gently before flicking his tongue over mine.

I tugged at the waistband of his pants and slid my hand in, wrapping my fingers around his bare, hard cock, my heart kicking up in excitement. He groaned at the same time I moaned against his mouth. His flesh was warm and satiny smooth. Sliding my hand down his shaft, I sighed quietly. I had fantasized about this cock for the past six goddamn months. Dreamed about it, lusted for it. Ash definitely exuded big dick energy, which I loved, but I was relieved to confirm that it wasn't *monster cock*, big dick. He was perfect.

"Gods, woman," he growled, sucking in a breath as I tightened my fingers around him. "You're going to be the death of me."

My fingers froze and I gasped, the shock of his words like a pail of icy water to my face. "Don't fucking say that." Immediately, the image of him lying in a pool of blood flashed through my mind, and just like that, nausea roiled in my gut. All the heated desire drained out of me as if it had never been there to start with.

Ash grew rigid, immediately grasping the impact of his words. "You know that's not what I meant, Elle."

I released my grip and moved my hand away, taking a step back. Fumbling to zip my leggings back up, I looked at him, biting my lip to keep my emotions in check. "I know."

"It was a slip of the tongue I should have never made."

I closed my eyes, hating myself for ruining the moment. "You deserve better than me, Ash," I whispered, the annoying burn of tears threatening to overwhelm me. "You deserve someone who isn't broken, someone whose emotions are not mercurial and unpredictable. Someone who can love you without fear. Someone you don't have to walk on eggshells around."

He pushed me against the tree, leveraging his weight to pin me there. "Listen, Elle." He curled his hand under my chin, "You know that talk we started earlier?"

My gaze flicked to his, and I nodded slowly.

"Let's finish it."

We climbed the short distance to the top of the trail in silence, tension hanging in the air between us. Ten minutes later, we stood at the summit, overlooking the valley below. The view alone was well worth the climb. A sea of brilliant color spread before us in a stunning display of nature's magnificence.

"I just love it here," I said quietly.

"I can definitely see why." Ash lowered himself down onto the rocky outcropping and pulling me down to sit between his legs. "Ready?" he whispered against my ear.

"Wait." I twisted around so I faced him, bringing my knees together between his. "I want to see your face."

He stared at me for a long moment, as if contemplating where to start. "My full name is Asher Valkyse."

Valkyse. What an unusual name. I'd never heard that surname before. It was crazy, and it should have bothered me more—we'd known each other for almost six months and I didn't know his last name. But I hadn't wanted to know it, because treacherous madwoman that I could be, I would have gone full-on stalker mode, searching for him online once I had that bit of information.

As if reading my mind, he said quietly, "You won't find any record of me, because I don't exist anywhere, not here in this country or in any national database."

I narrowed my eyes. "Why is that? Are you some kind of secret spy?" I gasped as another thought hit me. "Or a criminal? Oh god. Please don't tell me you're a serial killer."

He shook his head. "I'm none of those things."

"So how?" I asked, even as relief washed through me. "Who are you?"

"Do you trust me, Elle?" His green eyes studied me intently.

Immediately, everything inside me screamed yes, belting out a ringing endorsement. I trusted him. With every fiber of my being, I did. And that overshadowed any doubts or suspicions my rational mind threw at me.

"Yes, I trust you."

His eyes flashed with a mix of relief and happiness. "I told you before that there are things about me that I can't explain, but I need you to know that it's not because I don't want to tell you; it's just that you won't understand."

I propped my head on my knees. "Well I definitely *don't* understand."

He ran his fingers through his hair and looked off toward the valley, chewing thoughtfully on his lip. "How can I explain this without you thinking I am crazy?"

"Baby, have you met me? I can totally relate to crazy."

"My sole reason for coming to Hargrove was you," he said quietly.

"What?" My mind whirred with questions. "But I bumped into you at Crusoe's that night. Were you following me? Did you follow me home?"

"Fuck." He loosed a deep exhale. "I knew this wasn't going to come out right. Okay, tell me if I'm wrong."

I stared at him.

He leaned forward slightly. "I'm entirely certain that you feel an inexplicable feeling of *rightness* with me. As if you've known me for a long time. As if we *fit* in a way you never thought possible. Am I wrong?"

"No," I whispered, my heart hammering in my chest. "That's exactly how I feel. Like you're the missing piece to me."

"That's because I am. Just like you are *my* missing piece. There's a powerful connection between us, and that is how I found you. I was drawn to you by forces bigger than either of us that I can't really explain."

I swallowed slowly. As much as I wanted to scoff and turn my nose up at the notion, I couldn't, because Ash *called* to me in a way nothing ever had before. He felt *right* in a world that had only ever felt wrong.

He comes, and on his heels, your future.

I lifted wide eyes to him, certainty coursing through me. "You *are* the *he* the woman from my dream was talking about."

"Elle." He ran his fingers along my jaw.

"Ash." My heard raced wildly as another piece of the puzzle suddenly slid into place. "It was *you*." My eyes filled with tears. "How could I have not realized until now?" My fingers shook as I touched his lips. "Say the words."

"Which words?"

"The ones you always spoke to me when I wanted to die. I know you know what I'm talking about."

His green eyes glittered with heavy emotion as he leaned forward and pulled me closer, resting his forehead against mine.

"Be strong, Elle. Live. Fight the darkness."

Gooseflesh erupted all over my body as the world around us spun and faded away. My heart jackhammered in tumultuous wonder as I stared at him, a firm conviction settling over me that my life, as I knew it before, was over.

Chapter 24

ELEYSE

There are key moments that haunt your dreams—experiences so transformative that a mere thought, smell, sound, touch can trigger the mind's recall capability and rouse such a moment to the surface in a heartbeat. Not for one second did I doubt that this was one of them.

I stared at Ash, unable to tear my eyes away, my mind reeling. In my darkest days after Liam, when I was a spectral shell of a person, the silence and loneliness were crushing. But on the fringes of my grief, there was a presence—I acutely sensed it—refusing to let me wither away. I loathed it, resented it, raged at it, but at the same time clung to it because it made me feel *seen. Heard.* Reminding me that I was still alive. Urging me to go on. To fight. *The hope in my head*, I thought of it, my senses believing that it was the part of me who loved me so much and refused to let me give up on myself.

The missing part of me.

Staring at me now with so much devotion and scorching emotion in his emerald eyes that it rocked the very foundations of my entire being.

I leaped into his lap, flinging my arms around his neck and wrapping my legs around his waist. My throat burned, my emotions bubbling like a volcano on the brink of erupting. Crap. There was going to be ugly crying.

Ash clasped the sides of my face. "Let me explain."

"I don't care," I rasped, my voice stretched tight with the weight of poignant and exquisite heartbreak. "I just want your arms around me."

He obliged, holding me as if I was the most precious thing in the world to him. I buried my head in his neck as the floodgates blasted open.

A multitude of memories rushed to the surface. The brush of fingers in my hair as I bawled my eyes out in the parking lot at the gym. The whisper of a kiss on my brow as I lay on my bed hoping I never woke up. The calming touch of a hand on my back as I puked my guts out in the bathroom at work. The phantom hand in mine as I walked like a zombie through the trail near my house. The voice in my head feeding me strength, hope.

"Please don't cry, Elle." His fingers stroked my back gently. "Your tears gut me."

I cried harder, clinging to him, tangling my hands in his hair, afraid to leave even an inch of space between us.

"If I call you baby, will you stop?" he teased, rubbing his hands across my shoulder blades.

The tears continued to fall, but amid the rush of my tumultuous thoughts, in a moment of vivid clarity, my mind pinpointed the emotion fueling my outburst—*wonder*. All for the man in front of me.

"Ash." My voice was a hoarse murmur. I pulled away, lifting my shirt to wipe my face. Turning back to him, I let my gaze linger as I studied him, noting every detail, mentally tucking each piece away, wanting to remember this moment for the rest of my life.

"Mangy Cat was right." I brushed my lips against his forehead. "Love is a beautiful risk worth living *and* dying for. You are my beautiful risk, Ash. I'm ready. Ready to take a chance on life again, ready to let the pain and emptiness go. I can't ignore the pull inside me anymore. From the moment I met you, I felt it—this invisible thread joining me to you, and it yanks me closer each time we're together. I don't want to fight it anymore." I moved closer, clutching his shirt at his chest. "I know the *how* of all of this is way beyond my realm of understanding, but I don't care about that right now. All I can see right now is you. All I want right now is you."

"Fuck, Tialla." His mouth crashed down on mine, his hands gripping my waist and pulling me closer. His lips slanted over mine with a desperate reverence, his tongue parting my mouth and delving inside. I wrapped my arms around his neck, savoring the taste of him, the warmth of his mouth moving against mine.

He pulled away slowly and brought his hands to either side of my face. "You're so beautiful, Elle. Inside and out. The moment I first laid eyes on you, I knew you were made for me."

"I feel the same." I reached for his hands. "It's this inexplicable truth that lives inside me—that your path and mine are the same, that you are the way *home*, if that makes sense." I squeezed his fingers. "Tell me you're my guy, Ash."

His eyes flashed. "I'm your guy, Elle. Always. Just like you're my girl." He rested his forehead against mine.

"Let's go home."

"Do you trust me?" he murmured against my ear.

"From the very beginning," I answered without hesitation.

"Close your eyes, Tialla," he commanded softly, and as I did, his arms encircled my waist, bringing us both to our feet. His lips brushed against mine just as a loud popping sound filled my head and my body was gripped with crushing pressure. But just as quickly as it had happened—mere seconds—it was over.

I opened my eyes and staggered backward. A wave of nausea hit me and I grabbed Ash's arm, waiting for it to subside. As my body stabilized, I looked up and blinked slowly, confusion overwhelming me. Where the hell were we? A city in the clouds. That's what it looked like. Futuristic. Majestic. All around us, and beneath us, floating islands drifted among the clouds, each one teeming with lush vegetation and brilliant color. Structures of gold, silver, and crystal rose from the foundations—some tall and narrow with magnificent spires, others wide and dome-shaped, a few of them adorned with massive slabs of spiraling crystal that gleamed in the brilliant sunlight. As I peered at the different islands, I caught glimpses of sparkling rivers and cascading waterfalls, magnificent gardens with connecting stone bridges, all through which billowing tufts of clouds drifted.

Phantom whispers floated on the breeze, sending shivers through me.

Nor Ren al Renala cotur precvi.

"Ash," I said, my voice filled with amazement, "what is this place?" I looked at him to find him equally perplexed, his eyes wide with wonder as he met my gaze.

"Would you believe me if I said I had no idea?" His voice was a low whisper.

My jaw dropped. "What? How could you not know? You brought us here, didn't you?"

He rubbed his wrist gently, his brows furrowed in confusion. "This isn't where I intended us to go. It's the Ethere—the magic is doing its own thing."

"Magic?" My eyes widened. As I looked behind him, I gasped and clutched his arm, my nails digging into his skin. The city was spread out before us in a circular formation, and in the middle of it all, a mammoth structure moved, rising from beneath us, shooting upward into the heavens. "What is that?" I cried as it continued to ascend before suddenly grinding to a halt.

Ash turned, and together we stared at the tower-like structure looming above us. Six massive golden pillars fanned out in a circle, covered with flowering vines, stretching up to an ornate, crystal platform at the summit. Atop the crystal slab, golden sculptures of two monolithic creatures—the likes of which I had never seen in my life—were perched back-to-back, their impossibly wide wings spread open. Bird-like in form, but with slightly longer necks, each one bore a small horn, curving upwards at the top of their heads. Their tail feathers were multi-layered, trailing down the tower, almost the same length as their bodies. Atop their heads, rows of long feathers spilled out, snaking down the length of their heads and necks like manes.

"I've seen similar creatures, but not nearly as magnificent as these," Ash said quietly.

"Wait, what? You've seen *similar* creatures?"

Before he could answer, a loud chime rang out through the air, emanating from inside the tower. I peered closer and spied luminous, spherical shapes through the pillars, hanging from the inside base of the platform, spiraling down through the center of the tower. Another chime pealed, followed by one more, and then the space around us shifted. The air splintered, and just like before, crushing pressure consumed me before abruptly ceasing.

Nausea once more rolled through me, and I hunched over, concentrating on not throwing up. Ash's hand snaked around my waist, holding me steady for a minute until my stomach settled. I straightened to find that we were standing in my kitchen.

I turned confused eyes to him. "What the hell was that? And how did we end up back here?"

"It's like the magic *wants* to reveal itself to you," Ash said quietly, more to himself than to me.

"Back up, baby." My eyes threatened to pop out of their sockets. "What magic are you talking about?"

He stared at me for a long moment, his green eyes glittering like emeralds. "You can't tell me you don't feel it, Elle. The cat, the woman with violet hair, Arazul . . . me—everything is connected."

My body erupted in chills at his words. Connected. The knowledge slammed into me. Ash was the missing link. I'd been completely clueless about what any of the strange things happening to me meant, but him being part of it made sense. What it all meant, though? I was at a loss.

"Do you understand what I'm trying to tell you?"

"Ash." My voice rose three octaves higher. "I have no idea what you're trying to say. You're gonna have to spell it out for me."

He clasped both of my hands in his. "I want you to put aside all that you've learned and consider for a moment that other realms exist in the universe—realms that contain not only civilized life and supernatural beings. . . but also magic."

He had to be joking, but even as I thought that, I was sure he wouldn't fabricate something like this. Not to mention that the part of me that claimed him as my own *sighed* in acceptance, as if finally, everything was falling into place.

"Think back to everything the cat told you, everything that the woman with violet hair and Arazul said to you, what you told me about Maya, your strange vision of Mags."

"And Liam," I whispered.

He frowned. "Liam?"

I swallowed slowly. "Yes. Last night when I relived the memory of his death, there was something new. It was terrifying, but what he said—it made no sense."

Ash crossed his arms, one hand rubbing his jaw thoughtfully. "What were his exact words?"

I closed my eyes and conjured the jarring memory. "*The Shadow King and Queens breathe again, Agaia. Winther comes. Catraia stirs. The Third Age looms. The Bells of Galeseira call you home.*"

He was silent for a long moment, considering my words. "He called you Agaia?" he asked quietly, his face blanching.

I nodded. "Do you know what it means?"

He ran his fingers through his hair. "Agaia, Catraia, the Third Age—I am familiar with, but the others I've never heard of."

I stared at him, twisting my fingers together in front of me. "Will you tell me what you know?"

He nodded. "I will tell you what I can." Reaching for my hands, he pulled me toward him. "But there are certain things that aren't mine to tell."

I looked at him with a question in my eye.

"You'll find out soon enough. I promise."

I beckoned for him to follow me into the sunroom. "I just realized something." I came to a stop in front of the couch. "Mangy Cat told me that there would be three tragedies, three visits, and three voices of reason." I stared at Ash, the truth of it apparent. "You were my third voice of reason. How did you know I needed you?"

He tucked my hair away from my face. "The bond that exists between us—the same one that allowed me to find you—it lets me see when you're experiencing extreme emotions."

"It's how you were always there for me before," I whispered.

He nodded, kissing my forehead as he pulled me down onto the couch next to him.

"Okay," I said tentatively. "Mangy Cat. Who or what is it?"

Ash cocked his head. "Well, where I'm from, the Mavigos, as we call them, are the divine will of the universe. Entities responsible for keeping the balance all across the cosmos. I believe the cat is a manifestation of them."

We are the life force of the universe, arbiters and overseers of that balance. The multiple voices that had issued from inside the cat had spoken those words with smooth aplomb. Oh god. The scrappy-looking stray really was telling the truth.

Ash shifted his body on the couch to face me. "This is what I can tell you. The origins of your true identity will be revealed to you soon, but it's something I can't share with you." His eyes pierced through me, and his lips twitched, as if struggling against the words he wanted to speak. "You are not from this world, Elle. You come from the same part of the universe as I do."

My nails dug into his hand as his words washed over me. *Not from this world.* He was confirming what Arazul, the violet-haired woman, Mangy Cat, Mags. and Liam had, in some form or the other, said to me, but it still rattled me.

"It's called the Sangelis." Ash pried my fingers from his skin and held them gently. "The Gods brought you here as a baby to keep you safe. You are destined for greatness, a being of extreme power, one who will shape the future of the Sangelis. The time for you to return is close; it's why all these strange things are happening to you. Your power is awakening inside you."

I stared at him, my mind a blur of thoughts. The Sangelis. Both Mags and Arazul had mentioned that name. Yes, all my strange encounters had spawned proclamations that this world was not where I belonged, that I had a powerful destiny, that I was powerful. But to hear Ash say it, it made it feel *real*, like it wasn't a mistake or crazy thing I'd hallucinated.

"But what about my parents? Were they not from here?"

"They were."

My eyes flew to his at the cryptic tone of his response. "Wait. What are you saying? That they weren't my parents?"

"Listen, Elle." He squeezed my fingers. "The truth is complicated, and it's not something I can divulge. In all the ways that matter, your parents were your parents. And nothing will change that."

My parents were my parents. But how could that be if this was not where I was from? I closed my eyes, mulling his words over in my mind. A quiet calm enveloped me, filling me with the assurance that Ash was right. Nothing could ever change the bond I had with my parents. They had belonged to me, and I to them.

"What about you?" My eyes flitted up to meet his gaze. "How do you fit into all of this?"

"You tell me." Hs gaze was so intense my heart thudded in my chest. "What do your senses tell you? Trust yourself, baby; you know the answer."

Mine.

A possessive declaration from the depths of my soul. Mine. That's what he was.

"In this Sangelis, you and I are meant to be together?" My pulse pounded in my ears as I waited for him to answer.

"Regardless of place, you and I are inevitable," he answered, sending full-body shivers through me.

In that moment, I *knew*—the same way I knew how to breathe, or blink, or think—that what he said was nothing but the simple truth. What I felt for Ash was deeper than physical attraction. It was an instinctive compulsion I couldn't and didn't want to fight.

"The place we just saw," I said, gripping his fingers, "I know this might sound stupid, but it . . . called to me."

His eyes flew to mine. "To me as well, but I've never been there before."

"You said something about magic being responsible?"

He nodded slowly. "Where I'm from, magic is a reality, the source of it powerful and matchless. It's responsible for creating life and maintaining balance in the Sangelis."

"And you can use it?"

His thumb grazed my knuckles. "Yes. It's how I was able to travel across realms to find you. This magic is a part of who you are as well. The power you have inside you has been dormant all these years, but an awakening has begun."

My eyes widened as I absorbed his words, but not in denial. Something was happening to me. I felt the stirring inside.

A thought struck me. "Does your magic have anything to do with why you never stay longer than a day or two?"

He intertwined his fingers with mine. "In part. Being away for any longer than two days will drain my power, but I also can't stay away for too long because of who I am and the responsibilities I shoulder."

Who he was. Of course. He had a life—his real life—outside of the limited time he spent with me, and god help me, that filled me with longing and jealousy.

As if sensing my thoughts, he pulled me toward him until his face was inches from mine. "It changes nothing, Tialla. Even when I'm not with you physically, you are always in my thoughts."

He placed his hand against my cheek and I leaned into his touch, his warmth seeping into my skin, his long fingers strong, yet gentle as he lightly stroked my face.

My body dipped forward as he suddenly jerked his hand away, clutching his wrist, as if in pain.

"Are you all right?" My gaze flew to his hand, my mouth dropping open. "Your . . . your wrist is glowing."

"Fuck," he muttered quietly.

"What is it?"

He turned rueful eyes to me. "Know how I just said that if I stay too long, it drains my magic?"

I nodded, my eyes flitting to his wrist once more, his skin pulsing with a faint blue light.

"If I use my magic while I'm here, it drains me faster. When we were swept away to the city in the clouds, it must have taken a considerable amount." He leaned in, gently clasping my neck. "I hate to say this, but I have to go." Frustration and regret lined his face. "I wish . . . I wish I had more time. Every time I leave you, it gets harder."

"It's okay, Ash." I wrapped my arms around his neck. "Just promise me you'll come back to me."

He ran his thumb across my jaw. "I promise, Tialla. As soon as I can." He lowered his head and kissed me, his lips soft and pillowy against mine. "If you hear my voice calling out to you," he whispered against my lips, "don't be afraid."

My mouth dropped open. "You can do that?" Why was I surprised? Of course he could do that. He had before. But not since I'd met him.

"Now that you know about me, there's no need for me to hide it from you."

"I hate when you leave." A pang of sadness clawed at my insides.

"Soon, Elle." He tangled his fingers in my hair. "Things will change and we will be together." He brushed his lips against mine one last time before slowly getting to his feet.

"I want to watch you go." I fought the urge to touch him again.

He nodded, and as I stared at him, his eyes began to churn with emerald flames. "Until I see you again, Tialla." He touched his wrist, swirling his fingers in a clockwise patten, his eyes never leaving mine.

I gasped as he abruptly disappeared, the space where he stood cold and empty, a replica of the place in my heart that was filled with warmth and happiness when he was with me.

Chapter 25

ASHER

Catraia, I called, sitting on the edge of Elle's bed.

The Lonefera's countdown pulsed gently on the wall above the ornate headboard. Almost six months gone.

I am here, Asher, she replied.

I stared at Elle's face, her serene expression unchanged since her consciousness was yanked away from me in the present and flung back to the past. Slowly, I reached my hand out and touched her cheek.

I can feel how deeply you miss her, Catraia said. *Just as I can feel the stable power of your bond rippling through the both of you.*

Are you reliving her memories alongside her? I asked.

I'm guiding her consciousness and keeping it stable where it is, but I am on the fringes, observing and learning.

Where is she now? I asked.

With you, she said. *Climbing a mountain . . . along with other things. Learning truths you revealed.*

Climbing a mountain? My eyes flew to Elle's face. Almost six months. That would put her into October. Our hike in the mountains. The memory of Elle's back against that tree—her legs wrapped around my shoulders, her pussy grinding against my face—flew unbidden into my mind, and a surge of desire tore through me. Fuck. It was the first time—well, in her world—that I'd tasted her, and she was just as delectable as the night she came to me through the Senshifter.

"Bash," Treye's voice rang out, cutting through my thoughts. I turned as he stepped into the room, excitement on his face.

"Ice and I found something in the library," he said. "You're going to want to see this."

I made to follow him out of the room, turning to look at Elle one more time.

Treye cleared his throat, drawing my attention. He pointed toward my crotch with a grin. "You might want to wait until whatever thoughts you were having die down."

I looked down to find myself still hard from my memory of Elle.

Treye stepped backward out of the room. "Please don't tell me you were thinking of having your way with her lifeless body."

I grimaced and adjusted my cock. "Don't worry, Treye. It won't come to that."

He chuckled. "I sure hope it doesn't. Especially with all the Gods coming and going around here."

Sorin and Arazul had been back twice since Sorin's dramatic entrance to see Elle. At the moment, all three of them—Sorin, Arazul, and Eolith—were in Breonwinn, Arazul's sanctum in the celestial plane, meeting with Twylos, Goddess of the Elements. Both Arazul and Eolith were convinced that the God of Chaos and the Goddess of the Night would band together with Kaliope and Gargmoin, and they wanted firsthand assurance that Twylos would not.

As I stepped into the library, Faron looked up from the polished stone table littered with scrolls and ancient texts.

"You have to see this, Ash." He slid a weathered scroll toward me.

I pulled out a chair and lowered myself onto it. "What am I looking at?"

"Ice and I have been looking through the old history of Ariadna, specifically the past Gloweyen Sovereigns."

"Right," Faron said. "Treye dug up the history of Rywin and Verah Valkyse from thirty-nine thousand years ago and I looked at Drakus and Symia Solanis from fourteen thousand years later."

Treye plopped into the chair next to mine and pushed a thick book toward me. "Here's a question," he said, stroking his trimmed beard. "The beasts of your Gloweyen bond—how did you learn about them?"

I frowned. "From Arazul and Eolith. After Elle came to me through the Senshifter and I sought out the Goddess Mother, she and the Great Creator told me about the celestial star etching, and what it meant for me and Elle. At that time, my coronation was already behind me, with the Ethereal Harmonies returning the two labrals after they read me. I knew what those two labrals signified. Eolith and Arazul filled in the gaps, explaining more about the Gloweyen connection. Why do you ask?"

Faron furrowed his brows. "Well, the one thing that the two sets of Gloweyen Sovereigns had in common was this." He handed me the scroll from on the table, and Treye pushed his book closer, pointing to a sketch at the bottom corner of the page.

"We think the beasts of their Gloweyen bond were *actual* beasts," Treye said.

I stared at the sketch of the creature on the scroll Faron had passed to me, flicking my gaze to the book on the table. "These are locarels. Creatures bonded to and protected by Eolith, but yes, they were also the symbols of the Gloweyen sovereignties. Ternyen, that's what it's called—the symbiotic connection that the Gloweyen Sovereigns had with them."

"Exactly." Treye's eyes were bright. "These were the beasts of their Gloweyen bonds."

"You're right," I said quietly.

"Wait, what?" Faron's jaw went slack. "You knew?"

I scrubbed my hand across my jaw. "It doesn't work the same way for Elle and me. At least, I don't think it will."

"What does that mean?" Treye turned in his chair toward me.

"Vix and Magnus—the beasts of our Gloweyen bond—are a part of us. They live inside us, where our power resides."

"Stop right there." A look of incredulity stretched across Treye's face. "Vix and Magnus? They have *names*?"

"Well, no—yes," I said. "Elle named them. She didn't like the idea of some nameless creature living inside her. She named hers first and then decided that she had to give mine a name as well."

Treye threw his head back and laughed. "I haven't formally met our future queen yet, but Gods, I really like her."

Faron chuckled, folding his arms across his chest. "Of course you would."

I smiled. "Okay, we're getting sidetracked here. What I was trying to say is this. At Elle's coronation, when we officially become joint Sovereigns of Valkyse, we are supposed to set the beasts of our Gloweyen bond free in Alonai, the lake of rejuvenation in Falayen. This is how we amass our Gloweyen powers. This is where things were different for the previous Gloweyen Sovereigns. They didn't have beasts *inside* them. When the Ethereal Harmonies returned matching labrals for them, their locarels emerged at their coronations and bonded with them. It was only after their coronation that they experienced Ternyen."

"So you don't think there will be physical beasts for you and Elle?" Faron's pale-blue eyes were thoughtful. Knowing him, he was probably running through various possibilities in his head.

I shook my head. "The beast of my bond awakened inside me the night Elle came through the Senshifter before my coronation."

Treye cocked his head. "So do you communicate with Magnus?"

"The beast of my bond—"

"Magnus," Treye interrupted.

I glared at him. "Magnus . . . is an extension of my power, and responds to me the way the rest of my power does, so no, I don't communicate with him in the traditional sense."

"But," Faron said. "I'm sensing a but."

"Definitely a but," Treye added.

I glared at them both. "*But* Elle communicates with Vix."

Treye chuckled. "Of course she does."

"The two of you are going to get along splendidly." Faron smiled and inclined his head toward me. "Drive Ash nuts."

"I can't wait." I shook my head. "Between, you, Tora, and Elle, there won't be a dull moment to spare."

"Hey, that's the way life should be," Treye said. "Anyway, back to what you were saying. Elle communicates with Vix."

I nodded. "Yes. She talks to Vix, feels her respond, sees the image of a big, slitted crimson eye when she calls her. When the God of Chaos took her in the Void and then at the market, she felt Vix's rage and protective power coursing through her."

"And you don't feel that with Magnus?" Faron asked.

"I do, but only where Elle is concerned. He responds to her, but it's more reactive than anything."

"It's because she talks to Vix." Treye drummed his fingers against the table. "I bet you anything that's what it is. She's more in tune with her."

"That being said," Faron mused out loud. "You think that Vix and Magnus will continue to be a part of you and Elle when you set them free in Alonai? What does that even mean? Set them free?"

I frowned. "That's the part I'm not really sure about. The lake of rejuvenation is the pure essence of the Ethereal Harmonies. We physically consummate our union there after her coronation, and so do the beasts of our bond."

"Wait one sweet celestial minute." Treye's slitted eyes were as round as saucers. "Vix and Magnus get it on? How does that even work?"

"Sadly, I didn't get specifics, but I'm thinking we unleash them inside us and they take over."

Treye clasped his hands together. "Please, Bash, for the love of all the Gods, provide us with us much detail as possible about what happens. I am entirely curious to know how *that* all unfolds."

"My days of kissing and telling are over, my friend," I said, crossing my arms.

"And sharing." Treye pointed his index finger at me. "You were definitely a handful in the unhinged days, as Faron and I so affectionately refer to that time."

I groaned. "Don't remind me. I'm not proud of who I was back then."

"But the women all loved you." Faron leaned back in his chair. "No doubt, they all secretly hoped to be the one to win your heart, to be your queen consort."

"Poor gals." Treye shook his head. "Little did they know that before Bash was even born, that position already belonged to someone else."

A surge of longing and possessiveness coursed through me as I thought of Elle. From the moment she had walked into my life, everyone else had faded away, and I belonged solely to her. It was as simple as that, really.

"Back to the previous conversation," Faron said, cocking his head, "don't you think it strange that your Gloweyen bond with Elle is different from the other Gloweyen Sovereigns?"

"I think it's because of the celestial star etching." I ran my hand through my hair. "The scale of power that we hold. We are chosen to be high Sovereigns over all of Ariadna, something that has never before happened. Unfortunately, there's no precedent for that. I don't think even the Great Creator and the Goddess Mother know what's supposed to happen. Only the Mavigos do."

"It makes me wonder if Tora knows, but can't say." Faron frowned, absently touching the scar above his lip. "What you told us about her taking your memory, this oath she spoke of—what more does it prevent her from saying? We know nothing about the First Age, and we are preparing for a war that will bring us face to face with ancient ones and dark Gods from that era."

"We're going in blind," Treye said.

I leaned forward on the table, resting my forearms against the edge. "Tora said that the craleic oath will be broken when Elle absorbs the light strain of the Old, Arcane Magic. When that part of her transformation is complete, we will have answers."

Faron grunted. "Hopefully it's not too late. It won't just be Tora we'll be looking to for answers; it'll be Lorien too. All this time, he's known, and he's never mentioned anything."

"If the craleic oath prevented him, how would he?" Treye asked.

Faron's question mirrored one that had been running through my mind since Tora returned the memory she took from me. I'd known Lorien pretty much all my life. The Lord of Dramhelm Manor had always been loyal to the Valkyse sovereignty. Next to Uncle Andreo, he was my closest advisor and mentor. I considered him a friend. And yet, in all the time I had known him, he had never mentioned the ancient celestial star etching, although, according to Tora, nothing prevented him from doing so with someone who was a part of it. Then again, Tora was the only one I'd told about the celestial star etching once the veil lifted and I was able to go to Elle. One thing was clear—once Elle was through this and the rebounding curse was broken, I needed to have a long talk with Lorien about what he knew.

As for the beasts of our Gloweyen bond, I was almost certain that Vix and Magnus would always reside within us. Elle and I—we weren't like the other Gloweyen Sovereigns who had shared a Ternyen connection with their bonded locarels. Our beasts were part of us. And why would that be the case if they weren't meant to be?

But perhaps I was trying to convince myself that's how it would be. Because buried in the back of my mind was the not-so-distant memory of a futuristic city in the clouds, a feeling of belonging, and two monolithic sentinels, wings spread wide, keeping watch.

Chapter 26

ELEYSE

DECEMBER 23: ONE YEAR, THREE AND A HALF MONTHS AGO . . .

"Do you want some more eggnog, Ovi?"

"Hmm?" I said, completely lost in my own thoughts, barely aware of Aggie talking to me.

Fifty-five days. That's how long it had been since I'd last seen Ash.

Fuck. I was dying inside. I didn't know how much longer I could go without laying eyes on him.

I had *spoken* to him every day since, though. The night after he left me, I was sitting on my couch with a tub of ice cream when I heard his silky smooth voice in my head.

Elle . . .

Soft, sultry, my name a caress against my mind. Although he had warned me before he left that I might hear his voice, I was so not ready. My skin immediately erupted with gooseflesh, my heartbeat ramped up in speed, and my senses became hyper-acute. As mind-blowing as it was for me to grasp, he could *see* me when he spoke to me, and I hated that it wasn't the same for me.

Every night after that, almost like clockwork, his voice would brush against my mind. I found myself living for those moments. Sometimes we would talk for a few minutes, sometimes he would stay talking to me until I fell asleep.

Although he never mentioned anything about it, I sensed an underlying current of tension in him when we spoke. Something was happening where he was and it had him on edge. He always brushed it off and assured me everything was all right, but I couldn't shake the feeling that something was wrong. And for some reason, that terrified me.

Whatever it was, it had kept him away. I went about my day-to-day life, but I felt lost and aimless, unsure what the hell I was even doing. The stirring inside me was restless, impatient, anxious to break free, and I didn't know how to settle it. Only when I was talking with Ash did it go quiet, as if his voice was the balm that soothed it into submission.

Ariadna. That's where he was. The first time he'd said the name, my heart had trilled, and a feeling of contentment had rushed through the gaping cracks inside me, flooding them with warmth. A vision of a forest lake popped into my mind, and I saw myself barefooted, walking along the water's edge, the bank strewn with silver leaves and violet blossoms. All around me, the most enchanting melody rang out, leaving me delirious with want.

Was it possible to yearn for a place you'd never been? To long for a life that you didn't know existed? I reckoned yes. Sometimes, I'd ask Ash to just talk to me about his life, and I'd close my eyes and listen, soaking in every word, my mind transporting me with unbelievable detail to the places he described.

Home, that stirring inside me whispered. I could smell the air, taste it. Hear the leaves as they rustled through the trees. Feel the magic in the air as it kissed my skin. And every day, the restlessness and hunger grew, like a bird that had outgrown the confines of its tiny cage. I longed to fly.

"Where in blazes are you?" Aggie's voice cut through my thoughts, her brown eyes flashing as she stepped in front of me.

"Sorry, Aggie." I extended my glass for her to top off my eggnog.

A small smile quirked her lips. "Dreaming about your handsome man-god again?"

I blushed, taking a quick sip of my eggnog. "I wish you could meet him."

She patted my hand lightly. "Don't sweat it, Ovi. If it's meant to be, it will happen." She sat on the couch in her sunroom next to me, her face suddenly growing serious. "Listen, I know tomorrow is Christmas Eve, and I just want to put this out there. If Ash doesn't show up, I want you to stay here with me for a few days."

My body tensed as I stared at her, holding my breath and letting her words wash over me. My skin grew prickly and hypersensitive, jagged tendrils of sorrow scraping against my heart.

The wicked burn of tears punched its way to the surface, my nostrils flaring as I sucked in a breath. I needed Ash. I hadn't said a word to him, not wanting to put him in an awkward position if he was unable to leave.

"Thanks, Aggie." My voice was a scratchy whisper as I swallowed the vicious lump in my throat. "I'd like that."

On my lap, my phone buzzed and I reached for it, my heart skipping a beat at his name lighting up the screen.

Ash.

I'm standing in front your house, but your lights are off inside, it read.

I lifted excited eyes to Aggie's. "He's here," I said, my voice a high-pitched twitter. "Can I bring him in to meet you?"

"I'd love nothing more, sweet girl. And I'm so happy I insisted that you dress up." Her brows furrowed in a frown. "That reminds me. When was the last time you went to Nina's?"

"Aggie," I growled.

"Never mind, never mind." She shooed me away. "Go on out there and get him."

My thumbs flew against the keyboard on my phone. *I'm next door at Aggie's. I'll meet you out front.*

"I'll be right back," I said breathlessly, sprinting toward the foyer.

I slipped on my boots hurriedly, my fingers shaking as I worked the zipper. A jittery rush of excitement pummeled me as I pulled my coat on and opened the door. The moment my feet hit the front porch, my heart careened in my chest. He stood at the top of the driveway, the sight of him ripping the breath from my lungs. Tall, imposing, wisps of soft, dark hair drifting across his forehead. Even from this distance, I could see the brilliant flare of those emerald eyes. The evening shadows sharpened the knife-edge angles of his jaw and cheekbones, burning the image of him into my corneas.

Dark angel.

Mine.

A long-sleeved shirt—sleeves rolled up past his forearms—clung to his broad frame, tucked into slightly tapered, form-fitting dress pants.

Of their own accord, my feet took off down the driveway in my high heels, and as I barreled into him, he lifted my legs and hooked them around his waist before gripping my thighs.

I trailed kisses across his face, tangling my fingers in his hair. "You came." My throat burned as tears threatened to swallow me.

He lowered me to the ground, one hand tightening on my waist as the other cupped my cheek gently. "Of course I came. I know how difficult tomorrow will be for you. Four days, Tialla. That's how long I can stay. I'll have to leave briefly after the second day to avoid draining my magic, but I will be back."

"Are you serious?" I squealed, wrapping my arms around his neck. "I don't know what to say."

He rested his forehead against mine. "I fucking missed you, Elle. This time, even more so than all the previous times, despite the fact that we spoke every day."

"I missed you too," I said, brushing my lips against his.

Suddenly remembering where we were, I tugged on his arm and pulled him down the driveway with me. "Come. I want you to meet Aggie."

He snaked his arms around my waist as we got the front door. "You look gorgeous, by the way."

"I know." I brushed my hand across my figure-flattering A-line dress. "Aggie made me dress up."

I opened the door and stepped inside, slipping off my coat and bending down to unzip my boots.

"Don't bother with that, Eleyse." Aggie poked her head in from the kitchen. "Leave those gorgeous boots on so your man-god can finally get a chance to enjoy you not looking like a hobo."

"Aggie!" I blushed as I heard Ash chuckle behind me.

"Don't worry, baby," he whispered in my ear. "You're the sexiest hobo this man-god has ever seen."

I swatted at him, letting out a soft huff. Taking his hand, I led him to the kitchen where Aggie stood at her island adding more cheeses and meats to her charcuterie board.

She looked up as we walked in, her face immediately lighting up with a welcoming smile. "Finally, I get to meet Ovi's handsome angel." She shot Ash an appraising look, her eyes drifting slowly across his form.

No question about it, Aggie had a commanding presence, oozing intimidation and confidence, but Ash met her gaze full-on, a soft smile curving his lips as he returned her scrutiny. Two alphas coming face to face, each sizing the other up. That's what it looked like as I watched them assess each other.

"Please, call me Ash," he said warmly, reaching his hand out.

She shook it, her handshake firm. "He's even more devastating up close," she said to me, slowly fanning herself with her hand. "I'm warm just thinking about the toe-curling sex you're going to have."

"Geez, Aggie," I cried, heat rising to my face.

Ash laughed, reaching for my hand as he turned to address Aggie. "If it's not toe-curling, why even bother, right?"

She smiled. "It's the only kind worth talking about."

"Okay, can we stop talking about sex?" I hissed.

Aggie chuckled, opening a container of blue cheese-stuffed olives. "I like watching her squirm," she whispered.

I groaned, rolling my eyes.

We stayed at Aggie's for another hour, the conversation flowing easily between her and Ash. It warmed my heart to see them hit it off. As we made our way to the front door to leave, she pulled Ash back, and from where I stood buttoning my coat, I could see their heads together, their expressions solemn as they spoke. Finally, she smiled and reached for his hands, giving them a gentle squeeze. He lifted her hand to his lips and lightly kissed it before making his way toward me.

Aggie drew me to her in a hug. "Listen, Ovi. Now that you won't be alone over Christmas, I think I'll go into the city for a few days. I haven't seen Carolyn and Daphne since our trip and it will be nice to catch up."

I pulled away to look at her. "You didn't have to stay because of me."

"I know I didn't have to, silly child. I *wanted* to."

Tears sprang to my eyes. "Thank you, Aggie. That means a lot."

"Remember what I told you before." She squeezed my hands. "Live, Ovi."

I squeezed back. "I will."

Chapter 27

ELEYSE

"What were you and Aggie talking about before we left?" I asked as Ash and I strolled arm in arm toward my house.

"She just warned me not to hurt you." He tightened his grip on me. "She cares about you, and I'm happy you have her."

"I'm sensing a but?" I studied his handsome face in the soft moonlight.

He was quiet for a moment as we crossed the street and walked toward my driveway. "I know you trust and confide in her, but I just want you to be careful what you share with her."

My heart dropped. Why would he say that? Did she say something? Did he not like her?

He stopped walking and turned me to face him. "I'm not saying this to worry you, but to protect you. The things that are happening to you—they're extraordinary and will sound far-fetched. Not everyone will be inclined to believe you. When I say be careful, I mean listen to your intuition. And this doesn't just apply to Aggie. If it doesn't feel right to share something with someone, don't."

"I trust Aggie, Ash. She is the one who urged me to be open-minded about all the strange things happening to me. Plus, I didn't tell her everything. I didn't mention anything about what happened the last time you were here."

He grazed my cheek with his thumb. "I'm not trying to make you doubt how she feels about you. It's clear that she cares about you." He brushed his knuckles across my jaw. "Honestly, baby. Trust your intuition. Go with your gut. Promise me."

"One hundred percent, my gut tells me I can trust her."

He kissed my forehead. "Then, that's all there is to say."

I looked up at the sky, my breath catching at the brilliant display of stars in the cloudless expanse. The moon hung low, dreamlike and cyclopean, the lambent orb a magnificent shade of orange ringed in a gossamer-soft halo of opaque light.

Somewhere overhead, an owl hooted. An inquisitive cry, as if it wondered why we courted the silky darkness. A gentle breeze drifted across my face, pebbling my skin and sending shivers scampering down my body. It had yet to snow, and God help me, I hoped it didn't. I hated white Christmases, the very thought of it filling me with sickening dread. Snow was a symbol of wanton destruction, of heartless brutality—there was nothing pure or innocent or cleansing about it.

As if sensing the dark turn in my thoughts, Ash pulled me to him, one arm across my back, the other clasping the back of my head. "Stay with me, Elle."

My eyes flicked to his, and instantly, the shadows in my mind scattered, leaving only him and the resolute promise of security. I scrambled to latch on to it, surrendering to the strength and assurance blazing in his gaze.

Leaning into his warmth, I inhaled slowly, my fingers fisting the unbuttoned collar of his shirt. "Do you remember what you told me that first night you took me to dinner?"

The air around us thickened, and goosebumps tore across my skin, my body shaking as the sensation of phantom fingers caressing my flesh consumed me.

His eyes flared a glittering shade of emerald. "I haven't forgotten. I made you a promise, baby." He traced my bottom lip with his finger. "A promise to make all your sinful fantasies come true."

"Ash," I choked out against the lump in my throat, fighting the salient burn making its way to the surface. Goddamn it. The emotion had come out of nowhere. I cleared my throat, swallowing my blistering tears. "I'm glad you made me wait. You were right. About everything. Sex was just a tool for me—an attempt to feel something that would chase the emptiness away, if only for a little while."

"And now?" He gripped my hair and brought my face closer.

I brushed my lips against his. "I'm ready. To take a chance on life again, to let the pain and emptiness go."

His pupils dilated, fervid shadows dancing across his face. "What else?" His voice was a sexy rasp, a cocktail of smoke and sin. I couldn't decide whether I wanted to sip and savor or gulp and swill.

My breath hitched under his heated gaze, and for the life of me, I could not look away. His lips curved in a slow smile, rousing the beast inside me, spurring my heartbeat to frenzied heights.

"Oh, angel. I'm ready for you. Ready to do sinfully dirty and indecent things with you. I want to lose track of space and time and explore all the decadence that magnificent body and cock of yours have to offer me."

His eyes blazed, and his grip on my hair tightened. "Fuck. I love it when you talk dirty to me."

"I'm tired of cold showers and taking matters into my own hands." I trailed my palms across his broad chest.

He growled, reaching behind me to cup my ass and pull me to him. "That makes two of us."

A soft moan escaped my lips, and my body writhed, fighting to get closer to him. I couldn't look away if I tried; the raw desire blazing in his gaze completely commanded my attention, making me forget everything else. My heart thudded erratically and my pulse quickened under his predatory scrutiny. My entire body tingled in anticipation, the air around us charged with dangerously high-voltage levels of unslaked need.

He grabbed my thighs and hoisted me up with ease. I'd never seen someone move so fast. In less than a second, we'd crossed the driveway, and my back was pressed against the front door.

"Shit." I fumbled in my bag for my keys, distracted by the throb of his erection against my thigh. My hips tilted, and keys forgotten, I slid myself against his hard length, savoring the exquisite friction between my legs as I moved against him. I closed my eyes and moaned, my hands slipping between us to stroke his cock through his pants.

"Something you want there, baby?" His breath was shallow as his fingers gripped the backs of my thighs.

I looked up at him through half-lidded eyes, a surge of triumph rushing through me at the unfiltered lust on his face.

Fuck.

That mouth.

Those lips.

I grew wetter just picturing their warm suction between my legs. I leaned forward and kissed him, drawing his bottom lip into my mouth and sucking gently.

Pushing against the door with my back, I moved my hands down to the hem of my dress, slowly tugging it up to my waist. Pulling the fabric of my lacy thong to the side, I slipped my fingers between my legs, my movements deliberate and lazy as I stroked myself, my gaze fastened to his face.

A muscle ticked in his jaw, and he exhaled sharply, his eyes glued to my fingers.

"Something you want there, baby?" My voice was low and sultry as I threw his words back at him.

"For the love of fuck," he growled, twisting the handle on the front door and barreling into the house, carrying me as if I weighed nothing.

"Wait, what? How?" I stared at him in confusion as he slammed the door shut.

"Does it matter?" he said gruffly, striding toward the kitchen.

All thoughts of how he'd opened the door evaporated with the predatory look in his eye. My heart raced in excitement, something inside me ecstatic that at last, the beast had come out to play.

He lowered my ass onto the edge of my kitchen island, spreading my legs wide as he stood between them. My heartbeat hammered in my ears as he smiled sinfully, pushing my chest down with his hand until I was flat on my back. Dragging a stool toward him, he sank into it, at the same time sliding my body further up the island.

Slowly, he slid his hands up my thighs to my hips, taking my dress with him. Hooking his fingers into the skimpy lace of my underwear, he tugged, tearing it from my body. I gasped, shifting my weight onto my elbows to look at him.

"You want to watch what I do to you?" His long fingers dipped between my legs into my slick arousal.

"Hell yes." I bit my lip to stifle a moan. I stared at the veins running along his forearms, slipping my fingers down to trace them.

One at a time, he lifted my booted legs, hooking them over his broad shoulders, all the while staring at me.

"Tell me what you want, Tialla."

"You know what I want," I whispered, my chest rising in shallow waves.

He smiled wickedly, his eyes crinkling at the corners. "You're not growing shy now, are you?"

"Not a chance." I lifted my hips off the island, angling for his face. "Your mouth, your lips, your tongue—on my pussy. That's what I want."

"Demanded like a true goddess." His eyes grew darker as they dipped lower.

"If I'm a goddess, you are the god who will destroy me." My breath hitched. "I want you to fucking ruin me, Ash."

His smoky voice washed over me. "Oh, trust me, Tialla, I intend to. When I'm done with you, you'll never doubt who you belong to."

I laughed, my voice husky with desire. "Oh, angel. I knew I was yours the first moment I laid eyes on you." Gripping his hair, I shoved his head down between my legs. "Now stop talking and take me to paradise."

His breath skated against my skin, and then his mouth was on me, his lips closing over my clit and sucking. I arched my back, my fingers digging into his hair. He released his suction, moving his mouth over me.

"Fucking nectar of the Gods," he rumbled, his fingers spreading me wider to grant him more access.

His soft groans as he feasted on me drove me wild. His tongue lapped at my entrance, teasing, probing, and then it was inside me, plunging in and out, the pointed tip brushing against my sensitive walls.

I lifted my hips restlessly, my eyes glued to the sight of him devouring me like he hadn't fed in forever. I touched his cheek with my fingers, and he lifted his head, a sheen of my arousal glistening on his lips. Looking at me, he dragged his tongue down my clit—once, twice, until I cried out. He fastened his mouth around the sensitive bud, swirling his tongue slowly as he added suction.

I lifted my hands and grabbed my breasts, my fingers reaching for my sensitive nipples.

"Ash!" The sensations swept me away, climbing and climbing, until my climax was just a stone's throw away. The heat of his mouth, tongue, his fingers moving inside me, the vibration of his groans against my skin—I was on fire. I flexed my legs, my hips grinding against his face, a bead of sweat prickling my brow.

"Fuck. I'm going to come." I arched my hips, my body bracing for the manic onslaught. I moaned, and in the next breath, the sensations came to an abrupt halt. I opened my eyes, confused and disoriented, heat swimming in my head.

He moved his mouth away, sliding up my body, trapping my hands above my head.

"What the hell, Ash?" Frustration flared through me.

"Not yet," he drawled, a devilish smile lifting his lips. "I'm going to take you to the brink again and again, and when I finally let you come, it will completely melt your mind. You won't even be able to string two sentences together."

My eyes grew wide. "You're gonna fucking edge me?"

"Is that what it's called?" he said nonchalantly, his eyes flashing with humor.

"This is not funny. Why are you torturing me?" I tugged on my wrists, trying to free my hands. "I've been waiting seven months for this. You're lucky I don't stab you in the back with these stilettos."

His eyes narrowed. "Trust me, baby. You don't know what torture is. Seven months is but a drop in the bucket." Capturing both my wrists with one hand, he slid the other down my body. "I'll make a deal with you." His tongue trailed down my neck. "I'll let you come the fourth time." His fingers slid between my legs, delving into my slickness again.

My hips thrust forward, seeking the silken magic of his touch. His fingers teased my clit, stoking the fire in my belly to life once more. He brought his mouth to mine, and immediately I opened, tasting myself on his lips as his tongue slipped inside. I sucked greedily, my hands desperate to touch him, but his hand still held me captive.

My mind raced. This fucker thought he knew my body? Ha. I'd show him. As he continued to work me with his fingers, I stilled my movements, clenching only my inner muscles in even pulses. I slowed my breathing and focused on the feel of his mouth on mine, our tongues tangling, his fingers swirling against my core, hitting that goddamn sweet spot with every rotation.

The pleasure inside me intensified, and sweet merciful God, it was all-consuming. It was all I could do *not* to move my hips. He broke the kiss, and my eyes flew open, missing the contact at once. His emerald eyes stared into mine, and bloody hell, I lost it. That gorgeous face was my undoing.

He smiled softly as he continued to touch me, and my breathing ramped up.

"You can't hide your desire from me," he whispered. "I know you're close."

My breath hitched, my eyes drifting shut as I focused on the building pleasure fluttering through me. Okay, so I'd have to wait two more times. I could do it.

I whimpered as the delicious pulsing intensified, rocking my hips, feeling my release approaching.

"Ash," I moaned, and just like before, he withdrew his fingers before letting me finish. On instinct, I locked my legs around his waist in a death grip, grinding my hips against him, taking the friction any way I could get it—his thigh, the edge of his cock, the leather of his belt, the fabric of his pants. I laughed and moaned in his face as my orgasm erupted, shaking me to my core. My body arched and spasmed as I shook with the force of my release.

His soft chuckle drifted to my ears. "You little thief," he growled in mock menace. "You totally stole that from me."

"I totally did, baby." I sighed as he released my hands. Winding my arms around his neck, I brought my mouth to his, tasting the warm amusement on his lips.

He pulled me up with him, wrapping his arms around my legs as he carried me to the sunroom. Lowering me to the ground in front of the couch, he turned me around, his fingers deftly working the zipper at the back of my dress. He lifted my hair, trailing kisses down my neck as he slid the fabric off my shoulders. It fell with a soft swoosh to the floor.

I shivered as his fingers grazed against my back, unclasping my bra. His teeth gripped the strap at one shoulder, easing it down, repeating the action with the other side, until my bra joined my dress at my feet.

He turned me once more, and I stood in front of him, wearing nothing but my knee-high stiletto boots. The hungry look in his eyes was enough to send fresh waves of desire rolling through me.

"You are so fucking beautiful, Elle." His voice was heavy with need. He walked me backward, guiding me to the sofa's edge. As I sat, he kneeled at my feet, lifting one of my legs over his shoulder. Slowly, he unzipped my boot, tugging it off my foot. Repeating the action with the second one, he leaned back on his heels and let his gaze drift over me.

Quickly, he rose, pulling me to my feet with him. I stood facing him, my body trembling with desire. He was so much taller than I was. Standing in my bare feet, the top of my head barely came up to his shoulders.

"Oh god." My fingers shook as they reached for him. "You have no idea how much I've fantasized about undressing you."

"I'm all yours, Tialla." His voice was all silk and shadows, his eyes blazing with restrained hunger.

I tugged his shirt out of his pants, slipping my fingers underneath, running my hands across his hard stomach, and then over his chest. Taking my sweet-ass time, I undid each button, savoring the slow reveal of golden skin. I ran my fingers down the center of his chest before reaching my hands up and slipping the material off his shoulders.

I stared at his broad form, the curve of his biceps, the rippling muscle across his chest and stomach, the sexy V at his hips. Fuck. He was perfect. Made-in-heaven perfect. Or in a laboratory perfect. My body grew warmer as I studied him.

"I heard someone say once that women weren't visual creatures like men." I ran my palms across his chiseled chest. "That we didn't get aroused by sight." I stepped closer, teasing my nipples against his torso. Shit, he was tall. "That person was a bloody idiot, because I've never been so aroused by what I see."

He brushed his fingers across my collarbone. "The feeling is mutual, baby."

I moved closer, yanking on his belt to undo the buckle. I unzipped his pants and slid them down. His erection jutted against his boxers, and I swallowed the moan before it floated past my lips. I dropped to my knees, my eyes flicking up to meet his. His body was rigid, his fists clenched at his sides.

"Don't you fucking deny me this." I reached for the waistband of his underwear and pulled it down. His cock sprang free, almost hitting me in the face. Holy shit, he was perfect. Girth. Length. Every vein running down him. I wrapped my fingers around his shaft, his skin warm and smooth as I glided my hand down every glorious inch. He sucked in a breath as I cupped his balls, and I smiled, fisting his cock with my other hand. Swirling my finger across the tip, I swiped the thread of precum, spreading it around the sensitive ridge. I lowered my head, slipping my tongue out to lick the tip. He groaned softly, his fingers gripping my hair.

Spurred on by his response, I wrapped my lips around the head of his cock and sucked, sliding my mouth down his length.

"Fuck," he growled, his fingers tightening in my hair. I lifted my eyes to meet his as I moved my mouth over him, my hand working in unison to grip all of him. Hollowing my cheeks, I sucked harder as I slid my mouth up and down, my hand taking on what my throat couldn't.

Who would have thought that being on my knees with a cock in my mouth would make me feel powerful? But as I stared up at Ash, my beautiful man-god, completely at my mercy, his eyes a vortex of lust and wild need as he held on to my hair for dear life, I felt invincible.

"Elle," he groaned, closing his eyes in contentment.

I sucked harder. He shuddered, his hips thrusting slowly. I moaned, urging him on. His body tensed, and he pulled away, lifting me to my feet.

"I wasn't done," I protested, feeling the scowl settle over my face.

His lips quirked in a cocky grin. "You can suck my cock to your heart's content later." He cupped my breast, his thumb rolling over my nipple. My back arched and I leaned into him, seeking more of his touch.

My eyes drifted across his body once more, my blood heating as I drank him in. He was so mind-numbingly sexy—a magnificent specimen of a man—and I glowed in triumph that he was mine, at least in the here and now where nothing else mattered. I reached for him again, twisting my fingers in his thick, dark hair. His hard length pressed against my stomach, and I pushed closer, wanting more.

"Close your eyes," he whispered, and I obeyed, my palms flat against his chest, my heartbeat pounding in my ears as the seconds ticked by.

"You can open them now," he said a few moments later.

As my eyes flew open, I gasped at the sight in front of me. Soft light spilled from a sea of candles hovering around the room, suspended in midair by . . . *nothing*. On the floor, where my couch was before, was a mass of plush blankets and pillows, spread out luxuriously, decadently inviting.

I wrapped my arms around his neck. "You truly are fucking magic."

"Hardly, baby." He walked me backward and lowered me down onto the blankets with him. I shimmied up the pillows, opening my legs to welcome him. Our breaths were frenzied and shallow, and when he kissed me, it was savage and wild, our tongues and teeth going to battle, victor take the spoils.

I matched his intensity with my own, wrapping my legs around his hips and gripping his ass with my hands. Holy hell, he was hard and sculpted everywhere. I couldn't draw for shit, but man, would I kill for him to pose for me.

His mouth traveled down my body to my breasts, his tongue circling and flicking over one nipple while his fingers caressed the other. I moaned and arched my chest up to meet him, gripping his hair as he moved his mouth to my other breast.

His voice was low and guttural as he pulled away and looked at me. "Show me what you want, how you want it, Tialla. This is all about you."

He read my body like an open book as we clung to each other skin to skin—fingers, lips, mouths, tangled limbs all seamlessly undulating within the spiraling vortex of our turbulent passion. I couldn't get enough of him. I moaned, begged, bit, clawed, whispered in his ear all the depraved things I wanted him to do to me, embodying the wanton hellion he had awakened in me seven months ago. God only knew what deep, dark tomb she had been hibernating in before that.

He indulged me, teasing, taunting me as we kissed, our exploration of each other a playful banter and single-minded discovery rolled into one. I couldn't pry my eyes away from his mouth—sensuous and alluring—as his lips slowly snaked a path down my body. The touch, taste, smell, sound, sight of him in his hedonistic splendor waged a full-fledged assault on my senses.

My heart flailed madly, and I reveled in the feel of his hard, chiseled body against mine, his reverent worship of every inch of me with his hands and mouth. He set me ablaze, my body humming and vibrating on the same sphere of existence as his.

His hand slid lower until his fingers plunged into my wetness, and I gasped as he began circling his fingers slowly over me. *More! More! More!* my mind screamed, and something primitive inside me roared with a savage hunger when I began to pulse around his fingers.

"Ash," I moaned.

His fingers swirled over my clit. "Tell me, Tialla."

"Please fuck me." I reached between our bodies to wrap my fingers around his rigid cock. "I need to feel you inside me."

His lips curved. "When you ask so prettily, how can I say no?"

He nudged my legs open wider with his knees and lined himself up at my entrance. Slowly, I guided him into me, shuddering with pleasure as his length slowly filled me. Sweet merciful god. The feel of him sliding into me was my undoing—more mind-shattering than my darkest fantasies.

"Gods, Elle," he groaned, his voice a strangled rasp. "This is magic; *you* are magic." His hips rocked against mine, pushing deeper into me, and I met him thrust for thrust, matching his tempo in our primal dance, our eyes locked together as we raced toward our fevered destruction.

Tightening my legs around him, I shivered, pulling him even deeper into me. We moved together in a frenzied rhythm, my body on fire now as the silky length of him slammed into me. I bit down on his shoulder to keep from crying out, and he paused for a moment, searching my face.

"No inhibitions." His eyes smoldered as they held my gaze. "Don't hold anything back from me. I want all of you."

My heart raced at his words and at the raw desire in his eyes, and I kissed him with parted lips, my tongue searching for his. He deepened the kiss and we began our carnal dance again, my body meeting his thrusts with a wild abandon.

"Harder," I cried out, my fingers digging into the muscles on his back.

"Have at it, baby." He rolled onto his back, pulling me on top of him. A surge of power coursed through my body as I pushed myself up to a sitting position on top of him. I surveyed him from that vantage point—this beautiful, powerful man beneath me, at my command—and a wave of unbridled lust coursed through me.

He reached out his hands and cupped my breasts, pinching my nipples with the sweetest amount of pressure. I threw my head back, reveling in the pleasure rippling through me at his touch. "Don't fucking stop."

His cock pulsed inside me and I began to rock my hips, controlling how fast and hard I wanted to go. Grabbing my waist, he pulled me down with each thrust, deepening the contact. I ground my hips against his and began to move faster. His thumb slid between us to where our bodies were joined, finding my clit. Pleasure exploded inside me, my body writhing at the contact as the momentum continued to build. He lifted himself onto his elbows, and the shift in position made me see stars, pushing him deeper inside, allowing me more control in maneuvering. I straddled that exquisite line between pleasure and pain, greedily taking all he gave me. Leaning forward, I rubbed my nipples against his chest, cupping his face in my hands and kissing him. His emerald eyes were dark and stormy, and I delighted in watching the pleasure playing out on his face.

We locked gazes, beads of perspiration glistening on our skin. Faster and harder we moved, and as the heightening sensations rocked my body, I could not tear my eyes away from his. An image flashed in my mind of the two of us in another place and time—bathed in a pool of light and color, performing this same frenzied dance—and as the floodgates of my climax burst open and overpowered me, I saw myself screaming out his name in that vision as I screamed out his name in the present moment. He shuddered as he found his own release, emptying himself inside me. He gripped my arms tightly and moaned my name, pulling my body down on top of his. I refused to let go, clinging to him for dear life, convinced that if lightning were to strike me dead right now, I would die happy.

I interlaced my fingers with his, my body jerking and shaking with the aftershocks of my orgasm. Flipping me onto my back, he shifted onto his side and kissed me tenderly. My hands wandered over his hard chest and shoulders, traveling up his neck before tangling in his hair. His heartbeat thundered against mine, and his hand stroked the side of my breast, trailing down to cup my ass.

We lay there in sated silence, watching the flickering candlelight cast lazy shadows on the wall, our bodies appeased, our warm limbs tangled together.

He kissed my fingertips. "Are you okay?"

I nodded. "More than okay." A flood of emotion rushed in, causing my voice to crack.

"Hey." He rolled, turning us on our sides.

My vision blurred, and I swiped at my eyes.

"It couldn't have been that bad." His voice was light and teasing.

"Fuck, Ash," I cried, tears slipping down my face. "I'm in so much trouble."

"Tell me, Elle." His eyes were filled with worry and concern.

I shook my head. "No. That'll only make it real."

He brushed his palm across my jaw. "You can tell me anything, Tialla."

Anything. Bloody bastard. He was right. There was nothing I couldn't share with him. He was the missing part of me. I gripped his fingers in mine, my throat burning with the weight of the words waiting to be spoken.

"I fucking went and fell in love with you."

His eyes flared as he sucked in a breath, a myriad of emotions washing over his face.

"This was no itch that needed to be scratched. This was passion and power. Hope and healing. I know this might sound ridiculous, but it wasn't just our bodies that joined. It was our hearts and souls too. I felt that connection snap into place, felt the rightness of it all." I gulped, inhaling a deep breath. "I am in love with you, Ash, and I'm scared to death that it will destroy us both."

His body stilled for a moment, but then he lowered his head and kissed me, wrapping me in his arms. The reverence and tenderness in his touch made my heart ache. "I know how terrified you must be, Elle, but I want you to know that I'm here with you every step of the way." His green eyes shone with fiery intensity. "I have been in love with you for longer than you know, Tialla. Heart, body, and soul." My body felt boneless as his heated gaze bore into mine, the depth of his emotions seeping out of him. "Trust me, baby." He rested his forehead against mine. "Love is our salvation, not destruction."

My heart skipped a beat at his words, and I pulled him closer. After living for so long like a wraith wandering through life aimlessly, I didn't ever think I'd welcome love again. Aggie was right about Ash. He was a game changer, and as for what he just said—God help me, I fucking believed him.

Chapter 28

ELEYSE

DECEMBER 24: ONE YEAR, THREE AND A HALF MONTHS AGO . . .

My bladder was about to burst. I groaned and opened my eyes, the weight across my middle adding to the pressure gripping me. As the fog cleared in my mind, last night came rushing back.

Ash.

I looked down to see his forearm curled around my waist. I was lying on my side, and from the furnace heating my back, so was he. I closed my eyes, wanting nothing more than to wiggle closer into the warmth of his body, but I needed to pee, like yesterday.

Lifting his arm away as gently as I could, I scooted over to the edge of the blankets, daring to peek back at him. His eyes were still closed, his chest rising and falling steadily. I suppressed the urge to touch his face, my body screaming at me to get my ass moving.

Quietly, I made my way through the sunroom, rushing past the powder room, opting to use my bathroom upstairs. *Don't pee, don't pee, don't pee,* I chanted, making a mad dash the last ten feet as I darted through my bedroom.

I groaned in relief as I plopped onto the toilet and relieved myself. Frigging close call. After I was done, I headed to the bathroom sink, washed my hands, and brushed my teeth. I stared at my face in the mirror. Despite my smudged makeup, I liked what I saw. My eyes were bright, a smile hovered on my lips, and I looked lighter. Happy.

I was in love with Ash. I *loved* him.

My heart thundered in my chest just thinking about it. Last night was so much more incredible than I could have ever imagined. God, I had never had this much sex in one night before. We had both been insatiable, hungry for each other. Fast, hard. Slow, tender. Light, teasing. We'd shifted from one extreme to the next with ease, like two selkies changing skins. It was after four a.m. when we finally settled down to get some sleep.

I washed my face and wiped my makeup off, ran a hairbrush through my long, dark hair, slipped on my robe and belted it, and then headed back downstairs. The clock in the kitchen flashed 8:45. My feet skidded to a halt at the entrance of the sunroom, the breath whooshing out of me as I caught sight of Ash. He lay on his back, a blanket loosely covering his hips. His eyes were still closed, and I moved toward him, drawn to him as I always was. God, he never ceased to take my breath away.

I stopped at the edge of the blankets, slowly crawling on my hands and knees before lowering myself on top of him, straddling his thighs. My gaze snagged on a raised, crescent-shaped mark on his hip. I traced my thumb over it, the skin there soft and smooth. A birthmark. Or a scar.

At my touch, he cracked an eye open and looked at me, a lazy smile drifting across his face as his hands drifted up to cup my ass. "Is this for me?" He tugged the hem of my robe. "A pretty present, even wrapped up with a bow?" His fingers trailed up to the belt of my robe.

A wave of desire flanked me at the seductive tone of his voice. Beneath me, his cock twitched, and I gyrated my hips over him, my body moving with a mind of its own. He pulled the bow I had knotted on my robe, gripping the material and sliding it off my body.

His eyes flared with lust. "Fuck. I will never get tired of looking at you."

I lowered my upper body and brushed my lips against his, my eyes widening in surprise. "You taste like mint and berries."

His lips quirked in a smile. "You have an aversion to mint and berries?"

"No one tastes like mint and berries in the morning." I stared at him, trying to work it out in my head. He hadn't moved since I left him. At least I didn't think he had. I gasped. "Is it magic? Like how you opened the lock on my door? The candles? The blankets? You can make things happen without moving a muscle."

His fingers trailed circles on my thighs as I sat back upright and rested my hands on his stomach. Grabbing a pillow, he fluffed it and placed it behind his head. "There are varying degrees of magic, but yes, all those you mentioned were possible because of magic."

I raised my brows. "How does it work?"

"Well, simple magic is the most basic magic I can wield. Anything pertaining to my physical needs, I can take care of with simple magic. Basic hygiene, satisfying hunger, thirst."

"What if you needed to use the bathroom?"

"I can choose to use it, or I can use simple magic."

My jaw dropped open. "Holy crap, that's incredible. Can everyone use magic in Ariadna?"

He shook his head. "No, not everyone can."

"So what you're saying is that you're special."

"Different." His hand slid up my shoulder. "Houses, too, can be imbued with simple magic to take care of anyone staying there."

I stared at him in wonder. There was still so much that I didn't know about his life and the world he was from. Over the past month and a half, he had told me bits and pieces, and I sensed it was more to not overwhelm me rather than keeping anything secret from me. I still had a lot to learn.

I trailed my fingers over his chest, marveling at the ripple of muscle against my skin. Slowly, I moved lower, tracing every one of his abs, smiling as his body clenched against my fluttering touch.

"Do you want me to tell you about other types of magic?" His fingers slipped between my legs, igniting the flame inside me once more, stealing my curiosity away.

"Later," I gasped, placing my hand over his as I watched him stroke me. "For now, I just want your cock and your fingers to work their magic." I lifted slightly onto my knees, reaching beneath me to grip his hard shaft. With one swift move, I guided him inside me and lowered my body until he was fully sheathed.

He rolled and flipped me over, pinning me between his arms. "That's my favorite kind of magic to wield."

I sighed, my body melting into a puddle as I let him sweep me away with him.

It was past noon by the time we got out of bed. A quick shower turned into a lazy session of hot, steamy sex—both figuratively and literally—and by the time we finally left the house to head into town, it was almost two p.m.

As we sat at the popular Mystic Diner on Bell Avenue watching people scurrying past on the streets—most of them laden with last-minute Christmas presents and packages—the excitement in the air was palpable. In the diner, Christmas carols blared over the speaker system, while people around us laughed and chatted. The air was light and airy.

I gritted my teeth, fighting the sudden stroke of sadness strumming my heart like the bow of a cello drawing out a mournful bass melody. Since my parents' death, not one Christmas Eve had gone by that held any real joy for me. This day was forever tainted with the horror of their loss.

Lowering my eyes to my food, I swirled a French fry through the dollop of ketchup on my plate. I looked up to find Ash studying me thoughtfully as he took a bite of his steak sandwich.

"Is it any good?" I inclined my head toward his food. "I mean, does the food here even compare to what you eat on Ariadna?"

He swallowed the bite he was chewing. "It's not bad," he said, "but it's . . . different than what I'm used to. The food on Ariadna bursts with flavor, tastes fresher." He took another bite. "You'll see for yourself." He tilted his head to the side. "Soon."

Soon. I still found it hard to believe that there was another reality that awaited me. All I had known was this life. The life that for so long I had longed to escape. Especially on days like today that were a stark reminder of what I'd lost.

Ash reached across the table and touched my hand. "There's something I want to share with you," he said softly, drawing my gaze to his. "I think it'll help you understand why I can relate so deeply to your sadness." He hesitated for a moment before continuing. "I haven't mentioned this before, but like you, I lost both my parents on the same day."

My eyes widened. What? He'd talked about loss multiple times before, but I hadn't wanted to pry. What had he said the first time we met? That he knew what it was like to feel dead inside? "I . . . I'm so sorry, Ash."

His eyes swirled with emotion. "It was my birthday." He huffed a laugh. "What a day, right? I was lost for a long time after their deaths, but I realized that's not what they would have wanted for me. So now, every year on that day, I start the day off by remembering the things I loved most about them."

Fuck. He looked so vulnerable in this moment. It couldn't have been an easy thing to share such an intimate glimpse into his life.

He traced slow circles on the back of my hand. "There is power and healing in remembering why you loved someone you lost. With my father, my love for him was grounded in his patience, humility, and steadfast belief in the inherent goodness of others. With my mother, it was her compassion and the wild, carefree way she embraced life. Nothing daunted her; she was fearless."

His face lit up talking about them, and the bittersweet emotion pouring out of him made my heart clench.

He squeezed my fingers. "Tell me about your parents, Elle. What did you love most about them?"

I exhaled loudly, glancing out the window. Across the street, a little boy walked between his parents, laughing as they held on to his hands and swung him between them. Pure, uninhibited innocence. I couldn't even remember what that felt like.

I looked up at Ash, his eyes filled with encouragement and

understanding. "I was so young when they died. Sometimes I feel like I don't truly remember who they were, that my mind has created memories, impressions, wishes, to fill the gaps."

Absently, I stirred my glass of water with my straw. "When I close my eyes and allow myself to remember, the love is what hits me the hardest. They loved each other so much, and they loved me. That love was a living, breathing thing with a life of its own." I fidgeted with a strand of my hair. "Music is the next thing. My life with them was filled with it. They were both opera singers. They breathed and lived music, and according to them, even from before I learned to speak, I was drawn to that world."

As I glanced up at Ash, I was taken back by the depth of emotion on his face—compassion, understanding, devotion, longing. That look slipped past my defenses and into my heart, prying loose the hold the thorny claws of grief held me in.

"Love and music. Don't you see, Elle? You carry that with you; you carry *them* with you, even though they're no longer here." He intertwined his fingers with mine. "You've given this day so much power over you, and I can assure you that never in a million years would your parents have wanted that for you. Healing comes when you let go of the attachment to your grief, to the significance you apply to things. Do you think your parents would be happy that you hated Christmas? That they would be okay with how completely broken you are this time of year? Do you think their hope for you would have been for you to spend your life mourning their loss and not finding happiness?" He squeezed my fingers. "These are all questions I asked myself about my own parents regarding the dark choices I made after their deaths, and I know with certainty that a path filled with darkness and misery is not the one they would have wanted for me. And so I chose to change. I honored them by moving on and finding purpose in my life, becoming someone they would be proud of."

You betray the ones you love with your self-loathing and contempt for life. Arazul's words rattled around in my mind.

Ash, Arazul, the violet-haired woman, Mangy Cat, Aggie—they were all right. I lived my life as if I was the sum of all my losses and nothing more.

Grief, guilt, anguish, anger—I had assimilated them into the very core of who I was. I was so caught up in my own despair that I never really stopped to think about what my parents, Mags, and Liam would have wanted for me. I just focused on what I wanted for myself—to suffer, to die.

I didn't want that anymore, though. I wanted to live. To love. To be happy. I wanted a life like that with the man in front of me.

"I want that, Ash." I leaned forward, tears blurring my vision. "I want to live. To make them proud, to find purpose in my life. I want a chance at happiness. I want *you.*"

He reached out his hand to brush my tears away. "So claim it all, baby. Every single thing. Including me. Yours for the taking."

My heart stuttered, grappling with the mindless fear that suddenly lashed out, fighting for dominance over my emotions. I looked into Ash's eyes, locking onto the love and devotion swirling there, and I did what I had been unable to do since the day my parents died.

I let go.

I didn't want to be afraid anymore. I wanted to be free.

"I love you, Asher Valkyse." I lowered my head to kiss the back of his hand still intertwined with mine.

His eyes flared, a shimmer of green ringing his bright irises. "I love you, too, Tialla."

I smiled at him. "There is so much—"

"Ellie?" a voice rang out.

My entire body froze. I turned toward the edge of the booth we sat in to find two piercing hazel eyes gazing down at me in surprise. Blinking slowly, my heart ramping up in speed, I stared up at the mass of curly brown hair; the smooth, tawny skin; the tall, willowy frame; the smile that had captured the hearts of so many over the years. It couldn't be. My eyes slid back up to her face, hungry now as I drank in as much detail as I could. Everything about her looked the same, down to the small, serrated, crescent-shaped scar on her jaw she had gotten from falling onto a bottle cap when we were fourteen.

"Char?" I said, my voice a hoarse whisper, the air around me stifling and hot.

I slowly slid from my seat, standing to face her. My mind was a blank, shock and dread washing over me, quickly clearing a path for shame and guilt.

"Holy shit, Ells, I thought I'd never see you again." She threw her arms around me and pulled me to her.

She smelled exactly the way I remembered. Like brown sugar and vanilla. Like warm summer nights spent outdoors watching fireflies flitting through the tall cattails at the edge of her house. She smelled like home. Safety. Friendship. I fought the urge to hug her back. I didn't deserve her embrace, the warmth seeping out of her as she held on to me.

Charlotte.

Right here. Standing in front of me. Surprise didn't even begin to describe what I felt. And for the life of me, I didn't expect the sharp ache ripping through me, stemming from a pain anchored deep in my heart. A sense of wrongness overcame me, my stomach roiling in rebellion.

Something was missing.

Someone.

Liam.

Our entire friendship, Liam was the glue that held the three of us together. And while we were inseparable as a threesome, there was another entity that came into existence outside our precious trinity. Liam and me. And the horrid realization coursing through me now as I stood there with my other best friend's arms around me was that without Liam here, being with Charlotte felt *wrong*.

Fuck. I was a horrible person.

It wasn't her fault that Liam had died. Or that I had the emotional fortitude of a gnat. She didn't deserve the way I had cut her out of my life afterward. Yes, first and foremost, it was to save her life. After the elevator accident that had almost killed her, I knew I needed to cut ties with her, but maybe on some level, I was selfish, too, because she was too much of a reminder of what I had lost, and I couldn't handle that.

"Charlotte, I'm . . ." My throat constricted with emotion.

She pulled back, gripping my shoulders as her hazel eyes stared intently into mine. "Don't say it, Elle. I understand why you left. It hurt like a bitch, but after the accident, it didn't surprise me that you bolted. Was I angry? Yes. Did I worry about you? Absolutely. Was I afraid that you might not even be alive? Of course. But this is not the time or place for us to unpack any of that. Let's just focus on you and me in this moment. The past can wait for its reckoning."

I nodded as she clasped her hands in mine and squeezed.

She turned to look at Ash, her eyes flickering with surprise as she appraised him slowly. "Wow, Ells, you sure know how to pick them. First, Liam, and now this gorgeous specimen." Her hand flew to her chest. "Damn, girl. Leave some for the rest of us."

"As if." My lips twitched in a smile. "You've gotten every guy you wanted since we were twelve."

She rolled her eyes. "I think you're exaggerating a little."

I shifted my gaze to Ash, his eyes warm and supportive, something unspoken passing between us that filled me with calm. "Ash, this is my oldest friend, Charlotte. Char, this is Ash."

Ash stood, reaching out his hand in greeting. "Nice to make your acquaintance, Charlotte. I've heard wonderful things about you."

Her brows lifted. "Wow. Imagine that. And here I thought Elle had forgotten all about me."

I flinched, a surge of guilt twisting in my gut.

Charlotte looked at me with curiosity, arching a perfectly shaped brow. "So, is Ash . . . just a friend? Cause I'm sensing a whole lot more brewing between the two of you."

Charlotte. Blunt as ever, even after all these years.

I smiled. "He's more than a friend." I met Ash's gaze. "Much more."

She cocked her head and looked at me, a range of emotions washing across her face. For the briefest of moments, a glimmer of something I couldn't quite place sparked in her gaze, but it was gone so quickly, along with my unease, that I doubted it was even there to begin with.

Her face lit up with a bright smile, and she squeezed my hand. "I'm really happy you moved on, Elle. I didn't—"

"Charlotte," a voice called out, and I turned my head toward the front door where a tall man with blond hair and a pretty, petite redhead were looking our way.

"Oh, crap. I've got to run," she said, reaching for her purse. "Give me your number, Elle. I'll be in Hargrove for another two weeks and I'd love to catch up."

My heart thudded again. Catch up. Did I want to catch up? I shook my head, chasing the terrible thought away. I owed her that much. I rattled off my digits, and within ten seconds, my phone buzzed in my bag.

"Now you have mine too," she said. "I'll be in touch after Christmas." She reached for my hands again. "I know how much you hated this time of year, but I hope things have changed and that you've found some peace with everything."

I swallowed, biting the inside of my cheek to prevent myself from tearing up.

"It was lovely meeting you, Ash." She nodded in his direction before pulling me to her in a hug. "We'll talk soon, okay? I hope you have a good Christmas this year, Ells."

"You, too, Char."

She brushed a kiss against my cheek, and with her signature poise and confidence, made her way to the front and out the door.

Soon. I would see her soon.

Warm fingers drifted across my skin, trailing down my spine. I snuggled in closer, draping my leg sideways across Ash's hard body, seeking out the heat that always drifted off him. His lips brushed against my hair as he pulled me in tighter, his palm cupping my shoulder. Inhaling slowly, I closed my eyes and breathed in the heady, crisp smell of him.

My mind wandered to Charlotte. Seeing her had rattled me, had stirred up emotions I'd kept suppressed for a long time. I didn't want to go there, to delve into the past and conduct a postmortem on everything I had done to wrong her after Liam died. It wasn't the place or time, but soon enough, I would have to face it. I couldn't hide from it anymore.

My stomach twisted with dread, and for the life of me, I couldn't figure out why the thought of seeing her again made me so uncomfortable. It was Char. I had known her for as long as I'd known Liam. She was my friend. I needed to push my misgivings aside, do the right thing, and face the music. I owed her that.

It was clear when we left the diner that Ash sensed the turmoil inside me. He hadn't pushed, but instead had quietly let me lead. My leading meant that we had not left my bed since we got home. I was needy and demanding, clinging to him as if any second now, he would disappear, and in typical Ash fashion, he had gone above and beyond to assure me he wouldn't. His slow, patient kisses, the way he made my body sing for him, the tender possessiveness with which he claimed me, the reverence in his touch—all deliberate and intended to set my mind at ease, to assure me that he was mine and there for me in whatever way I needed.

"I take it Christmas is not a thing in Ariadna." I trailed my fingers across his pecs, feeling them tighten under my touch.

"No, it isn't." He closed his hand over my straying fingers. "But we do have Cadavweira, the Celebration of Light and Harmony."

"Cada . . .?"

"Cadavweira. It's a four-day long celebration, culminating with festivities, gift giving, and the welcoming of the new year." He shifted us both onto our sides so we were facing each other. "It's a time for reflection and rebirth, for gratitude and giving."

"I love that." I slipped a leg between his. "What's the history behind it?"

His expression grew thoughtful. "Well, the origins stem from the history of the Gods of the Sangelis. It's said that at the dawn of the New Age, when Sorin, Summoner of Light and Darkness, came into existence, he was unable to summon light. Except for the stars and moons that lit up the skies at night, the Sangelis was covered in darkness for four thousand years until a goddess—the Goddess of the Ethereal Harmonies—blended her power with Sorin's, making it possible for him to harness the light. The union of their power caused a massive surge in the heavens, creating two entirely new constellations that align once every century.

"Those constellations were eventually named after them, and as time passed, Cadavweira became not just a celebration of the union of light and harmony, but also a celebration of the symbolic journey we travel to find enlightenment in our lives, making our way out of the darkness into the light."

I stared at him, a deep sense of longing sweeping over me. "That's really beautiful. Does each day of the celebration symbolize something?"

He nodded, brushing his finger across my collarbone. "Day one and two are days of reflection that both end with a promise. On day one, you make a promise to surrender some source of darkness in your life. It could be a bad habit, negative thought, person. On day two, you make a promise to commit to something that will feed your soul and bring you joy. Day three is a day of gratitude and giving, for gathering with friends and family, and celebrating life. Day four is the festival of Light and Harmony—a celebration of light, magic, music, and new beginnings."

A tingling chill danced across my skin. "I . . . I don't know why that resonates so deeply with me."

Ash kissed my fingers. "It doesn't surprise me that it does. You do belong to that world, after all."

It still blew my mind to think of that, and yet I'd already accepted it as the truth. "I wish I knew what my story was."

Ash exhaled, pulling me closer. "I promise you, Elle. You'll find out."

"Does who I am have something to do with the violet-haired woman?" I rested my head on his bicep.

His eyes flashed with surprise. "Why do you ask that?"

"Because just like you call to me on a deeper level that I can't understand, she does too. From the first night she came to me in my dream, I felt it. I didn't feel that sense of connection with Arazul or Mangy Cat."

Ash smiled, tucking tousled tendrils of my hair behind my ear. "You will find out the truth soon enough, Tialla. I promise." Shifting his weight onto his elbow, he reached behind him for a flat, silver box. "I have something for you. Don't think of it as a Christmas present, but just as a gift from me to you."

I stared at him, a rush of blood flooding to my head. "Ash," I said, unable to find the words as he placed the box in my hand. I'd never seen anything like it before. The silver rippled across the surface as if it were a living thing, shifting back and forth, like waves on a restless sea. "What is this?" I traced a ripple with my fingers.

"This is zidiurrh. The most precious metal on Ariadna."

"It's beautiful." The fluid motion of the metal was entirely mesmerizing

He nudged my fingers. "Open it."

"You didn't have to get me anything." I peered up at him. "I didn't get you something."

He tilted my chin. "I know I didn't have to. I wanted to. And it's something given freely, with no expectation of anything in return. Everything I need is right here. Please get that through that beautiful head of yours, okay?"

I nodded, shifting my attention back to the box. It fit perfectly in the palm of my hand. I unlatched the small clasp at the front and opened the lid. A small gasp escaped my lips at the sight of an elegant bangle-style bracelet resting on a bed of red velvet.

My jaw dropped as I stared at the four purple, gem-studded flowers at the top, branching out into silver leaves weaving around the band. My fingers traced the design gently, lingering over the purple flowers. "It's so beautiful, Ash."

He reached for the box. "May I?"

I nodded, and he carefully lifted the bangle out, unhooking the clasp. I reached my left hand out and he slid it on, locking it into place.

"Perfect." He brought my hand to his lips. "Just like the one wearing it."

He traced the violet flowers with his thumb. "I had it made specifically for you, and it is imbued with the magic of Ariadna."

My eyes widened. "What does it do?"

He stroked the clasp. "Think of it as a talisman. The magic makes it so that it will always stay on your wrist and will act as a source of protection." He clasped the side of my face, a silent plea in his eyes. "I want you to remember something, Elle." His tone was serious, tinged with an undertone of urgency.

"What is it?"

"You are precious to me; there is nothing—absolutely nothing—I wouldn't do for you. I can't always be here, though, and as much as I wish I could change that, it's not possible. Not yet, anyway. I need you to start relying on and trusting your instincts more." He placed his hand over my chest. "The power that lives inside you—it is awakening, and it will not lead you astray. It's an extension of who you are."

Heed the voice that stirs in the deep reaches of your soul. That's what Arazul had said to me.

Ash's eyes blazed. "I am honored to call you mine, Tialla, but you are so much more, and I need you to know that and understand the significance of it."

"What do you mean?" My brows furrowed in a frown. "What am I?"

"You are the hope of the Sangelis." He rested his forehead against mine. "And it's almost time for the promise of who you are to become a reality. I know that none of that really makes sense to you right now, but that is going to change, and when it does, your life will never be the same."

I sucked in a breath, a shiver of apprehension at the unknown gripping me. "How will I know when it's time?"

He looked at me, his expression serious. "The Gods of the Sangelis will come calling."

Chapter 29

ASHER

PRESENT DAY SOLNIESS, THE VOID . . .

"Can I ask you something, Eolith?" I clasped my hands behind my back as we walked on the grounds of Solniess. My gaze drifted up to the curtains of colorful tyvosi moss spawning in droves and draping down the wide branches of the buswyn trees around us. Through the foliage, the sky was bright and cloudless, the same as it always was.

"Of course, Asher," the goddess replied, her voice warm and melodic.

"There's something I've wondered about for a while." I turned my head to look at her.

"Oh?"

"When Elle told me about the first time you visited her in her dream, she said that you told her that you had slept for more than a century and that you were both back where it all began—in the In-Between. Is that where you were all the time you were gone from Ariadna? In the Cradle of the In-Between?"

I studied the Goddess of the Ethereal Harmonies intently. Not that long ago, Eolith was more than just a figurehead in Ariadna—she had played a very active role alongside the Cloryals, her daughters. But that suddenly changed about a hundred and twenty years ago when she disappeared, and the Cloryals took over full responsibility as Keepers of the Ethereal Harmonies.

It hadn't been easy seeking her out after Elle came to me through the Senshifter, but I'd made discreet inquiries, and in the end, Eolith had come to me. Yet, up until the veil lifted, it was always in my dreams.

"I had a moment of weakness, Asher." Her eyes flashed with regret. "For which Arazul had no choice but to sequester me until the veil lifted."

I blinked slowly, my body growing still. "He did *what*?" What madness was this? What had she done for the Great Creator to take such drastic steps?

"I'm not proud of my actions." She took my hand, her steps coming to a halt. "I gave up a future with my daughter because I believed in the promise of the Light Age and the role Elle would play in making that a reality." Her fingers tightened on mine and her facial features twisted, agony lining her expression. "But giving her up left a hole in my heart that never healed, even with my four daughters. I began to doubt the ancient celestial star etching. Thousands of years had passed and none of the other signs had come to pass. I just wanted to see her. I pleaded with Arazul for that—just one glimpse—and he agreed to take me to her."

She leaned against the knobby trunk of a rasienda tree, her silver eyes swirling with pain. "The moment I laid eyes on her—more essence than physical form—I felt the demand deep within my soul to hold her, to love her, to raise her. She was *mine*, after all."

My chest constricted with the hot tang of sorrow. I didn't know what it was to be a parent, but the strength of the bond between a mother and child—I understood that. I could only imagine what torture it must have been for Eolith to willingly give up all she did with Elle.

Her fingers twisted in her lap, plucking at the gossamer threads of her silver gown. "I . . ." Her lips quivered. "I used my power against Arazul. I summoned my magic to me and flung it at him. The blast caught him off guard, but he recovered before I could breach the barrier and get to Elle. He tried to reason with me, but after seeing her, all my resolve evaporated. I was at war with myself. I *knew* what the greater good was, but I also wanted my child. And so I pleaded with Arazul to put me in tecleios. It was better for me to slumber than to continue living with the torture of not having Elle with me. At least I could be with her that way."

Tecleios. The sleep of the Gods. It would explain why she only visited me in my dreams when I sought her out.

I tilted my head to the side. "How did he explain that to the other Gods?"

She smiled wistfully. "I had attacked him. The evidence of my power would have lingered like a shroud around him, so he summoned the other Gods of the Sangelis after securing me in the Cradle of the In-Between and explained that he had sentenced me to an indeterminate period of tecleios because of what I'd done. They could see the remnants of my power still clinging to him. To attack the God of Gods is punishable by annihilation, so really, tecleios was a light consequence."

I looked past her toward the ocean in the distance. "Sorin must not have been happy about that, I'm sure."

A lopsided smile curled her lips. "So he told me when I went to tell him about Elle. He sought Arazul out and threatened to prevent the suns from rising across the Sangelis unless Arazul took him to see me."

My brows lifted. "I don't imagine that went well."

Eolith shook her head. "It didn't. Things became heated between them and the Mavigos themselves intervened to put an end to it. Sorin said that's when he knew something was at play. The Mavigos do not involve themselves with the affairs of Gods unless something monumental is at stake. He just didn't know what it was."

I furrowed my brows, catching my lower lip between my teeth. "You must have had some level of awareness even while in tecleios. You visited me in my dreams on more than one occasion."

She pushed off from the rasienda tree and stepped toward me. Her violet hair shimmered in the sunlight, the shade of it so similar to Elle's. Linking her arm with mine, she started walking. "There again, the Mavigos played a part." Her tone was soft, contemplative. "It is common belief that the Gods have the power to command a Senshifter. Not entirely so. The Mavigos must first relax their hold on the flow of time before a God can imbue a Senshifter with their power. They disrupted my tecleios on the eve of your coronation and explained to me that divine intervention was inevitable. Two times I would have to imbue a Senshifter with my magic. In the present moment, and then again at another point in the future that they would make known. Both moments had to intersect to change the flow of time and allow Elle to travel from her present to your past."

My eyes widened. The Mavigos had played a part in sending Elle through the Senshifter?

As if seeing my surprise, Eolith squeezed my arm. "You were on a dangerous path after Kaliope murdered your parents. One that would have altered everything. Only Elle held the power to change that. At least, that's what the Mavigos believed. Too much was at stake, and sending Elle back in time to you was the only way to change your mind so you wouldn't go through with your plans."

She stopped walking, grasping both my hands in hers. "Grief and sorrow can cloud a person's judgment, can make them contemplate and commit acts they never would have otherwise. This was a rare and dangerous attempt at a course correction, but it carried risks. Tora could have refused the Senshifter access. Elle could have refused you. You could have turned her away. But even though things progressed and you both gravitated to each other that night, you still had to make a choice about your intended plans. And in the end, you chose her."

I exhaled loudly, my mind reeling with the magnitude of what she had said. At what point did I truly change my mind about going through with my plans? Was it when Elle first slipped through the Senshifter? Was it after my senses claimed her as mine? Or was it at my coronation itself when the Ethereal Harmonies returned the two labrals and I remembered the dream Elle had told me about? What if she'd never mentioned that? Would it have made a difference?

Truth be told, the moment she looked into my eyes for the first time, I was done for, but perhaps, it wasn't any *one* thing, but rather a combination of all the things that had unfolded after she stepped into my room.

When it came right down to it, one thing was certain. Elle was the catalyst—the clarity I'd needed to choose a different path. If that night had not happened, nothing would have stopped me from getting my vengeance.

Eolith and I resumed our walk in silence. The overwhelming importance of the celestial star etching was not lost on me. The direct involvement of the Mavigos in overseeing and guiding the flow of events was proof of that—intervening with Arazul and Sorin, with Eolith while she was in tecleios, with Kaliope when they stayed her execution after she murdered my parents, with Elle in the human world.

I threw a sideways glance at Eolith. "Why is it so important to them?"

She pressed her lips together, her expression thoughtful. "I asked the same question. Their response was that the ancient celestial star etching was a symbol of hope, a promise given at the end of the First Age eons ago, a promise to right immeasurable wrongs and atrocities. What the outcome will be is not set in stone; there are multiple possibilities, but ensuring that all the players are at the table so to speak, that everything aligns to set events in motion, is their responsibility."

I pursed my lips. "Were you aware when Arazul took Elle from the Cradle of the In-Between and carried her to the human world?"

Eyelids fluttering closed, she slowly shook her head. "Arazul did what he had to do. He deepened my slumber at that time, and I don't fault him for that. I would have interfered in her life. To know that my daughter was alive and growing up without me, I wouldn't have been able to stay away, even more so considering the tragic losses she had to endure."

We came to a stop at an ornate stone fountain, intricate carvings and embellishments woven around the circular base. At the top, a sculpture of Sorin and Eolith towered proudly. Locked in an embrace, the love and devotion in their gazes hard to miss even through stone, it sent a pang of sadness to my heart. Their story was, in a word, tragic. It had to be unbearable—an immortal existence, unable to share it with the one you loved.

"After Liam died," Eolith was saying, "the Mavigos came to me again, showing Elle to me. What I saw broke me. She was a shell of a person, buried under the weight of loss and heartbreak. All I wanted to do was wrap her in my arms and tell her that it would be all right. But I couldn't.

That's when I came to you. Just as she had been your salvation, I knew you would be hers. It's only after the veil was lifted that Arazul woke me out of tecleios and I was able to go to her for the first time."

A bitter laugh escaped my lips. "It doesn't seem fair. You and Sorin, me, Elle. So much loss and heartache. I know what lies ahead won't be easy, and I'd be lying if I said I wasn't afraid. Not for myself, but for Elle, Ariadna, the Sangelis."

"Our losses and heartaches make us stronger." She gently squeezed my fingers. "Remember what the Mavigos said. The celestial star etching is a symbol of hope, a promise to right wrongs. You and Elle *are* that hope, Asher. The two of you together will be unstoppable. Cling to that, to your love for each other. Love is the most powerful force in the cosmos. It will light your path forward."

Her words echoed in my mind. Nothing had changed in my feelings for Elle. Heart, body and soul, I loved her so completely. I prayed to the Gods that when she remembered what happened in those five months I was gone from her life that she felt the same.

Chapter 30

ASHER

PRESENT DAY SOLNIESS, THE VOID . . .

"She's entering the rocky period." Treye stepped onto the balcony and plopped down in the chair next to mine.

I turned my head, peering into the room to stare at Elle's form on the bed. She was into the month of April on Earth. A little less than a year to go. When I returned to Ariadna after spending Christmas with her, things became infinitely more complicated. The beast of my bond—Magnus—was restless and temperamental, and that restlessness bled into my everyday life, making me miserable and agitated. Only after I spoke with Elle every night would he settle, but by the next morning, I'd be in the same position again.

A large part of the agitation Magnus experienced then had to do with the fact that Vix had not yet become awake and sentient within Elle. He could sense her presence beneath the surface of Elle's dormant power, but could do nothing to connect with her until she awakened. That drove his need to be with Elle, his claiming of her a placeholder until he could establish a connection with Vix.

My problems with Magnus, though frustrating, paled in comparison to the sequence of events that unfolded in quick succession during that six-month period after visiting her at Christmas. But in all honesty, even after that, things never really settled down for me to feel any measure of calm. I was always on edge.

I clenched my jaw, folding my arms across my chest. "That was a really shit time." It was hard to keep the bitterness out of my voice. "And it was even harder keeping it all from Elle. I know she sensed the turmoil I was experiencing, but she had no idea what was really happening."

"Kaliope really dug her claws in then." Treye's slitted eyes were hard as he stared out at the ocean. "Bri, Shae, Rem—they'd still be alive if I'd been more diligent."

"Treye. Enough. We've been through this countless times. Nothing you could have done would have changed the outcome."

"I should have known Bri would break," he said softly.

I released a slow exhale. "People do desperate things for love."

"The brotherhood should come before that." His voice was firm, impassioned. "The Dulogrien's first loyalty is to our Sovereign, to Valkyse."

"Spoken like someone who's never been in love." I rubbed my palm over my knuckles. "No one should ever be put in the position where they're forced to choose between love and other sworn allegiances. And that, my friend, is on Kaliope, not you."

We sat in silence, the air heavy between us. My hatred for Kaliope flared out of me like a beacon, the memory of every unforgivable thing she'd done to me and those I cared about churning in my mind.

Bri had been a good man, trustworthy. He was the newest member of the Dulogrien, recruited personally by Treye. He was the only one Kaliope managed to detect, thanks to Gargmoin. Bri had not yet been inducted into the brotherhood, and as such, had not yet been endowed with the mental shields that went into effect once induction occurred.

As a result of Gargmoin's powerful mind manipulation abilities, Bri was exposed. Kaliope captured his betrothed and tortured her, threatening to kill her if Bri did not cooperate. Bri divulged the details of his current mission, and in so doing, brought about the deaths of Shae and Rem, two more of my Dulogrien. In the end, his betrayal of the brotherhood was all in vain. Kaliope still ended his life and that of his betrothed.

The situation was volatile after that, with Treye exercising extreme caution, even pulling some of the brotherhood out of Kindrik. Treye and Gilham were the only two of the group who were not entrenched in deep cover missions; everyone else was planted in key covert positions, either in Kindrik or Kaliope's fortress in Clawkier Dreve, on the outskirts of Proscette.

After what happened with Bri, Kaliope intensified her focus, inserting even more spies within Valkyse's borders, using bribery, extortion, and fear to get others to do her bidding. I had to be infinitely more careful when it came to visiting Elle, as Kaliope's spies reported to her daily on my comings and goings.

The one thing that was predictable about Kaliope was her unpredictability. I'd learned that the hard way over the years. There was no rhyme or reason to some of the things she did, almost as if she rolled out of bed and went with whatever chaos-inciting, half-baked idea that was rattling around in her head that day.

Her unpredictability was dangerous, and was the reason I could never let my guard down. Expect the unexpected. That was my mantra when it came to her. The element of surprise, coupled with her killer instincts, meant that more often than not, she was successful in her attempts to wreak havoc. She was a shit disturber, and excellent at it.

The heavy tread of hurried footsteps approaching pulled me from my thoughts. I turned my head just as Faron's face appeared at the balcony door, his features lined with worry.

"Better come quick, Ash." The urgency in his voice was unmistakable. "I think the time for peacefully watching over Elle is over."

Treye and I both bolted out of our chairs. "Why do you say that?"

He cocked his head. "Well, when four of the six Gods of the Sangelis are waiting in the Goddess Mother's library, requesting the immediate presence of the Godslayer, it sort of gives that impression."

"Holy shit," Treye blurted out, scrubbing his hand over his face. "Go. Faron and I will stay with Elle."

My heart thudded as a sickening dread settled in my gut. I quickly made my way to the bed, dropping a kiss on Elle's brow.

"This is it." I squared my shoulders and turned to Treye and Faron. "I feel it. Faron is right. Quiet time is over."

"Jaraya and Cazril have aligned with Kaliope and Gargmoin," Arazul said flatly, his expression hard and unreadable.

We were seated around the stone table in the Goddess Eolith's library—four Gods of the Sangelis and me—grim expressions all around. Twylos, Goddess of the Elements sat next to Eolith, her curly green and blue hair a stark contrast against her dark, tawny skin and copper eyes. Arazul had forced her hand in choosing a side, declaring that war was imminent. As we had hoped, she chose ours.

"I take it the Goddess of the Night knows who Elle is?" I looked between Sorin and Eolith.

Sorin's eyes flashed a rich shade of amber. "Yes, she does. And that made it easy for her to pick a side." He folded his arms across his trinzum breastplate, looking at Eolith with sadness in his eyes. "There is no one she hates more than Eo, and now that extends to my daughter, whom she has never met." He arched a brow at me. "You never know with Cazril; he is flighty. He can go either way, usually, depending on which way the wind is blowing, but you made it easy for him when you put a hole through his gut."

"And I'd do it again in a heartbeat," I purred in satisfaction, narrowing my eyes.

"Jaraya and Cazril working together with Kaliope and Gargmoin are a dangerous combination." Arazul rose from his chair and walked toward the window.

No shit. Three masters of manipulation, pettiness, cruelty, deception. There was nothing about this war that was going to be pretty. As for Gargmoin, he was the wild card in all of this. I still didn't know what was in it for him, what Kaliope had guaranteed him.

I steepled my hands on my chest. "Do they all know about the celestial star etching?"

Arazul sighed. "Yes. The details of the ancient celestial star etching are common knowledge now. Kaliope is using it as a recruiting tool to gather allies, focusing on one specific word in there to assure others that the outcome can be swayed in her favor."

I furrowed my brows, running through the words of the star etching in my mind. "Let me guess. That word is *if*?"

Arazul nodded, taking his seat once more. "*If she, whose name is lost, can claim the Ankhira and harness the power of the Ethereal Harmonies, she will have dominion over Shadow and Light and will take her rightful place in the Sangelis.*"

My eyes flicked upward. "I have to ask. This Ankhira that the star etching speaks of, is it the power of all four Phanteras combined?"

Arazul's eyes flashed silver as they pierced through me. "If I told you that no one, including me, knows for certain what the Ankhira is, would that change anything? This war *can* be won without the Ankhira."

I blinked. The God of Gods—the one who had protected the celestial star etching since the dawn of the New Age—didn't know what the Ankhira was?

I folded my arms across my chest. "Well, you can rest assured that simply because the celestial star etching speaks of it, Kaliope will turn the Sangelis upside down to find out what it is. She will make it her mission to claim it before Elle can."

Arazul's expression was thoughtful as he assessed me. "What makes you think that the 'she' spoken of at the end of the celestial star etching is even the same person as the Celestial Songbird? I have pondered the true meaning of the star etching since the beginning of my time, and even I don't know the entire truth. Everything about the First Age was annihilated, and every surviving ancient one found themselves bound by an unbreakable oath that prevented them from speaking of that era. The Mavigos are the only ones who know for sure, and they have never revealed the truth to me, despite my many attempts at finding out."

"What about Gargmoin?" Sorin asked quietly, narrowing his eyes. "He is an ancient one—a powerful one at that—who wields the dark sway of the Old, Arcane Magic."

Arazul shook his head. "Even if he does know, he is bound by the craleic oath and cannot speak of it."

I cocked my head. "Tora told me that while the ancient ones may be bound by the craleic oath when it comes to speaking of the First Age, they could share details of the celestial star etching with those who were part of it. Wouldn't that mean that if Gargmoin knew what the Ankhira was, he could share that knowledge with Kaliope?"

"I'm with the Godslayer on this one," Sorin replied. "That sick fuck would spill his guts to her if it got him one step closer to the power he craves."

"Can I say something?" Twylos interjected, her curls bobbing as she moved her head.

Arazul inclined his head toward the Goddess of the Elements. "You have the floor, Twy."

She smiled, her eyes bright as she regarded the God of Gods. "You said that you don't know for certain what the Ankhira is, that there are things about the celestial star etching that you're not entirely sure of. What do you *think* it all means? You are the greatest and most powerful of us all, Ara. Tell us what you believe. Your wisdom matters to us."

The Great Creator's eyes flared as he considered Twylos's request. He moved back to the stone table, taking his seat once more. "In order to do that, I need to share my thoughts about the First Age of the Sangelis." He leaned forward in his chair, spreading his palms on the table. "I believe that the end of the First Age was a catastrophic event that tore apart the fabric of the cosmos. It was unplanned and unexpected, bringing about extinction-level destruction and loss of life. The Mavigos told Eo that the celestial star etching was a symbol of hope, a promise given at the end of the First Age eons ago to right immeasurable wrongs and atrocities. Do I think it's a coincidence that the craleic oath ends when the Celestial Songbird completes that phase of her transformation to absorb the light strain of the Old, Arcane Magic? Absolutely not. The celestial star etching calls Catraia the anchor, the bridge between light and darkness. But the

Celestial Songbird is a bridge too—the bridge between all three ages—the First Age, the New Age, and the Light Age. What that means is left to be seen, but it's only a matter of time before all three ages collide."

Arazul was right. All three ages were going to collide. The events of the First Age were significant. Why else would such lengths have been taken to erase it from existence, only to drag it back into the light when Elle completed her transformation? What was her role as far as the First Age went?

"As for the Ankhira," Arazul continued, "I do believe it's a weapon that is powered by the unity of all four Phanteras, a weapon to wield the vast power of the Ethereal Harmonies, but what that weapon is, I don't know. One thing is certain. Somebody knows, and we should all be worried about the knowledge of it falling into the wrong hands."

A shudder snaked through me. Rest assured, Gargmoin would have told Kaliope all that he was at liberty to say about the celestial star etching based on what he was knowledgeable of. As for the Ankhira, it was a game changer; I felt it in my gut. Not for one second, though, had it crossed my mind that Elle wasn't the "she" spoken of in connection to the Ankhira. If not her, then who? Whose name was lost? Regardless, Arazul was right. The knowledge of the Ankhira could not fall into the wrong hands.

"This brings me to more pressing matters." Arazul's expression darkened.

A sickening feeling of foreboding clawed at my insides.

"Jaraya and Cazril have granted Kaliope access to their sanctums in the celestial plane of the Void. She knows that your and Elle's consciousness and shadow selves are here."

Dread swarmed in, sinking me like a stone. "No!" Rage clouded my vision. "How did she even find out?"

"The blame for that lies with me, Godslayer." Sorin pushed his chair back and stood, his rugged features highlighted by the flare of his essence around him.

My pulse pounded in my ears. "What did you do?" My power flared as it rushed through my veins.

"Don't, Asher." Eolith reached for my hand across the table. "Let him explain."

Sorin and I glared at each other, and I clenched my fists, itching to hurl my power at him. If he had knowingly placed Elle in danger, I would kill him with my bare hands.

"Got all that power under control, cub?" He smirked, baiting me.

"Enough, Sorin." Eolith flashed furious eyes at the Summoner of Light and Darkness. "We are all on the same bloody side."

Sorin lifted her hand to his lips. "I'm sorry, Eo. You're right." He turned to look at me once more. "One of Jaraya's spies in Madwen eavesdropped when Eo came to tell me about Elle. She reported back to her mistress."

I turned desperate eyes to Arazul. "You are the Great Creator. You have to do something. Elle still has almost a year of time left to relive through her consciousness. Kaliope cannot be here. She will actively try to get to me, to her. Please tell me that Gargmoin cannot follow her here."

"He cannot enter the Void," Arazul said, his expression somber. "And as for Kaliope, she's already made an attempt to infiltrate Solniess."

I closed my eyes, a sinking feeling dragging me under.

Eolith's voice was quiet, composed. "She captured a joranda and tried to use dark magic to control it, but the life force of all my zaragals are bonded with mine, and I was able to summon it back to me and undo all the damage she had done."

"I will see to Kaliope," Arazul said, his glittering expression hard. "She doesn't belong here in the Void and is a blistering distraction we do not need. As intently as she might try, she will never breach Solniess."

"Why can't we just end her and be done with it?" Twylos asked, her copper eyes flashing. "It would eliminate so many problems for everyone. We are Gods of the Sangelis. She is but a mortal."

The Great Creator sat upright in his chair. "A mortal with a path protected by the Mavigos. We may be Gods, but even we do not oppose the divine will of the universe."

"You think that's what happened with the First Age, don't you?" Twylos tilted her head to the side. "You think one of the old Gods defied the Mavigos and paid for it?"

Arazul frowned. "I don't know what happened with the First Age, but that is a possibility. Are you willing to risk the wrath of the Mavigos and possible annihilation to find out? For whatever reasons, things must unfold the way they were set out in the ancient celestial star etching, and we must abide by that."

I gritted my teeth and held my tongue. Why were the Mavigos so intent on ensuring that the celestial star etching was fulfilled? What would happen if it wasn't? A shudder went through me. I had a nagging feeling that we wouldn't want to find out.

Chapter 31

KALLOPE

CELESTIAL PLANE OF THE VOID: PRESENT DAY . . .

My eyes burned with rage. That odious piece of shit. I would eviscerate him for his treachery.

Only a fool would trust the God of Chaos, but after what Ash had done to him, I'd been convinced he was firmly on board, his rage and inflated ego demanding nothing less than cold retribution.

I'd thought myself secure in Clocero, Cazril's sanctum in the celestial plane, but the deceitful prick had simply stood there, his eyes bugging out with insipid curiosity and intrigued surprise when I was suddenly whisked away.

The ground rumbled and shook beneath my feet. I was still in the Void; that much, I was certain of. The chamber I was in was monstrous, enveloped in warm light and yawning nothingness as far as my eyes could see. To add to my frustration, whatever power lining the walls of my prison had rendered my magic useless.

The light shining down on me encased everything it touched, irking and perturbing me to no end. The darkness that clung to me, quarrying and nesting within my heart, recoiled in hostility, hissing to be free. No doubt about it, I was in the presence of a God of the Sangelis, and I had a pretty good suspicion which one.

I shuddered as the culprit approached, the power he exuded provoking my senses into flagrant—albeit silent—protest. His form was the same one he had assumed the first and only time I had encountered him: the day I was released from Glanag. I hadn't shown fear then, and I sure as shit wasn't going to now.

He was tall and imposing, his light-brown hair falling just below his broad shoulders in soft waves. His features were sharp and angular, his face ageless and enthralling in its appeal. There was nothing even remotely inconspicuous about him. He was power personified. His stride was confident and purposeful, his eyes two pools of silver fire. As he walked, his cloak of light billowed around him, and despite my antipathy for who he was, I could not smother the part of me that was compelled to obey.

Smirking defiantly as he drew closer, I braced myself for whatever reprisal he was about to unleash. I refused to bow my head in his presence—I knew that would rile him—and I smiled at the blazing fire in his eyes as he glared at me. I was done with being at the mercy of any higher power; I would do whatever I wanted and wreak as much havoc as it took to get to the top.

"Well, isn't this a surprise, oh Great Creator, Arazul." I met his gaze with unabashed brashness.

"I see respect and humility in the presence of the Divine is still beneath you," he observed dryly, his voice deep and powerful as it reverberated around me.

"Oh, what? Did you expect me to simper and act demure in your presence?" I pouted my lips in mockery. "Sorry to disappoint you, Great One, but I couldn't give a shit about respect and humility in your presence. We both know there is nothing you can do to me because you are a steadfast rule follower, and to do anything to me would break one of your divine rules." I wagged a finger slowly in his face. "Thou shalt not go against the Mavigos." I clapped my hands together gleefully, basking in triumph and condescension as I drank in his unamused reaction. "In fact," I continued, lifting a finger haughtily into the air, "I would even venture to say that in bringing me here, you are breaking that very rule. Wouldn't you agree?"

"Enough!" Arazul commanded, and although every fiber of my being fought to oppose him, I was forced to obey. He regarded me with distaste, his eyes blazing as he drew closer. "Your presence in the celestial plane of the Void goes against my rules for order and civility."

My skin singed in his proximity, the scar on my cheek burning as his power flared. "Civility?" I snorted in derision. "I'm sorry. When did I ever give the impression that I cared one whit about that?"

"That's right." His silver eyes flared. "Mindless destruction and senseless mayhem—that's more your signature move."

He moved closer, the power emanating off him driving me to my knees. I gritted my teeth, fighting him every step of the way, seething with fury that I wasn't strong enough to withstand his compulsion.

"Make yourself comfortable. You'll be here for a while."

Fists clenched in a death grip, I glared daggers at him. "You can't keep me imprisoned." What I wouldn't give to rip his fucking head off.

He narrowed his eyes. "Watch me. As long as the Celestial Songbird is unable to defend herself, you cannot touch her. You were brazen enough to enter the Void. While you are here, you are a slave to my rules. The Celestial Songbird is untouchable."

Godsdamned *Sviyen Cielta*. I was sick of hearing about her.

I spat at his feet. "What a joke. As if she stands a chance against me. She is weak and pathetic."

He cocked his head. "And yet the Ethereal Harmonies claimed her . . . as did Asher Valkyse."

The blood rushed to my head, my face heating as unfettered rage pumped through my veins.

"Let me be clear," I said through gritted teeth. "I will use whatever means available to me to wage war against your sorry excuse for a chosen one. I have my own interpretation of the celestial star etching: crush the bitch at all costs and take *my* rightful place in the Sangelis with Asher Valkyse at my side. And by the looks of it, I'll achieve that in no time. From what I hear, the little cunt has no control over her magic, not to mention that darkness has taken root inside her. Ha. For all we know, she might end up joining me before all is said and done."

Arazul took an abrupt step forward—eyes flashing—gripping my jaw with his fingers. "Your arrogance, Kaliope, your lack of humility and utter disregard for balance and order are why you will not prevail. And as for the celestial star etching, I have my own interpretation. The Celestial Songbird will come into her own and defeat you, taking her place as the High Queen of the Light Age, alongside her King. It was always meant to be *her*, not you."

"We'll see about that," I ground out. "The first chance I get, I will break her into tiny little pieces, both physically and mentally."

"I tire of your venomous prattle." He turned his back on me. "If I were you, I'd use this time to reflect on your plans for war. There is still time to change your mind."

"No fucking chance."

He sighed in resignation. "I didn't think so."

He walked away from me, and my roars of fury echoed in my ears as he disappeared, leaving me in the light-filled chamber alone.

I closed my eyes, forcing myself to calm my explosive emotions.

Gargmoin.

There was still a chance that my connection to him was intact despite Arazul's magic. I had to try and reach him. There was nothing he wouldn't do for me. I delved inside and yanked on my magic, but it was cut off from me, as if a great divide had been erected to block my access.

I screamed in frustration, even more rattled that there was nothing around me that I could take my rage out on. Nothing I could smash or destroy.

My thoughts shifted to Ash, my stomach twisting as Arazul's taunt from earlier replayed in my mind. He had claimed *her*. Snakelike ribbons of jealousy lashed out, sinking their venomous fangs into my heart. I closed my eyes, savoring the burn, committing the pain to memory. The joke would be on everyone. Ash would be mine. I had seen it. With Gargmoin at my side, it was possible.

Gargmoin—the answer to making my wildest dreams come true. Our coming together had always been inevitable. I had been the one to save him from the infernal stasis in which he had been ensnared for Gods-know-how-long—deep in the bowels of the Phantom Pocket Between Realms—tortured and tormented by the ghosts of his iniquitous and traitorous past.

During my imprisonment in Glanag, the whispers in the darkness had trickled knowledge of his existence to me: a great and terrible power long forgotten and lost to the Sangelis, the truth of who he really was obliterated from the annals of history before the destruction of the First Age. Just the mention of his name had unnerved and agitated the Hagdern—those cantankerous and aggravating beasts charged with guarding the prison. And when the shadows in the darkness had wrapped their opaque cloak around me, allowing me to slip unnoticed through that tenebrous void riven in the deepest chasm of Glanag, I had followed. They'd shown me the way into the Phantom Pocket Between Realms to find him.

The whispers and shadows revealed the dark spells that would release him from his prison and indenture him to me. Who or what he truly was, I didn't care; as long as he could help me get what I wanted, that was all that mattered.

He was a haunted and pitiful shadow when I found him, but I brought him back to life. Those bloody whispers—so similar to the ones that lived inside me—never shut up, taunting us both with other tantalizing secrets, painting for us vivid visions of grandeur, revealing the details of the ancient celestial star etching to us.

He had coldly asked for only two things: to be able to slake his bloodlust and to be the one to end the Celestial Songbird's life. I had promised him both. In return, he would do my bidding and help me retrieve the Phanteras, the sacred artifacts that would grant me supremacy over all of Ariadna.

But that was before I knew who all the players were. Now, more than anything, I wanted to be the one to crush the creya, to watch the life leave her eyes at my hand.

My release from Glanag was a freedom of significant proportions. Armed to the teeth with knowledge, my first order of business had been releasing Gargmoin from the wards keeping him within the confines of the prison. It was child's play, much easier than I'd expected, as if the universe itself had lent a hand to make it a reality.

Since then, Gargmoin had far exceeded my expectations. Everything I had commanded of him, he had done without questioning, savoring each kill and depravity he committed, executing every task with precision and relish. With him leading my armies into battle, victory was almost guaranteed.

He was bound to me. We had sealed our bargain in blood, and blood oaths, once made—especially those sealed with dark magic—were impossible to get out of. Together, we would shake the very foundation of the Sangelis and bring it to its knees. This was my destiny.

Fuck the Celestial Songbird.

The bitch was as good as dead.

Chapter 32

ELEYSE

JUNE 8: TEN MONTHS AGO . . .

"What's going on in that head of yours?" Aggie's eyes narrowed as she stared at me. "I can see the cogs spinning out of control, and let me tell you, it terrifies me."

My eyes snapped to hers, simultaneously gripping the glass of lemonade in my hand.

"Bloody hell, you're in a mood today," she muttered, leaning forward in her chair. "Is it the lack of sex? I would think you of all people would know how to work a vibrator, for heaven's sake."

I glowered at her, setting my glass on the table a little too loudly even for my own liking.

"Come on, talk to me, Ovi." She reached her hand across the table and squeezed my fingers. "I can't help you if I don't know what's bothering you. Is it Ash? Is his absence weighing on you?"

I exhaled slowly and chewed on my bottom lip, trying to find the words. "I don't know what's wrong with me, Aggie." I shifted my gaze to her flower beds, searching for a distraction. She had wasted no time in getting her landscaping going once spring hit, her perennials already in bloom in their rich charcoal mulch beds.

I tapped my foot restlessly against the floorboards of her front deck, trying to quiet my mind. She was right. I was in a mood today; had been since I woke up this morning with a heavy cloud of unease hanging over me.

Ash and I had talked last night, and although the conversation itself

278

hadn't been anything out of the ordinary, there was an underlying note of tension in his voice that had set me on edge, seeping into my subconscious, unsettling me.

Something had happened since he was last here, six weeks ago—something that had prevented him from visiting me again. We spoke every night, and although he gave me his assurances that everything was okay, that *we* were okay, I couldn't shake the feeling that there was more he wasn't telling me because he didn't want me to worry.

I'd sensed it in his voice after he gave me the bracelet on Christmas Eve. He was worried about something. True to his word, he had stayed with me for four days, and it had been more than I could have ever hoped for, but just before he left, he'd reiterated his warning to me about being careful and trusting my intuition to lead me.

Since Christmas, he'd visited three times, but his frustration about not being here with me had been evident for the past six weeks, and only kept growing as time wore on.

Fear.

That's what I sensed, and although he never came out and said it, the quiet desperation in his tone when he said goodbye every night told me everything I needed to know. He was scared of something.

My mind drifted back to one of our last in-person conversations. He had been unusually quiet, and the weight of his unease had settled over my heart like a wrecking ball ready to unleash havoc.

"I want you to promise me something, Elle." The serious tone of his voice had brooked no argument.

"Okay . . . What is it?" An ominous tug pulled at my insides, causing my entire body to brace.

His words were soft but steely. "The bracelet I gave you—I want you to promise me that if ever it should turn cold—and when I say cold, I mean like a band of ice around your wrist—call out for me and try to find a safe place to hide until I come for you."

My heart thudded in my chest. "Ash, what are you saying? What are you scared of?"

"Elle." His eyes shone with a silent plea. "Just promise me. It's a precaution. I can't be here with you all the time, and I need to ensure that you're safe."

My heartbeat accelerated, the blood thumping loud in my ears. "Safe from what? What do you need to protect me from?"

His voice was a disquieted whisper. "I hope that as long as you're hidden away on Earth, you'll never have to find out."

I jumped as Aggie's touch on my hand yanked me back to the present.

"Heavens, I haven't seen you so on edge before." Worry lined her features.

I frowned. As much as Ash consumed my thoughts, he wasn't my only source of unease. Charlotte was in town again, and we had arranged to meet for dinner and drinks later this evening. My unease about Ash made it so that I didn't want to deal with anything else.

After Ash had left at Christmas, Char and I had met, and it was every bit as difficult as I had expected. There were tears, hard truths, a release of anger, grief, sorrow. That night put me through the emotional wringer, sucking me dry. No amount of mental steeling could have prepared me for that conversation.

I had abandoned my best friend, and done so under the guise of saving her. She had tried her best to find me, but I'd been good at not leaving a trail. And as much as I hated to admit it, I'd had no plans of finding or reconnecting with her. I couldn't afford to lose anyone else. It was horrible to say, but in a messed up way, I'd already mourned losing her when I left. For the life of me, I couldn't understand why I didn't want to reopen that chapter of my life and welcome Charlotte back in. My angst was driving me mad, but it refused to go away, refused to let me feel remorse.

When Ash and I bumped into her at the diner, she'd been in Hargrove for a short work stint. Now she was in town again for a week and I'd agreed to meet.

I stared at the bracelet on my wrist. Having it against my skin made me feel close to Ash. "I miss him." The quiet admission slipped past my lips, bringing with it the prickle of tears. "I can't explain it, Aggie. We've talked every single day, but I walk around with this ache inside me, this gut-wrenching pain because he's not here. It's different from any kind of loss I've felt before. It's a restlessness, a mindless hunger, an all-consuming need to be put back together."

Aggie's brows knitted, her expression thoughtful. "Have you considered visiting him? If he can't come to you, maybe you can go to him."

I frowned. "It's not that simple."

"What's not simple about it? You hop on a plane and you just go."

I was silent. I hadn't told Aggie all the things Ash had revealed to me about the Sangelis and who he was. Always there, in the back of my mind, was his warning telling me to be careful about what I said. Aggie just assumed that we talked on the phone every day, and I'd said nothing to suggest otherwise.

He'd told me to trust my intuition, and my gut told me that Aggie could be trusted, but I didn't want to offload any more of my crazy onto her. She was pretty much my only friend, and I didn't want to burden her any more than I already had.

"You know you can confide in me, right?" she said, as if reading my bloody mind.

I squeezed her fingers. "I know."

She patted my hand. "Everything will be all right, Ovi. You just have to keep going. One foot in front of the other."

I nodded, my fingers absently tracing the purple flowers on my bracelet. The metal was warm against my skin, and that soothed me, setting my mind at ease that I was safe with Aggie.

"Are you ready for your dinner with Charlotte tonight?"

"Not really." I slouched down in my chair. "But at least it can't go any worse than the last time we met." At least I hoped it wouldn't. God help me, I couldn't handle a night like that again.

Aggie sat up straight in her chair. "Do me a favor, will you?"

My eyes flicked to hers.

"Go home, look at yourself in the mirror, and summon that goddess that Ash sees in you. Let that confidence and self-assurance settle into you. Wrap it like a second skin around you. Wear something that makes a statement, and go out tonight with the intent to reconnect with a dear friend. Put the past aside. People are drawn to the energy you put out—bad or good—and respond accordingly. Go out with a positive attitude tonight."

I looked at her and nodded. She was right. Negative energy was heavy, draining. I would do it—shake the gloom off and have a good time. Tonight, I would be Ash's Tialla.

The evening unfolded infinitely better than I'd expected. Charlotte and I had dinner at a Thai restaurant I loved, and the conversation was light and filled with banter, much like old times. None of the heaviness from our previous reckoning seeped in, likely due to the two cocktails I'd swilled while waiting for her to arrive. By the time she got there, my head was warm and fuzzy, and I slipped into the skin of a confident goddess with ease. Most of dinner was spent with her catching me up on everything she'd been up to the past few years.

We left the restaurant, our arms linked as we sashayed down the street, and my heart was the most content it'd been since Ash was last here.

"So tell me about Ash," Charlotte said as we came to a stop at a pedestrian crossing. "How did you two meet?"

I pushed the crosswalk button. "We actually met at a bar near my work. I bumped into him—literally—and we got to talking, and the rest is history." Okay, that wasn't *exactly* accurate, but I didn't need to give all the details.

"No way." Her hazel eyes sparkled with interest. "And the long distance thing works?"

I looked both ways as we crossed. "It surprisingly does."

"So where's he from?"

I cocked my head. "Out west."

"And you guys see each other often? From the looks of it when I saw you two at the diner, things seemed pretty intense."

Holy shit. I didn't want to talk about Ash. It felt *weird* talking about another man in my life with Charlotte.

I dipped my head in a quick nod. "Things are serious."

She squeezed my arm. "Any plans to change your relationship from long distance to a more permanent kind of arrangement? A ring in the future, perhaps?"

I needed to get off this topic fast. I didn't want to talk about my feelings for Ash. "I haven't thought that far ahead." I tilted my head to look at her. "Where are we going, anyway?"

"I figured we could go dancing, just like back in the day." A wicked smile curved her lips.

I threw my head back and laughed. "I don't think I'd even remember how. It's been so long."

"Fuck, Ells." She linked her fingers with mine and pulled me down a side street. "You were untouchable on the dance floor. Liam and I loved to watch you dance. Hell, everyone loved watching you dance. The moment you stepped onto the dance floor, you owned it."

"I don't know, Char." I furrowed my brows, slowing my steps. "I'm not the same person anymore."

She stopped abruptly, turning to face me. "Well, tonight you are, and I'm not taking no for an answer. A group of people from the office are going to be there and I got us VIP passes."

"Where exactly?"

"A club called No Inhibitions. Been there before?"

I shook my head. "Haven't been there, but I've heard of it. Definitely the place to be on a Saturday night."

"Well, let's go. I think it's just down the next street." She rubbed her hands together in glee. "This is going to be so much fun."

I groaned. "I don't know about that. My buzz is wearing off already."

"Good thing that's a quick thing to fix," she said with a wink.

I smiled, a twinge of sadness piercing my heart. The last time I had gone dancing was when Liam was alive. God, we were good together on the dance floor. But I'd always had fun with Charlotte as well. I could do this. For old time's sake, I would go. It wasn't as if we would be alone, anyway. Her friends would be there too.

The line to get into the club was wrapped around the building, but with Char's passes, we slipped in without having to wait. She pulled her phone out to message her friends from work, and they guided her to a cordoned-off section on the second level. A group of ten or so milled around, laughter and conversation filling the air. Bottles popped, glasses clinked, and music filled the night.

A tall, blond-haired man stepped behind Char, wrapping his arms around her waist. "You came!" he shouted over the music, and she twisted to face him, planting a kiss on his lips. I recognized him as the guy who had called her name at the diner on Christmas Eve.

"Wouldn't miss it for the world, Will." Her bronze skin glistened in the recessed lighting as she reached for a bottle of bubbly on the table in front the seating area. Pouring two glasses, she handed one to me. "Everyone, this is my friend Elle," she shouted, gesturing to me.

I was met with waves and friendly faces, and I smiled and waved back, acknowledging everyone in the group.

"Now drink up, so we can go dance," Char said in my ear.

I looked at the glass in my hand, the bubbles fizzing and popping as I lifted it to my lips. What the hell. Dancing had always been an escape, a freedom of proportions, and god knew I needed a distraction and outlet to release my frustrations tonight. I downed the drink, and Char took my hand, leading me down the stairs to the dance floor.

Excitement lit me as we wound our way through the crowd, restless energy wrapping itself around me as it always did when music seeped into me, settling into my bones. Holding on to Char's hands, I closed my eyes and swayed softly, letting the music lead, move me, sweep me up in its thrall. I was glad Aggie had encouraged me to dress up. From my straightened hair to my smoky makeup to my mid-thigh V-neck bodycon dress clinging to my gym-hardened body, I felt powerful and confident, as if the world itself bowed to the magic humming inside me.

Char and I weren't on the dance floor that long before her friends found us. The blond-haired hottie—Will—made a beeline for her, and she willingly slipped into his arms, her lithe body clinging to his as they moved to the music.

The atmosphere was light and welcoming, laughter and conversation bubbling amongst the group, even as the music blared above us. Everyone was relaxed and enjoying themselves, and I found myself drawn into conversation, settling into the comfortable camaraderie within the group.

With my inhibitions lowered, I was wholly unprepared for the searing panic that gripped me when an arm snaked around my body from behind me and a palm squeezed my ass. I twisted, but the arm tightened its grip around mine as whoever it was ground their torso against me.

I gasped, lifting my foot and bringing the heel of my shoe down hard on my assailant's ankle. An angry yelp reached my ears, and I tried to free my elbow to force it into his ribs, but couldn't move.

Fear washed over me, and I looked up to see one of the guys in Char's group move closer in my direction. He pulled me to him, yanking my assailant's arm free, and in one swift stroke, blasted his fist into my attacker's face. I turned to see a light-haired man on the floor, blood spurting from his nose. He sprang to his feet, his fists in front of him as he lunged, aiming for my savior's head. The latter dodged the blow easily, shifting with ease and landing an uppercut blow to the attacker's chest.

The bracelet on my wrist went cold, sending a chill down my spine. I had to get out of here. I searched the dance floor for Char, but she was nowhere in sight. Neither was Will. It was so crowded around us, I wasn't even sure anyone even realized a fight was in progress. I pushed my way through the throng, my heart hammering in my chest.

I should have never come here. I made it off the dance floor and raced toward the exit, the overwhelming need to leave drowning out every other thought in my head. As I rushed by, I scanned the crowd for Char but couldn't find her. I reached into my clutch for my phone, my fingers shaking as I unlocked it and searched for her number.

Pushing the exit door open, I stepped out onto the sidewalk, doubling over as I took heaving gulps of air. Searching my contacts, I found her number and dialed, but it went straight to voice mail. I texted her a message to let her know I was leaving and made my way down the sidewalk, heading back in the direction of the restaurant where I'd parked my car. All the while, the bracelet on my wrist remained cool—not a band of ice like Ash had mentioned, but cold, nonetheless.

I was halfway to the parking lot when I heard a voice shouting from behind me. I ignored it and quickened my pace.

"Hey!" the voice called again. "Wait up!"

The streets were far from deserted, and I chanced a look behind me. I sagged in relief. It was my savior from the club.

"Are you all right?" he asked when he caught up to me, his dark hair, so like Ash's, brushing against his forehead. His eyes were a piercing sapphire blue that I couldn't look away from.

"I'm sorry for taking off and leaving you to fight my battles." I flashed him an apologetic smile. "I couldn't breathe and needed to get out of there."

"It's okay." His lips tipped up, setting off a dimple in his left cheek. "The bouncers got a hold of him shortly after that."

"I . . . I couldn't find Charlotte." I picked up my pace again, the parking lot within sight in the distance. My scalp prickled with unease, the events from earlier still swirling in my mind.

"I saw her leave the dance floor with Will," he said, his sapphire eyes twinkling. "I figured they went to find somewhere more . . . private?"

"Ohhh . . ." The silence chewed up the space between us.

"Did you and Charlotte come together?" he asked. "Maybe we should wait for her; I wouldn't want her to be worried about you."

"No, I met her here." I fished in my clutch for my car keys. "Plus I left her a message letting her know I was leaving."

"From what I heard the others saying tonight, she and Will have been playing this game of hot potato for months now." He flashed me a grin that lit up his features, highlighting how unnervingly gorgeous he was.

I smiled. "Sounds like the games Charlotte likes to play." I inclined my head as we approached the entrance to the parking lot. "My car's at the back end of the lot."

He nodded. "I'll walk you there. Women can't be too careful these days. Too many crazies out there." He stuck out his hand. "I'm Ty, by the way."

I shook his hand, noting that his grip held the right amount of firmness. "Nice to meet you, Ty. You and Charlotte work together?"

"No, I actually just met them all tonight. Hit it off with a few of them earlier and then stuck around as we were having a good time."

The bracelet on my wrist sent a jolt of ice to my skin, causing the hair on the back of my neck to raise. I looked over my shoulder, searching the shadows for any sign of the guy from the club. Was he out there somewhere watching us?

We were almost at my car now, and my body sagged in relief, craving the safety of my warm bed and Ash's voice in my head.

I pushed the button on my remote to unlock my car. "Thank you again, Ty."

"It was nothing at all." He walked the rest of the way with me to the driver-side door.

The cold pouring out of the bracelet into my skin sent an icy chill straight to my heart, stopping me dead in my tracks.

A band of ice around my wrist.

Fuck.

I gasped just as Ty spun me and blew a handful of gold dust in my face. Ash was a whisper of a thought in my head as blackness engulfed me, and I slipped away.

Chapter 33

ELEYSE

S hooting pain seared through the side of my head as awareness flooded in, drowning me in a cacophony of chaos. My eyes burned as I struggled to adjust to the glare from the lone fluorescent bulb overhead. Where the hell was I? Groggily, I stirred, my body heavy and slack. The world spun before me as I peered around at my surroundings, unable to focus my vision.

A blast of pain tore through my skull as I moved my head, and I cried out, my fingers gripping something jagged, the grooves rough, like unplaned wood. Ever so slowly, awareness filtered back in, my body slumped in a seated position in a hard, unyielding chair. I tried unsuccessfully to move, and in a shudder of horror, I realized my hands were tied to the arm rests. My feet, too, were restrained.

Panic gripped me, and my heartbeat kicked up into a gallop, flooding my senses with fear. The bracelet on my wrist was icy cold against my skin, and my mind reeled with cries for Ash. *Please come for me*, I beseeched.

"Finally. You're awake," an eager voice piped in from the shadows in the corner of the room. "I apologize—I used way too much shimelyx on you."

Shimelyx? What the—

Slowly, a figure stepped forward, and I squinted as Ty—if that was even his name—moved into the light. I shook my head, trying to remember. He had walked me to my car. Glittery gold dust. He had blown it in my face. I didn't remember anything after that.

He sauntered toward me purposefully, his curious gaze washing over me. "*What* are you, sweetheart?" His eyes narrowed as he studied me, his fingers tracing a trail down my arm over to my hand. My eyes tracked the movement, and my heart thudded at the floating green haze hovering over my wrist, binding it to the chair. My head snapped to my other hand to find an identical green band there.

He cocked his head. "The moment you walked up those stairs at the club, you called to me like a bloody siren. You're human, but also *not* human. I'm intrigued. I mean, what are the chances that you just happened to be in the same place as me at the same time?" His eyes flashed and a smile curved his lips. "Those fuckers have to know about you. *She* has to know about you." His voice dropped to a whisper. "And yet she never mentioned you."

"Who are you?" I asked, a dull throbbing still splitting my temples.

"What do you mean?" He looked at me as if I was slow. "I'm Ty."

I stared at him, at a loss for words, completely unsure what to make of him.

My eyes widened as I took in my surroundings, looking for an exit, an escape, anything. But there was nothing. Just a windowless room with four padded walls and a metal door affixed with a heavy-duty deadbolt.

"Where is this place? What do you want with me?"

"Oh, I just want to see what happens next," he said, as if it was the most obvious explanation in the world. "That bracelet on your wrist is brimming with magic, not to mention I can see the faint shimmer of your essence around you. I'm willing to bet that someone is going to come looking for you. I'm dying to find out who." He smiled, his eyes sparking with excitement. "As for where we are, this is just some place I found in the middle of the woods."

I stared at him. I couldn't figure out how I felt. My senses were going haywire, curiosity superseding every other emotion, pushing them out of the way. He had to be like Ash. He had magic. But how? And who was it that he thought knew about me?

I forced myself to meet his gaze. "Where are you from?"

"Vancouver." He crouched in front of me. "Have you ever been? It's a lovely place, Elle."

His voice uttered my name like a caress. I narrowed my eyes. "That's not what I meant. You have magic. Where are you really from?"

He studied me, an irksome grin on his too-handsome face. "Let's just say that I'm a *long* way from home." His hand cupped my cheek gently. "This might hurt a little, sweetheart, and I apologize in advance, but now that you're awake, I need to get into that head of yours. I just want a little peek." He brushed his thumb over my lips. "I got nothing while you were out cold, which is curious as fuck. I mean, really—who the fuck are you? I have to know."

I pulled my face away, but he gripped my jaw with one hand, the other hand trailing to the spot between my eyes, his fingers pressing into my skin. Darkness swam at the edges of my vision as pain tore through me, ripping a scream from my lungs.

"Goddamn it," he growled, letting me go. "Nothing." He licked his lips slowly. "Now I'm never going to be able to let this go. A human strong enough to keep me out? Impossible." He swatted my nose lightly, almost affectionately. "You are quickly turning into an obsession, love."

Adrenaline pumped through me and my heartbeat kicked up, everything around me becoming brighter, more vivid, just *more*. Unease. Calm. Unease. Calm. I kept shifting between those two emotions. What the hell was going on?

Suddenly, the bracelet on my wrist tingled against my skin, and tendrils of warmth seeped through my arm, winding its way through my body. I inhaled slowly as the air around me thickened, growing heavy with charged frissons of electricity. The fluorescent bulb above my head flickered and buzzed before shattering, throwing the room into darkness.

Immediately, the room was filled with a stream of amber light which trailed from Ty's body. I stared at him in shock, my mouth hanging open.

Eyes flashing with glee, he winked at me. "Here we go." He stood to his feet, rubbing his hands together.

Above us, a loud rumbling sound reverberated, and the chair I sat in clattered as the room began to shake. A rush of raw, untamed energy crashed into my senses, flooding the space with crackling sparks of blue light and something so undeniably mind-shattering that fear and awe rocked me: *power*. Terrible, wrath-fueled power.

Shadowy tendrils of mist filled the room, blotting out the light, and in a crack of booming thunder, a shape took form, illuminating the room once more, tearing a strangled cry of relief from my lips.

Ash.

Like I'd never seen him before. A terrifying, avenging dark angel—no—dark God, his eyes swirling with emerald fire.

Ty's eyes widened in surprise, but he took a step forward, that arrogant smile still clinging to his face.

Ash turned to look at me, his eyes flaring even brighter as his gaze drifted over me, settling on my hands and feet bound to the chair. The room vibrated and shook, bits of plaster shaking loose from the ceiling as the shadows and lightning surrounding him thickened.

"Oh my. It's been a long time since I've seen a display of power like this." Ty smiled, his gaze hawkish as it settled on Ash.

"If you hurt her, it'll be the last time you see anything," Ash growled, his jaw clenching as he glared at Ty.

"This little sweetheart?" Ty stepped closer to me. "Who'd ever want to hurt something so precious? She's like an adorable little puppy. Tell him, love." He looked at me encouragingly, his blue eyes twinkling. His voice dropped to a whisper. "Actually, you might want to leave out the bit about me trying to get into your head. I suspect he might not like that."

Ash's eyes narrowed, his magic flaring around him. "Get the fuck away from her."

Ty lifted both his hands in surrender and casually stepped backward to lean against one of the padded walls. All the while, that assessing, smug expression lingered on his face.

Ash stooped in front of me, his eyes filled with rage. "Are you hurt, Tialla?" The tenderness in his voice was at wild odds with the fury emanating off him in waves. His gaze never left Ty's.

I shook my head, my heart racing that he had come for me. He placed his hands over mine, whatever magic he commanded undoing the one that held me in place. Lifting my hand, he kissed my palm, tingling warmth radiating through my hand, swirling and lingering there. His touch was gentle as his eyes searched my body for any signs of trauma. Slowly, he undid the restraints at my feet.

"The magic of the Sangelis showing up here, in this tucked-away world," Ty said, speculation riddling his words. "Too strange, too wild, to be a coincidence." He pushed off the wall, his eyes flashing as he regarded Ash, still crouched in front of me. "You're powerful; I can feel it. And she smells like you—like yours—but it can't be what I think it is because she has no real magic that I can sense. Her *humanness* is overpowering. There is something special about her, though."

He lifted his hand, and a blast of his magic hurtled toward Ash, hitting him in the side of the face. I jerked in my chair, reaching out for Ash as he rose to his feet, unfazed by Ty's attack.

"Whoa, killer." Ty raised his hands again in supplication, that infernal smile still tugging at his lips. "I'm just testing the waters to see what I'm up against. If I wanted to hurt you, you'd know it."

Ash rolled his head, opening his mouth slowly to adjust his jaw. "You wield the Old, Arcane Magic." His voice was tinged with surprise.

A glimmer of curiosity crossed Ty's face. "You're young, but your magic is . . . other. I want a taste."

I looked between them, completely clueless about what they were referring to.

"Come and get it." Ash's eyes flashed as his chest flared and he stood tall, his hands clenched at his sides.

Ty closed his eyes, and I froze as his body began vibrating, a forcefield of light building around him.

"Ash," I squeaked, my skin erupting in gooseflesh at the wave of power filling the room.

"Don't worry, baby," Ash said serenely, his gaze glued to Ty.

I gasped as Ty's eyes flew open, two streams of golden light shooting from them.

Calmly, Ash braced his hands in front of him, palms out, reaching for the magic Ty was blasting at him. My eyes widened as Ash curved his hands, harnessing the golden light and shaping it into a ball.

Ty retracted his magic, his face aghast as he looked at Ash, who stared at him with a smile lifting his lips. The ball of light in Ash's hands was the size of a basketball, indigo shards of lightning flickering through it.

"You wanted a taste of my magic, right?" Ash's irises flared bright emerald as he stared at Ty.

The air around us grew charged with scorching energy, and with unwavering certainty, I knew it was Ash's doing.

Ty's jaw clenched and his face flashed with disbelief and what I swore was fear. "A fucking Godslayer?" he cried. "Those fuckers didn't. Did Winther teach them nothing?"

Next to me, Ash froze, his gaze narrowing on Ty. "What do you know about Winther?" He released his hold on his magic, the ball of light dissipating as his hands fell to his sides. His body was deathly still.

Winther. The name that Liam's specter had mentioned. But what the hell was a Godslayer?

Ty smirked. "I know enough to know that it's time for me to make my way back home."

He took a step forward, and I almost jumped out of my skin as his body suddenly splintered into countless shards of light, swirling around the room like a flock of starlings in formation.

A seductive whisper brushed against my ear. "We'll meet again, love. I am certain of it."

In a shrill, screeching chime, the shards of light were sucked out of the space, leaving Ash and I reeling in silence.

Ash closed the distance between us, sweeping me into his arms. "Brace yourself, baby."

I closed my eyes as the air around us splintered and we, too, were sucked away.

When I opened my eyes, we were standing in my bathroom.

Ash's touch was gentle, but at the same time possessive. "Are you all right, Elle?" He was my Ash again, all traces of ire, vengeance and heart-stopping power gone.

"I need a shower." I clutched at his black vest as I waited for the wave of nausea to pass. "I feel drained."

Pushing the glass shower door open, Ash reached in and turned the dial to warm. The powerful spray blasted the glass, and my skin itched in anticipation, driven by the mindless need to be enveloped in its energizing, cleansing warmth.

Ash's eyes flared, and my clothes slid off my body, pooling on the floor at my feet. "Let me do this for you, Tialla." His tone was beseeching as he pulled me toward the shower. "Let me take care of you. I should have gotten there sooner, but I couldn't find you after you lost consciousness."

My voice cracked. "You came for me, Ash. Just like you promised you would."

Pulling his shirt and vest off over his head, he quickly removed the rest of his clothes. He led me into the shower with him, and I splayed my hands on his chest as the water soaked into my skin. Tilting my head back, Ash wound his fingers through my hair, massaging my scalp under the warm spray.

I lowered my head, my gaze drifting to the water slinking into the drain. "Who was he?" I whispered, pressing my forehead against his chest.

His body grew rigid. "I'm not sure."

"Is he like you? Does he come from the Sangelis?"

"Yes, that much I can say for certain."

"He knew about Winther." I absently stroked the red, crescent-shaped mark on his hip. "He also mentioned others who knew who I was, as well as someone he called 'she.'"

Ash stiffened. "She? What did he say specifically?"

I peered up at him. "That *she* had to know about me, but she'd never mentioned me to him."

Ash was silent, his face inscrutable.

"Why did he take me? He seemed surprised that our paths had crossed. Who could he have been talking about?"

"All questions rattling around in my head too," Ash said quietly.

"He knew you would come for me." I touched the bracelet on my wrist. "It was almost like he was using me as bait. And it was strange. I felt his emotions—he wasn't sure if he wanted to hurt me or protect me."

Ash brushed his lips against my forehead. "I promise, Elle, I'll get to the bottom of this." He grabbed my shampoo and lathered my hair, reaching for my loofah and body wash next, gently scrubbing every inch of my skin.

When he was satisfied with his work, he turned the shower off and pushed the glass door open. As my feet hit the bath mat, a blast of warmth enveloped me, immediately drying my body and hair, as well as his. I barely reacted, this display of his magic trivial compared to what I'd witnessed earlier.

As he led me into the bedroom, he turned the sheets down, lifting me off my feet and tucking me into the bed before climbing in after me. Lying on my side, I leaned into the warmth of his chest as his arms wrapped around me.

The chaos in my mind settled, my thoughts fluttering home to roost. Ash was powerful, his magic more mind-blowing than anything I could have imagined. Ty—whoever he was—had been afraid of him. Ash could have killed him. For *me*. That reality clattered around in my head. I'd seen the truth of it in his eyes. His magic was terrifying and powerful, and while my brain told me I should be afraid, a surge of pride and satisfaction bubbled up from the depths of my soul, enveloping me. This vengeful creature was mine.

I shifted to face Ash, my hands reaching for his face. "What's a Godslayer? Was he talking about you?"

Ash sighed, his face lined with weariness. I could tell he didn't know how to answer me, and suddenly, it didn't matter. I didn't want to talk anymore. I didn't want to get dragged down more rabbit holes of magic and mind-melting revelations. I needed Ash's warmth, his strength.

Needed his arms around me, his voice in my ear, his touch on my skin. I needed the safety and calm I felt only with him.

I brought his head down to meet mine, my lips brushing against the lush fullness of his. My mouth parted as his tongue swept in, and I laced my fingers through his hair, a moan escaping as his warm length grazed against my stomach.

He poured himself into that kiss, every stroke of his tongue an apology, every drag of his lips a declaration of his love, every nip of his teeth a promise to always keep me safe. I pulled him on top of me, reaching between us to guide him inside me, wrapping my legs around his waist as he sank into me.

There were no spoken words, our bodies communicating what our voices didn't as we clung to each other with quiet desperation, undulating slowly, chasing a release that had nothing to do with carnal pleasure and everything to do with soul surrender.

As my climax ripped through me, a rush of emotion cleaved me in half, filling me with the exquisite certainty that what existed between us was ageless, inevitable, unrelenting. "I love you," I whispered as his mouth crashed against mine, muffling the moans that drifted past my lips as he gripped the side of my face and thrust into me.

"I love you, Elle." His body shuddered with his release, his limbs clenching for a moment before growing slack.

There were no other words as we held each other, each touch and kiss passing between us a silent language only our hearts could decipher. I lifted his fingers and placed them against my temple, and understanding what I was asking for, he applied gentle pressure, slivers of warmth bleeding into my mind as fatigue washed over me and I drifted to sleep, wrapped in the arms of the man I loved.

Chapter 34

ELEYSE

A UGUST 9: EIGHT MONTHS AGO . . .

Holy frig, it was hot. I couldn't remember a heatwave this bad, ever. Restlessness had driven me from the house to my back deck, and although I was shaded from the sun under my gazebo, it did absolutely nothing to alleviate the stifling heat simmering around me. Even the trees stood limp and lifeless, robbed of any kind of breeze to stir their leaves and branches.

I peeled myself—quite literally—from my lounge chair and reached for my iced water. Moaning in contentment, I brought the chilled glass to my temples and slid it down my cheek. Who the hell would even want to—

Fuck!

I jumped, falling off my chair, my heart jolting in shock.

Lying on its side on the patio stones in front of me, leisurely grooming its fur with not a bloody care in the world, was Mangy Cat.

"What the hell?" I glared at the feline still absorbed in its lazy fur licking and clearly ignoring me. "You almost gave me a heart attack."

The cat's eyes flicked to mine, and with an agile movement, sprang to its feet and stretched its front legs leisurely. "Hello, Eleyse." It sat on its haunches, tail swishing back and forth. "We told you we'd be seeing you again."

It was hard for me to believe that this woeful-looking creature was the divine will of the universe. The Mavigos, as Ash had referred to it. I got to my feet and dusted my hands off. Gross. They were so slick with sweat, the dust had turned to a filmy paste.

"I think I'll go inside. It's too hot out here." I cocked my head as I looked at the cat. "Mangy Cat, if you are the all-powerful will of the universe, can't you do something about this god-awful heat?"

The cat narrowed its eyes at me before blinking slowly. "Is that the best moniker you could come up with? It's not exactly endearing."

I shrugged. "Hey, if you wanted endearing, you could have chosen to show up as a puppy, or a chipmunk, or here's an idea—a non-mangy cat."

"Beauty is in the eye of the beholder, Eleyse," the cat said with what I swore was an exasperated eye roll. It watched with keen interest as I slid open the patio door. "Are you going to invite us in?"

Invite it in . . . For a hot second, every vampire movie I'd ever watched flashed through my mind. I needed to *invite* the cat in. Shit. What to do?

"We don't *need* to be invited in." I jumped at its words, turning to find it standing in my kitchen. "We were just being polite."

I narrowed my eyes. "Okay, you're allowed in the house, but don't scratch my furniture or pee in my plants."

"You amuse us, Sviyen Cielta." A gurgling sound much like a chuckle emanated from the feline. Crossing the kitchen, it made a beeline for my sunroom. It paused in front of my piano before jumping onto the piano bench and lifting its front paws to look at my sheet music.

"We see you're creating again." A heavy purr vibrated through its body. "Good, Eleyse. The melodies are healing. Don't for one second think they're not. You've witnessed that twice now. Writing the song allowed you to open your heart to love. Singing it made you realize you were in love. Music is a powerful force between you and the other half of your soul. You might be the Sviyen Cielta, but his voice carries the magic of the ancients too. You experienced that in the aftermath of revisiting your third earthly tragedy."

Sviyen Cielta. Ash had told me it meant Celestial Songbird, and was tied up with the pieces of my identity he could not reveal.

The cat turned and peered at the sheet music once more. "We think it's missing something."

I stared at the piece of music. It *was* missing something. I'd been working on the song for over a month and just couldn't finish it. I'd felt a compulsion to write after the night Ash had rescued me, but I hadn't been able to achieve the catharsis I was chasing. I kept drawing a blank every time I sat at the piano and couldn't move forward.

"Maybe it's not yours to finish." The cat hopped off the bench. "Don't forget to sing it when it's done, though. The magic happens when the songs are sung."

I stared at the cat as it made its way over to my fireplace. I had to admit. The little bugger was starting to grow on me. But even as I thought it, I had to remind myself that what I was looking at was in no shape or form even remotely a representation of the power residing within.

"As for why we're here," the cat said, turning to me once more, "we have a pressing matter to discuss."

My eyebrows shot up. What pressing matter could it possibly have to discuss with me?

"As a boy, your human father discovered something in the waters of Greece in southern Crete. Something that he treasured very much and passed on to you."

I furrowed my brows. The cat was right. My father had found something while snorkeling as a boy on a holiday to Greece. Something that, by his account, had strangely shot itself out of the sand into his hand, as if it had *wanted* to be found by him. That same something was sitting in a box above my fireplace mantel.

"What about it?" I walked toward the cat.

"It is time for it to be returned where it belongs."

"I'm sorry?"

The cat turned, and with one swift leap, jumped onto the mantel, nudging a carved wooden box with its head. "That this came to reside with your family was no coincidence. It is an integral part of the life force that completes who you are, after all. A very long time ago, it was ensconced in this world for safekeeping, very much like you, actually. With your impending return to the Sangelis, this must make its way home. It is not safe here anymore."

"What are you saying?" My mind was at a complete loss.

The cat pawed at the box. "You will return it, and in return, you will see a glimpse of the world you belong to."

My brows shot up. "Y—you're sending me where?"

"To Ariadna," the cat said matter-of-factly, "but when we said a glimpse, we meant a glimpse. You will only have a short time before you must return. Hide the box, and then make your way back through the portal."

I frowned. "Why can't I just give it to Ash the next time he's here?"

"Because it has to be you who returns it. Eventually, it will all make sense. Everything in its own time."

Shit. I was actually going to see this mysterious world that until now was surreal and unreachable. "Can I see Ash when I'm there?" A rush of hope flooded me.

The cat shook its head. "The other half of your soul will only be a distraction. This needs to be done quickly. Are you ready?"

I blinked. "Wait, what? You mean like *now*?"

The cat stared at me as if I was the stupidest person it had ever met. "Yes, *now*, Eleyse," it said, its voice softening. "Take hold of the box."

I stepped forward and grabbed the box, cracking the lid and peering inside. The unusual-looking rock glowed in its blue, velvet-lined casing. The sight of it never ceased the take my breath away. Smooth, with a texture and appearance similar to marble, it was about two inches in diameter and an inch thick—round, but not symmetrical. It was silver and black with an unusual geometric pattern all around it—tiny teardrop shapes contained within hexagonal borders. A soft, blue light drifted off it in hazy waves. Ever since I could remember, looking at it—touching it—had filled me with humming contentment, but maybe it was because it was something precious to my father that I'd felt that way.

It was hard to believe that something like this actually existed in nature. Mags had said my father always believed it was out of this world, and it turned out, he was exactly right.

"What is this, really?" I turned to look at the cat still sitting on my mantel. "What did you mean when you said it completes who I am?"

"That's not important right now," it replied dismissively. "Your connection to the object inside the box was never meant to be realized in this world—just preserved." The cat placed a paw on my shoulder. "You need to get going. Close your eyes for a moment and then open them. The first thing you see will act as the portal to send you where you need to go."

Shit. This was really happening. "Um . . . okay." I bit my lip.

Mangy Cat moved toward me and blew a breath of air in my face. "If you encounter anyone, do the same thing to them, and make your way back through the portal."

"I blow in their faces? What will that do?" I clutched the box to my chest.

"It will stun them momentarily and wipe their mind of your presence. Now close your eyes."

"Bossy much?" I grumbled, closing my eyes.

"Open them now."

I opened them, my eyes landing on the bowl of chocolate almonds on my coffee table. Seriously?

"Chocolate almonds it is."

Before I could say a word, the cat pushed me forward and I was sucked into the glass bowl.

Ash . . .

The second I stumbled out of the portal, I was assaulted by his presence. For a moment, I could not move. My senses were on overload, my entire body shaking, my legs wobbly and weak. I grabbed the edge of the bookshelf beside me as I breathed in his smell that was permanently imprinted in my senses. It was a glorious addiction.

Slowly, I looked around, my jaw dropping open in awe. I was standing in a tall and spacious study. Opulent and beautiful. As my eyes flicked to the floor, my heart flew into my throat at the sight of the most extraordinary-looking cat, the size of a goddamn Bengal tiger, sprawled on the rug in front of me, eyeing me curiously.

"Mangy Cat?" I whispered as the animal stretched and got to its feet. Oh god, I was going to be mauled to death, shredded to ribbons on this beautiful, very expensive-looking rug. I inched backward until I was pressed against the wall. The cat moved forward and sniffed me, nudging its head gently against my hand. God, it was fearsome to behold, but so beautiful, snowy white with swirls of royal blue on its body and face.

Slowly, it backed up, dropping its front paws to the floor and lowering its head, almost like it was bowing to me. It flicked its gaze to mine, and I was done for. Emerald-green eyes stared back at me, so similar in shade to Ash's. Wait. There was no way . . . The cat lifted its head and licked my hand, a low, guttural rumble reverberating from its throat. It sat back on its haunches, studying me.

I gripped the box in my hand, the feel of the wood snapping me back to reality. Right. I was supposed to hide the box and get out of here. I looked around me. A large desk was positioned in the middle of the room, behind which a very tall, masculine-looking chair in leather and dark wood was positioned. My mind conjured an image of Ash sitting there, and even in my imagination, my heart fluttered.

Three armchairs flanked the front of the desk, and in the corner of the room, a strange obelisk sculpture stretched all the way to the ceiling. It was covered in peculiar swirling patterns that lit up intermittently with indigo-colored light, fading in and out from top to bottom. The entire room was lined with bookshelves.

Keeping a cautious eye on the cat, I crossed the floor to the bookshelf in the far left corner and crouched down. Surveying the contents of the shelf, I pulled out three smaller books, sliding the box to the back and carefully replacing the books. Unless someone went looking for those books specifically, they wouldn't find the box.

This had to be Ash's study; I just knew it. I moved over to his desk, scattered with books and sheets of paper, and my eye caught something scribbled on one of the loose sheets at the front of the desk near his chair. *Who/what is Winther? First Age?*

I froze. *Winther.* That was the name the ghastly specter of Liam had mentioned, the name Ty had uttered in disgust. What the hell was the First Age, though?

"Snooped enough?" a deep voice asked quietly from behind me, splintering the silence.

I jumped, but before I could run, someone grabbed me from behind, pressing something cold and hard into my neck.

"Don't even think about moving, or I will slit your throat," the voice commanded.

My body went slack.

The next few moments passed by in a blur. One minute I was in the clutches of someone with a blade at my throat and the next, the blue and white cat was roaring and pouncing, bowling the intruder over.

"What in Medra's name are you doing, Tryxie?" The man's voice rang out in irritation, trying to push the cat off him. "It's me, girl."

I crouched against the desk, grabbing a letter opener and holding it out in my hand.

"I told you it wasn't Kaliope or one of her spies," another voice said calmly from behind me, startling me further. I spun around to see two other men in the study with me. They were dressed for stealth—all black from the neck down, and armed to the teeth with swords and daggers. How had they gotten in here? Both men in front of me had shoulder-length ivory hair and powerful builds, and when I looked at their faces, my heart lurched. Their eyes were *slitted.* What the hell?

I backed up against the bookcase, my heart hammering, letter opener still in my hand. The man on the ground managed to get the cat off, and the blue and white feline slurped him on his neatly trimmed beard as he got to his feet. His hair was a rich, chestnut color, cropped short around his face. His eyes, too, were slitted as he regarded me curiously.

"Please, I apologize for earlier." He showed both his palms to me in submission. He moved a step closer, and I immediately retreated, but I was already against the bookshelf and there was nowhere else to go. The cat, as if sensing my apprehension, padded over to me and nudged my hip with its hand as it looked back serenely at the three men standing in front of me.

"Forgive our friend," the one who had made the comment about spies said. "He can be a little hasty."

"Ha. My hastiness has saved your life on more occasions than I can count," the short-haired one retorted, his face softening as he looked at me.

I stared at him, captivated by his gray, slitted eyes. The other one who had talked—his eyes were bright green. The one who hadn't spoken had piercing baby blues, his skin the color of rich chocolate. The latter was staring at me intently, and something about his expression stirred some feeling in me.

He moved his hands animatedly, and the other two nodded. What the hell? Wait. He couldn't speak. He was signing. Even stranger, I understood what he had said: "This must be the one. I can sense it."

I moved closer. "Which one is that?"

A look of shock flitted across his face, and then he began signing back at me. I wasn't looking at his hands, but the words he was speaking were still registering in my brain. As if they were coming to me from his mind as he was relaying them.

"The one our Sovereign loves."

I blinked, surprised by his answer. Sovereign? What did that mean? Were they talking about Ash? "Who are you?"

"We are part of Ash's inner circle," the gray-eyed one answered. "I am Treye, the most dashing of the bunch as you can see, and that hideous fiend over there is Gilham." He gestured to the one with the green eyes, who was anything but hideous. "The blue-eyed devil is Ovix. You are Eleyse?"

"I am." I looked between them in confusion. Ash's inner circle? He had never mentioned them to me before. There was so much about him that

I still didn't know, so much that he hadn't told me.

A bright flare at the door pulled my attention. Shit. The portal. I had to get back. The urgency of the call yanked me.

"Well, it was nice meeting the three of you." I scurried toward the flare of flashing light, "But I have to go."

"Is that a portal?" Treye asked, a bewildered expression on his face.

"Uh-huh." I stopped in front of them. "Sorry about this." I moved close enough to blow in their faces as I darted toward the waiting portal. I looked behind me to see the three of them frozen where they stood, their expressions suspended in surprise. On the floor, the cat—Tryxie, as Treye had called her—looked at me, blinking lazily.

I dropped my voice to a whisper. "I hope to see you again, beautiful girl." And with that, I stepped through the swirling light.

Pulled through my bowl of chocolate almonds, I tumbled unceremoniously onto the floor of my sunroom.

Mangy Cat sat on my coffee table, regarding me calmly. "Good job, Eleyse. Everything is as it should be."

My mind erupted in a vortex of chaos. "Oh my god, I have so many questions."

The cat sauntered toward me, its eyes flashing silver. "Not right now, sweet Eleyse." It pounced on my chest and quickly blew a breath in my face. "It'll all come back to you when the time is right."

I blinked and shook my head slowly, staring at the upended bowl of chocolate almonds on the coffee table.

What the hell? When did I come in from outside?

Chapter 35

ELEYSE

SEPTEMBER 15: SIX AND A HALF MONTHS AGO . . .

I touched my palm gently, absently tracing the skin in the middle with my thumb. I rolled to the other side of the bed, inhaling deeply, dousing my senses with the lingering smell of Ash from last night. Longing and sadness cinched my heart, threatening to snap the fragile threads of my composure. Every time he left, it got harder. The restlessness and agitation were unreal, clawing at my skin with needlelike pincers, driving me insane with the irrational need to break free of the confines of my life.

Time slipped by slowly as I tossed and turned, my thoughts scattered and uneasy. We hadn't talked mind-to-mind tonight, and although I tried to dismiss it since he had only left this morning, I missed hearing his voice before I went to bed.

Throwing the covers off, I pulled my robe on and headed downstairs. The moment my foot hit the bottom step, I felt it—dual thrums of power, each with its own magnetic signature, both of which I'd experienced individually before, but not in unison. I quickened my pace, heading toward the source.

My heart thudded in excitement when I spied a shock of curly violet hair in my sunroom.

"Leida mata," her melodic voice rang out, her words warming an unlit place inside me.

I stared at her form, surrounded in an ethereal haze of light and power, that mesmerizing melody reverberating from inside her. Next to her stood Death—no, not Death. Arazul. The guardian of the Sangelis, as he had called himself.

The power drifting off the both of them was enough to drive me to my knees in obeisance, but before my body could surrender, they both stepped forward, each one holding a hand out to me. My fingers curled around theirs, and a surge of raw energy pulsed through me, threatening to ignite and scorch my senses.

"Do you know why we're here, Eleyse?" The intensity in Arazul's gaze caused my heart to stutter.

"You are Gods of the Sangelis." The certainty of my words rattled deep in my bones. Ash had told me this was coming; he had prepared me for this moment.

"And you are our secret," the violet-haired woman replied.

Secret of the Gods. She had called me that the very first time she had come to me in my dream.

She brushed her fingers against my cheek. "Tonight, sweet Eleyse, you will learn the truth of who you are and the powerful future that belongs to you.

Full-body shivers rocked me, the hair on my skin standing on end.

I lifted my chin to meet her gaze. "I am ready."

Every cell in my body *hummed,* even as my mind was overrun with raw, naked shock. My tongue was as heavy as lead in my mouth, my throat tight and constricted. Around my head, heat radiated in erratic pulses. My body was rigid and wound tight, my limbic system unable to regulate my emotions and my physical response to them.

My *mother.* I stared at her—Eolith, Goddess of the Ethereal Harmonies—her eyes shining with so much emotion I was drowning in them. She was my *mother.* Even as my brain struggled to process what I'd just heard, my senses did not suffer the same impairment. No, on the contrary, they rejoiced in acceptance, the chamber doors of my soul flung open for the first time, flooded with light and celebration, and at long last, peace.

I looked between *her* and Arazul, their silver eyes blazing as they waited patiently for me to react, and I longed for Ash. He had told me that the secret of my identity wasn't his to divulge, but god, I wished he was here now. If only I could see the strength and assurance in his eyes, everything would be all right.

I turned to face Arazul, my lips quivering as I tried to find the words. "So . . . so my parents weren't really my parents?"

He lifted his hand and stroked my cheek. "I poured the essence of who you are into their lifeless child's body. Tamped down all your power and radiance, ensuring that they remained dormant and unresponsive within you. All souls are immortal, Eleyse. A mortal body is just a temple. By human standards—DNA, physical makeup—you *were* their child. In every way that matters, you were theirs. But you were also always so much more."

My mind flashed to what Ty had said about me—that I was human, but not human. He had said my *humanness* was overpowering, but he could still sense I was different, could see the faint glimmer of my essence. This explained why.

"A mortal existence has a different flow than an immortal one," Arazul continued. "Life, death, the soul's afterlife, and in some cases, rebirth. You are born of the Gods, the first of our kind, destined for an immortal life. Housing your life force and all your power in a mortal's body was only ever meant to be temporary. Upon your return to the Sangelis, your mortal body will undergo a series of transformations until, at last, you will become the powerful being you were always meant to be."

My goddess mother stepped forward, tucking my hair behind my ear. "Do you remember what you said to me the first time I asked you what your heart told you I was?"

I nodded. "Life, redemption."

"Do you feel the truth of it?" She brushed her lips against my forehead.

I closed my eyes, allowing my senses to guide me. It was like I had told Ash—just like he did, she too called to me on a deeper level I didn't understand. She felt like a warm hearth on a cold winter's day, like a cool spring in the stifling heat of summer, like the soothing hum of a lullaby crooned to a sad heart. She felt like *home*. Like *mine*. And I *wanted* to be hers.

She opened her arms to me and I stepped into her embrace, feeling the tears on her cheeks against my skin.

"What about my father?" I lifted my head to look at her. Sorin. Summoner of Light and Darkness. "Ash mentioned him before when he told me the story of Cadavweira. How with your magic, you helped him to harness the light he wasn't able to wield on his own."

She placed her palm against my cheek. "Love has a way of creating light in a dark world."

I saw it—the depth of emotion flickering in her eyes for the God who was my father. "You loved him, then?"

"And I love him still." A sad smile lifted her lips.

"After all this time, he still doesn't know about me?" It was hard to fathom the true length of my existence. For thousands of years, the essence of who I was had been *alive*. It was mind-blowing, really.

She shook her head. "Keeping you safe and hidden until the time was right was our priority." She looked at Arazul, sadness etched on her features. "Sorin would have never given you up if he knew you existed. Arazul and I made the choices we did to protect the future that you would usher in—one that is bigger than anything I personally wanted."

The protector of my future. That's what Arazul had said he was. My eyes flitted to his. All these years, he had watched over me. I needed to know. "Why did you come to me each time I lost someone? Then again when I tried to end my life all those times? You never said a word. You made me believe that *you* were responsible."

He sighed, his eyes filled with sadness. "I couldn't interfere in your life here, but I needed to make sure that your losses did not have detrimental consequences—did not awaken your power. It needed to stay dormant, and I had to make sure that it did. But in all honesty, I hated seeing you so broken and lost to the darkness. Seeing you allowed me to dull some of your emotions. It would have been infinitely more heightened if I didn't. Trust me, little bird, this world is not ready for power like yours. As for the *nine* times you tried to end your life, my purpose was simple: to ensure you lived."

The sting of tears blurred my vision as I stared at him, my throat tightening as a swarm of emotions blasted through me. "I hated you for who I thought you were. For what I thought you had done."

"It's all right, Eleyse." He tilted my chin. "I can take your hate. Darkness was never meant to be your path; you are a child of the light. To watch you slip away into nothingness was something I wasn't willing to let happen. While this world served as a refuge for you, it also became a prison, and for that, I am sorry."

I smothered a sob and wiped the tears from my cheeks. "Do you truly believe I am who you think I am? This chosen one who will usher in a new age to the Sangelis?"

Arazul smiled, his eyes shining with intensity. "It is not a matter of belief, it just *is*. You are marked by the Mavigos. Each living thing in the vastness of the universe serves a purpose in life. Each soul holds within it the truth of their existence. To honor that truth brings self-actualization, the ultimate attainment of one's purpose. What does the truth in your soul whisper to you, little bird? Ask it who you are meant to be. It will answer you."

I didn't need to ask it to know. The acceptance of who I was roared through me, ringing out for me to hear.

I swallowed, dropping my hands to my sides. "What happens now?"

"Only the Mavigos know how and when," Arazul said. "But you will leave this world and return to the Sangelis."

"The time is close, leida mata." My moved forward and cupped my cheeks. "The restless pulsing of the Ethereal Harmonies tells me that it is. No matter what happens from here on out, know this. You are loved. So very much. And you are never alone." She leaned forward and kissed my cheek. "We will see each other again soon, soladeo."

Arazul squeezed my shoulder gently. "Hold on to your light, little bird. You will need it."

My heart ached as I watched them fade into the air itself, the yearning for something more threatening to engulf me. They were right. *Soon.* I could feel it too. Something inside me was stirring. And it was ready for what awaited me. Ready to go home.

Chapter 36

ASHER

PRESENT DAY SOLNIESS, THE VOID . . .

The light of the Lonefera coasted over my skin before drifting to Elle. My heart was heavy, my thoughts dark as I lay on my side next to her shadow self, staring at her beautiful face, contemplating all the grisly possibilities from here on out.

Arazul had assured me that Kaliope was not a threat to us as long as we were in the Void, and while that was a relief, I refused to let my guard down. *Expect the unexpected.* It was burned into my brain. That psychotic bitch did not play by anyone's rules, and I was not going to underestimate her.

Cazril and Jaraya had both demanded entrance to Solniess—Jaraya to summon Sorin, and Cazril to demand Arazul's judgment for what I had done at the Torannon market.

Eolith had turned them both away, but they refused to leave, encamping themselves on the borders of Solniess. The fact that they couldn't get in didn't make me any less uneasy; on the contrary, their close proximity only exacerbated my already-agitated frame of mind.

Events unfolding in the Void weren't the only worries on my mind. What awaited us the moment our consciousness left Solniess and returned to the present weighed on me. Would Lorien be able to reverse the effects of the rebounding curse? Would Kaliope and Gargmoin be waiting? Would Elle return to me with all her memories intact? But perhaps the thing I feared most was the thing I tried not to think about at all—would she hate me when she remembered the events of those last five months?

"I'm sorry, Tialla." I brushed my lips against her head. "I'm sorry I abandoned you when you needed me the most."

Do you really believe that? Catraia's voice rang out in my mind.

I closed my eyes, resting my chin on Elle's head. *You haven't seen what happened yet.*

From what I'm sensing, there are a lot of things you don't know either.

She had me there, but the things I did know . . .

Listen, Asher. I don't need to see what happens next to know that what you say is not true. From the moment you walked into her life, you were there for her, bringing her back to life. Every moment you spent with her was crucial. You tell yourself not to underestimate Kaliope, but you underestimate Elle—her strength and her love for you. Trust her, Asher.

Shame coursed through me. When it came to Elle, I was a slave to my fear. I feared losing her, and that drove my every decision. The night she revisited Liam's death, I had been in Chantilis for Faron's and Astrid's birthday celebration, and the moment my labral grew hot and I felt the abject pain and despair leaking out of her, I'd taken off without an explanation to anyone.

The night she was taken, I had been in Averon with the other Sovereigns to discuss an alliance in preparation for war, but when I felt her call out for me, felt her terror through my labral, I abandoned everything to get to her. I had been so consumed with keeping her safe from the evil lurking in Ariadna that it had never crossed my mind that there were forces on Earth that could touch her. Saving her had cost Ariadna that alliance, but I would do it all over again if I had to. She was the most important thing in the Sangelis to me. And that in itself was terrifying.

It was because I feared losing her that I stayed away those last five months after Kaliope found out about my visits to Earth. It was the only way to keep her safe, to lower the chances of Kaliope finding her.

Catraia was right. I was underestimating her strength and love for me. My need for control refused to let me be at the mercy of feelings beyond my influence.

The sound of a throat clearing drew my attention to the entryway of Elle's chamber, where Faron and Treye stood. I kissed Elle's brow and sat up.

"You don't have to leave her," Treye said softly, "but can we talk?"

I nodded, swinging my legs onto the floor, but staying next to Elle.

Faron pulled two armchairs closer to the bed from the corner of the room and he and Treye sat, facing me. He leaned forward, his forearms on his knees. "We were just on the grounds with Eolith and Sorin—which by the way, they insisted we call them—and Sorin said something very interesting." His eyes were bright with excitement.

"Good interesting or bad?"

Treye cocked his head, looking at Faron. "Not sure yet. Just interesting."

I wasn't sure I liked where this was headed.

"He was talking about you, actually," Faron said. "About the Mavigos giving you the power to slay Gods."

I narrowed my eyes. "Okay . . ."

"He said that in the Entombed City of Magana, there is an obscure reference to a Godslayer in one of the hidden chambers of the ancient temple there."

I froze, my heart thudding in my chest.

"Get this." Treye steepled his fingers on his chest. "The name of that Godslayer is *Winther*."

"What?" My jaw dropped open. "Are you sure?"

"That's what he said." Faron leaned back in his chair. "Treye said that was a name you were looking into based on something that happened when you were on Earth with Elle."

"Yes." I rubbed my jaw, my thoughts flying to the night Elle was taken.

Elbows pressed against the armrests of his chair, Treye leaned forward. "What was the exact phrase Elle told you about?"

"'The Shadow King and Queens breathe again, Agaia. Winther comes. Catraia stirs. The Third Age looms. The Bells of Galeseira call you home.'"

"Wait," Faron said, his expression thoughtful. "Isn't Agaia what Tora calls Elle?"

I nodded, turning to look at Elle's profile on the bed. "But it's also what my senses claim her to be. It means *storm* in Hasheyn."

Faron shifted in his chair. "Do you think Winther means something that refers to you?"

I frowned. "No. It's not a Hasheyn word. That phrase was a message to Elle. A warning, almost." I turned to Treye. "Ty—the being from the Sangelis who took Elle that night—he mentioned Winther. At the time, I didn't understand what he meant."

"Wait, what?" Faron's jaw was slack. "Back up a bit. There was a being from the Sangelis on Earth? One who took Elle?"

I nodded. "He happened to be in the same place she was one night, and his senses triggered him when he spotted her. He took her in an attempt to find out more. The protective bracelet on her wrist alerted me that she was in danger and I rushed to her. He recognized my magic right away, just as I did his."

Faron's eyes sparked with disbelief. "What are the chances that another being from the Sangelis would be on *Earth*?"

"And not just any being." Treye narrowed his eyes. "From what you said, Bash, he wielded the Old, Arcane Magic."

Faron tilted his head. "Light strain or dark sway?"

I clenched my jaw. "A blend."

"What?" Faron cried. "What the fuck does that even mean?"

"That it's not black and white?" I cracked my knuckles. "Trust me. I'm just as curious as you to find out. Elle said that when she was him, she felt his emotions—that he wasn't sure if he wanted to hurt her or protect her. I don't know enough about the Old, Arcane Magic to grasp what the implications are of someone wielding a blend." I sighed. "He knew I was a Godslayer. And in the moment he realized it, he mentioned Winther. He said, 'Those fuckers didn't. Did Winther teach them nothing?' I've thought about it on repeat since then, and the one thing that keeps nagging me is that he had to be talking about the Mavigos. With what Sorin just told you both, it makes a little more sense. Winther is—*was* a Godslayer, like me. The Mavigos clearly bestowed that ability before."

"Gods," Faron exclaimed. "There's so much to unpack here."

"You can say that again." Treye exhaled loudly, interlocking both hands behind his head. "I can't help but think that the First Age is the missing link. The other things Elle told you about—Catraia, the Third Age—we know of. But who are the Shadow King and Queens? And the Bells of Galeseira? I've never come across any mention of that before. Do they belong to the First Age?"

I rubbed my fingers across my temples, trying to ease the dull throbbing there. Ever since Tora's letter and the memory she had returned, one unsettling thought had plagued me. The ghosts of the Sangelis's past—ghosts we knew nothing about—would come back to haunt us.

"All three ages will collide." Faron pinched the crease between his eyes. "You said that the Great Creator referred to Elle as the bridge between all three ages. What if this is an example of that?"

Treye's fingers tapped against the armrest of the chair. "Tora and Lorien. They have to know something."

Faron stretched a knee out in front of him. "Along the lines of what Treye said about the First Age, here's the thing I can't stop thinking about. We all love Tora fiercely. She is the beating heart of Torannon. If she is indeed as old as the First Age, she could have settled anywhere in Ariadna or the Sangelis, really. Same with Lorien. Why did they choose Valkyse? Was it intentional or a coincidence? They both knew of the ancient celestial star etching. But nothing in there suggests where the High King of the Light Age would come from, or his queen."

Eyes fixed on Faron, I flashed back to Tora's letter to me. *I have been loyal to the House of Valkyse since its inception, for I have always known that greatness would arise from within.*

"She knew." My voice was a low whisper. "In her letter to me, she said that she had always known that greatness would come from within the House of Valkyse."

"Holy shit." Treye looked between Faron and me. "Forget the Gods of the Sangelis. Tora and Lorien are the key to unlocking all of this. They wield the light strain of the Old, Arcane Magic, plus Lorien is the keeper of that magic on Ariadna. The knowledge of the First Age lies with them."

"Which begs one monumental question." Faron's gaze flicked to mine. "What the fuck happened to bring about the end of the First Age?"

I nodded. "And what can we expect in this war when it comes to the dark Gods and ancients of the ages? We literally have no idea. I can't stop thinking about it."

"Right." Treye chewed on his lip. "What happened to the Gods of the First Age? Annihilation by the Mavigos? Or are they in tecleios? We know the sleep of the Gods is a real thing. Maybe that's where they've been all this time."

Faron lifted his index finger. "Or maybe this Godslayer, Winther, had something to do with their fate."

"What if they scattered to other worlds across the universe." I reached for Elle's hand on the bed beside me. "This Ty, he was on Earth. He mentioned someone else knowing about Elle as well. What if there are more of them in different civilized worlds, biding their time, waiting to return?" Ty's words scraped across my mind. *I think it's time for me to make my way home.* He was so intent on finding out who Elle was, but who in blazes was he?

Faron swiped his palm across the back of his neck. "Only the Mavigos would know any of this for certain."

I grunted. "They're not exactly forthcoming with providing information. They might be all-knowing and all-powerful, but we can't rely on them to provide us with answers. We have to do that on our own."

Treye's brows lifted. "We start with Tora and Lorien. The Entombed City of Magana is ancient, long believed to be a relic of the First Age. For Medra's sake, WorDalg is conscripted there, and we know that old fuck wields the dark sway of the Old, Arcane Magic. It's an easy picture to paint. All roads lead to the First Age."

"And what about Valkyse's Phantera?" Faron piped in. "Do you think it's a coincidence that it's buried within the Entombed City of Magana? I find that hard to believe. I would even venture to add that all roads lead to the First Age *and* Valkyse. Tora, Lorien, the source of the Old, Arcane Magic, the Phantera, Ash, Eleyse—all centered around Valkyse."

Faron and Treye were both right. Valkyse was at the center of the ancient celestial star etching. The Mavigos had told Eolith that the star etching was a promise given at the end of the First Age to right immeasurable wrongs and atrocities. We just needed to bide our time and wait for Elle to absorb the power of the light strain of the Old, Arcane Magic as part of her transformation. Once the craleic oath was broken, we would have answers. At least I hoped to fuck we did.

"For all we know, Kaliope might be the least of our worries," Treye snorted.

"Can you imagine?" Faron released a huffed laugh. A shadow promptly fell over his face, and he scrubbed his jaw with his hand. "Actually, no. I don't want to. The thought of something worse than Kaliope scares the shit out of me."

Treye sucked his teeth. "You can say that again. She and Gargmoin together are the stuff of nightmares. I don't even want to think about all the other unhinged horrors we *don't* know about joining their happy troop of psychopaths. We already have the Goddess of the Night, the God of Chaos, WorDalg, Kurglokh and his Soulshredders, that snake of a Sovereign, Madio Averon. It doesn't look good."

My eyes flashed as I looked between my two closest friends, my brothers-in-arms. "Elle is the key to winning this war. I feel it in my bones, and my senses are never wrong." I reached for her hand at her side. "We protect our girl at all costs. Catraia is right. We should not underestimate her. She is the hope of the Sangelis, and we will fight for her. That is my command, now and always."

"With our lives." Treye placed his fist against his heart.

"Agreed." Faron mirrored Treye's gesture. "With our lives, we will protect her."

Chapter 37

ELEYSE

NOVEMBER 20: FOUR AND A HALF MONTHS AGO

A tear dripped off my cheek onto Ash's bare chest. The weight of my sadness was crushing, wrenching the air from my chest. Two months ago, he had spoken the words that had pierced my heart with the brutality of a serrated wedge of glass and embedded itself there.

Soon, I may not be able to return.

He had been here twice since then, but the heaviness and frustration radiating off him each time was overpowering and infectious, injecting a heart-wrenching sense of desperation into each moment we spent together. Funny how the certainty of a fast-approaching demise had the ability to make you cling to each minute because you feared it could be the last.

"Elle." Ash's voice was calm but commanding as he flipped me onto my back and shifted onto his side next to me. "Tell me." His fingers trailed down my cheek, his eyes reflecting the same sorrow I felt inside.

I placed my hand over his. "I hate this, Ash. Every time you make love to me now, it feels like you're saying goodbye. And not that it isn't amazing or that I don't love the intensity of it, but my heart can't take it. I don't want to say goodbye. I don't want to wake up one day and be cut off from you. When you're not here, the fact that I can still talk to you and hear your voice makes your absence bearable, but if I were to lose that?" My eyes filled with tears and my throat tightened as my emotions surged.

He closed his eyes, his face lined with anguish. My breath hitched as he pulled me to him, burying his face in my neck.

My lip quivered. "Tell me, Ash. What do I not know? There is so much you don't say, and I know it's because you don't want me to worry, but don't I have a right to know?"

"I'm sorry, Elle." He pulled back and looked at me, his voice tinged with regret. "I've tried to keep you safe, but it's getting harder."

"Tell me." I pushed against his chest. "Keep me safe from what?"

He loosed a breath, raking his hand through his hair. "There are those in the Sangelis who would hurt you because of who you are."

"Because of this great power I will supposedly wield?"

He nodded. "And because you are precious to me."

I frowned. "Who are you in Ariadna? You've told me stories about your life and traditions, about your friends and your family—your sister and your uncle—but there's a lot you don't say as well. I haven't forgotten what Ty called you that night. Godslayer. What does it mean?"

"Does it matter?" His finger traced the shell of my ear. "I am myself the most when I'm with you."

"It matters," I whispered. "Tell me."

He was silent, his expression guarded as he absently traced my collarbone with his thumb. Slowly, his eyes flicked to mine. "I am Asher Valkyse, son of Arlon and Harwen Valkyse, brother of Gwynn, nephew of Andreo, love of Eleyse." His voice dropped to a low murmur. "I am also the Sovereign of Valkyse."

My eyes widened. *Sovereign.* Why did that sound familiar? A memory rattled loose as an unfamiliar voice perforated my subconscious. *This must be the one . . .* A man's voice. Speaking about me, to me. *The one our Sovereign loves.* I shook my head, clawing at the wisps of the memory, but there was no trace of it for me to latch onto.

I stared at Ash. "Sovereign? As in . . . a king?"

Ash nodded. "Four dominions divide Ariadna, each one ruled by a Sovereign. I am the Sovereign of the Dominion of Valkyse."

I closed my gaping jaw, swallowing slowly. A king. It shouldn't have shocked me—my mother and father were *Gods.* "Is that why you have magic?" I asked, my voice a low whisper. "Why you're so powerful?"

He nodded. "Magic is inherent in Sovereign bloodlines, but in addition to my Sovereign powers, I was also bestowed with the powers and title of Godslayer by the Mavigos."

My eyes widened. "What does that mean?"

"Exactly what it sounds like. I have the power to kill Gods."

Sweet Jesus. I swallowed slowly. I couldn't even fathom the magnitude of what he was saying. "So Arazul, my . . . *parents* . . ."

"Just because I hold that power doesn't mean I will use it mindlessly." His knuckles grazed my forehead. "Yes, I am powerful, but your magic? That is beyond anything I wield. Everything you've learned about yourself so far makes it clear that you have an even more powerful future ahead of you. Arazul called you the hope of the Sangelis because that's what you are. Your birth was foretold *millions* of years ago by the Mavigos. Your parents are two of the most powerful Gods of the Sangelis."

My heart thudded in my chest. It was pretty wild and mind-blowing to have it laid out like that, but even as my rational, *human* mind flared in disbelief, that *certain* part of me from the deep reaches of my soul reared up and swallowed my doubt whole, as if to say, No *way. Not on my watch, you don't.*

Ash knotted a tendril of my hair around his finger. "Even as you live your life here, far removed from the Sangelis, it has begun. A great darkness is threatening the peace of the realms, and is growing in power every day. The person behind it all murdered my parents in cold blood years ago."

My eyes flicked to his, my body frigid as I gripped his hand. "Oh god. I'm so sorry, Ash."

He intertwined our fingers. "She has a twisted, unnatural obsession with me, and if she were to find out about you . . ." His voice trailed off, his eyes tortured and pained as his thoughts ripped him away from me.

Jealousy flared at the thought of another woman claiming any kind of rights to him, but to hear that this person had inflicted soul-crushing pain on him—molten, red rage rushed through my veins.

Ash curved his hand around my waist, pulling me closer. "Every time I visit you, I risk her finding out. She is getting more tenacious, inserting her spies everywhere to watch me. Elle, I can't put you in danger. Especially from her. Your power is locked to you here. Until the Mavigos return you to the Sangelis, I am putting you in harm's way every time I visit, every time I reach for you in my mind."

I shook my head, a surge of heat rushing to my face, my blood thumping in my ears. "Don't you dare, Ash." I pounded my fist against his chest. "I have a choice, too, and I don't care. I choose the risk. I choose us. Even if you can't visit me anymore, don't you fucking stop reaching for me in your mind. Arazul might call me the hope of the Sangelis, but *you* are the hope in my head. Don't take that away from me."

"I'm sorry, baby." His eyes pooled with regret. "You are the most important person in the universe to me, and I will do whatever I have to do to keep you safe. Even give you up. And I'll do that because I know it won't be for long. The Mavigos will return you to the Sangelis, and I'll be right there waiting."

He reached for my hand and I pushed it away, my breathing ragged as anger inflamed my senses. "So that's it? You get to make the decisions and I have no say because you're doing it for my own good?"

"Elle," he said, his voice tortured. "Do you think this is what I *want*? Fuck, no. If it were up to me, I would never go back. I'd stay with you until the Mavigos decided it was time. But this isn't just about you and me. This is bigger than *us*. Your mother—a powerful goddess—made the hard sacrifice to give you up because she believed in the promise of your future. I believe in that same future—one where you are at my side and we usher in peace to the Sangelis. Giving you up now is short-term pain for long-term gain. I need you to understand that and be on board with it."

"What about my sacrifice?" Bitterness coated my tongue. "What if I want to sacrifice my safety because you're worth the risk to me?"

His eyes flared. "That's not going to fucking happen. You're not even trying to see things objectively."

"I'm sorry, Ash. I'm not okay with this." The chaos in my head drowned out any rational thought. I rolled away from him, pushing his arm off as he reached for me.

"What are you doing?" The heft of his gaze bore into me as I raced to my walk-in closet and grabbed a pair of leggings and a tank top.

"I need some air." I hurriedly yanked the leggings on. "I have to clear my head, so I'm going for a run. And no, I don't want company."

He exhaled slowly, but I ignored him as I headed to the bathroom to pull my hair into a ponytail. When I stepped back into the room, he was sitting up in bed, his expression unreadable.

"Listen." The resignation in his voice was impossible to miss. "I know you're angry and hurt right now and need your space. But that bracelet on your wrist—don't you fucking ignore it if it goes cold, do you hear me?"

My eyes met his, and the momentary flash of fear in his gaze unsettled me. Part of me wanted to crawl into his lap just to feel the safety and comfort of his arms around me, but my anger won out and I turned away and walked out of the room. I pulled my sneakers on at the door and headed outside.

Sacrifice. My entire life was marked with the sacrifices others had made for me—my goddess mother choosing to give me up, my parents moving away from the city after I was born to give me a good upbringing, Mags giving up her music dreams to raise me. Even Liam, although he'd never said it, had turned his back on his hockey dreams for me. And now Ash. What the hell made me so special? Why did I deserve their sacrifices? I would have never asked any of them to make the choices they did.

My feet pounded the pavement as I ran toward the trail, completely oblivious to everything around me. Ash said I wasn't seeing things objectively, but what did that even mean?

This is bigger than us. His words echoed in my head. Was it? Once Liam died, I'd only ever had *me* to think about. My actions were my own and had no repercussions for anyone else. I was alone.

You are the hope of the Sangelis, Arazul's words floated in. Shit. Would people die if I didn't become who I was meant to be? Would horrible things happen? I wasn't used to having people depend on me for anything.

You were made from pure light, created to wield the light, Mangy Cat had said to me. I wasn't even sure what that meant, but no doubt, it was monumental. *You were born for greatness, but that greatness does not extend to this world. Here, you cannot blossom and thrive.* Arazul's words grated against my nerves, driving the point home. This world was not where I belonged. This world was not where I was needed, or would achieve my true potential.

I was just past the trailhead when my heart lurched. *What if he's gone when you go back and you never get to say goodbye? Is this how you want to leave things?* Panic and fear gripped me, and I spun on my heel, racing like the wind to get back, praying to my goddess mother and Arazul to not punish me for leaving the way I did.

I threw open my front door, slamming it behind me as I toed off my sneakers. The silhouette of his fully clothed body came into view at the entrance to my kitchen and I sagged in relief, closing the distance between us and leaping into his arms. He lifted me by the thighs as I wrapped my legs around him, gripping his body as tightly as I could.

I trailed kisses down his face. "If this could be the last time I'm with you, I don't want to spend it being angry."

He walked us to my sunroom, lowering himself onto the piano bench before gripping my face with his hands. "I don't want you to feel that your choice is being taken away, Elle. That is not what I'm trying to do."

"I know." I swiped at the tears blurring my vision. "You were right. I wasn't seeing things objectively. I know this isn't something you're doing lightly. If you can sacrifice, so can I. You, my goddess mother, Arazul, Mangy Cat—you all have a vision of me that far exceeds anything I see for myself, and if that's what it takes, I will give you up to make that vision a reality, simply because you believe in it."

"I fucking love you, Elle," he said gruffly, pulling me to his chest. "Don't for one second forget that. Promise me."

"I promise, baby." I threaded my fingers through his hair, feeling the steady thump of his heartbeat against mine. I furrowed my brows as my eyes snagged on the sheet music resting on the music rack of my piano. "Hey." I pushed forward and reached for one of the pages. "Did you do this?"

He traced my smile with his fingers. "You've been stuck on this one for a long time. I tried to finish it for you while you were asleep."

It's missing something. The words floated in my mind from somewhere. He had finished the song for me. I looked up at him with wonder as the overwhelming need to sing it coursed through me. "Will you sing it with me?" I asked hopefully. "I can sing my piece and you can sing yours."

He smiled, warmth flooding his eyes. "I'd be honored, Celestial Songbird."

"I'm still not sure what that really means." I climbed off him and slid onto the bench next to him. Head cocked, I gestured to the piano. "Do you play?"

"I think I can figure it out." He winked and turned around beside me.

Grabbing the two pieces of sheet music, I placed them side by side on the music rack. "This song was supposed to be about you," I whispered. "Music is the language of my heart—you know that. I just wanted to express how much you mean to me, but I got stuck."

He leaned over and brushed his lips against my forehead. "Hopefully you like the ending, Tialla."

"I'm sure I will love it." My fingers slowly slid across the keys as I began playing, the opening melody filling the room. I closed my eyes for a moment and gave myself over to the music.

The walls close in, the loneliness gnaws
Tearing at my heart with razor-sharp claws
The shadows lengthen, the silence roars
Swallowing me whole in its monstrous jaws

My heartbeat slows, the blood cools in my veins
Slowly I succumb to this tempest of pain

I lose my grip on reality and free fall into the darkness
I slip through time, descend into madness

But then I see you take form through the veil of my tears
Slashing a path through my thicket of fears
Until suddenly you're there standing at my side
Gathering me to you, arms open wide

And your voice is a beacon guiding me home
From the desolate shores I drifted and roamed
I feel your breath on my cheek in the waning light of day
And my heart feels at peace when you smile and say

Ash's fingers slid across the keys, the transition from my piece to his seamless. He began singing, picking up where I left off, and I tumbled headfirst into the ensnaring magic of his voice.

I'm here, I crossed time and space to find you
Beseeched the Gods and fates to reach you
To be with you
There is nothing that will ever keep us apart
No greater power than the one that guides our hearts

And though the night grows dim and hope seems to be gone
I'll lead you through the darkness and back to the dawn
I'll be your strength, I'll carry you, forever and a day
However long it takes you to find your way.

The music gently faded, and I sat there, tears streaming down my face, overcome with emotion. He was what was missing in my song. And now it was perfect.

"I love it." I choked on a sob, throwing my arms around his neck. "Singing the songs is what gives them their power. That's one of the things Mangy Cat told me that day on the trail. Ash, your voice is pure magic. It gives your beautiful words so much more meaning."

He slid his thumb across my jaw. "I'm happy that I did it justice. I wanted to inject how I feel about you, the lengths I will go for you."

I reached for his face, pulling it down onto mine, my lips moving against his reverently. He deepened the kiss, parting the seam of my lips with his tongue, gripping the back of my head with his hand. Heat coiled low in my belly, radiating through my core, and I climbed onto his lap, straddling him.

The fire roared to life as the madness took control, whipping me into a tangle of hot, desperate need.

"No slow and gentle," I growled in his ear as I reached for the sides of his T-shirt and tugged it over his head. "I want it rough and hard."

His eyes flared as he gripped my head with his hand, trailing his lips down the side of my neck. "Tired of making love, baby?"

"Never." I arched my back as his hands gripped my ass and pulled me against his hardening length. "I just want you to fuck me."

He smiled, his teeth snagging on the corner of his bottom lip. "I hope you're not overly fond of these leggings."

Before I could answer, they fell off my body in shreds without him even touching me.

I glared at him. "You didn't have to destroy them."

He shrugged. "You said you wanted it rough and hard."

His eyes flashed again, the flecks of gold in his emerald orbs flaring like little slivers of lightning. The air shifted, power rippling around him in soft waves. I gasped, excitement whipping me into a frenzy as I drank him in. He was slipping into the skin of the dark and dangerous God who had saved me that night, and fuck, I was here for it all.

My heart raced as he gripped my tank top and ripped it off my chest. Cupping my breasts, he rolled my nipples between his thumb and forefinger before pinching. I bit my lip to keep from crying out.

He rose from the bench, lowering my feet to the floor as he unbuttoned his pants. My eyes followed the path of his hands, settling on his jutting cock as he pulled his pants off. I slid my fingers out to stroke his shaft, but his hand snapped around my wrist, bringing it to his chest.

"The only part of you that touches my cock is your pussy." His voice was a husky snarl, and my heart tittered in response, my blood heating as it glimpsed the beast lurking beneath the surface of his control.

"Show me how you want it, baby." He flipped me around so my back was pressed against his chest. Of their own accord, my hips moved, and I arched, pressing my ass against the warm, silken length of him. Taking a few steps forward, I dropped to my hands and knees, lowering my arms until my face touched the floor. Looking behind me, I smiled and beckoned to him with my finger, wiggling my hips wantonly.

"Fuck." He was on his knees behind me in a heartbeat, his hands gripping my ass as the tip of his cock lined up with my entrance. "Gods," he rasped. "You're always so fucking wet."

My eyes fluttered closed as he rubbed the tip of his dick over my clit, a scream ripping from my lungs when he pulled back a fraction and slammed his cock inside me with one swift thrust.

"Is this what you want?" He slid all the way out and slammed into me again.

I arched my back in response, pushing my hips back to meet his next thrust.

"Are you going to come on my cock, baby?" His hands gripped my ass as he set a punishing pace, thrusting into me again and again.

Stars swirled before my eyes, but I welcomed them, harnessing the pleasure and pain as I reveled in the dual sensations morphing into one entity within me. This was what I wanted—to strip the emotion out of it, to focus only on the feel of him and what he did to my body.

"Harder," I cried, the ravaging slide of his cock igniting every nerve ending in my body, setting me ablaze. He obliged, his fingers sinking into my hips as he pushed deeper.

"Gods, you feel so good." He tilted his hips and slammed into me again, hitting that sweet spot that made my toes curl. Reaching an arm around and under me, his fingers stroked my clit.

I whimpered at the sensation, twisting my head around to look at him. His emerald eyes were fiery as his gaze met mine, and I reveled in the sight of the beautiful face I loved, the magnificent body that commanded mine, the arms that made me feel safe and cherished, the lips that offered pleasure and also kissed my tears away.

I gasped as sadness barreled through me, halting my wild lust in its tracks. His body stilled immediately, a multitude of questions swirling in his eyes. I moved forward as he pulled out of me. Scrambling onto my knees, I turned around and crawled toward him, climbing into his lap.

"Slow and gentle," I whispered, wrapping my hands around his neck. "If this is the last time we're together, I want it slow and gentle."

He stroked my jaw with the utmost tenderness. "Slow and gentle makes you cry."

"Thanks for the reminder, asshole." My eyes welled and the burn of tears tightened my throat.

"It kills me when you cry, Elle."

He lowered his head and kissed me, and I parted my lips, welcoming the reverent worship of his tongue. He lowered me to the floor, magically covered now with soft blankets, and my back arched as I reached for him, our gazes locked as his body settled over mine.

I wrapped my legs around his waist and guided him into me, tears slipping down my cheeks as he began to move. "I love you, Ash," I whispered, brushing my lips against his jaw.

He reached for both my hands, intertwining his fingers with mine. "I love you, too, Tialla. Don't forget that, not for one second. You are my world, Elle." His voice cracked with emotion, and something inside me broke, my tears pouring out of me as I wrapped my legs tighter around his waist, needing to be one with him, to slip inside his skin as he was in mine, to savor every second of the precious time we had left.

Even when release claimed us, I refused to let go, trailing kisses across his skin, whispering, "I love you," over and over again, my heart breaking into a million pieces because I didn't know when I'd get to say it to him again.

He didn't know for sure when it would happen, but the same part of me that had embraced the truth of my identity and the truth of who Ash was to me—it *knew*. It whispered the truth to me.

This would be the last time I'd see him . . . for now.

Chapter 38

ELEYSE

DECEMBER 17: THREE AND A HALF MONTHS AGO

I closed my eyes, sinking into myself, seeking out my source of strength. *I will not cry. I will not fucking cry. I will not lose my shit in the middle of a crowded café.* Bringing my bracelet to my lips, I kissed the top of the violet gemstone flowers, letting their warmth sink into my skin.

From the depths of my soul, a flutter of calm seeped out, wrapping its wispy tendrils around my heart in a soothing embrace. Love, so intense, flooded me—not mine for Ash, but his for me. I smiled, brushing away the tear sliding down my cheek.

Gone.

He was gone.

Not just physically, but entirely. The last time I'd heard his voice in my head was twenty-one days ago, and the days since then had been the longest of my life. I walked around with a hollow ache in my chest, the sadness at times threatening to sweep me away. Only hope kept me going—hope that I would see him soon, that I would see my goddess mother again, that I would return to the world where I belonged.

Even as the weather got colder, I refused to give up running, haunting the trail every day with the hope of seeing Mangy Cat again. I never did. All the wild and mysterious things happening to me had ceased, gone quiet, eerily so—the calm before the storm.

Christmas carols rang out from the café's speakers, and my heart clenched as my mind flitted to last Christmas when Ash was with me. What a difference a year made. How I wished I could relive my time with him.

I looked up as the bell on the café door dinged. Charlotte sauntered in, waving as she spotted me. I plastered a smile on my face and waved back.

We had seen each other just once since that night at the club. I hadn't told her what had happened to me, and she'd apologized for not being there when I left. It was as Ty had said—she and Will had found somewhere more private—a coat closet somewhere inside the club.

"Elle." Her voice was smooth, silken, laced with her signature sophisticated grace.

I slid off my stool and hugged her, taking in the curiosity in her eyes as she studied me.

"What's going on here?" She wrinkled her nose as she waved her hand in a circle in front of me.

I frowned as we both took our seats. "What do you mean?"

"There is some serious dark energy wafting off you." Her eyes narrowed. "Did something happen?" She gasped. "Wait. Did you and Ash break up?"

I stared at her in confusion. Was that a spark of . . . *happiness* in her eye? No. I was seeing things.

"Something like that," I mumbled, reaching for my tea.

"I'm so sorry, Elle." She gripped my hand. "What happened?"

I clamped my jaw as the hair on the back of my neck prickled. What the hell was happening? A feeling of unease snaked through my body and the bracelet on my wrist grew noticeably cool against my skin. "I . . . I don't really feel like talking about it."

She touched my arm. "Oh, absolutely. I didn't mean to pry. If you need to talk, I'm always here."

I smiled gratefully. "Thanks, Char."

She unzipped her coat and hung it on the back of her chair. "Honestly, though, this is why I never get into serious relationships. You and Liam scarred me for life. I'd never want to love someone so deeply only to lose them."

My smile froze on my lips, a sinking unease settling in my stomach.

She squeezed my fingers. "Don't get me wrong. Yours and Liam's was a love for the ages, but not everyone is lucky enough to have that. And you even had another chance at it. I don't think I would have been able to put myself out there again after a loss like that. I mean, Ash was smoking hot, and I'm sure he was a great guy, but it must have been hard for you knowing that he would never compare to Liam."

I blinked rapidly, my fingers clenched as heat rose to my face. "You don't know Ash or the type of man he is." My words were clipped, my body tensing in anger.

"What more do I need to know?" Her eyes widened as she looked at me. "You guys broke up, and recently, too, by the looks of it. Liam knew how difficult this time of year was for you. He would have never done that. He always put your feelings first."

Something about her tone set my teeth on edge, a trace of resentment that filtered through about Liam putting my feelings first.

"Liam and I were together, Char. We put *each other* first."

She nodded placatingly and looked away, but not before I saw the reaction she couldn't hide.

"Did you just roll your eyes?" I asked, that sickening feeling solidifying in my gut.

"Oh, come on, Elle. We both know that Liam was the selfless one in your relationship."

My body froze as shock washed over me. Had she really said that?

"What's that supposed to mean?" My face was hot and flushed, my pulse thudding loudly in my ears.

"Well, it's not like it's a surprise. We both know he loved you more than you loved him. Let's not do this."

"Do what exactly?" My nails dug into my palms. "Sounds like you have a lot you need to get off your chest."

She pursed her lips. "Come on, Elle. From the moment Liam broke Terry Bernard's nose for you, he was under your spell. It's like he couldn't think for himself. Everything you wanted, he did. His entire life was dedicated to making you happy. He loved you unconditionally, and as a result, there was no room in his life for anyone else, for others who might have shown him the love he deserved if he gave them the chance."

Her words were like a punch to the gut. I stared at her, my mind reeling from the venom of her comments. What the hell? *Hold on for one hot second*, my brain screamed. I shook my head, sickened by the thought slowly formulating in my mind. It couldn't be. Had she been *in love* with Liam? How the hell had I not seen it before? Our entire friendship, the three of us were always together, but Char and I had never really spent a lot of time together *without* Liam. And then, after we got engaged, she pulled away from us, almost as if she couldn't stand to be around us anymore.

"I didn't know you felt that way about him," I said softly.

She smiled, patting my hand lightly. "Listen. I didn't mean to come off so harsh. This is all in the past. Let's leave it there."

I couldn't. "Do you really feel that way? I loved Liam with my whole heart. He was my entire world. And as for you—Char, there is nothing I wouldn't have done for you."

A flash of anger lit up her eyes. "Is that seriously how you see things? Elle, I love you, girl, and this might be tough to hear, but you are the most self-absorbed person I have ever met. The world did not revolve around you and your grief, and yet you were the only one who didn't see that. You took off and left without a word to me, cutting me completely out of your life as if thirteen years of friendship counted for nothing."

I blinked, my heart aching from her weaponized words. Each one of them had sliced through me with cruel efficiency.

I slid from my chair, reaching for my coat.

"Not yet." She grabbed my hand. "I need to say this."

"Charlotte, don't." My voice was cold, even to my own ears. My skin prickled, my pulse thundering in my head.

"I know you loved Liam in your own way," she said, her voice lethally calm. "But you and I both know that if it hadn't been for you, he would still be alive. Everyone who loves you dies—a fate that yes, I know, I narrowly avoided."

Damn. She had dipped that arrow in tar, lit it, and sent it flying straight at my heart.

"So what?" My chest was tight, the lump in my throat painful as tears streamed down my face. "All this time, you were just pretending to be my friend?"

The couple at the table next to us turned to stare, but I didn't care.

She shook her head. "No. We *were* friends. We had a lot of fun together. But I loved Liam more, and when it came to your selfishness, I looked the other way for him. Because *he* loved you."

What? I couldn't believe this. "So why even come up to me last year when you saw me at the diner? If you felt this way about me, you could have just walked away without even saying hello."

She let out a strained laugh. "I could have, but you, me, Liam—there's so much history. We're tethered together. In some fucked up way, it makes me feel like I can still feel his presence when I'm with you."

I closed my eyes, the chaos in my mind threatening to tear me apart. "Goodbye, Charlotte." I grabbed my coat and slipped it on. "I'm truly sorry you feel that way. I never in a million years meant to do anything to hurt you."

Without waiting to hear what she said, I turned on my heel and ran out of the café, bursting into tears as soon as the cold air blasted my face. Mindlessly, I made my way to my car, grief crippling my senses, my heart numb from the beating it had just taken.

As I slid behind the wheel and slammed my car door, I stared straight ahead, my breath misting in the cold air, my hot tears turning frigid on my cheeks. Was she right? Was I self-absorbed? Had my grief so completely consumed me that I was a shitty person to the people who loved me? Did I ruin Liam's life?

I lowered my head onto my steering wheel and let the anguish consume me. Heavy sobs racked my body, stealing the breath from my chest. I wasn't sure how long I sat there, raw agony pouring out of me, but my fingers were numb and my face frozen by the time my well was dry.

I wiped my eyes and started my car, pulling out into traffic and heading home. Fuck. I missed Ash so much. Was it wrong for me to long for him, to crave the comfort and peace I felt in his arms? Was that selfish? Did he think that about me too? Did I give nothing back in return?

In less than five minutes, Charlotte had brought my world crashing down, had presented me with an image of myself so wretched and vile it made me sick to my stomach. I didn't even think I could look myself in the mirror without hating what I saw.

Was this what Mangy Cat had meant when he told me that I would suffer loss again? Ash was gone and I didn't know when I would see him again. My entire friendship with Charlotte had been based on a lie, the pain of which had ripped away years of happy memories, leaving me hollow and frozen inside.

As I turned down my street, loneliness and longing gripped me, and the dam burst again. I pulled into my driveway, my body sagging with heaviness as I exited the car and trudged to Aggie's house. Being alone wasn't a safe option for me tonight—not in this frame of mind.

Before I even knocked, Aggie opened the door, her eyes filled with worry as she took in my appearance. Without saying a word, she pulled me into her arms and closed the door, and I held on to her small frame and fell apart again.

"It can't be that bad, Ovi." She stroked my hair as her other hand rubbed circles across my back. Without saying another word, she led me to her sunroom, sitting on the couch next to me, holding my hand as I tried and failed to stanch my tears.

Her quiet presence was soothing, providing the comfort I so desperately needed. What the hell would I have done if she weren't here tonight?

With a slow squeeze of my fingers, she stood to her feet. "I'll make us some tea." She headed to the kitchen, her confident steps echoing throughout the room as she strode across her expensive hardwood floors. She returned a few minutes later, setting the teacup on the side table beside me. "Just get it all out, and when you're done, I'll be right here. If you feel like talking, I will listen, and if you don't, I'll still be here."

It must have been an hour before I was ready to talk. I told her everything that had happened with Charlotte, even going back into the past to revisit my friendship with her and Liam. All the while, she was silent, letting me talk and air my feelings.

"How could I go through my whole life and not know that someone I cared so deeply for felt this way about me? Is what she said true? Am I so out of touch with everything and everyone around me?"

Aggie's eyes flared. "Let me stop you right there, sweet girl." She gripped my hands, her expression serious as she looked at me. "You are kind and compassionate, loving and caring. Despite all the tragedy in your young life, you still managed to hold on to that. Yes, after Liam, you tried to push the world away and keep everyone out, but when you let people in, you bring so much *joy*. I am speaking from experience, Ovi. You're funny and smart, sarcastic and spirited, but *all* in an endearing way. And you have such a bright, beautiful spirit. It broke my heart when I first moved here to see you in so much pain, but bit by bit, you came out of your shell, and then once Ash came into your life, you *blossomed*. It was incredible to watch."

I clutched her fingers, my throat tight with emotion as she leaned in closer. "Your parents, Mags, Liam—they saw the true you. Ash and I see the true you. The you that Charlotte sees is colored by her own jealousy and resentment, and yes, I know the things she said hurt, but her truth doesn't match with anyone else's version. Trust me, I have seen a lot of horrible people in my time to know that you are not like that. If Ash were here, he would tell you the same thing."

My breath hitched as a pang of sadness tore through me. "I miss him so much, Aggie."

"He'll be back. I'm sure of it. That man is crazy about you."

Her words hung in the air, sending ribbons of guilt slashing at me. I had told her that Ash and I were still together but that he had to leave for a little while, and she hadn't pushed, leaving it up to me whether I wanted to share more.

She reached for her cup of tea on the coffee table. "The same offer I made last year stands this year. You can stay with me over Christmas if you'd like. However long you need."

I threw my arms around her. "Thank you, Aggie. That means a lot to me."

I felt so much gratitude for her presence in my life. She was the only person I had left in this world, and I would never forget her kindness and her friendship. My senses still sang with warmth toward her; I would happily trust her with my life. Deep inside, I was sure I could trust her with everything, but I didn't know how to broach the subject and explain the truths I'd learned about myself. She deserved the whole truth from me, and as my mind settled and I sank into the comfort of her presence, I made a promise to myself to tell her.

Chapter 39

ASHER

Guilt riddled me as I stared at Elle's face, everything about her features peaceful and unruffled. Fuck. I hated this leg of her journey. Mostly, because there was so much I didn't know about what she'd gone through in those five months I was away from her. I hadn't been able to see her, talk to her, go to her, the ability to connect with her through my labral completely locked down. As for what I did know about that time, none of it was good.

I stared at the Lonefera on the wall. She was into March now on Earth. Mere weeks before she ended up in Ariadna. Those five months away from her were longer than the ninety-seven years I'd spent waiting for her after she came to me through the Senshifter.

Once Kaliope got wind of my visits to Earth, using my labral had no longer been an option. I was still able to sense Elle—although everything was muffled and faint—through Magnus. What came through broke my fucking heart. Pain and heartache—it consumed her.

Constantly throughout the day I would will my feelings for her through our Gloweyen bond, but with Vix not yet awake inside her, I had no idea if she even sensed my presence or feelings that way. In those five months, as my worry and fear for her grew, so too did my rage and hatred for Kaliope.

She had used Gargmoin's dark magic to intercept my labral—specifically *where* I was using it, and it had placed me on Earth. Ovix, one of my Dulogrien, had been the one to confirm the details

339

to Treye of what Kaliope knew. Once she found out I had spent time away from Ariadna, she had commanded Gargmoin to keep track of any abnormalities in my labral usage.

Even now, I wasn't sure how Gargmoin had been able to intercept the magic signature of my labral. I didn't even know such a thing was possible. He had abilities I wasn't sure anyone fully knew of, but I was certain that Tora knew a whole lot more about him that she wasn't able to say.

A knock on the open door pulled me out of my thoughts, and I looked up to see Faron standing there. "Better suit up, Godslayer," he said, brows lifted. "Arazul has granted Jaraya an audience with Sorin at Solniess. They're in the south garden. If you ask me, things are about to get nasty." His lips tipped up in a tight smile. "Treye and I think you should be the one to escort her in. Just so she knows she has to behave."

I frowned. "Why did Arazul relent and grant her an audience?"

"She's threatening to throw off the harvest season in Ariadna by tampering with the moon cycles."

I clenched my jaw as I strode toward the bed. Leaning over, I brushed a kiss against Elle's head, breathing in the redolent, floral smell of her hair before reluctantly pulling away. I'd have much rather stayed here with her than have to deal with the petulance and pettiness of Gods not getting their way.

"Don't let her out of your sight," I said to Faron as I marched out of the room.

He nodded. "I won't."

The sound of arguing reached my ears as soon as I walked onto the footpath leading to the south garden.

"No, Sorin," Eolith's voice rang out. "I will not."

"Eo," the Summoner of Light and Darkness pleaded. "It will rile her more if she sees you."

"Absolutely not. Solniess is *my* sanctum and I will not hide from the likes of her. Do not ask me again."

I stopped in front of them. The angry flare of Eolith's magic curled around her like a serpent ready to strike.

"I have to agree with Eolith." I folded my arms across my chest. "She is the Goddess of the Ethereal Harmonies. Apart from Arazul and the Mavigos, she answers to no one."

"Nobody asked you, Godslayer," Sorin growled, the amber of his eyes flaring. "Would you not ask the same of my daughter if it meant protecting her from the likes of Kaliope?"

I cocked my head. "If Elle were in possession of all her powers and Kaliope made the mistake of coming into her house, I'd sit back and relish the sight of her ripping the bitch to pieces."

Sorin grunted, the barest glint of approval flashing in his eyes. He reached for Eolith's hand. "I can see why you're so taken with him. He's vicious when it comes to the ones he loves, just like you."

I turned at the sound of footsteps behind me. Treye strode toward us, his expression grim. "Do you want me with Faron, Bash?"

I shook my head. "With me for now. Not quite sure what to expect."

Sorin loosed a heavy sigh. "It's Jaraya. You can expect a scene."

"Can I ask something?" I stared at Sorin curiously.

He stroked his chin. "I gather you'll ask even if I say no?"

I ignored him. "Why did you marry? None of the other Gods have."

He looked off into the distance. "Because that was the only way I could harness my power. Although I summon light and darkness, when I came into existence, I could not do that on my own. I needed to merge my power with that of another God. I thought the Goddess of the Night would help me harness both sides of my magic, but her price for helping me was that I marry her. She wanted an unbreakable alliance between Gods, and desperate to claim my power, I agreed. Yes, I was able to summon the darkness as a result, but the light eluded me for thousands of years. It was only after I fell in love with Eo that I was able to summon it. It's only then I realized that to love is to harness the light. And even more mind-bending, our love gave birth to its own constellations in the Sangelis!"

"So that part of the legend of Cadavweira is true," Treye said, his voice filled with wonder.

Sorin nodded. "You will find that there is often a grain of truth to every legend."

The air around us turned blustery and cold, the trees on the perimeter bending and flailing in the powerful gust. In a matter of seconds, Arazul appeared before us in a blinding flare of light. He, like Sorin, was wearing an ornate, heavy trinzum breastplate, but underneath, he wore a thin, zidiurrh-laced shirt. His pants, too, were lined with the same indestructible material. In the sunlight, the zidiurrh sluiced back and forth across the fabric as it clung to his form.

"Are you ready for me to usher her in?" Arazul's silver eyes flashed as he regarded the Summoner of Light and Darkness.

Sorin stepped forward, his massive form rigid as he took up his position at Eolith's side. His eyes flitted to each of us. "Jaraya will go on the offensive as soon as she gets here. It won't just be about me. She will try to provoke and anger whomever she can into acting against her. Keep your wits about you." His gaze lingered on me. "No needless violence."

I smiled through gritted teeth. "As long as she behaves, the Goddess of the Night has nothing to fear from me."

Sorin grunted and then turned to nod at Arazul.

The Great Creator inclined his head toward me. "She cannot get to Eleyse. Once I let her in, she will not be able to step foot out of the perimeter circle I place around her. She is a powerful God of the Sangelis, one whose power is vital and cannot be replicated."

I frowned. "So what are you saying? That there's no one who can take her place?"

"Precisely. The moons across the Sangelis are responsible for many facets of life. Without her to harness the night and control the cycle of the moons, there will be devastating consequences. No matter what happens, show restraint, Godslayer."

Treye and I exchanged glances, and from the look he threw my way, we were both thinking the same thing—they were expecting something dramatic. We needed to be on our guard.

Arazul stepped forward, a thin stream of blue light emanating from his index finger and settling on a spot about ten feet in front of us. On the ground, shadows swirled and writhed within the bounds of a light circle about five feet in diameter.

The shadows lagged and grew slothful, and a few seconds later, a spray of flaming red shards shot into the air within the circle, spinning at breakneck speed before abruptly dissipating. Out of the haze that followed, a figure emerged. A form-fitting red gown clung to her tall and willowy form, her shimmering silver hair fanning out behind her as she moved. A diadem of stars stretched across her forehead, accentuating her glowing alabaster skin and silver-white eyes, so cold and empty as they fastened on all present.

"Well, well, well." Her singsong voice dripped with sickly sweet venom as she tossed her hair behind her. "What a gathering we have here." She turned her piercing gaze to Sorin, a muscle clenching in her jaw as her eyes drifted to Eolith at his side. "Hello, *husband*. You've been busy." Her tone leaked contempt, her face drawn in a tight scowl as she narrowed her eyes. "A daughter with the likes of *her*, an outcast Goddess spurned by the Great Creator himself for striking out against him?"

"Watch your tongue, Jaraya." Arazul's tone was lethally calm. "It doesn't take much to incur my ire anymore."

"So I heard." She tilted her head with an air of defiance. "Caz told me that you imprisoned Kaliope Tandor without just cause. You better watch out, Ara, or you'll find yourself with a rebellion on your hands."

She was baiting him, that much was clear. He refused to engage, simply looking at her, his stance relaxed, his expression unreadable.

Sorin folded his arms across his chest. "Say what you came to say and take your leave, Raya."

"Don't you dare tell me what to do," she spat, her eyes flaring with rage. "I will leave when I'm damn well ready." She shifted her gaze to Arazul. "We Gods have lived in peace and boredom for too long. It's about time that we shake things up, inject some intrigue and adventure into our humdrum existence."

Arazul clenched his fingers. "You do not want to ally with Kaliope

Tandor and Gargmoin, Jaraya."

"What did I just say about not telling me what to do?" she snapped, her head tilting to the side to look at me. A slow smile curved her thin, red lips. "The Godslayer himself. You definitely are pretty to look at. I'm sure you'd be an infinitely better fuck than my husband. I can see why Kaliope wants you."

I stared at her, my eyes flat, refusing to react.

"That's enough." Eolith stepped forward, her essence flaring around her, her silver eyes blazing with anger. "If you've said what you came to say, I'd like you to leave."

The Goddess of the Night whirled, fixing her bitter gaze on Eolith. "Oh, Eo, you clueless dear," she drawled, her mouth set in an exaggerated pout. "I didn't come here to say anything so much as to make a statement. It does a far better job at making intentions clear, don't you think?" She cocked her head. "I brought presents." Her eyes lit up, her smile wide as she clapped her hands gleefully. "For the both of you," she said, pointing to Sorin and Eolith.

The hair on the back of my neck rose in warning.

"Now, I'm not sure how this is going to work, but I'm assuming since I'm the only one locked in this circle, my presents will be trapped in here with me too?" She frowned. "They're a bit on the large side, but sometimes you need to go big to make the right statement."

A feeling of dread settled in my stomach as I summoned my power to me, keeping it close to the surface. Whatever was coming would not be good. From the rigid stances of the others, it was clear we were all on the same page.

"Dear husband," she said whimsically, "what is the perfect gift for a philandering, disloyal piece of shit? I thought long and hard, but I think I got it right."

"Jaraya," Sorin growled. "What did you do?"

"My gifts are all from the heart, dear." A smile of pure malice lit up her face. "Not *my* heart, of course. Both of yours." She lifted her index finger in front of her. "Just one second."

My heart thudded when Sorin dropped to his knees and roared, clutching his chest.

"No!" His eyes grew wide with horror as he turned to look at the Goddess of the Night. "No, Jaraya. Not Rodan."

She smiled, a wicked gleam glinting in her eyes.

My mind reeled. Rodan? The bladrawan? That was the name of Sorin's zaragal—a behemoth, stallion-like creature with golden scales covering its body. What had the Goddess of the Night done?

We didn't have to wait long to find out. A second later, the sanctum shook as Sorin's cherished zaragal dropped to the ground at Jaraya's feet. The perimeter shield around her grew larger to accommodate the creature's massive size.

My jaw was slack as I stared at the slain bladrawan—the last of its kind—the only zaragal tied to the Summoner of Light and Darkness. All the other Gods of the Sangelis had multiple zaragals, but not Sorin. His deep connection to Rodan was well known across Ariadna. Jaraya had *killed* it. Out of spite.

Zaragals' life forces were bonded to the Gods they belonged to. This was a fresh kill, executed in the moment for maximum effect. Sorin had literally felt its death mere moments ago.

"Rodan!" He scrabbled toward the creature, whose lifeless black eyes stared skyward.

"I know how attached you were to your precious bladrawan, *my love*. What better way to convey exactly how I felt having my heart ripped out as a result of your betrayal. It's really too bad that none of the Gods of the Sangelis were blessed with the power of resurrection, isn't it?" Jaraya looked pointedly at Arazul, who, with a flick of his hand, pulled the bladrawan forward, out of the light circle.

"You really are a heartless bitch," Sorin hissed, stroking the golden scales at the top of his zaragal's head.

"Don't you fucking forget it," she snarled.

"Enough, Jaraya," Arazul commanded.

"Jaraya," Sorin roared. "Stop this." He sprang to his feet and hurtled toward the circle, only to be shot backward.

Her lips peeled back in a sneer. "What I've done is already done, and there isn't a thing you can do to prevent it. Now before anyone thinks of doing something stupid and retaliating, you know what will happen if something should happen to me. We can't all be as fortunate as Eo to be blessed with *four* daughters to step in for her when she proves herself incompetent." She cocked her head, tapping her index finger against her lips. "Oh wait. Was it four? I mean, technically, it is *still* four, if you count Sorin's bastard."

My anger flared inside me, even as Eolith's face blanched, her eyes wild as she stared at Jaraya.

With a dull thud, a body landed at the Goddess of the Night's feet. Eolith sagged, a loud, keening wail of agony rushing from her lips. I stared in horror at the sight of Medra, Patroness Cloryal of Valkyse, her pale silver eyes devoid of life, her lustrous lavender hair limp and slick against her head.

Jaraya bowed her head in mock sorrow. "Lucky thing she wasn't a full goddess. Not everyone is fortunate enough to have a Godslayer on their side. And before you get any ideas," she said, her eyes snapping to me, "if you so much as touch me, someone *you* care about will be next."

I clenched my fists, the power sizzling inside me begging to be released. She deserved to be put down for what she had done.

A roar of rage bellowed from behind me as a blast of magic shot out of Eolith, aimed at the Goddess of the Night. It bounced off the perimeter circle Arazul had constructed.

"I think that's my signal to leave," Jaraya said gleefully. "Everyone's all full of fury and bloodlust. I love it. It will make what's coming so much more entertaining. See you on the other side."

"Ara, you can't let her get away with this," Eolith pleaded, her eyes wild as she stared at the Great Creator.

A muscle ticked in his jaw. "I promise you, Eo, she will pay for this. But for now, we have to let her go." His eyes were pained, filled with bristling emotion. With a sweep of his hand, the perimeter circle disappeared, taking the Goddess of the Night and her mocking laughter with it.

Eolith dropped to her knees in front of Medra, lowering her head onto her daughter's chest. Heaving sobs wracked her body as she mourned, each strangled cry tearing at my heart. As Sorin wrapped her in his arms, she fell apart completely, lost to the sorrow that had claimed her.

I watched helplessly, my rage threatening to consume me. Another Kaliope. Vindictive, petty, and cruel. And a powerful Goddess. How could the Mavigos let any of this stand? Why give me the ability to slay Gods if I had to stand helplessly by and watch the Gods abuse their power because they believed they were untouchable? Where were the checks and balances in that? The justice?

As if reading my thoughts, Arazul clasped his arm on my shoulder. "The tide turns with the Celestial Songbird, Asher. Eleyse is the hope of the Sangelis. In more ways than one. Remember that."

In the heat of my frustration and disbelief, I did not notice Faron flagging me until Treye nudged my shoulder. Hurriedly, we both made our way toward the edge of the garden where Faron waited, panic and fear swirling in his eyes.

He pulled me and Treye to the side. "You need to come now, Ash. It's Elle. Something's wrong."

I beat Faron and Treye back to Elle's chamber, my pulse roaring in my ears the entire way. Eolith and Sorin had enough to deal with at the moment without adding this to their plate. I skidded to a halt at the sight of the Lonefera flashing red as it scanned Elle's features, emitting an unsettling humming sound.

Catraia, what's happening? I asked, panic swirling through me.

Her voice rang out calmly in my mind, instantly settling my shot nerves. *Gargmoin's darkness inside her is tightening its hold. It knows her time reclaiming her lost memories is almost up.*

I turned inward once more. *What do we do?*

Everything Elle needs right now is in this sanctum, Catraia replied. *Her parents, and you. As the Lonefera counts its way down to Gargmoin's magic hitting her, talking to her will help keep the darkness at bay. But I will tell you this, Asher. When she relives the moment Gargmoin's magic hits, and I return her consciousness here, the darkness inside her will put up a fight. Even now, it's sinking its claws in, trying to expand its reach.*

I closed my eyes, frustration seeping out of me. *Why does his magic affect her this way?*

Because there is a similar power signature between them both, just like there is a similar signature between yours and his. To fully understand it, you need to figure out who Gargmoin truly is. There is much about him that is shrouded in shadow.

Dread coiled in my gut. What the fuck? A similar signature between Gargmoin's magic and mine and Elle's? Was that why my magic was ineffective against him at Cazara Torannon? Why Tora had not wanted me to touch him?

Rest assured, Asher, Catraia added, *the bond between you and Elle is much more powerful than any other source of magic, similar or not. We will rid her of Gargmoin's darkness around her soul. For now, you need to do what you do best and show her you love her. Use your Gloweyen connection. Although Vix slumbers while Elle is in this state, she can still feel you.*

I sat on the edge of the bed and covered Elle's hand with my own. "Fight it, Tialla," I whispered. "You've endured so much in your young life. You don't even see how strong you are. You've got this, baby. I know you do. Just come back to me. I'm right here waiting for you."

Even as I said the words, heaviness settled over me like a sodden storm cloud. Kaliope. Gargmoin, Jaraya. One thing after the next. The odds were heavily stacked against us.

That kind of thinking will do you no favors, High King of the Light Age. Catraia's tone was clipped, chastising. *Elle has not even begun to sink into her powers. And neither have you. You and I—we are both her anchors. I anchor her power, and you anchor her soul. You would be wise to heed me* on this. As the one gifted with that position, you need to unwaveringly do one thing—when it comes to her power, who she is as a person, the paths she must walk, the choices she will make, the crown she will wear.

What's that? I asked.

Believe. The moment you stop doing that, you will destroy everything, and you will lose her.

Chapter 40

ELEYSE

MARCH 24: SEVEN DAYS AGO . . .

Ash, I called out in my mind. *I don't know how much longer I can do this.* I lay back in my tub, my eyes closed, the water covering my body as scaldingly hot as I could physically tolerate.

Aggie had been my only lifeline these past few months. Unable to bear the loneliness and sadness that clung to me like a second skin, I had thrown myself into work—staying late, taking on extra projects—simply to keep my mind busy. As long as I was working, I wasn't thinking—wasn't thinking about Ash, about my goddess mother, about Charlotte, about the truth of my identity, about the future that was still waiting for me.

I worked myself ragged during weekdays so that by the time I went to bed, I was already half asleep. I had a rigid schedule that I followed to a fault. I'd go for a run first thing each morning, then into the office at seven; leave at seven at night; hit the gym afterward on Mondays, Wednesdays, and Fridays; hot yoga on Tuesdays; and dinner with Aggie on Thursdays.

Aggie and I usually went into town on Saturdays. Shopping, movie, theater, culinary experiences, pottery classes—we always found something interesting to keep us busy. She understood that distraction was the name of the game and did her best to keep me occupied.

Sundays were my chores and errands day. I'd start the day off with a long run, followed by housework, then errands. I'd stay out until the stores closed and then head home.

Weekend nights were the most difficult for me. They were

my *miss-Ash-like-crazy* time—the only time I allowed myself to give in to my feelings and revel in the memories we had made together.

I sighed and turned the hot water on full blast. Tears sprang to my eyes as I imagined the feel of his hands in my hair, his lips against mine, his skin on my skin. There were times I swore I felt his presence close by, heard a whisper in my ear, felt phantom arms around me. From the depths of my soul, that part of me that had claimed him as mine rang out with reminders of his love, filling my heart with a bittersweet assurance that I still belonged to him and he to me.

I'd taken Mangy Cat's advice. I'd turned to singing the songs—*his* songs. The two he'd sang to me. They were the only things that eased the stinging anguish in my soul. And although it was my voice singing the words, it was always his that I heard in my head.

Shutting my eyes against the sting of tears, I whisper-sang the words, listening as they bounced off the walls in the echo of my quiet bathroom.

I promise it won't last, the piercing pain you feel inside.

Did he know that his words would be what I needed to see me through after he left?

Like sea-washed glass, tumbled smooth by steady tides.

I could still remember every inflection, every emotion-laced cadence, every soulful detail of his smooth, smoky baritone.

Let the sand and currents shape you as time in its power transforms you.

I'd meant it when I told him I'd never heard anything more beautiful. His voice was *magic*.

And you emerge changed, your jagged edges polished and planed.

It called to mine in a completely different way than the spoken word did.

The burning truth imprinted on your soul, a broken spirit can always be made whole.

It was because music was the language of my heart.

So close your eyes and let the pain and sorrow go.

Let the evening light surround you in its healing glow.

And when the darkness fades with the coming morn

You'll awake at peace as you find yourself reborn.

He'd said it was the song his mother sang to him. As I sang the words, I pictured him as a little boy in my mind's eye, sad and forlorn, snuggled tightly in the arms of his mother as she sang to him, soothing his pain and righting his world the way he had done for me with the very same words and melody.

My throat clogged with searing emotion, the heat of my bathwater suddenly too stifling, too unbearable. I could hardly breathe. Reaching for my towel, I stood and stepped out of the tub, the exposure to the air prickling my skin and sending a chill down my spine.

Quickly, I dried myself off and headed to my closet. Grabbing a pair of soft yoga pants and a comfy tank top, I changed hurriedly before blow-drying and brushing my hair.

I was just about to head downstairs when the bracelet Ash had given me went deathly frigid. *A band of ice around your wrist...* My heart rattled a bone-shaking warning. Oh no.

Before I had time to process my thoughts, a loud, frantic banging at my front door stopped me in my tracks.

"Ovi!" Aggie's muffled, but panicked voice rang out.

Oh, god. What was happening?

Gathering my hair into a quick bun, I raced down the stairs and unlocked the deadbolt, pulling the door open.

Eyes wild with terror, Aggie scrambled inside the house and shut the door, turning the deadbolt. "Call out for him, Ovi." She gripped my hand. "I'm willing to bet your bracelet is freezing your bloody wrist off. Call out for Ash."

Ash! I screamed in my mind, *I need you!* What the hell was happening? I had told Aggie everything at Christmas, and not once did she ever make me think she didn't believe me. But she was scaring me now. Why would she ask me to call out for him when she knew what it meant? Who had she been running from?

"Be very quiet," Aggie said softly. "I think they're looking for *you.*"

What the fuck?

"Who?" I asked, my voice a strangled whisper.

"Look through the peephole," Aggie rasped, her warm, brown eyes muddy with trepidation.

Slowly, I placed my eye to the door, scanning for what had Aggie so spooked. I swallowed a scream when I glimpsed two monstrous beasts, the likes of which I'd never seen before, walking in the street, sniffing the air, as if they were searching for something.

Tall. Wolf-like. Terrifying.

That's all my brain managed to process. Holy shit! My heart flailed madly in my chest. What the hell kind of abominations were these things?

One of the beasts turned its head in the direction of my house, and to my utter horror, began walking up the driveway.

"We have to go, Aggie," I cried, my voice shrill with fear.

"You have to hide." She grabbed my arms. "And then wait for Ash to come for you. That's what he told you to do, right?"

"We have to hide. Basement. Now. I have a hidden room down there."

Together, we bolted for the basement, racing down the stairs. Adrenaline pumping, I scrambled in the darkness toward the back wall. Grabbing my phone from my back pocket, I turned the flashlight on, feeling with my hands for the hidden entrance to the crawl space. In a brain-addled fit of terror, I scraped my fingernails against the wall, searching for the telling groove in the concrete.

I'd just found it and pushed on it when my front door upstairs smashed open. A frenzy of footsteps sounded from the main floor above, stomping and thudding, as if they were running through the house. I almost wet myself with fright.

"I'm sorry, sweet girl." Aggie's eyes pooled with sadness and regret. "I believe everything you told me. You *are* special, Ovi. You have to live long enough for Ash to find you."

"We have to live long enough," I whispered. "Come on."

A loud, low voice rumbled from the main floor, the words as clear as day. "The human is here. I can smell her."

I forgot how to breathe, staring at Aggie, fear paralyzing my body, rendering me useless. Her eyes sparked with resolve as she rushed forward and pushed me into the crawl space. She pulled the door closed just as the sound of my basement door blasting open reached my ears.

"Stay, Eleyse. Don't you dare come out," she commanded softly. "You have to live."

No. No. No. Aggie. No. This couldn't be happening. What was she doing?

Through the door, a jarring scraping reverberated against the wall, and I almost threw up when I realized it was the sound of talons. Aggie's muffled voice rang out, but I could not make out her words, and then she screamed—the most god-awful, hair-raising sound—her cries ringing out over and over again, filled with undeniable agony. I shoved my fist into my mouth and bit down on my fingers to silence my own wail, my entire body shaking uncontrollably as I crouched there like a coward on the cold concrete floor.

The booming footsteps receded, heading back to my main floor, and as the seconds dragged by slowly, I stayed frozen, terrified to move even though nothing but silence echoed through the house.

You need to move! my mind screamed. *You can't take the chance that they come back.*

I slowly pulled open the crawl space door, squinting as the light from the basement hit my eyes. Aggie must have turned it on after she pushed me through the door.

My body shuddered as soon as I crawled into the basement, my senses stormed by the tang that hit my nose.

Some smells you never forget—the organic redolence of freshly-cut grass, the earthy petrichor of rain on a warm spring day, the fragrance of lilac bushes lifted on a summer breeze, the sickly sweet smell of death. The latter hung heavily in the air.

A scream froze in my throat, wrenching the air from my lungs. Aggie lay on her back in the middle of the floor, her brown eyes blank and still. Blood leaked out of her stomach where she had been sliced through from one side of her body to the other. She was gone.

I burst into tears, my hand clamped over my mouth as I unraveled, my heart aching with anguish at the sight of my dearest friend. Death had taken from me again.

"I'm so sorry, Aggie." I scrambled on my hands and knees to get closer to her.

A scuttling movement from the floor above stopped me in my tracks, and I listened with bated breath, expecting footsteps again, but there was only silence.

I needed to move. I closed the distance to Aggie, cupping her still-warm cheek gently. Closing her eyelids with my hand, I leaned over and brushed a kiss against her forehead. "I love you, Aggie," I rasped, tears scorching my cheeks. "Thank you for *everything*."

I hurried over to the basement window, climbing onto the side table as I slid it open. Cautiously, I peered outside. The woods behind my house were nothing but seeping blackness and writhing shadows. I jumped when booming footsteps sounded once more from the floor above me. Shit. They were back. I couldn't stay here.

Pushing myself through the window, I slid it closed quickly once I was outside. Looking around slowly, I judged the distance from where I was to the edge of the woods. Ten seconds. That's all I needed. I would climb a tree and hide and wait for Ash to find me. I was a good climber. Yes. That's what I would do.

I took a deep breath, and before fear could cripple me, I bolted, tearing toward the tree line.

My heart turned to ice when behind me, a high-pitched shriek of alarm pierced the air, ramping up in intensity. Oh god. They had found me.

Chapter 41

ELEYSE

Oh, the fucking irony. I was going to die in these woods. A gruesome, torturous death. Aggie's sacrifice was going to be in vain.

I ran like the wind, my heart tattooing an erratic and demented rhythm, the thrum of my terror pounding in my ears. I gasped for air, my lungs burning from the intake, but I couldn't stop. They were coming.

The night was cold and thick with the smell of fear. My fear. My time was up. I could hear them behind me—their unworldly caterwauling getting closer with each move I made. I darted through the trees blindly, the primal urgency to get far away from them tantamount in my mind.

Amid the tangle of the corpulent forest canopy, the tiniest sliver of moonlight filtered through, just enough for me to make out a way ahead. *Holy shit! Don't turn around; just keep going, keep moving.* I kept my eyes in front of me, my legs on fire as I pushed myself forward.

The squat, weeping foliage lent a slight advantage, allowing me to maneuver through the trees with more agility, but even so, the blasted beasts were still faster. Shit! They were right behind me. I could almost feel their scorching breaths on my neck.

Too late, I saw the tangled tree roots, and my feet splayed out from under me, sending me sprawling face-first into a mound of desiccated leaves and pine needles. My arm snagged hard on a tree branch, snapping my shoulder back, but I managed to pull free. Scrambling onto all fours, my hands slipped on a patch of muddy leaves and my chin smacked the ground with a thud.

The sound of shallow breathing and a low growl floated in from the dank shadows. Too close. Fuck! My manic heartbeat pounded in my ears.

I flipped onto my back, ready to pounce to my feet and go down fighting, but terror kept me frozen on the ground, my fingernails digging into my palms as I gripped the mucky leaves beneath me.

A figure stepped out of the darkness, striding slowly toward me. I'd only caught a glimpse of their monstrous forms through the peephole earlier, but this was far more vivid. Glowing red eyes and sharp, ragged teeth—too many of them—drew closer with each rattled breath I took. I gasped, paralyzed with fear as it kept coming. It stood on hind legs—a massive, towering beast. With a head bearing a remote likeness to a wolf and elongated tusks protruding from its upper jaws, it was terrifying to behold. Its eyeballs bulged out of its sunken face, eyes spectral and luminous, emitting a ghastly red glare that pierced through me when it fixed its menacing gaze in my direction.

Long, thick quills protruded from the top of its head and across the length of its spine. It was a four-legged beast with wings—wings so massive and powerful, with spikes along the top and bottom. With one foul swipe, it could shred me to pieces.

Sweet baby Jesus! From which circle of hell had this demon spawn escaped? My heart sputtered and jerked as if debating whether to simply give up the ghost. Fuck, yes. Heart failure definitely seemed like the most palatable way to go.

Through the trees, more eyes glowed red in the darkness, and one by one, more beasts stepped out of the shadows to join the demon in front of me, their macabre faces quivering with predatory excitement. Terror, so heart-stoppingly gripping, drenched me from head to toe. There wasn't going to be anything left of me for anyone to find.

The first creature bared its jagged teeth, lifted its head to the sky, and let out a bloodcurdling shriek. The others followed suit, the night awash with the power of their malevolence. The first beast spoke, and my heart plummeted at its thunderous words: "Feast, my brothers."

It dove toward me and I scrambled backward, but not before one of the spikes on its wings tore into my thigh, ripping through my flesh. I screamed as the pain sliced through me in waves.

The beast threw its head back and laughed triumphantly. It was toying with me, the twisted sack of shit.

Time and my heart seemed to stop. My body went slack as my life flashed before my eyes. I cried out for Ash, for Mangy Cat, my goddess mother, Arazul—anyone—to help me.

No sooner had the plea left my mind when a blinding blue light shot through the darkness, casting a wall between me and the ghastly beasts. The leader of the pack hurled himself against it, only to be catapulted backward.

I froze as a voice in my head whispered urgently, "Get up, Elle! Run! Now!"

Ash. He was here. He had come.

For a second, my body sagged in relief, only to be replaced with a surge of adrenaline as it rushed through me. I pulled myself to my feet and started running, gritting my teeth against the pain slicing through my leg.

"Don't look behind you, Tialla," Ash's voice commanded. "Get to the cliff. It's up ahead."

My heart rallied, clinging to his voice like a lifeline. He had come for me! How didn't matter. The only thing that mattered was that he was here.

Faintly, I made out a haze of light in the distance, and I bolted as quickly as I could in that direction. Shrill screeches of terror and pure agony pierced the silence of the night, and my heart flailed madly in my chest, every nerve in my body sentient now of the acrid fear that had invaded and permeated the air. But it was no longer my fear; it was theirs—the beasts who hunted me. Perverse pleasure filled me at the thought of the nightmare hunting them—my monster, my avenging dark angel.

The trees fanned out into a small clearing, and the moon shone radiantly against the backdrop of night, a refulgent beacon in the darkness beckoning me forward. Up ahead, the cliff loomed large against the moonlight, and I caught a glimpse of the river below.

"Don't stop. Jump!" Ash commanded.

As I neared the edge, terror took hold of me and I slowed my pace.

"Jump, Elle. Nothing will hurt you. I promise. Quickly now."

I let go of my fear and darted toward the cliff—my faith in Ash steadfast and absolute—and the last thing I saw as I hurled myself over the edge into the darkness was the water below—dark and roiling and ominous—reaching up to swallow me in its murky depths.

"Are you going to eat that?" a disembodied voice asked from somewhere nearby.

I squinted against the glare of fluorescent lighting as I grabbed my head to stop the jackhammering searing through my temples. Slowly, the world in front of me came into focus. A hospital room. What was I doing here?

An IV tube was attached to the back of my hand, the IV bag near my bed slowly drip-dripping god-knows-what concoction into my bloodstream. What was wrong with me? I shook my head, trying to clear the fog clouding my mind. The door to the room was open, and the pitter-patter of feet, soft conversation, and beeping call buttons drifted in from outside.

How the hell had I ended up here? I tried to remember, but everything was jumbled, and my mind refused to settle.

"Are you going to eat that?" the persistent voice asked again, and I turned toward the speaker in the bed next to mine. A woman with mousy brown hair and hazel eyes regarded me eagerly, glancing at the covered food tray on my side table. I absently shook my head and she reached for the tray, scooping it onto her own table.

"You're a decent gal." She flashed me a toothy grin, and I managed a wan smile in acknowledgment as she dug into the Jell-O enthusiastically. Have at it, lady.

Footsteps approached, and a nurse in green scrubs strode toward my bed, her silver-blonde ponytail swishing behind her as she walked. "Ah, you're awake. How are you feeling . . . gosh, I don't know how to pronounce your name, dear."

"That's okay," I said, my voice a hoarse whisper. "It's like Belize, but without the B. Eleyse." I rubbed my temples as she looked at my chart.

"It's a lovely name, Eleyse. How are you feeling?"

"Umm. . . a little groggy. How did I get here?" I looked around the room, searching for something to spark my memory. "I don't remember anything."

She patted my hand gently. "You're on some pretty strong pain meds, so things might feel a little hazy right now. You had a pretty nasty laceration on your thigh when you were brought in. It was laced with a venom the lab said they'd never seen before. Miraculously, we were able to neutralize it in time."

Venom? What the— I moved the blanket aside and noted the thick bandages wrapped around my left thigh. Suddenly, it all came flooding back. Aggie. The chase from my house into the woods. The terrifying beasts. Ash's voice in my head. The river.

There were only bits and pieces after that. Ash holding me on the bank, telling me he loved me. His lips on mine. The terror and pain in his emerald eyes. Me begging him to go back to my house and see if there was a chance he could heal Aggie. Everything was hazy and jumbled after that. Flashing lights, sirens, voices talking urgently, and then darkness. Cold, sweeping darkness.

"Do you know who brought me in?" I sat up, adjusting the bed to an upright position.

The nurse shook her head. "Someone called in your location anonymously. When the EMTs got there, they found you unconscious on the riverbank." Her eyes were sympathetic as she regarded me. "Now that you're awake, the police will want to talk to you."

My eyes widened. "The police?"

"Of course. Someone clearly attacked you and then left you for dead."

My mind reeled. What was I going to say to the police? It wasn't as if they would even believe me about the beasts that attacked me. Not that I would say anything about that to begin with. Was this what Ash had meant when he said there were those who would harm me if they knew about me? Shit. Never in a million years could I have imagined anything so terrifying.

I shuddered as I recalled the monsters' cries of pure terror and agony. Ash had done that. My beautiful love was a force to be reckoned with, and something told me that this was but a mere fraction of his power.

I fidgeted with the IV tube on my hand as the nurse made notes on my chart. "How long have I been here? Do you know if anyone reported seeing anything else?"

"You've been here two days." The nurse lowered the chart, cocking her head. "I haven't heard news of anyone seeing anything else." She rubbed her hand lightly across my forehead, her lips pursed as she studied me. "I know this must be a lot to take in, dear. Why don't you just get some rest, and I'll let the police know they can come by this evening." Her brows furrowed as she adjusted the IV bag. "Is there someone I can call for you, Eleyse? You didn't have anyone listed as an emergency contact."

A pang of emptiness curled in my gut as an image of Ash swirled in my mind. Where had he gone? Had he left again? He'd said before that using too much of his magic here drained him quickly, making it imperative for him to return to Ariadna. That had to be what had happened. But what about Aggie? Had he been able to do anything for her?

I looked up at the nurse and exhaled slowly. "No, there's no one."

"All right, then." Her voice exuded warmth and kindness. "If you need anything, just buzz. My name is Janice."

"Thank you, Janice." I smiled at her and pressed the button to recline the bed as she stepped out of the room. My roommate was fast asleep in the bed next to mine, the contents of my food tray long gone.

Out of the corner of my eye, I caught some movement near the door, and thinking Janice had returned, I turned my head.

Terror—unbridled and manic—surged through my veins. What the actual fuck! A wide, hulking . . . thing . . . devil stood inside the room quietly watching me. It was as tall as the ceiling, wider than the doorway, its skin a blackish-green that glistened with a sickly hue under the fluorescent lighting. Its eyes were as black as coal, its lips curled in a thin, cruel smile.

The blood rushed to my head, and I tried to scream, but only a squeak came out. What the hell was happening?

The thing stepped closer, a menacing glint in its eye. "Your time is up, human. Your life is mine."

Oh god! My body was rigid and clammy as horror punched through me like a surging tidal bore. Shit! Shit! Shit! I scrambled to press the buzzer to summon the nurse's station, but before I had even lifted my hand, a blast of heat shot toward me, searing into my chest. My skin was on fire, and a sharp, agonizing pain ripped through my head. As quickly as it had started, it was over, and everything went black.

Chapter 42

ASHER

PRESENT DAY SOLNIESS, THE VOID . . .

I had done what Catraia had advised. As the Lonefera steadily counted down the remaining weeks, I'd barely left Elle's chamber. I'd talked to her, held her, sang to her, reaching out to her through our Gloweyen connection. I sensed Vix's presence within her, responsive on some level to my efforts, and that bolstered my spirits.

Although the Lonefera had continued to flash red, the unsettling humming had stopped, only to resume when the countdown revealed that seven days were left, coinciding with the attack on Elle at her house and what had happened to Aggie. Catraia had confirmed that Elle's frame of mind as she relived that incident, coupled with the relentless darkness clinging to her, were coming to a head.

Eolith and Sorin hadn't been here much, having to deal with the fallout of Jaraya's actions. Valkyse no longer had a patroness Cloryal, and the moment we returned to the real world, that would become a pressing problem.

In the time they were here, they too had spent quality moments with Elle, talking to her about their history, how they fell in love, feeding her glimpses of themselves and their love for each other, which, after all this time, was still unchanged.

I looked up.

Five, the Lonefera flashed.

This was it.

Five days ago, Gargmoin's magic had struck Elle as she lay in her hospital bed. Two nights before that, I was in Torannon when my senses had reeled in warning that she was in danger. I'd heard her voice in my head, calling out for me.

Although my connection to her through my labral had been locked down, the magic laced into the bracelet on her wrist was still active. If she was in danger, it was set up to alert me. In the event of something like that, getting to her was my main priority.

Kaliope had already found out about my visits to Earth. In the back of my mind, although I hoped it wouldn't happen, I feared it was always just a matter of time before she found her way to Elle.

Within a minute of the bracelet alerting me that she was in danger, I received word from Treye in Kindrik that Kaliope had dispatched nine of her Manatocht warriors. *Nine* ghastly beasts to deal with one human woman with no magic to protect her. She'd wanted a bloody massacre.

Without hesitation, I'd reinstated my connection to Elle through my labral and used the portal to get to her. Crippling panic and fear had swarmed me when I saw her flat on her back in the woods—those lethal beasts closing in for the kill—emotions that were quickly replaced with rage as I summoned my power to me.

Throwing a shield over the woods to prevent outsider detection, I'd used my power to create a wall between Elle and the beasts, calling out to her to run. I had shown no mercy in unleashing my retribution, ripping each beast to shreds before moving on to the next one. I'd burned them all to ash, leaving no trace of their presence in the woods.

In my rage, I'd almost been too late in reaching her as she jumped over that cliff, but I'd managed to swoop her away just before she hit the water.

Fuck. The emotion that had rushed through me to have her in my arms again—it was overpowering. I swore I'd heard Magnus roar inside me.

She'd been so cold, her body shivering uncontrollably, her eyes wild with both fear and relief. It was only then that I noticed the blood seeping out of her thigh. I'd just started healing her when she pulled my hand away, begging me to go to Aggie, to see if I could heal her. I didn't want to leave her, but my magic was flagging, and I knew she'd never forgive me if I didn't do as she asked.

Drawing as much poison out of her wound as I could, I placed her safely on the riverbank and called in to emergency services to report her location. Assuring myself that she was all right, I kissed her and told her I loved her, promising to be back as soon as I could.

I'd found her bracelet in the woods when I was exacting my vengeance. Like a beacon, it had called to me. The clasp was broken, snapped off somehow in her flight from the beasts. That, in itself was troubling; the magic imbued inside it was supposed to be unbreakable. In the frenzy of everything that followed, I'd forgotten to slip it back on her when she was on the riverbank.

By the time I got to her house, my labral was painful against my wrist, warning me that I needed to get back to Ariadna before I depleted all my magic. Horror and regret coursed through me when I found Aggie. There was nothing I could do to save her; my magic was not powerful enough to bring her back. Not even a wisp of her essence lingered.

My heart ached for Elle, at the pain she must have felt at losing the remarkable woman she had come to care for so deeply. Aggie's death would have wreaked havoc on her. Guilt, that she was responsible for yet another life, would have plagued her.

As I knelt in the basement paying my respects, my senses prickled. A small gray cat sat in the corner, looking at me. Elle's Mangy Cat. The *Mavigos*. It was a far cry from the powerful form they had assumed when they bestowed the powers of Godslayer on me.

"You have done well, son of Ariadna," the cat said calmly, multiple voices resonating from within its body. "This is as far as you go, though. Your earthly travels are over. Return with haste to the Sangelis; your magic is spent."

"I can't leave her," I pleaded. "She needs me."

The cat blinked lazily. "The Celestial Songbird will find her way to you, to where she belongs. We must bid you goodbye, Godslayer. There is much to take care of here, loose ends to tie up. We'll see you again soon."

"Is she one of those loose ends?" I inclined my head toward Aggie.

"Have you seen the place? The Dark Shen beasts made quite a mess. All the carnage must be wiped away."

"You never mentioned that there were other beings from the Sangelis here?"

The cat blinked slowly. "And yet you found out all on your own. All traces of the Sangelis on Earth leave with the Celestial Songbird. Brace yourself, Godslayer. It begins."

Before I could say another word, I found myself reeling through time and space, and when I opened my eyes, I was back in Ariadna.

After replenishing my magic in Falayen, I quickly realized that I could no longer access the portal to Earth. They had locked me out. My anger and frustration at not being able to go to Elle was reaching a breaking point. Desperation, worry, and fear consumed me. She was all alone, with no one to turn to. The last thing I wanted was for her to think I had abandoned her.

I summoned Eolith, and with Uncle Andreo's help, we created wards of protection for Elle, using her broken bracelet, which still contained traces of her core essence. Eolith weaved in access to a portal to Ariadna should Elle be in danger again. We weren't certain it would work, but my suspicion was that the Mavigos had deemed it time for her to return to the Sangelis. If I couldn't be there to protect her, I wanted to be sure that she would be safe. Even though the bracelet couldn't be on her wrist, it was still doing its job, watching over her.

I returned with Eolith to Medra's temple on Somel. She wanted me there when she told her Cloryal daughters the news about Elle. That's where I was when Kaliope sent Gargmoin.

The sound of flurried activity at the door yanked me out of my thoughts and back to reality. Eolith, Sorin, Arazul, Treye, and Faron filed into the room, their expressions solemn as they looked at the numbers on the wall. According to the Lonefera's countdown, we had less than an hour left.

"How are you feeling?" Eolith asked, her silver eyes flashing with trepidation.

"On edge." I ran my hand through my hair.

Sorin's eyes flashed as he moved toward me, reaching out his hand to clasp my arm. "She has the most powerful Gods of the Sangelis fighting for her, as well as the Godslayer himself. We will save her."

I nodded, hating the nervous energy pulsating through me.

Catraia, I called in my mind.

I am here, Asher, she promptly replied. *Be ready. Her consciousness is fraying; I am doing my best to keep her grounded, but in that moment when I guide her back to the present, I will rein her in and cut off the source of her power so the darkness can't siphon off her true magic. It means that she won't be in control—the darkness will be. It does not answer to me, and it does not want to be separated from her. We must contain it.*

I communicated to the others what Catraia had said, a heavy feeling churning in the pit of my stomach.

"Together, we can do this." Arazul's voice brooked no debate. "Gargmoin's magic will not prevail inside her. He might have been the catalyst to usher her to the Sangelis, but his power does not belong with her. We need to subdue it as quickly as possible and leave the Void so that the rebounding curse can be destroyed."

He turned to look at Eolith and Sorin, standing on opposite sides of the bed near the headboard. "Your combined essences are what created her. The moment the Lonefera runs out of time, blast her with your light, Sorin, and the healing magic of the Ethereal Harmonies, Eo. It will not hurt her, but it will make Gargmoin's darkness recoil."

Flitting his eyes to me, he nodded. "Once time runs out, I need you to yank on your Gloweyen bond. Flood it with as much emotion as you can so that she's drowning in it. Call to her beast. We need every part of her to be filled with the power that makes her who *she* is. Do not stop until we neutralize her darkness. While the three of you are on the offensive, Treye, Faron, and I will go on the defensive, countering whatever attacks Gargmoin's darkness throws at us."

He lifted his hands in front of him, moving them in a circular motion. His gaze drifted to Treye and Faron, standing on either side of me at the foot of the bed. "I will deflect her retaliations as best as I can. Treye, use your stealth and shadow magic to focus on the dark tendrils of her essence." From his curving hands, three orbs of swirling trinzum floated free, hovering in midair. "Faron, use your matter manipulation to create shields of trinzum as needed. Remember, whatever we do, we cannot harm her, so temper your power."

I sucked in a breath, my jaw muscles clenched as my eyes fastened on Elle's still form. There was no movement or change in facial expressions. She was just as serene as she was when Catraia guided her back to the past, six hundred and ninety-eight days ago. She had relived it all. Had reclaimed all her memories. The moment her consciousness returned to the present, those memories she had made in the five days she had spent in Ariadna would also come flooding back.

The air around us was tense and rife with restrained bands of our collective power as we watched the minutes slip away. As the Lonefera counted down the seconds of the last minute, Catraia's voice seeped into my mind. *We cannot fail, Asher. This is our only chance.*

The moment the Lonefera hit zero, a coordinated symphony of magical medley unfolded as Elle's body arched on the bed, her back bowing, her eyes flying open. I yanked on our Gloweyen bond, inundating our connection with memories of our time together, baring my emotions and feelings for her as I reached out to Vix and Magnus.

The melody within Eolith hummed in perfect harmony as she directed it at Elle, the violet tendrils of her pure essence folding her daughter in their embrace. Sorin's light magic streamed out of him, his blinding-white essence merging with Eolith's to cocoon Elle, and together, they interlaced their essences with hers.

My heart faltered as I took in Elle's eyes from where I stood at the foot of the bed. They were completely black. The two dark tendrils of her essence stood coiled above her, poised to attack. Beside me, Treye invoked his invisibility, and I watched as blue shadows lifted off the floor, mimicking the shadowy tendrils of Gargmoin's darkness.

The dark essence flared, shooting toward Eolith, but Treye's shadows intercepted, deflecting the shot. Again, her darkness attacked, this time toward Sorin, but Treye directed his shadows once more, just as Faron manipulated one of the trinzum orbs to stretch into a full-body shield in front the Summoner of Light and Darkness.

Slowly, Elle rose to a sitting position, the darkness swirling in her eyes riling Magnus and setting my teeth on edge. I watched the tendrils as they reared back defensively, a high-pitched hissing sound issuing from them as they moved in different directions, each one acting independently.

I flicked my head quickly toward Faron. "Far, focus on the dark tendril on the right. Treye, take the left."

Elle growled, the sound rumbling from her throat menacing and animalistic as she sent both tendrils snapping toward my face. Treye's shadows met one of them full-on, coiling around it and squeezing, while Faron threw a shield of trinzum in front of the other.

I have cut off her core power from her, Catraia said in my head. *Gargmoin's darkness is in control, but you need to reach her.*

With both tendrils of Gargmoin's darkness lashing out and meeting resistance from Faron and Treye, Elle roared, sending a blast of power shooting from her eyes toward me.

Arazul's magic flared from his position between Eolith and Treye, erupting in a flicker of shooting sparks in front of me, swallowing her power whole.

"That wasn't very nice, Tialla," I said.

Her dark gaze snapped to mine, her face contorting as if she was in pain. "Tell them to stop. They're hurting me."

Don't listen to her, Catraia commanded. *It's the darkness talking.*

"Come back to me, Elle," I cajoled. "I've missed you."

Her eyes flashed. "Why would I want to come back to you? You abandoned me. Left me like everyone else in my life."

My heart stuttered. Is that how she really felt? My biggest fear was that she would hate me for precisely that reason.

Asher, Catraia snapped. *Focus. You haven't reached her yet.*

I shook my head. "The last thing I wanted to do was leave you, Elle. You know that."

"But you did anyway." Her eyes flared once more as a blast of power shot toward me.

Arazul's magic whipped out, absorbing most of it, but I jerked my arm back as the sting of Gargmoin's dark magic grazed my shoulder.

"It's just as well." Her lips slowly lifted, her smile laced with venom. "I'd be better off with someone else. You're pathetic. Plus you're a lousy fuck."

I couldn't help the laugh that escaped me. "Is that so?" My lips twitched before curving in a smile. "Maybe I need to remind you precisely how *lousy* I am?" Conjuring as many memories as I could of her with her head thrown back in wild abandon, her body writhing as she screamed my name, as she screamed that she loved me, I shoved them down our bond, savoring the moment she registered them. Her body grew still and her eyes fluttered madly. For a moment, I glimpsed the whites of her eyes and the gray of her irises.

"Come on, baby. Fight the darkness."

She shook her head, battling internally for control. "Help me." Her dark tendrils lashed out again, only to be restrained by Treye and Faron.

"Soladeo," Eolith cried, her voice shaking with the force of her emotion. "You are powerful, my love. You were made to rattle the Sangelis to its core and rebuild it stronger with your magic. I believe in you, leida mata."

"We have yet to meet formally, my daughter." Sorin's amber eyes flared with emotion. "But the first moment I laid eyes on you, love so inconceivable flooded the chambers of my heart. I will fight to the death for you."

An ear-splitting scream streamed from her lips as the darkness gripped her, her body flailing wildly on the bed as she grappled for control.

Now, Asher, Catraia cried. *Go to her.*

I lunged forward, wrapping my arms around her tightly as my body sank onto the bed next to her. "Look at me, Elle," I commanded.

Her eyes were shut tight, her body shaking as she tried to fight off my hold. "Ash," she whimpered, her hands reaching out blindly for me.

"Remember who you are, Tialla. You have all your memories back now. You know the truth. Come back to us."

"Catraia!" she cried, her hands gripping her hair.

I am here, Eleyse.

"The whispers won't stop," she sobbed. "I'm not strong enough to fight them. They're going to swallow me whole. I can't hold on much longer."

She screamed as the two dark tendrils of her essence flared toward me, writhing as they tried to pry my body away from hers. Treye's shadows smothered one of the tendrils while Arazul's power surged once more, rendering the other tendril limp.

"There is only so much we can do to target the darkness without hurting her," Arazul said. "It knows that."

Sorin roared in frustration as the combined essences of his and Eolith's power continued to flow into Elle. "How do we muzzle it, Arazul? There has to be a way."

Can't you release any of her power to her? I asked Catraia, desperation strangling my control. *Give her a chance to fight off the darkness?*

I cannot, Asher. The moment I do, the darkness will seize it. Remember what I told you before. I am the anchor. I protect her at all costs, even from herself. If she cannot defeat it, you know what I must do.

Terror, so heart-stopping, seized my heart. *No, Catraia. There has to be another way.*

Keep feeding your Gloweyen bond. Remember, the beasts of your bond exist to preserve and protect your union.

Elle's body grew limp in my arms as a gravelly wheeze escaped her lips. "Ash," she rasped, her voice barely audible. "I'm sorry." Her body convulsed as the dark tendrils lowered and wrapped around her face, coiling their way around her body, like a spider cocooning its prey, sealing her away from me.

"No, Elle!" I roared, fear gripping me in its clutches. "Fight it, baby. You are powerful. You can do this."

Shit. I held her tighter, my heart clenching in my chest. I looked at Arazul helplessly.

"She is ultimate power, Asher," the Great Creator said. "The darkness recognizes that. It's parasitic, feeding off her essence. Catraia cannot release a single grain of her power to her. The longer we wait, the more resilient the darkness becomes. It will swallow her whole and incapacitate her, waiting for her power to be released. As long as the darkness remains, all paths lead to her destruction. We need to end this now." His voice was calm, a stark contrast with the wild panic rattling my nerves. "Don't let go of the connection to your Gloweyen bond. It is the key to her salvation."

Our Gloweyen bond. That bond wasn't just Elle and me. It included Magnus and Vix too. Treye and Faron were right. Elle was right. The beasts of our bond were separate from us although they lived inside us.

I stared at Elle, her lifeless form completely shrouded in shadow. A flare of anger and resolve surged through me. Fuck the darkness. Her entire life had been shrouded in it. We hadn't gone through everything we had only to succumb to defeat. I would get my girl back.

I closed my eyes, delving into my wellspring of power, visualizing myself at that vast lake, diving in. *Magnus,* I called as I summoned my power to me, seeking out the beast of my bond. I smiled as I felt him stir, heard the chuff of acknowledgment as he surged to the surface. And then, as plain as day, two slitted crimson eyes flew open, regarding me intently. My Goddess was right. There was absolutely a method to her madness. I'd be sure to let her know when this was over.

My breath slowed as I conjured the powerful memories of Magnus's and my response to Elle and Vix, sending them down our bond. I separated my emotions from his, flooding the bond with his and my feelings. It had to work. I refused to accept any other outcome.

"Come back to me, Elle." I poured more of Magnus's and my feelings for her down the bond. The way she lit us up inside with her laugh, her smile, those eyes that saw through to our soul. The way we felt when we were with her, when we were away from her, how we felt when she was sad, happy, aroused, excited, afraid. The sheer joy and contentment she and Vix filled us with.

She exhaled a rattled breath and her body went limp, completely encased in the dark tendrils of her essence. Even as fear tightened its grip on me, I didn't relent. I refused to give up, pouring everything I had into our bond.

That's when I heard it—as loud and clear as if it were happening right next to me—a shattering roar from inside Elle as Vix surged, inundating her with power. Before I had time to even process what was happening, Magnus answered Vix's call from inside me, and together, they drenched our Gloweyen bond with powerful bands of their brilliant essence, wrapping their combined magic around us.

My jaw dropped open as I looked at our bodies glowing in a blinding haze of amber. Holy fuck. Vix and Magnus were doing this. They were acting of their own accord, not as part of *us*.

The dark tendrils hissed and slid from Elle's form, shrinking and falling limp in front of her. Elle gasped and opened her eyes, her gray irises bright as she reached for my face.

"Now!" Arazul commanded. "Back to Cazara Torannon."

He closed his fist, and the chamber around us faded as our shadow selves were ripped from Solniess, flung out of the Void, and reunited with the real world once more.

Chapter 43

ASHER

PRESENT DAY ARIADNA, CAZARA TORANNON . . .

Everything happened in a blur of activity once we jolted back into our physical bodies in the library at Cazara Torannon. Lorien, already positioned in front of Elle, leapt into action, wielding the light strain of the Old, Arcane Magic, drawing Gargmoin's darkness out of her.

Beads of perspiration dotted his forehead as he exerted his magic, his hands outstretched in front of Elle. I grimaced as the air around us erupted with a myriad of shrill, scattered whispers, unintelligible at first but gradually slowing until three phrases rang out on repeat.

The song of the Siccharis is lost. The Light Age will never be. The Dark Age of the Sangelis rises from the ashes.

My body froze from where I was sitting on the sofa next to Elle. Before I even had time to process the words, Elle rose to her feet, the dark tendrils twitching at her sides.

I stood quickly, vaguely aware of Faron and Treye entering the library and standing ready at the door.

Lorien didn't waver as his gaze flitted to mine. "I need to end this now before those tendrils flare to life again." A burst of gold lit up his eyes as his steady voice filled the room. "Tri agwei Carasmas veo."

To the abyss of the Carasmas you go. What in blazes did that mean?

A stream of magic burst free from his fingers, siphoning the lax dark tendrils of Elle's essence in spooling, shadowy threads and transferring it to a small crystal chest lined with vertical bands of zidiurrh. The whispers fell silent, and the chest turned bright green, the dark tendrils contained inside.

Lorien pulled his hand away and picked it up, studying the trapped shifting shadows. "It is done, Ash," he said, pulling me to the side. His body heaved and his breaths were uneven as he clasped my arm. His golden eyes flashed with assurance. "You did all the heavy lifting with getting her to this point and neutralizing the darkness so that I could draw it out of her. I have only a small window to destroy this, so I must take my leave now. We'll see each other again soon. I know you have questions, especially after the ramblings we just heard. With the approaching Convergence, time is not our friend."

"Yes, there is a lot to do and discuss." My mind wandered to the multitude of things I wanted answers for. "Thank you, Lorien."

"Anything for the High King and Queen of the Light Age." His eyes shone knowingly as he lowered his head in a show of obeisance. "Come find me at Dramhelm Manor after the dust settles. For now, go be with your queen."

I nodded, clasping arms with him.

With a flourish of magic, he disappeared, the darkness that had threatened Elle's life and the future of the Sangelis gone with him.

I turned to see Gwynn and Elle locked in a tight embrace.

"It's over, Elle," Gwynn exclaimed. "Gargmoin's darkness is gone."

"I can *feel* it," Elle whispered, her arms wound tight around Gwynn. "The heaviness is gone. And I have all my memories back. There's so much I have to tell you."

"I can't wait to hear all about it." Gwynn laughed, a tear slipping down her face.

Uncle Andreo stood behind them, his gaze meeting mine. He smiled, lifting his brows, relief knitted across his features. Although mere seconds had passed for them, the significance of what had happened was not lost on anyone.

I shifted my stance as Treye and Faron came to stand on either side of me.

"That was something." Treye clasped my shoulder. "For a moment there in her chamber, I was afraid we wouldn't be able to save her. I'm just glad it's over and Lorien managed to rid her of Gargmoin's darkness."

I loosed a slow exhale. "Yes. Thankfully."

"I wonder what he has to do to destroy it," Faron mused. "And will it be gone for good?"

"Add it to the list of questions I have for him." My mind was swimming with all the things I wanted to know.

"Smolders," a sultry voice called from behind me.

My body froze.

Tora.

I turned, my gaze locking onto hers immediately at the entrance to the library, her expression lined with a cautious indecision I'd never seen on her face before. She was flamboyantly beautiful as always, wearing a sequined blue and lavender gown, her green and silver hair floating airily around her shoulders.

With Lorien back at Dramhelm Manor, she had clearly wasted no time in returning. She regarded me intently, willing me to make the first move. I knew what she was waiting for; I could see it in the rigid way she held herself—as if she was scared to breathe, hope pooling in her golden eyes that hadn't blinked once since I turned to look at her.

I crossed the distance between us, coming to a stop in front of her as I lowered my hand to her cheek. "There is nothing to forgive, Tora." I reached out and pulled her toward me. "I will always be in your debt."

She wrapped her arms around my waist, a strangled sob escaping her lips. In my entire life, I had never seen this raw vulnerability from her. Not even when my parents were killed. To say this was out of character for her was an understatement.

I brushed a kiss against her head, leaning down to whisper in her ear. "We have a lot to talk about, and I know there are things you can't say, but I'm hoping there are things you can."

"You have my word, Ash," she said with a nod.

Feeling my skin prickle with awareness, I turned to find Elle looking at me. The moment our eyes met, the world around us melted away and it might as well have just been the two of us standing there, relief, longing, desire, gratitude, desperation bouncing back and forth between us as our gazes clashed.

She took a step forward, and then another, and then she broke into a run toward me, leaping into my arms with the unflinching assurance that I would catch her. I gripped her thighs as she wrapped her legs around me before crashing her lips onto mine.

"I fucking missed you." She tangled her hands in my hair, tightening her grip around me, her lips skittering kisses across my jaw.

I wrapped a hand around her neck, my blood roaring in my veins at the feel of her in my arms. "You have no idea how much I missed you, Tialla, how hard it was to watch you lying there, not being able to talk to you, to see your smile, hear your laugh."

"I did what Gwynn said." She clasped each side of my face in her hands. "I enjoyed falling in love with you all over again. I truly did." She lowered her head and kissed me, parting my lips with the tip of her tongue. I felt the love pouring out of her as she clung to me, her cheeks wet with the shimmer of tears.

She pulled back slowly and looked at me, her eyes clouding with grief as the memory hit her. "Aggie." A strangled whisper wrenched from her soul.

Regret drenched me. "I'm sorry, Elle. It was too late to save her."

Her face crumpled as she buried her face in her hands and cried, each anguished sob flaying my heart apart.

There was so much for us to unpack, to discuss, analyze, mourn, celebrate—I didn't even know where to start.

I sensed the moment the air shifted around us, heavy with the power of Gods.

"Leida mata," a melodic voice said from behind us, and we turned to see Eolith, Sorin, and Arazul standing there. At some point, everyone else had filed out of the library, giving Elle and me a moment alone.

But now the moment was over. The Gods had come calling.

ELEYSE

Could a heart be filled with heartbreak and joy at the same time? Flooded with both aching sorrow and unspeakable happiness? Guilt and contentment? Could those dueling emotions live in the same soul?

Aggie was gone, and the weight of her loss dragged me back into the pit of despair I'd come to know intimately for so long. But as I lay broken in that darkness, there was Ash, his light shining above me, showing me the way back home. To him. To my newfound family. To love.

Love. I saw it in the way he looked at me. Saw it now in my goddess mother's eyes and my powerful father's smile. To come face to face with the truth of a heritage far beyond anything I could have possibly imagined was surreal.

"Soladeo," my mother said, taking my hand as Ash lowered me to the floor. "This day is one I never thought would come—when the three of us would be standing here together in acknowledgment of the wondrous gift you are, the one created by our love." She reached for Sorin's hand, her body relaxing as she leaned into his touch. "For so long, I dreamed of the day I would be able to tell your father about you, and now, at long last, everything has been laid bare and you are back in the Sangelis where you've always belonged."

"Soladeo mata," my father said, covering my hands with his.

I had stared at his face so intently in Gwynn's book on the Gods of the Sangelis, puzzled then by the strange sense of kinship I had felt to him. Broad and hulking, his massive form towered over me. He was even more striking in person, both terrifying and exquisite, but that sadness that had bled through the page and touched me was gone.

His eyes softened as he looked at me. "In my entire existence, I never imagined I could love another being as fiercely as I love your mother, but the moment I saw you at Solniess, that changed. As for your Gloweyen

King," he said, turning to look at Ash, "there is no question about the depth of his devotion to you. For that and nothing else, he has my loyalty. I look forward to spending more time with you and becoming better acquainted. Even with a war looming, I would like that."

"I'd like that too," I said, as he pulled me to him. Eolith wrapped her arms around me, too, and I stood cocooned in the shelter of my parents' embrace, my heart bursting with fragile contentment.

I turned to Arazul next, the sight of his familiar face momentarily jarring as it resurrected my memories of him throughout my life.

"We meet again, little bird." His eyes were filled with warmth as he regarded me.

"We do." I shivered reflexively, my senses vibrating as they responded to the power radiating from him. "Thank you for watching over me all these years."

Traces of sorrow shadowed his features. "I'm sorry that I couldn't have done more to spare you pain and heartache."

I cocked my head. "Although I spent so much of my life hating your presence, I'm grateful that you refused to let me die."

"Like everyone in this room, I believe in the promise of who you are, Renala Cielta."

Celestial queen.

At the feel of Ash's hands on my shoulders, I turned my head, my body instinctively leaning in his direction, like a flower seeking the sun.

"What of Kaliope?" His voice was lethally calm, at odds with the tender swirl of his thumbs against my shoulder blades.

Arazul's eyes hardened. "The moment your and Eleyse's consciousness returned here, I released her from the Void. I don't need to tell you, Asher. We should expect no respite from her; if anything, swift retaliation because she was thwarted in the Void might be the more likely reaction. Be ready."

Ash nodded, his lips pursed in a grim line. "Noted. Expect the unexpected."

I shuddered, a spine-chilling malevolence scraping its icy talons down my spine. No respite. I hated the sound of that.

After my parents and Arazul left, Ash and I returned to the others, where Tora had conjured a veritable feast.

My heart was full as I sat next to Ash in the lavish dining room, listening to the laughter and banter that flowed freely between everyone at the table. The Sangelis had gifted me with something beyond my wildest dreams: *family.* Ash, Gwynn, Tora, Andreo. My true parents, even Arazul. Everyone around the table belonged to Ash's family, and by extension, that included me. Faron, Treye, Gilham, Ovix, even Faron's twin sister, Astrid. I was excited to get to know them, to welcome them into my life.

When Ash had introduced me to Treye, Gilham, and Ovix, I'd felt the strangest jolt of recognition, but it wasn't just me; I'd seen it in their eyes, as well, as if we had met before. I warmed to them immediately, and I remembered Mangy Cat's counsel to always trust my senses.

As I sat there with a smile on my face, a small sigh escaped my lips. Everything about the moment was perfect, meant to be savored and cherished—the windowless room with tall ceilings and carved stone pillars ushering in breathtaking city views and brilliant starlight, the soul-haunting music playing softly in the background, the mouthwatering smells and tastes of good food and drink, the warmth and acceptance from the people around me, the feel of Ash's hand in mine and the look in his eyes that set my heart racing whenever our gazes collided. My soul was overflowing with happiness.

And in that moment, I realized something—happiness could only be achieved in the moment. The past was gone, the future indeterminate—both out of my control—but the present moment, that was *mine* to choose. I could *choose* to feel however I wanted and let those feelings sweep me away—for better or worse—but it was *my* choice.

After a life of heartache and loss, punctuated with fragile moments of true happiness, I knew what really mattered. It was as Mangy Cat had told me that day on the trail—*See past the sorrow and pain of each loss and focus on the happiness, the love. From great sorrow comes redemption.*

I closed my eyes and let myself remember. My parents, Mags, Liam. Their fierce love for me, the beautiful music they'd filled my life with, the laughter, the acceptance, the sacrifice. Tears sprang to my eyes as love so powerful swept through me with the force of a gale wind. I thought of Aggie and every precious moment I'd spent with her that had healed and nourished my soul, stitching me back together. I thought of Ash and all the memories I had recaptured of our love story, and my journey from darkness back into the light.

Mangy Cat was right. Had been right all along. The words echoed in my mind, bringing a smile to my face. *Only when you see and accept love for what it is—a beautiful risk worth living and dying for—will you be free from the chains that bind you, and steer the course of your future.*

Love had saved me—being loved, and allowing myself to love. I would never forget.

I stood on the balcony in Ash's bedroom, Tryx sprawled at my feet, her soft fur brushing against my leg as she lay on her back for me to scratch her belly.

Catraia, I called as I looked out across the harbor and the twinkling lights of the city.

I am here, Eleyse, she replied. *Right where I've been the entire time.*

Contentment wrapped its wings around me at the sound of her voice. *Did you see all of my memories as I relived them?*

I did. There was much I learned about you from the time that was lost to you.

I shifted uneasily, digging my fingers into the balcony railing.

You can ask me anything, Eleyse. I already sense the questions stirring in your mind.

I chewed on my bottom lip. *Did. . . did you hear the things the whispers said to me?*

Yes. I heard them.

You are the truth diviner, Catraia. Is what they said true?

There was a long pause in my mind. *It doesn't work that way, Eleyse, not when it comes to proclamations about things that have not yet occurred.*

My heart thudded in my chest, fear scattering venomous seeds of doubt across the fertile landscape of my mind.

As with all things, anything is possible, but you cannot let the possibility of something happening smother you as you breathe. You must fight for what is yours. Heed the words of the Mavigos. The moment you give up on love, all is lost.

I jumped as two arms snaked around my waist, pulling me close. My body sank into his, already aware of who was holding me. Slowly, I exhaled, my heart still clenched in the vise of my fear.

"Something's wrong." His chin rested on the top of my head. "Your essence gives you away."

I turned in his arms, placing my hands on his chest. "Just thinking about what lies ahead."

"The only thing that matters is that we're together. Your coronation, completing your transformation as the Songbird of Valkyse, retrieving Valkyse's Phantera, the Convergence and impending war—we'll face all of it as a team."

I shivered at the mention of war. There was still so much for me to grasp and learn. A team. I had that now. And no matter what, I would never be alone. Catraia was with me, not to mention Vix.

My eyes widened as I looked at Ash. "Have you felt Magnus's presence since what happened at Solniess?"

He brushed the shell of my ear with his finger. "No, but I feel a placid lull over my wellspring of power."

I gripped the fabric of his shirt. "Me too. As if she's happy now that they're reunited. She saved me, Ash. She *and* Magnus."

"It was the most incredible thing to witness." The flecks of gold in his emerald eyes flared.

A burst of triumph exploded within me. "I knew she was a separate entity from me like Catraia, and not just part of my power."

He chuckled, tracing my smile with his thumb. "Yes, you did, baby. You were absolutely right."

My heart somersaulted. "I still love it when you call me that."

He lowered his head and skimmed his lips across my jaw. "I know."

We stared at each other, a million unspoken things passing between us, and the reality of everything we needed to process and deal with pushed its way to the surface. I shoved it all down and locked it away. Not tonight. That was tomorrow's problem.

I slid my arms around his neck. "I love you, Ash. Always and forever."

"Always and forever, Tialla mata." He scooped me into his arms and headed into the bedroom, lowering me to floor in front of the bed. "I love you, Elle. Don't ever doubt that."

"I never did." My fingers tugged at the buttons of his shirt, my body impatient to feel his skin against mine.

A smirk tugged at his lips. "You know I won't be able to prove to you that I'm not a lousy fuck. We still have to wait until your coronation."

Eyes closed, I ached into his touch. "We both know that wasn't me talking. Plus you've proven to me time and time again that we don't need to fuck to get to paradise."

He growled, stripping our clothes away with his magic, every part of us—heart, body, and soul—bared to each other. And as he lay next to me after lowering us onto the bed, I knew I was where I belonged. Where I would always belong. At his side.

In the aftermath of our intimate reacquaintance, when nothing but the sound of his steady breaths and his heartbeat against my ear lulled me, the uneasiness crept its way forward, pecking at my mind like a crow at a dead carcass.

Over and over in those tumultuous last moments in Solniess—like a litany, the dark whispers had chanted the words now burned into my brain. I didn't know if I would ever forget.

Your Gloweyen King will fall to the darkness, Agaia. Even now, it searches for him, intent on claiming his soul. His love will be ripped from you, and as the shadows twist and shape him in their likeness, you will lose your light and doom the Sangelis. So sayeth the Book of the Timplaris.

Chapter 44

KALIOPE

P RESENT DAY ARIADNA . . .

The wind howled, whipping blasts of sand and tree debris at my face as I stood in the shadows. The terrain in Senna was dry but mountainous, prone to sandstorms in the windswept spring seasons.

Under the cover of two dense bracwood trees, I stared unflinchingly at the cazara on the rise, warm exterior lights flanking the perimeter of the property. The faint hint of clesia blossoms mingled with the sharp smell of pine and crisp night, invoking a sickening nostalgia.

From inside my coat, Zaval stirred, poking his head past my upturned collar to peer into the darkness in front of us. The banguar had been glued to me since I'd returned to Clawkier Dreve from the Void, refusing to leave my side.

As soon as I had been released from Arazul's detainment, Gargmoin had commanded me to meet him here. Like the uncommunicative shit he was, he had given no details, just issued the message that this was where I needed to be.

I sucked my teeth as I searched the shadows for him and came up empty-handed. Who in blazes did he think he was to keep me waiting? The bastard knew I had things to do—a war to plan, people to torture, havoc to wreak. Everything needed to be in place before the Convergence. I was still seething from my failure in the Void. I would pay Arazul back tenfold for that.

I sensed Gargmoin before I saw him. The signature of his power was distinct, charged with its own special frequency of destruction and chaos. I fucking loved it.

"Shadow Sorceress." His voice was flat and glacial, as it always was. Not once had I ever seen a flicker of emotion on his face, heard a different inflection in his voice. Every part of him was as dead and cold as his eyes.

"What are we doing here?" I pulled my sleek beyngyle coat tighter around me.

His eyes narrowed at my tone as he crossed his massive arms around his mammoth chest. "The witch who lives here may have answers we seek."

My brows lifted as I stroked the scar on my cheek with my thumb. What the fuck? "What kind of answers?"

"Answers that may light a path to the Ankhira." He snapped a thick branch off the bracwood tree in front of him as if it were a twig, hurling it behind him.

My mind whirred as I stared at him. Interesting. Never in a million years would I have thought to look *here* for answers about something as consequential as the Ankhira. The bitch who lived here was a hateful old shrew. The last time I'd laid eyes on her was the day I was sentenced to Glanag. She was one of many who had come to revel in my demise. I remembered them all, every single one of them. And oh yes, their time would come. I would wipe the smirks off all their faces with their own brackish blood before I made them choke on it.

"Are you coming?" Gargmoin's voice boomed, jarring me out of my happy reverie.

"Tell me what you know," I demanded as we strode toward the cazara. "Don't leave anything out."

He grunted but obliged, and all the while, I was giddy, unable to contain my excitement that my path to victory lay so close to home.

I chuckled quietly. "I'm coming for you, Grandmother. Hope the tea is on."

Acknowledgments

As a reader, one of my favorite things to do is read the "Acknowledgments" section at the back of a book. It warms my heart and gives me goosebumps to read about all the people who support and see a writer through their writing journey. As I've often said to many people, writing can be a lonely path to travel, and having that base of people in your corner, rooting for you to just keep going, can make the world of difference. Knowing someone believes in you and your story can be that push you need, particularly in moments when you don't believe in yourself.

Writing book two in the series came so much easier for me than book one, but along the way, I had my own little fan club cheering me on, providing me with encouragement and kind words that I will cherish forever.

To my sister, Tams, as always, thanks for being my biggest fan. Thanks for always being there when I needed you to read something or just to brainstorm and get your opinion. Most of all, thanks for being the best big sister a girl could ask for.

To Stacey and Maegan—I love you guys. I'm so blessed to have you both as friends, and I'm eternally grateful for all your love and support while I was writing Songbird's Remembrance. Thanks for loving Eleyse's and Ash's love story as much as I did. We will definitely have to repeat the chapter-by-chapter book review session with book three!

A special shout-out to Kyle—lover of the fantasy genre—who was completely unfazed by reading my fantasy-romance, and really enjoyed the story, world building and characters, especially Queen Crazy,

Kaliope.

To Sarah, thanks for reading and brainstorming, and for promoting my story to others. I'm happy I took your suggestion to start book two with Kaliope. She really brings out the unhinged and crazy in the room!

To Alex, thanks for being a great critique partner and an awesome friend, and for taking the time in the midst of writing and publishing your own book to help along the way with mine. So happy for your successes with your story!

To my editor, Jess McKeldon—once more, thank you. Thank you for all your hard work in editing book two, and for loving my story and cheering me on. What more could a writer want in an editor? I still have your lovely message to me about book one stuck to my office wall and look at it often when I feel my story is crap.

To you, the reader, who took the time to read Ash's and Elle's story—I hope I was successful in doing what I set out to do—to provide that *feeling* and experience that only books can. In writing this series, I wanted to give back what, for all my life, books have given to me. Even if it was to just one person, it was totally worth it.

And finally, to Andrew and my wildlings—thanks for loving and supporting me, and being proud of me for finally taking the plunge to let my stories live out there in the wide, wild world.

About the Author

L.S. Taal is a Canadian author who lives in Atlantic Canada with her family. A lover of the written word and vivid, lush storytelling from a young age, her biggest complaint is that there are not enough hours in the day for all the stories waiting to be read.

When she is not creating worlds and stories of her own, she can be found either spending time with her family, hiding from said family with her head stuck in a book, or writing music.

www.ingramcontent.com/pod-product-compliance
Lightning Source LLC
Chambersburg PA
CBHW051314250626
47155CB00007B/2319